D1548867

The Abinger Edition
of E. M. Forster

Volume 17

The Prince's Tale

and other uncollected writings

E. M. Forster

Edited by
P. N. FURBANK

ANDRE DEUTSCH

First published in 1998 by
André Deutsch
A VCI plc company
76 Dean Street
London W1V 5HA

CIP data for this title is available
from the British Library

ISBN 0 233 99168 9

Typeset by Derek Doyle & Associates
Mold, Flintshire.
Printed and bound in Great Britain by
WBC, Bridgend.

Contents

Introduction

E. M. Forster first made his mark as a book reviewer in 1914. It was a difficult moment in his life. The brilliant success of *Howards End* in 1910 had had a queer side-effect, giving him a superstitious feeling that he might be 'dried up' as a novelist. A new novel, *Arctic Summer*, ran into problems and had to be abandoned, and an 'Indian' novel, begun soon after his first visit to India in 1912-13, soon became stalled likewise. Late in 1913, in a swift burst of inspiration, he composed *Maurice*, his novel about homosexual love, but (or so he thought) there could be no question of publishing it; nor did it, as he had hoped, succeed in freeing him from his writer's block. 'My literary future,' he wrote to his friend Forrest Reid (15 March 1914), 'is an abyss into which I dread to peer.'

It was at about this time that R. A. Scott-James launched the brilliant though short-lived *New Weekly*, and over the months leading up to the First World War Forster contributed eleven articles and reviews, in the style that would always be characteristic of him: clever, imaginative and playful, yet fundamentally serious-minded.

There was another and deeper moment of frustration for him in 1919, when, returning to his Indian novel, more or less put aside during the War, he still found himself balked. The obvious escape was literary journalism, and during that and the following year he produced a flood of reviews (some eighty or ninety) for the *Daily News*, Middleton Murry's *Athenaeum*, H. W. Massingham's *Nation*, and the *Daily Herald* (of which he also, for a few months, became literary editor).

When at last, taking Leonard Woolf's advice, he returned once again to *A Passage to India*, grimly determined this time to complete it, whether it proved publishable or not, he for the time being cut out book reviewing. It was, however, an activity he always enjoyed and took seriously; and over the long years – half a lifetime, indeed – that were to follow, it was one of the main ways in which he would make his presence felt. He was always greatly in demand as a reviewer. Arnold Bennett told Siegfried Sassoon in 1922 that 'EMF was the best reviewer in London'; and Forster's friend J. R. Ackerley, looking back on the years when Forster was writing for him on the *Listener*, wrote that 'Morgan was, of course, our most brilliant and penetrating literary critic; to get a review or article from him, during my 25 years on the *Listener*, was the highest prize any literary editor could hope to win, the most unfailingly satisfying and delightful dish that could be offered to the intelligent reader.'[1]

The two collections of his reviews and articles that he made himself, *Abinger Harvest* (1936) and *Two Cheers for Democracy* (1951), have always had an admiring following, and it struck the editors of the Abinger Edition that it would be perfectly possible – there was material for it in abundance – to compile a third collection of the same kind. B. J. Kirkpatrick's Soho Bibliography of Forster lists well over five hundred contributions to periodicals, so that even these three collections are very far from exhausting what is available.

In editing the present selection I have done my best to follow the pattern of Oliver Stallybrass's Abinger Edition of *Two Cheers for Democracy*, adopting his notion of an 'Annotated Index', i.e. notes and index all in one. It seems to me to have some real advantages, though it forces one to be rather selective – some readers may think too selective – in what one decides to annotate. There was less need in the present volume for textual notes, since for the most part the articles have not previously been reprinted, and in any case I have always worked from the original printed version. It seemed helpful, however, to include a list of the books reviewed, as well as a list of sources. I have preserved the original titles of the articles, though no doubt as a rule Forster did not choose them himself.

1. J. R. Ackerley, *E. M. Forster: a Portrait* (1970).

*

It seems true that the book review, as a form of literary criticism, has flourished more happily in the Anglo-Saxon world than anywhere else. I am not thinking of the steam-rollering, Macaulayesque style of reviewing, which amounts to rewriting a book for the unfortunate author, but rather of a certain more informal kind of review: one addressed to a wide general audience and mindful of its practical function, and of the duty of decency and fairness to an author, but which turns into something larger and more creative, defining some quite original observation or law. Henry James's reviews were often of this kind, and so sometimes were George Eliot's. In our own century T. S. Eliot was capable of it, as was Auden; and it happened very frequently with Virginia Woolf, who found book reviewing, with its mockable conventions of solemnity and anonymity, particularly liberating.

E. M. Forster, one can fairly say, belongs in the same company. If anyone should doubt his remarkable talents as a book reviewer, they should look at an unpretentious item in the present collection, teasingly entitled 'To Simply Feel'. It is a review of some absurd sentimental poems by Ella Wheeler Wilcox, together with a totally forgotten work by a certain H. Fielding Hall. He treats the authors with amenity but sharp-eyed attention, has some engaging knockabout fun with them, but then, in the most natural way, moves into an earnest and gravely worded sermon. Edwardian writers, it will be said, were expected to sermonize, whereas it would be unthinkable for a serious writer now. Perhaps so. But Forster's novels also abound in sermons, arising naturally from their context, as this one does, and impressing one – precisely *within* their context – as profound insights.

It is indeed in the field of ethics, and ethical discriminations, that Forster's book reviews are most truly original. I am thinking, for instance, of his review of Middleton Murry's *Son of Woman: The Story of D. H. Lawrence,* a most devastating piece of demolition. It progresses very quietly as well as fairly, so that one hardly notices the point where the demolition-work begins. 'He [Murry] pleads – very convincingly – that we can only find relief from certain painful emotions by writing them down, and to one of his temperament there is no barrier between writing a thing down and offering it to the general public.' We are being given a hint here, of course, but an ambiguous one. It is only several paragraphs later that one fully grasps what he wants to convey, about the sheer awfulness of Murry. It has often struck one how savagely Murry's contemporaries talk about him, but it is Forster, though he knew him very little, who gets nearest to conveying the reason.

> The words flow on in a menacing spate, and the mind of the unbeliever is carried away by them for a little. Then it withdraws, and tries to take stock. What underlies these lavish comminations and absolutions? Does Mr Murry feel that he himself and all of us are in a state of peril too? Yes, he feels this, and perhaps he is right. But he also feels – and here one dissents – a profound complacency in his plight. He relishes being scared and tries to infect others with his *malaise.* So might an adept, emerging from the shrine, hint that he has seen mysteries too terrible to mention, proceed just to mention them, and so send his disciples trembling away.

Forster was a master of the dismissive. Could there be a more delicate insult than the one he offers to Maurice Baring? 'If only Mr Baring could give away a strawberry or some other edible trifle with each of his volumes, the still small voice of criticism would be stifled at once.' His puncturing of Sidney Lee's pomposity, in his Life of Edward VII, is equally and gorgeously unanswerable. 'Despite the restraints on boyish liberty and the educational discipline in which the paternal wisdom chiefly made itself visible to the son,' wrote Lee, 'the boyish faith in his dead father's exalted and disinterested motive lived on.' – 'Such a sentence,' comments Forster, 'pops when trodden upon, like seaweed, yet it would be wrong to say that it contains nothing. A diplomatic residuum survives – something gummy, something as subtle in its way as literature though it exudes from the opposite end of the pen.' This, in its nimbleness and inventiveness, exhibits in perfection what you might call the 'beautiful amusingness' of Bloomsbury prose. It is a significant trait in Forster that, when he employs a metaphor, he insists on faithfully following it through. But notice, too, the extreme accuracy of his analysis of Lee's prose.

> Read the sentence again, and do not try to find out whether the Prince liked his father or was cowed by him, whether he obeyed him or disobeyed, for these are not the points. Consider instead the repetition of the adjective 'boyish'. It is significant. In literature a repeated adjective does something, and it does something here too: it helps us to forget that we are reading about a boy.

More or less everything necessary, one feels, has been said here about a certain kind of royal hagiography.

Admittedly, Forster is at his most masterly of all when reviewing the second or third rate. Faced for the first time with 'modernist' works, such as those of Virginia Woolf and Gide, he was observant, honest and open-minded, but he did not feel really at home, and in retrospect his judgements strike one as rather hit-or-miss. It is significant, all the same, that, for Woolf, Forster's opinion counted for more than anybody else's. 'Morgan has the artist's mind,' she wrote in her diary for 6 November 1919, 'he says the simple things that clever people don't say; I find him the best of critics for that reason. Suddenly out comes the obvious thing that one has overlooked.' There was some awkwardness between them over her *Night and Day*. Clive Bell, Lytton Strachey and Violet Dickinson all praised it to the skies, but Forster wrote to say that he liked it less than *The Voyage Out*, and this, Woolf recorded, 'rubbed out all the pleasure of the rest.' When they met, however, and without backing down, he managed to explain his objections in a way that, for her, took all the sting out of them. *Night and Day*, he said, was a 'strictly formal and classical work'; thus it mattered, as it had not mattered with the impressionistic *The Voyage Out*, that the reader should care about the characters. She was appeased and decided it was not 'a criticism to discourage'.

Forster, Lionel Trilling wrote, was 'a critic with no drive to consistency'[2]. He was, Trilling complained, too relaxed as a critic, too inclined to take refuge in whimsy. He had magnificent and first-hand perceptions but too often refused or failed to follow them through. There is something in this, and we need not simply blame the genre of the book review. But it reminds us that, from another point of view, Forster was a writer of extreme consistency. He had a profound and entirely coherent philosophy. At the centre of it was Helen Schlegel's doctrine that 'Death destroys a man; the idea of Death saves him', and there was entailed in it an idiosyncratic attitude towards 'things'. Why he trusted metaphors to lead him where they would was because he believed that 'things' contained the truth, albeit a truth probably very unlike men's presuppositions. Schoolmasters and men of good will, he wrote once, were keen to tell us what Life is. 'Once started on the subject of Life they lose all diffidence, because to them it is ethical. They love discussing what we ought to be instead of what we have to face – reams about conduct and nothing about those agitating apparitions that rise from the ground, or fall from the sky.'[3] Forster once, when asked to face facts, asked how could he, when they were all round him? The thought quietly resurfaces in the essay on William Cowper in the present collection.

> Brilliant descriptions and profound thoughts entail disadvantages when they are applied to scenery; they act too much as spot lights; they break the landscape up; they drill through it and come out at the antipodes; they focus too much upon what lies in front. Cowper never does this. He knows that the country doesn't lie in front of us but all around.

It is one's impression that somehow or other, quite early on in life, Forster arrived at a vision of death as simply one item

2. Trilling, *E. M. Forster: a Study* (new & revised edn, 1967), p.141.
3. E. M. Forster, 'The Game of Life', in *Abinger Harvest* (1936).

in human existence among many, in no way its climax or denouement. The fact coloured his whole outlook, and there was indirectly connected with it the thought that things, and moments also, are infinitely various and should never be lumped. It is apt, then, that he was intensely taken by Giuseppe di Lampedusa's *The Leopard*, reading it first in Italian and then in translation, and that, being then in his eighty-second year, he wrote a most memorable and moving review of it. 'What a tribute to the urbanity of death!' it runs. 'The whole chapter scintillates with power and with a tenderness that is untroubled by pity.' He notes approvingly how the novel's hero, Prince Fabrizio, employs his last instants in 'separating the good moments from the bad', and it strikes him as a stroke of genius that the figure – the slim young woman in a brown travelling dress – whom the dying Prince imagines as having come to rescue him, should be a newcomer to the story, 'and not some character already docketed and staled!' The prose of this review is Forster's at its most achieved: spare, supple and delicately exploratory, imaginatively all alive ('See him [the Prince] out hunting and killing minute animals in an enormous landscape'), and rising on occasion to ravishing eloquence. How lovely is the sentence which ends 'he goes out into the garden which is scented almost to decay with the contending violence of flowers'.

It remains to mention two important items in this collection which were not book reviews: his Presidential Address to the Cambridge Humanists, on 'How I Lost My Faith', and the late essay, *De Senectute*, first read to the Cambridge Apostles. It is a treat, in the former, to see how effortlessly he skirts the snares that lie in wait for humanists, and especially the great trap of turning humanism into a religion. The calm self-observation in 'How I Lost My Faith' is equally acute. Forster entirely endorses his youthful attitude in the College Mission controversy; indeed it was the one he would take in all subsequent controversies, for instance the one with T. S. Eliot over D. H. Lawrence – a matter of referring intellectual debates back to daily life and human realities. Elsewhere, on the other hand, he registers a profound and significant change. Salvation, the theme which so dominates his stories and early novels, has 'disappeared from his thoughts, like other absolutes'.

As for *De Senectute*, one is reminded that Forster was one of the great phrase-makers of his era, and his 'Senatorial Heresy' deserved to be added to the collection. 'As a prophet or guide the Senator is quite useless. He can, however, be esteemed as an exhibit, and on that narrow pedestal a case for him can be made.' The discrimination between *absolutely* bogus claims for old age and those for which a 'case' can be made (there is also a 'mild' one to be made, we are told, for sexual impotence) is a most appealing joke. It also helps bring home to us how much, almost more than any writer one can think of, Forster's mind pullulates with discriminations. It was essential in his view that things that were separable should be separated. (That they should be 'connected' is implied too.) He patiently teases apart the aspects of Jesus Christ which profoundly appeal to him from the ones that he greatly dislikes. He notes, another nice discrimination, that the fact that his rejection of Jesus is not vehement 'does not save it from being tenacious'. He insists, in *De Senectute*, that the subject of old age must be kept clearly distinct from those of growing old and of death, and in the same essay accurately distinguishes wisdom from intuition, knowledge and sympathy, as a prelude to maintaining that wisdom is both 'an immensely important human achievement' and (as against received opinion) quite impossible to communicate. These late essays strike me as a model of good humour, good taste and applied intelligence. Rationalism has had few better defenders.

P. N. Furbank

Books

To Simply Feel

Can one feel too much? Ah, no, pants the heart. To feel everything always – for what else were we born? And most especially were we born to feel love. Away with reason – it chills. Away with art – it confines. Away with the world and the devil. Fling wide the floodgates to the natural emotions, and let them sweep us whithersoever they will. Let us rise, if it so happens, from a low emotion to a high one; but oh! let us always feel, and urge others to do the same, for feeling is life.

Thus counsels the heart. The Puritan has his answer ready, and may be left to give it. But there are other answers besides his, and it is interesting to attempt one. What is this Nemesis that waits on unqualified emotion? Why is the writer who tries simply to feel apt to simply feel before he has tried for long? Is it a coincidence that an emotion and an infinitive should so often split at the same moment? May they not be suffering shipwreck upon one rock, and, if so, what is the name of that rock? These questions, among others, are suggested by the two books under review.

Let us begin with Mrs Wilcox, the most widely read poet of our day. She tells us herself that –

> women's souls,
> Like violet powder dropped on coals,
> Give forth their best in anguish,

and it may be that she will yield something to the gentler fire of criticism. In *Poems of Problems* she continues a series that has already brought comfort to thousands of English schoolgirls and adult Americans – a series of verse utterances on the great things of this life and the next. Passion, Pleasure, Power, Cheer, Sentiment, Progress, and Experience have alike received treatment from her pen, and now it is the turn of eugenics and heredity. Here are delicate subjects, but she approaches them with the confidence of a capacious heart. Thanks to her intense feeling, she has access to Heaven, which proves to be far more unconventional than Dante or any of the Churches have dreamed. Mrs Wilcox knows what God really minds, as apart from what He is supposed to mind, and anticipates a semi-scientific Judgment Day, in which the unwed mother shall be preferred before the childless wife, and the unsound father be healed. Meanwhile, there is much to do on earth:

> From rights of parentage the sick and sinful
> must be barred,
> 'Till Matron Science keeps our house, and
> at the door stands guard.

Science is God; God, Science. Both are Love. Consequently, mankind will never dismiss its concierge – she will perform her duties so feelingly. She is not the slow spectre of the laboratories, athirst for truth, but an American lady of elevated morals, who knows right from wrong, she does hope, and is only too glad to lend the world a helping hand. Healthy and warm-hearted, she would make short work of the science of Anatole France. Monsieur Bergeret, it may be remembered, once lifted his eyes from his dishonour to the stars, and speculated whether Life may not be a transient blight in the universe – a local malady by which the earth has been attacked, and the earth alone. But then Monsieur Bergeret was dyspeptic and French. How can life be a malady when we all regard one another as cordially as we do? And anyway, why speculate at all, when to simply feel is sufficient?

Poems of Problems is an interesting document for the future historian of our society. It evidences a new demand on the part of the semi-educated public – a demand for frankness and unconventionality. No one can call Mrs Wilcox conventional. She airs subjects that orthodoxy would stifle, and the wideness of her circulation proves the need. But, though unconventional, she is never original. However scientific her

Heaven, it remains replete with angels and Biblical talk. In fact, she is offering new dogmas for old, as did the Reformation, and may exemplify to the historian the transition between subservience and independent judgement. The educated public completed that transition fifty years ago. The semi-educated – those who have learnt to read, but not yet how to read – are here seen making it. As a document, her poems are notable. As poems, despite their sincerity and feeling, they are not. Why? Before attempting an answer to this, let us turn to Mr Fielding Hall.

The receptacle for Mr Hall's emotion is cast in the form of a novel. *Love's Legend* tells of the honeymoon, estrangement and reconciliation of one Mr Gallio and Lesbia, his wife, intermixed with amorous episodes between the same adown a Burmese river. But all is subsidiary to feeling. The characters are bathed in feeling. It sprinkles the slightest of their actions, permeates the landscapes, and is threatened in the last sentence of the book for ever, ever, evermore.

Now, while agreeing with Mrs Wilcox that love is everything, Mr Hall draws a very different moral – so different that the two writers must hate one another like poison, and only a cold outsider can hope to read them both. If the lady is semi-Christian, the gentleman is neo-Oriental. Science, a matron for her, becomes a Pasha for him – Pasha Science, as full of feeling as ever, but different in other ways. Mrs Wilcox says that:

> In the banquet hall of Progress
> God has bidden to a feast
> All the women of the East.

Mr Hall denies that such an invitation has been issued; he knows that progress is fatal for females – it so increases their husband's difficulties, and in consequence their own. A man is public property, a woman the private property of a man. Let her be told this by her parents, and no more, lest conjugal bliss be marred.

He states the problem as follows:

> Suppose you engaged a peach or an apricot to come to you to be eaten, but when she came you found her fixed idea was that she was to be placed under a glass case on a sideboard. It wasn't fair to bring up girls like that, it wasn't fair to us. Society has no right to deliberately and intentionally pervert a girl in this way.

And he asserts that Nature decrees a double standard of morality for the sexes. Woman must be pure. Man may disport himself before marriage on the Boulevards. (What about the women with whom he disports himself? On this point Pasha Science is duly silent.) Woman takes. Man gives. Woman is the audience. Man the poet. These are hard lessons for a peach, nor does poor little Lesbia learn them without falling into the Irrawaddy and losing all her European clothes. She has also to learn that God, instead of being in the sky, as Mrs Wilcox supposes, is really inside one – a discovery unwelcome to her, but her husband will have no shirking. Now by an apt anecdote, now by persiflage or horse-play, now by intimidating silences, he leads her up to be all she should be. The quiet stream of her life joins the impetuous torrent of his at last, and they flow on together in one mighty river of broadening emotion towards the sea, whence – solemn thought – they will one day re-emerge in the form of dew, and it will all happen over again.

Mr Hall is a more skilful writer than Mrs Wilcox, but his lack of nobility makes him less pleasant reading. Like her, he assumes that the two sexes are fundamentally distinct (have either of these scientific emotionalists read a line of science?); but, unlike her, he preaches that men are never to blame, women always; and since he is personally male, his sermon becomes suspect. Were he cynical, he might be void of offence, but he writes in the name of high feeling and theosophy and marital love, which makes him very hard to bear. Those who imagine that Mrs Wilcox is mere silliness, would do well to glance at *Poems of Problems* – they will find among its crudities a real desire to elevate humanity. But those who have enjoyed *The Soul of the People* are advised not to spoil their recollection of that charming book by conning *Love's Legend.*

And now let us try to answer our question. Love is everything. So both these writers assert. They are absolutely right. It is. But Lord Bacon was also right when he wrote that the true atheist is he who has become cauterized by handling holy things, and it is from this point of view that they should be criticized. They fail not because their outlook is narrow or their facts wrong or their style weak – it is possible to have all those defects and yet win through – but because they misuse emotion. Professing to feel, they have merely handled and have tossed sanctities about like parcels, without trying to apprehend the contents. Love is not a word of four letters, nor God a word of three. Both occur on many a page of either book, yet are further than ever from us at the close. They can only approach us when they are instinct in the writer, when they are so completely in his possession that he scarcely thinks of mentioning them by name. Such a writer does not set out to 'feel', because feeling is his starting point. He does not eulogize the heart or decry reason. He does not treat of emotion, because it is bound to appear incidentally, whatever his theme. Emotion is not a theme. It is the central fire and the external glow, but it is not a theme, and those who persist in handling it as if it were are trying to enter the Kingdom of Heaven by calling, 'Lord, Lord!' and must remain, despite their protests, in the outer darkness. The fate of the emotionalist is ironic, and he will never escape it until he is less obsessed with the importance of emotion. When he is interested in people and things for their own sake, the hour of his deliverance has approached, and while stretching out his hand for some other purpose, he will discover – quite simply! – that he can feel.

[1914]

H. Fielding Hall, *Love's Legend*
Ella Wheeler Wilcox, *Poems of Problems*

A New Novelist

One of the men in Mrs Woolf's book complains: 'Of course we're always writing about women – abusing them or jeering at them or worshipping them; but it's never come from women themselves. I believe we still don't know in the least how they live, or what they feel, or what they do precisely . . . They won't tell you. Either they're afraid or they've got a way of treating men.' And perhaps the first comment to make on *The Voyage Out* is that it is absolutely unafraid, and that its courage springs not from naïveté, but from education. Few women writers are educated. A gentleman ought not to say such a thing, but it is, unfortunately, true. Our Queens of the Pen are learned, sensitive, thoughtful even, but they are uneducated, they have never admitted the brain to the heart, much less let it roam over the body. They live in pieces, and their work, when it does live, lives similarly, devoid of all unity save what is imposed by a plot. Here at last is a book which attains unity as surely as *Wuthering Heights,* though by a different path, a book which, while written by a woman and presumably from a woman's point of view, soars straight out of local questionings into the intellectual day. The curious male may pick up a few scraps, but if wise he will lift his eyes to where there is neither marrying nor giving in marriage, to the mountains and forests and sea that circumscribe the characters, and to the final darkness that blots them out. After all, he will not have learnt how women live, any more than he has learnt from Shakespeare how men perform that process; he will only have lived more intensely himself, that is to say, will have encountered literature.

Mrs Woolf's success is more remarkable since there is one serious defect in her equipment: her chief characters are not vivid. There is nothing false in them, but when she ceases to touch them they cease, they do not stroll out of their sentences, and even develop a tendency to merge shadow-like. Rachel and her aunt Helen are one example of this. Hewet and his friend Hirst another. The story opens with Helen. Helen, though an accomplished Bohemian, is discovered in tears close to Cleopatra's Needle – she is off for a holiday in South America, but does not like leaving the children. Her husband, a Pindaric scholar, beats the air with a stick until she has finished and can gain the boat, where Rachel, a pale idle girl of twenty-four, awaits them. Helen is bored at first. But at Lisbon they are joined by a kindly politician – he, like most of the minor characters, is sketched with fine foolery and malice – and he, by kissing Rachel, wakes her up. When he has disembarked, she expounds to her aunt, they become friends, and when the Voyage Out, so far as it is by water, has ended, she goes to spend the winter with Helen at Santa Marina. Below their villa in the English hotel dwell two young Cambridge intellectuals, Hewet and Hirst. The pairs become acquainted, and for a time there is a curious darkness, while one of the men – we know not which – and one of the women – we know not which – are nearing each other. When the darkness clears, Helen is definitely the confidante, Hirst the onlooker, and Hewet and Rachel have, in the recesses of a primaeval forest, become engaged to be married. The Villa acquiesces, the Hotel smirks, and, until the final note, we expect wedding bells.

If the above criticism is correct, if Mrs Woolf does not 'do' her four main characters very vividly, and is apt to let them all become clever together and differ only by their opinions, then on what does her success depend? Some readers – those who demand the milk of human kindness, even in its tinned form – will say that she has not succeeded; but the bigness of her achievement should impress anyone weaned from baby food. She believes in adventure – here is the main point – believes in it passionately, and knows that it can only be undertaken alone. Human relations are no substitute for adventure, because when real they are uncomfortable, and when comfortable they must be unreal. It is for a voyage into solitude that man was created, and Rachel, Helen, Hewet,

Hirst all learn this lesson, which is exquisitely reinforced by the setting of tropical scenery – the soul, like the body, voyages at her own risk. 'There must be a reason,' sighs nice old Mrs Thornbury, after the catastrophe. 'It can't only be an accident. For if it was an accident – it need never have happened.' Primaeval thunderstorms answer Mrs Thornbury. There is no reason. Why should an adventure terminate that way rather than this, since its essence is fearless motion? 'It's life that matters,' writes a novelist of a very different type; 'the process of discovering, the everlasting and perpetual process, not the discovery itself at all.' Mrs Woolf's vision may be inferior to Dostoevsky's – but she sees as clearly as he where efficiency ends and creation begins, and even more clearly that our supreme choice lies not between body and soul, but between immobility and motion. In her pages, body v. soul – that dreary mediaeval tug-of-war – does not find any place. It is as if the rope has broken, leaving pagans sprawling on one side and clergymen on the other, while overhead 'long-tailed birds chattered and screamed and crossed from wood to wood, with golden eyes in their plumage.'

It is tempting to analyse the closing chapters, which have an atmosphere unknown in English literature – the atmosphere of Jules Romains' *Mort de Quelqu'un.* But a word must be said about the comedy; the book is extremely amusing. The writer has a nice taste in old gentlemen, for instance. They talk like this:

> 'Jenkinson of Cats – do you still keep up with him?'
>
> 'As much as one ever does,' said Mr Pepper. 'We meet annually. This year he has had the misfortune to lose his wife, which made it painful, of course.'
>
> 'Very painful,' Ridley agreed.
>
> 'There's an unmarried daughter who keeps house for him, I believe, but it's never the same, not at his age.'
>
> Both men nodded sagely as they carved their apples.
>
> 'There was a book, wasn't there?' Ridley inquired.
>
> 'There *was* a book, but there never *will* be a book,' said Mr Pepper, with such fierceness that both ladies looked up at him.

> 'There never will be a book, because someone else has written it for him,' said Mr Pepper with considerable acidity. 'That's what comes of putting things off, and collecting fossils, and sticking Norman arches on one's pig sties.'

In the humour there is something of Peacock. When the ball at the Santa Marina Hotel turns into a bacchanal, and the aforesaid Mr Pepper executes a pointed step that he has derived from figure skating, there is an effect of cumulative drollery that recalls the catastrophe in Nightmare Abbey, when Mr Toobad fell into the moat. The writer can sweep together masses of characters for our amusement, then sweep them away; her comedy does not counteract her tragedy, and at the close enhances it, for we see that the Hotel and the Villa will soon be dancing and gossiping just as before, that existence will continue the same, exactly the same, for everyone, for everyone except the reader; he, more fortunate than the actors, is established in the possession of beauty.

[1915]

Virginia Woolf, *The Voyage Out*

Breakable Butterflies

Can it be that as the years roll by one becomes more entertaining to oneself? The notion seems too fantastic. Yet, while life on the whole remains as amusing as ever, less and less of the amusement can be ascribed to the efforts of others. They can provide beauty and pathos and seriousness; but when it comes to being light, quaint, dainty, semi-satirical and mildly allusive, surely one does it just as well oneself, either in solitude or under the stimulus of a cup of tea. For this reason, the incidental in literature must pass a very severe test. Unable to draw on our sense of reverence, it has to satisfy our standards of perfection. Since it does not attempt greatness, we require it to have all other qualities in every line – playfulness, brilliancy, form, good taste, atmosphere. These little plays of Mr Baring's first appeared in the *Morning Post*, and very lucky it was to get them, and very enjoyable would be the house party which produced them with the author as stage manager. One would go away in great elation. But when the plays are bound in a book and the acting rights are reserved, criticisms occur, such as 'Surely in my undergraduate days we used to be quite as fanciful about Euripides,' or 'After all, is it any better than what they got up at old Mrs Penny's?' When literature sets out to beat life in trivialities it takes on a very serious job, and perhaps only succeeds when it conceals something that is not trivial. Gilbert's *Rosencrantz and Guildenstern* is a good play as well as a skit on *Hamlet*. Mr Max Beerbohm's *Christmas Garland* contains among its verdure some exquisite blossoms of insight, and some very sharp thorns. But Mr Baring is neither a practised dramatist nor an acute critic. There is nothing to support him below the surface. When, like all men, he falls, the ice breaks and he goes in. Old Mrs Penny fell too, but she didn't go in because she was the hostess and our sense of obligation broke her weight; we said, 'At all events, she gave us lovely strawberries.' If only Mr Baring could give away a strawberry or some other edible trifle with each of his volumes, the still small voice of criticism would be stifled at once. As it is, one raises a quavering complaint – quavering, for the volume is full of quite jolly things.

'Caligula's Picnic' is a good example. The scene is 'A large banqueting table in the centre of a bridge, which stretches for three miles between Puteoli and Baiæ. The Emperor Caligula is reclining in the place of honour. There are hundreds of guests.' An excellent stage direction, promising fantasy and amplitude. But the ensuing dialogue does not follow it up. The trivialities about roast boar and the drama are not so amusing as life. Consider what it must have actually been to picnic with Caligula, the mixture of anxiety and elation; consider what the philosopher Philo did, historically, go through when he ran after the Emperor in the middle of house decorators and plumbers, trying all the time to justify the religion of the Jews. The atmosphere should be so rich in fun. But Mr Baring makes no play until he gets to the speeches. These are very funny; while listening to them one feels that the picnic is after all a success. There is the Prefect of Puteoli proposing the health of the Emperor, 'who with his knowledge of the Roman heart has had the happy, the graceful, nay more, the truly Imperial and truly Roman idea of joining the two cities by this elegant and monumental bridge.' There is the Prefect of Baiæ, who, having to propose the Army, compares the bridge to a battle. And there is the Army's reply:

> Citizens, my trade is to speak and not to act – I mean to act and not to speak. (Loud cheers.) I am a humble particle of what has so rightly been called the great dumb one. (Cheers.) I thank you all very much for drinking the last toast, and I in my turn have great pleasure in proposing the toast which comes next on the list, namely the toast of Literature (Cheers) . . . coupled with that of the divine Emperor, who, as we all know is a first-rate author himself. (Cheers.)

An elderly poet then rises to read his 'short epic in six cantos' called 'The Bridge'; but before he can begin Caligula gives a signal, and the guests are thrown into the sea. And here, for the second time in one little drama, Mr Baring trips. The catastrophe should be far more sumptuous and bizarre. Appropriate cries should proceed from the previous speakers, from the orators especially. But we are given a brief stage direction, and there it ends. Think of the catastrophe of *Zuleika Dobson*, when all the undergraduates of Oxford, except one, drown themselves. How satisfying! Perhaps that is why one has grown rather heavy-handed about 'amusing' literature: one is always comparing it with the incomparable achievements of Max. Butterflies, they do say, should not be broken on a wheel. And unbreakable butterflies, though they exist, are necessarily rare.

[1919]

Maurice Baring, *Diminutive Dramas*

Kill Your Eagle!

André Gide is a great figure in the literary horizon of France, but the English do not read him much. Both his merits and his defects alienate him from us. It is his merit that he cannot be labelled, and we have a coarse love of labels. Anatole France is 'satirical', Pierre Loti 'exotic', Paul Bourget 'reactionary', and each has secured in England the public that demands his particular brand. But Gide provides all three brands, and more besides, which we regard as unsatisfactory. Sometimes he is decrying religion and society, sometimes he turns out scented lyrical descriptions of oriental life, sometimes he upholds miracles and titles and the other trimmings, old and new, that Authority assumes. His outlook is so subtle and personal that he cannot keep long to the paths of other men, nor indeed to his own. He is always veering. And this brings us to his defect. He lacks strength. His work is terribly uneven. He loses interest and vigour in the middle of a flight and falls disappointingly to the ground. Much has been written about his philosophy, but surely the truth is that he has none. He is like some exquisite screen, perfectly designed but weak on its hinges so that it falls as soon as we stand it in front of the fire. The English like labels, but, very rightly, they like strength too, and Gide provides neither.

Le Prométhée mal enchainé, though full of originality, is not one of his best books. It is a fantasy about conscience. The eagle that feeds on the liver of Prometheus symbolizes the nagging moral force that each man carries in his breast, and that drives him to idealism and unselfishness, and also to pity his fellows when they are unworthy of pity and to help them when they do not want to be helped. As the power of conscience grows, the natural healthy impulses decline. The eagle, which began as a small, mangy bird, no better than a vulture, becomes in time magnificent; while Prometheus, originally a plump young Titan, shrinks into a sentimental neurotic, who abases himself beneath his tormentor and feels a morbid love for the terrific beak. The deeper his conscience stabs, the happier he is. The idea is brilliant, and characteristic of Gide, who is always hesitating between paganism and self-abnegation and unable to decide which is best. This time paganism wins. Prometheus in the end kills his eagle, and eats it at a Paris restaurant. It tastes delicious.

Afterwards, one of his friends asks him what is the use of having an eagle. He replies: 'You get a sport, dinner and some beautiful feathers.' That is to say, conscience, though it preys on a man, gives him something good that he would not have had otherwise. And the lesson of the book is, firstly, the importance of having a conscience; and, secondly, the importance of stifling it sometime or other and returning, richer for the experience, to the life of instinct. It is the book of a pagan who has made a profitable excursion into Christianity; it is written, as Gide himself put it, with a feather from the dead eagle's wing.

The idea is not well worked out. Led away by his fertile fancy, Gide tires himself by introducing other motives, until the main fantasy is enfeebled and obscured. Nor is he aided by his translator. Lady Rothermere has had the unhappy notion of rivalling the achievements of Ollendorff, and rendering her original literally. Gide is always a master of style, and it is sad that his delicate phrases should turn into 'but the introductions not having been asked for, without more ado the two men both sat down', or 'thus the reader will allow us to leave at present someone he will hear of sufficiently later on' or ' "Ah hah!" cried Prometheus, "you interest me enormously".' Indeed, some of the sentences must be quite unintelligible to readers who know no French; one has to retranslate them mentally before the meaning dawns. To be literal and to be lucid are two different things, but Lady Rothermere appears to identify them. Nor is she more lucid when she writes English all on her own. Her preface contains sentences such as 'Zeus, the banker, poses this disinterested act because his thought refuses or hesitates to admit it'. Truly a poser! No. Gide must not be judged on this inauspicious little volume. He has written far better elsewhere on the death of eagles, notably in *Les Caves du Vatican.* He has celebrated their victory in *La Porte étroite.* He has ignored their existence in *Isabella.* Let us get down our French dictionaries and grammars and tackle those originals. There are greater books in literature, but there is nothing exactly like them in French and nothing the least like them in English.

[1919]

André Gide, *Prometheus Ill-Bound*

Visions

Some nations see, others hear or think, and the English have never been good at seeing. The very word vision (Latin *video*) has in our language come to mean something that perhaps ought to exist, but certainly doesn't, like a legacy or an angel. 'I have a vision of a great united people,' say politicians, when they mean that what they do see is neither united nor great, and the visionary man is one who duly cowers before the practical. Can we rescue the valuable word to its proper sense? A vision has nothing to do either with unreality or with edification. It is merely something that has been seen, and in this sense Mrs Woolf's two stories are visions.

In the first she sees a mark on her wall just above the mantelpiece. Instead of getting up, as all well-conditioned Englishwomen should, and discovering that it is a ——, she continues to see it, rambling away into the speculations and fantasies that it inspires, but always coming back to the mark. Sometimes she thinks it is a hole – no. It seems to project, not a hole – like a tumulus more – tumulus – she begins to get rather sleepy – antiquarians – retired colonels – leading parties of aged labourers to the top and getting into correspondence with the neighbouring clergy, which, being opened at breakfast time, gives them a feeling of importance, and the comparison of arrow-heads. And on and on the sentence goes, until she comes back to the mark with a jump, sees it again, wonders whether it may not be a nail and rambles off again. It requires an intruder from the outside world before the mark can be actually examined and proved to be a ——. What does the reader think it was? His verdict, whether right or wrong, is not of the least value. For in this queer world of Vision it is the surfaces of things, not their names or natures that matter; it has no connection with the worlds of practical or philosophic truth, it is the world of the Eye – not of supreme importance, perhaps, but, oh, how rarely revealed!

In *The Mark on the Wall* there is, as Mrs Woolf sadly points out, a moral of a sort; she is a poor housekeeper, or the mark would not be there. But it is impossible to extract any moral from 'Kew Gardens'. It is vision unalloyed. Or, rather, there are two visions which gradually draw together (as when one adjusts field-glasses), until they grow unforgettably bright and become one. Flowers and men are the two items at which Mrs Woolf is looking, and, at first, they seem strongly contrasted. The flowers are down in their bed with a snail, the men, erect and sentient, are strolling past with their womenkind, and the possibility of tea. And the men sometimes look at the flowers, whereas the flowers never look at the men. But as the story goes on this difference becomes terribly unimportant, and at the end the flowers, if anyone, have the upper hand. They win not in any allegorical sense – Mrs Woolf is no pantheist. Their victory is over the eye: they cause us to see men also as petals or coloured blobs that loom and dissolve in the green blue atmosphere of Kew. One cannot quote from this extraordinary story, because it is constructed with such care that the fun and the beauty – and there is much of both – depend for their main effect on their position in the general scheme. But those who like it will like it very much, and those who do not like it are to be pitied.

They are to be pitied, but not to be despised. Mrs Woolf's art is of a very unusual type, and one realizes that quite good critics, especially of the academic kind, may think it insignificant. It has no moral, no philosophy, nor has it what is usually understood by Form. It aims deliberately at aimlessness, at long loose sentences, that sway and meander: it is opposed to tensity and intensity, and willingly reveals the yawn and the gape. Most writers seem to be so solemn even when being funny; they are so anxious to express their devotion to their art, and they frown when we do not attend to their jokes. Mrs Woolf, though she doubtless welcomes attention, is very careful to make no bid for it. She only says, 'Oh – here is something that I have seen,' and then strays forward. Forward it is, but those who are blind to the newer developments of English prose may not think so and may complain at the end that the authoress has left them where she found them. Which is, no doubt, exactly what she would wish to do.

The stories are not to be had through the booksellers. Those who would experiment in them should write to the Hogarth Press, Richmond.

[1919]

Virginia Woolf, *The Mark on the Wall*
Kew Gardens

Almost Too Sad?

The relation between foreign affairs and literary fashions is an interesting subject, though a depressing one. It really seems as if men – most men – don't love beauty, so ready are they to leave it at their country's call. It is indeed the first thing they leave. War is declared, and books written by the enemy immediately become either Satanic or contemptible, while books written by the allies are revealed as the utterances of angels. Russia has known either fate. In 1914 all Russian books were supernaturally good. People who had held back from them as being 'almost too sad', now rushed forward to adore their mysticism and humanity. Lemburg fell, Dostoevsky was wonderful. Przemysl fell, and Dostoevsky was sublime. But then Warsaw fell, and finally the Tsar, and readers in England began to suspect that the Russians could not write after all. With the advent of Bolshevism suspicion became certainty. The Russians grew 'almost too sad' again, and much else besides; they proved as bad as the Germans, and in some ways worse – even Nietzsche had not led to regicide. There was a slump in Slavs. And the negligible minority, who try to read a book for its own sake, felt yet again how utterly they were in the minority, how utterly cut off from the interests and passions that stir most men. Most men do not value beauty; it does not tickle their senses, or confirm their prejudices, it even makes them uneasy; most men, even in 1914, were not quite sure about Tchehov.

In spite of the Bolsheviks and of all the money that British investors have lost in Russian Imperial loans, Mrs Garnett has just brought out the seventh volume of her translation of Tchehov's stories. May the venture succeed, for it includes one of the best tales he ever wrote – 'The Steppe'. It is a great pleasure to read it in her version. 'The Steppe' is about a journey – the kind of journey that any of us might take, though somehow or other we never manage to take it. A little boy has to go to school. He starts in a carriage with his uncle and the village priest, is transferred on to a wool waggon, where he travels a few days with the carters, bathing, laughing, losing his temper, eating fish soup, getting wet through, and rejoining his uncle and the priest in a feverish condition, from which he soon recovers. They arrange that he shall be taken *en pension* by an old friend of his mother's, and that is all. The journey is over, nothing has happened, and yet we have experienced something unforgettable and great. Most writers would have concentrated on the fever, and made a huge crisis out of it, but Tchehov lets it flow by quietly with the other facts, nor does he give a single bad mark to the uncle for callousness, to the priest for superstition, or to the carters for incompetence.

He is neither melodramatist nor moralist. He is only concerned to make the journey interesting and to fill every sentence – not just the show sentences – with beauty. In consequence we are left with a sense of completeness. We have travelled through the world of his creation, and enjoyed its imaginative fullness, nothing has happened that might not happen in the world of daily life, but the particular sequence of events is not to be experienced this side of poetry. Tchehov (if one cares to label him) is both realist and poet. With one hand he collects facts, with the other he arranges them and sets them flowing. The imagination that he possesses is content with the earth and the sun and the stars that we know; it never attempts to gain beauty by distortion. And in 'The Steppe' it should appear without difficulty to the English reader for the reason that the general theme is not 'almost too sad' – is, indeed, almost jolly.

The other six stories in the volume are likewise beautiful, but they are sombre, and contain qualities that have been exalted (or condemned) as typically Russian. They reveal and endorse a highly uneconomic society, full of ne'er-do-wells and of ignorant idle priests, and riddled by a thoughtful but unconstructive intelligentsia. In 'Uprooted', Tchehov meditates on the millions of Russians who drift through life though they are ashamed of drifting, and his conclusion is:

> How amazed and perhaps even overjoyed all these people would have been if reasoning and words could be found to prove to them that their life was as little in need of justification as any other. In my sleep I heard a bell ring outside as plaintively as though shedding bitter tears, and the lay brother calling out several times: 'Lord Jesus Christ, Son of God, have mercy on us! Come to mass!'

Such a life is greatly in need of justification from the investor's standpoint. Dividends are impossible unless people work. And pity and forgiveness, though all very well in the Sermon on the Mount, seldom make for financial stability. Tchehov is of course, not an extremist like Dostoevsky, but his temperament is akin, and in 'The Letter' he gives the last word to a drunken priest who believes that nobody should be punished or blamed. And in 'The Bishop' and 'The Murder' he voices another heresy – that it is only in moments of extreme humiliation that we perceive the truth, whether about God or men. The Bishop, as he gains prosperity, loses touch with his fellows, and sees even his own mother become crafty and artificial: in illness and death he regains her. The murderer, Yakov, transported to Siberia, finds there the heavenly peace that he sought in vain during years of worship at home. Interested mainly in his art, Tchehov never underlines his opinions, but they are implicit in all that he writes and inherent in his conception of humanity, and they are on the whole not the opinions of the sound middle-class man. The slump in Slavs seems likely to continue, despite Koltchak and Denikin. Yet all the same:

> In the churring of insects, in the sinister figures, in the ancient barrows, in the blue sky, in the moonlight, in the flight of the nightbird, in everything you see and hear, triumphant beauty, youth, the fullness of power, and the passionate thirst for life begin to be apparent; the soul responds to the call of the lovely austere fatherland, and longs to fly over the steppes with the nightbird. And in the

triumph of beauty, in the exuberance of happiness, you are conscious of yearning and grief, as though the steppe knew that she was solitary, knew that her wealth and her inspiration were wasted for the world, not glorified by song, not wanted by anyone, and through the joyful clamour one hears her mournful hopeless call for singers, singers.

Sadness may triumph, but ugliness never. That is Tchehov's message to the Western world.

[1919]

Anton Tchehov, *The Bishop and Other Stories* (trans. C. Garnett)

The End of the Samovar

It would not be fair to judge this volume on its own merits. It is part of a great enterprise, the eleventh in a series, and it chances to contain but faint echoes of the masterpieces that have gone before. Dostoevsky seems fatigued, repeats himself, his humour often becomes facetious, his pathos mawkish; and the fatigue seems to have infected both his publisher and his translator. The publisher, for instance, has provided an inferior binding – at a moderate price it is true, but it would surely have been better to charge an extra shilling rather than spoil the appearance of a standard edition. And the translator, generally so fastidious, lapses into mechanical phrases and into unhandy and unhelpful expletives such as 'Tvoo!' which make Russian conversation even queerer than usual. No one who is ignorant of Dostoevsky should begin with this book. Those who know him already may read it with profit, for one or two reasons. Idolaters – they will profit particularly. Some of the stories (e.g., 'Another Man's Wife' and 'The Heavenly Christmas Tree'), are so feeble that they should dispel the superstition that Dostoevsky can do no wrong. It is a dangerous superstition, because only the more intelligent people hold it. The great Russian – least academic of men – is too often held up like a knout before the younger generation of English novelists, with the result that they flagellate themselves with him unskilfully, and mistake the weals that he has raised upon their style for literature. Abruptness, obscurity, sudden tracts of gibber-goo and tvoo – such is the legacy the master will leave English fiction, unless we are careful. As a stimulus he is invaluable, as a model he may be disastrous. He has penetrated – more deeply, perhaps, than any English writer – into the darkness and the goodness of the human soul, but he has penetrated by a way we cannot follow. He has his own psychological method, and marvellous it is. But it is not ours. And like all methods, it sometimes breaks down, and it is salutary to note the failure in most of the stories under review.

Here and there he succeeds. 'An Unpleasant Predicament' is one of those agitating tales that are more alive than life, and fill the reader with unbearable shame and gêne. Did you ever do the wrong thing in society? If so, imagine yourself to be Ivan Ilyitch, an important official with liberal aspirations, and to be walking home one night fairly full of champagne. You halt outside a little house where wedding festivities are in progress, and on learning that it is the abode of one of your own clerks, you think, in an evil moment, how nice it would be for him if you went in. You would cheer him, he will speak of your kindness and condescension in years to come.

> 'Of course, as a gentleman, I shall be quite on an equality with them, and shall not expect any especial marks of. . . . But morally, morally, it is a different matter; they will understand and appreciate it. . . . My actions will evoke their nobler feelings. . . . Well, I shall stay for half an hour.'

Your entry is inauspicious. The guests are appalled, the host is filled with an agitation that soon hardens into hatred. He sends out for champagne, which he cannot afford, and instead of being the life of the party, you sit swilling moodily upon the sofa. Everything goes wrong, and when the guests realise that you are 'a little top-heavy', they pass from awe into familiarity. Supper comes. You take Vodka, become hopelessly drunk at once, are insulted by a guest whom the host has to expel, collapse altogether into a plate of blancmange, become bestially ill, have to be installed for the night upon the nuptial couch. . . . etc., etc. To continue the catalogue is too cruel. Suffice it to say that you ruin your clerk, and that eight days later he asks to be transferred from your department. But you cannot get over it, even then, because Dostoevsky has not been writing about an imaginary Ivan Ilyitch, but about you. The force of his genius has dragged you into his pages, so that instead of reading a social satire or a farcical sketch, you have passed through a very painful and personal experience, and learnt a most necessary lesson. Never again will you venture out of your class . . . except in true humility, and for true love: that is the positive side of the Dostoevsky creed of which 'An Unpleasant Predicament' so scathingly presents the negative.

We approach the positive in 'The Dream of a Ridiculous Man', the last story in the book, and perhaps the best. A dream in Dostoevsky always is good – it was a form in which his genius most gladly worked. Think – to take contrasted examples – of the dream about the crushed reptile in *The Idiot*, and of Mitya's dream in *The Brothers Karamazov* about the weeping babe. The 'ridiculous man' dreams, like Mitya, of something that leaves him unreasonably and ridiculously happy, of a perfect and sinless planet to which he is transported, and which he corrupts until it turns into our world of sin. There should be nothing exhilarating in such a dream. Yet the emotion makes good, and a sense of joy and peace invades the reader in the final pages. In the first place we are cheered by a vivid memory of that golden age.

> They had no temples, but they had a real living and uninterrupted sense of oneness with the whole of the universe; they had no creed, but they had a certain knowledge that when their earthly joy had reached the limits of earthly nature, then there would come for them, for the living and for the dead, a still greater fullness of contact with the whole of the universe. They looked forward to that moment without joy, but without haste, not pining for it, but seeming to have a foretaste of it in their hearts of which they talked to one another.

And in the second place, though the golden age has been tarnished through the impurity of one man, though knowledge has been enthroned above feeling, and the consciousness of life above life, though suffering, inevitable, universal, has driven out joy and raised temples to Crucifixion – yet (so the dream teaches) there shall come in the end a glory the golden age never knew, when the same man shall learn to suffer not for himself but for others, and to love others as if they were himself. Then (this is illogical, but logic is part of corruption) – then paradise will return, return at once to our earth, inoculated for ever against decay, and men will again find in their daily life an uninterrupted foretaste of the heavenly. It is a beautiful dream, and it is full of essential, though not, of course, of official Christianity. Whether there is 'anything in it' is a question that each reader must answer for himself, but there is certainly much literature in it. Whatever our opinions, however great our inability to make these particular religious jumps, we must all admit that it seemed true while we were dreaming, and that a radiance followed into life after we had closed the book.

Thus the two sides of Dostoevsky – the critical and the constructive – both find expression in this miscellany. Different in spirit as are 'An Unpleasant Predicament' and 'The Dream of a Ridiculous Man', they both teach that we must love one another. An answer to their teaching could be attempted, but there is no space for it here. One must conclude by recommending the volume to all who have read the great masterpieces, and by congratulating the translator and the publisher upon their progress in their task. If the volume is not up to sample, it is just as well in a way, for it brings down Dostoevsky from the pedestal of omniscience and omnipotence where the idolaters would place him. He is a writer, not a god; and there is no writer, however great, whom any reader, however obscure, has not the right to criticize. Moreover, he is a writer who, for all his greatness, is a dangerous model for those who would write in England.

[1919]

F. Dostoevsky, *An Honest Thief, and Other Stories* (trans. C. Garnett)

Literature and History

The past has often been helpful to men of letters. When they do not feel quite up to the mark they can look at a chronicle or a museum, and ten to one some little creative spurt will result. Events that have happened long ago do acquire a certain air and even a certain shape; though the Muse has not digested them, she has given a preliminary chew, so that a washing bill, provided it belongs to a fifteenth-century convent, or a sucking pig, if given as a prize for the Hundred Yards in 1623, seems already matter for literature. So unexacting is the past, so irretrievably lost is the sequence of its facts, that the man of letters can either, like Mr Belloc, invent a sequence or he can hop from one fact until he conveniently encounters another, like M. Rodocanachi. Antæus-like, each time he thus hops, he feels an agreeable access of vitality, makes a little joke, sheds a little tear, evokes a little picture, throws a little light upon something small in our daily lives, and all the while suggests that the vitality is inherent, not derived, and that if he decided not to hop he could fly. One doubts it. Intermittent inspiration is so common; almost everyone is, for half a sentence, a fine novelist or a profound poet, and if the sentence would but finish there is no knowing where one would get to. As it is, one always gets to the ground, and only when the subject is historical can one pretend the ground is as lofty as the sky. Essays like these are, in fact, not quite on the square; they are neither history nor art, yet dodge criticism by hiding alternately under the robes of either.

This is the only censure that need be passed upon them. They are done very nicely – one can think of nothing as neat in English, though Diehl's *Figures Byzantines* occur as a possible rival in French. 'Open me where you will,' M.

Rodocanachi seems to say, 'you shall never find me inadequate.' He spreads a newspaper over brows that the Academy has three times crowned, he leans back in his commodious chair, and one reads:

> La vie coulait douce, insouciante, agrémentée de plaisirs. Une fois on édifia un château de bois que des chevaliers durent prendre d'assaut; dans une autre occasion, un groupe de gentilshommes montèrent dans une barque pour aller à la conquête d'une île; mais la barque chavira, les gentilshommes périrent tous noyés; le fils de celui qui avait organisé la fête était du nombre; le duc ne voulut pas qu'elle fût interrompue.

Here in a couple of sentences are gaiety, tragedy, irony, and an implied criticism of the period – the sixteenth century at Ferrara. What more will you? Fantasy? Very well:

> Virgile débarrassa Naples d'une invasion de sangsues au moyen d'une sangsue d'or qu'il jeta dans un puits. Il créa un marché où les viandes se conservaient pendant six semaines sans se corrompre. Il fit beaucoup mieux encore: il mit Naples dans une bouteille afin de la soustraire à ses ennemis. Naples n'en fut pas moins prise par les Impériaux. . . .

And the people who did or believed these things were once alive. This is history, not literature. And yet they raise emotions appropriate to a creative work, so it is literature, not history. Hither and thither the writer hops, from a blob of dates, via a flight of the imagination, into a financial transaction conducted in écus! The dates are right, the imagination isn't wrong, and only gradually does one realize that the form of his compositions is bastard and their appeal too shifting to be intense.

But the past has another possibility, a subtle and terrible quality which M. Rodocanachi's temperament will never convey. The past once was alive and it now is dead, and if a writer succeeds in expressing these facts simultaneously, as

Hardy does in *The Dynasts*, and D'Annunzio in *La Città Morta*, he has achieved a great literary effect. The expression must be simultaneous, there must be a complete fusion of all tenses, or the spell fails. Napoleon and Agamemnon are men and will not be men, were men and are not men at the same time; even in the flesh they were ghosts, leading phantom armies whose tramp can be heard, and the dust that now blows about the world, influencing us, is Napoleon and Agamemnon. The gates between the living and the dead fly open, as in Beddoes' strange play, yet though the passage has become easy it has lost nothing of its Miltonic horror. The tenses have not been fused in any philosophic sense; it is an æsthetic faith that has interwoven them, three in one and one in three, and made them a garment for poetry. And strictly speaking, it is only along lines such as these that Literature should have any commerce with history: otherwise she may suffer from the connection and have to caper more often than she bargained for.

[1920]

E. Rodocanachi, *Etudes et fantaisies historiques*

Frenchman and France

'Hasty generalizations are always tempting to travellers.' One must begin, as does Mrs Wharton, with some such apology before discoursing on national characteristics. But as soon as the apology has been made, how confidently one gallops forward, leaping over inconvenient facts, saluting convenient ones, tilting at generalizations that conflict, riding faster and faster with the blood of battle in the veins, and the sting of the wind on the cheeks. Norwegians are honest. Greeks don't wash. Never trust an Oriental. Faster, faster; until the apology has sunk beneath the horizon. And if, drawing rein, one looks back and remembers a Greek who did wash, or an Indian friend with whom one's purse and person were equally safe throughout a period of fifteen years – never mind; they are exceptions. They must not be allowed to spoil the fun of the ride. It would be too depressing to suppose that this exhilarating activity may be mainly waste of time, and generalizations but the cries of ignorant armies that clash by night.

Mrs Wharton's book takes the form of a sermon about the French addressed to good but rough Americans. Her tone is a little stern. She deplores the crudity of her countrymen, and is indeed almost as severe upon untravelled members of her race as upon unmarried members of her sex. France she knows well, and perhaps loves it better even than she knows it, and under the four heads of 'Reverence', 'Taste', 'Intellectual honesty', and 'Continuity' she builds up the French character for the benefit of the uninformed. But early on a regrettable misfortune occurs. As an example of French 'reverence', she refers to the national abhorrence of blackberries. Blackberries, she tells us, are never, never, never eaten by the French, and this not because of any lack of intellectual curiosity, but out of respect to some ancient sanction that forbade the eating of blackberries. This generalization seemed easy to test, so, meeting two French ladies, one from Normandy and one from the South, I asked their opinion. The answer in both cases was an indignant 'Mais on les mange tout le temps,' and the catastrophe rather shakes one's faith in Mrs Wharton.

Of course, the French people whom she has met happened not to eat blackberries, and the matter is in itself unimportant. But one immediately fears that the rule the example is supposed to support may be crumbling also, and that the French are not reverent either. Mrs Wharton faces this possibility under the heading of intellectual honesty, and solves it by a brilliant paradox: the French have both intellectual honesty and reverence, and correct the one by unconsciously secreting the other. But is there not another and a duller solution? May not some Frenchmen be reverent and others not? There was Racine, and also Voltaire; there is Claudel, and also Anatole France. The more one shakes a book of this sort, the more its leaves fall out. It has turned from the individual, the only reliable unit, to masses of individuals, and has to surmount contradictions that result, not from facts, but from its own unsound method. It makes epigrams of the 'door is both open and shut' type, when it merely means 'here are two doors, one shut and the other open.' Generalizations are sometimes necessary, for human intercourse and clarity of thought itself becomes impossible without them. But they are the desperate device of our weakness, of our inability to remember the various separate facts that we have encountered; they are horses that gallop us away from the country where we ought to have stopped, and where blackberries are eaten by some of the inhabitants though not by all.

When Mrs Wharton turns to geography she is, indeed, on firmer ground. The exposed Eastern frontier of France is a fact which has probably had its effect upon 99 per cent of individual Frenchmen, and made them nervous in peace time, desperate in warfare, and cruel in victory. Throughout the centuries France has been occupied in holding it or in providing an exposed Western frontier for the Germans, and no doubt this has differentiated her from countries whose barriers are more secure. Her culture, too (e.g., the Academy) provides generalizations that should hold good in the majority of cases. And for the main aim of the book – the promotion of sensitiveness in Americans – one can have nothing but praise. Yet the writer told us far more about the French in her novels that she has done here, partly because she is a first-rate novelist, whereas she is an indifferent generalizer, far inferior to Mr Clutton Brock, who has covered similar ground. What vivid pictures she gave us in *The Custom of the Country* of aristocratic life in the provinces! As a novelist dealing with individuals she was so remorseless, so logical. But as an interpreter of national characteristics she can argue thus:

> The French mean [by 'La gloire'] something infinitely larger, deeper, and subtler than we mean by 'glory'. The proof is that the Anglo-Saxon is taught not to do great deeds for 'glory', while the French, unsurpassed in great deeds, have always avowedly done them for 'La gloire'.

Where is the proof? May not the two words mean the same thing, and the Anglo-Saxon teaching be right and the French wrong? And, again, to illustrate the continuity of French art, she refers to the prehistoric cave drawings at Altamira, while admitting that there is really no connection, and that the caves are in Spain. Her book contains much interesting observation. But it is, as she says, hastily compiled amid war conditions, and would have been more appropriately published in the form of a diary, or, better still, used up as fiction.

The chief barrier between us and the foreigner is, of course, language. This is a dull remark – so dull that few writers consent to make it. It is much more amusing to talk darkly of racial characteristics, of mystic sympathies and antipathies, or to work for more than it is worth some local accident of climate or scenery. Since the war all the high falutin about nations' souls and habits and voices has greatly increased, and one longs for the cold, reasonable light of the eighteenth century to shine out again and dispel it. You cannot talk to France, nor can you listen to her. But you can talk to a Frenchman if he talks English or you French, and then the personal intimacy upon which alone knowledge can be based may spring up. The intimacy is its own reward: it is not a short cut towards knowing other Frenchmen, and it will have no effect upon the official relations between England and France. One is told that it will, and that a nation's foreign policy expresses the collective sentiments of its citizens. More high falutin. If – which Heaven forbid – relations ever become strained between the Court of St James's and the Quai d'Orsay, books would at once appear to tell us that between the Anglo-Saxon and the Latin an eternal gulf yawns, that blackberries are a symbol of it, and the Hundred Years' War a proof, and that our real affinity is with – I dare not finish the sentence!

[1920]

Edith Wharton, *French Ways and their Meanings*

Cousin X--

Most of us have, at one time or another, been taken to see an old gentleman, a distant family connection perhaps, who was highly but mysteriously spoken of in the circle of his friends. Cousin X (for so let us call him) lived in one of the more unusual counties, such as Worcestershire or Rutland. He sent a very notable pony cart, broader than it was long and painted gamboge, to meet us at the station. Yet he could not be called old-fashioned, because at his park gates we had to transfer out of the pony cart into a motor-car, which whizzed up the drive in no time. Our reception was polite but impersonal; Cousin X at once began to talk in a booming voice, mainly about conchology, and never stopped until it was time for his guests to go. He talked all through lunch, which, conchology apart, was a memorable meal, for the menu was a roast swan, followed by a small and badly made rice pudding. Moreover, the table was littered with appliances for ringing the bell or for letting out the dog, appliances which worked, but which took up a good deal of room. We departed quite sure that Cousin X was remarkable, but unable to equate him with anything that was remarkable in the world outside. Even his shells seemed to have come out of a special sea.

With feelings as mixed as the above does one peruse the works of Mr Doughty. He, too, is remarkable, but it is quite impossible to connect him with anything remarkable outside. When one thinks of other writers one forgets him, and vice versa. He, too, is highly but mysteriously spoken of by a small circle. He, too, is full of appliances that work but take up a good deal of room. His 'fame', to use a most inappropriate word, rests upon *Arabia Deserta*, a book of travels that is sometimes praised but seldom opened. Doughty visited Arabia in the seventies. It impressed him and (a truer measure of a man's worth) he likewise impressed it: the recent political successes of Colonel Lawrence in the Hedjaz were (one is told) facilitated by local memories of the romantic and intrepid Englishman, who had preceded him. But the wonderful tour is described in a style that is so gnarled, so affected, as to be almost unreadable; purple patches may survive in an anthology, but the book as a whole, despite its moral sincerity, is as dead as the sands that it chronicles. And if Doughty's prose is dead, what will be the fate of his verse?

> Wherefore be those too much to blame,
> that pinch;
> Of malice, rankling in ungenerous
> breast;
> (Which might themselves a cattle-crib
> uneath
> Devise:) at master-ártificers work;
> And with the venom of crude lips,
> deface;
> Who moved of hearts devotion, vows
> to Heavens
> High service a CATHEDRAL.

What does it all mean: What does 'uneath' mean? Why in the last line but one is there no apostrophe in 'hearts' and 'heavens'? Why does the last line but two end with a colon instead of a full stop? There is no answer to any of these questions. Cousin X is speaking, and interruptions are useless. There is nothing to be done except never to visit him again. One would renew the attempt if, beneath the tiresomeness, there was a beautiful or intellectual general purpose. But no beauty or intelligence can be discerned in the general purpose of *Mansoul.* It is the old hackneyed business of a visit to the under-world – so tiring, such a getting downstairs, so dark, magic mirror, etc. First of all we meet the Kaiser, 'a loathly leprosy blots his werewolf's face', then others of the dead. The conversation is such as is usual on infernal occasions. The shades ask the poet, with whom are associated two things called Mansoul and Minimus, how he came to be here while still alive, and he replies to them at length. Then they give their opinion on man's destiny. Zoroaster, Confucius, Buddha, Socrates, and the other heavies each utter appropriate redes. To hear them we have to burrow backwards and forwards under the earth, sometimes tunnelling the Mediterranean.

Finally we come to the 'Belges' war-wasted march', which entails more sharp words to the Kaiser, who now seems to be alive. A second vision follows – of British poetry – then a third, of a city of dreams: and Mansoul learns, as the result of his wanderings, that Faith, Love, Patriotism, Peace, etc., are English virtues, and that 'uneath', 'ment', 'derne', 'scruzed', 'tyned', 'stover', 'totty', and 'blebs' are English words. Obscure in its parts, commonplace as a whole, there is little to be said for the poem. It is the work of a man of high integrity and valour, but of a man who must be impervious to criticism and who has not – like that other contorted poet, Gerard Manley Hopkins – an inner fountain that gushes out through the rubble and the scree and makes an eternal melody. Even at his simplest, Doughty is not melodious.

> Pied daisies, crowned each with a silver
> fret;
> Starring 'mongst cups of gold, in thicket
> grass;
> With speedwell gentle, under woodbine
> bush.
> And meadows sweet, whose gracious
> plumes aloft,
> So nobly meek, our every sense doth greet.

How reluctantly the music issues! And – shifting to the pictorial standpoint – how feeble are the images! They neither transfigure nor recall any flower that we have known. The utmost they do is to remind us of other poems that we have read.

But while one criticizes, Cousin X seems to lift his leonine head and to intimate that if he thought it worth while he could stop his booming, and could explain why he was crabbed in his diction and obvious in his thoughts, why he constructed sentences upside down, and punctuated them inside out, why he quotes from Homer neither in English nor in Greek, but in Italian. Did he not once explain why he employed both a cart and a car to bring his guests from the station? It was that the lane was too rough for the motor and the drive too steep for the pony – a logical explanation, though somehow it raised more problems than it solved. Anyhow, Cousin X was sincere, independent, dignified. He lived his own life in his own way, fearing no man. And the same is true of Doughty. Judged by standards other than the literary, he ranks extremely high.

[1920]

C. M. Doughty, *Mansoul*

Where There is Nothing

True happiness consists in giving rather than in receiving. Riches are useless without love, and those who acquire them suddenly often spend them ostentatiously. Jews are very rich and very cynical, and cannot be trusted owing to their Oriental origin. The poor, ground down by captains of industry, must not expect help from the Church, which has greatly deteriorated since the days of her Founder. Much the same is true about Art. Art should be simple, even in a woman's dress. Imagine if the masterpieces in the Louvre were overloaded with ornaments! Old age approaches despite powder and rouge. Then what is our duty? Not to be faint-hearted. Every cloud has a silver lining, and life will lead us back through suffering to love. The battle is indeed to the strongest, but 'strength' does not necessarily mean 'material strength', indeed, rather the contrary.

Not Martin Tupper, not Mrs Markham, not even the late Lord Avebury, is taking the field. We are in no maiden lady's drawing-room where canaries twitter and the shafts of the afternoon sun fall upon a little tea-table, but in the tremendous council chamber of one who has known the world, and shaken it to its foundations, and who is certain of his place in history. Unborn generations will remember the name of Georges Clemenceau, nor can his contemporaries pronounce it without awe. His immortality is assured, whether in paradise or in the infernal ice, and he won it by his own efforts, not by the compliancy of circumstance. At the Last Judgment vast and solid is the material that such a man will provide. The triumph of France and the misery of Europe will be piled – into which scale we know not, but with the sound of thunder the opposing scale will kick the beam. The Sentence is about to be pronounced, the Heavenly

Hosts stand attentive. But at the last moment one of the subordinate angels – she who looks after art – will come up with *The Strongest* and one or two other novels in her lap, and Michael will raise them to his starry forehead, rapidly to absorb their contents. He will apprehend the foregoing maxims and the following plot:

Henri au Grand Sérieux (the name is not printed thus, but Michael naturally knows characters by their real names) – Henri au Grand Sérieux, after a turbulent and aristocratic youth, falls in love with the wife of Monsieur Parvenu, his friend. That love is returned and a girl born, whom Parvenu, immersed in his commercial schemes, is deceived by the Doctor into accepting as his own, although at first he exclaimed 'Impossible!' Madame Parvenu dies, and imagine the pathos of Grand Sérieux's position now! A father and a Frenchman, he has to watch his own daughter growing up in surroundings that he cannot approve, for it is terrible, the condition of the workpeople in Parvenu's paper factory, and his taste is bad and his ideals coarse, and worst of all, he destines his supposed child for a brilliant marriage which shall consolidate his position in society. Things come to a crisis with the arrival of the fascinating but corrupt Comtesse des Intrigues, whom Grand Sérieux has known in his unregenerate days and whom Parvenu hopes to wed. She interests herself in finding a mate for the girl. Terrific is the struggle, which is transferred to Paris and conducted with the heartlessness so characteristic of that capital. The countess is surrounded by her allies – Baron Cynico; the international financier, Quai d'Orsay, the gilded diplomat; Madame de Mimonde, the Abbé Tartuffe, and a host of others; and she leads the rout until the inexperienced girl is intoxicated. In vain does Grand Sérieux put forth his own candidate, an honourable Frenchman who has travelled in India, but seldom speaks. He is outmanoeuvred, and his daughter decides at the same moment that she will marry the diplomat and that strikes must be put down by force. She reaches these decisions against her better judgement, which she stifles by injecting morphia, so that at the final scene she is a trifle dazed. That scene, like the rest of the book, does not repay quotation, but 'I, not you, am her father' is its theme, and its concluding sentence is 'Now I will live for forgiveness.'

Thus far the Archangel Michael, and tosses the volume into the appropriate scale. But while it is falling we, who have not the sense of eternal values, may with propriety ask ourselves another question. Was the volume written sincerely? Say 'no', and nothing else need be said; the Tiger in 1898 was off his feed, so he turned out a novel. But say 'yes', and some interesting considerations ensue. The great and successful statesman whose iron will has modified history is giving us his impressions of the world where he was so active. The book now becomes as precious as the Confessions of Aurelius or the poems of Frederick the Great. France, Clemenceau's lodestar, for whom he would have died, for whom he has urged millions to die; France, for whose sake he has outwitted humanitarians and economists and ruined Europe – France is about to re-emerge from his mind in the form of fiction. One reads with an awe which seems to have sustained most critics to the end. But at last a new emotion asserts itself: boredom; France and its contents appear to be dead. Pinch the book where you will, and it does not move. Not only are the characters 'dead' in the technical sense, being mere bundles of qualities, but the scenery, the social face of Paris, is also defunct, which is most surprising, considering the writer's career. He, to whom all sections of society must have been open, reads as if he had never been anywhere or seen anything. Compare his account of a costly evening party with Miss Daisy Ashford's, or, if this test be too severe, with anything out of Alphonse Daudet or Thackeray. Hum of life, vividness of details – he transmits neither. Vague rhetoric and clumsy satire are all that he achieves, until one cannot believe that Georges Clemenceau was ever invited to any evening party, costly or cheap. The chapters about the factory and the modiste's are equally extinct, and the pall is provided by the cloud of sentimental morality of which specimens have already been given, and which envelops the whole affair. Is it thus that he conceives our civilization?

The obvious reply is 'No. He conceives it otherwise, as his

actions prove. Do not make so much fuss. He happens not to be a good novelist, and there the mystery ends.' But does it end? May not Clemenceau have correctly transcribed his most sacred visions, and his books and his life be one? Human nature is so eerie that the possibility must be contemplated. The Paris he fought for may be the Paris he depicts. The Justice he talks about may, like the Justice he writes about, be nothing but the moral perspiration that is incidental to an elderly man. His acts, like his art, may be built round a void, and if we could enter his mind, we might find in it only the feeblest image of the world that we love. Little is known about the psychology of 'greatness', for, naturally impressed by the men who rule our fortunes, we adopt in all ranks a modest attitude towards them. We assume that a statesman who feels strongly about France feels a France that is fine, and that his sensations are more vivid than our own, although he may not be able to express them artistically. Yet hints to the contrary occur, and *The Strongest* confirms them. Its mediocrity is so complete as to suggest that Clemenceau sees our lovely and tragic earth as a half-lit picture where youths kill one another and emperors fall and boundaries are readjusted in terms of universal insipidity. All is relative, and of course his Germany is less valuable than his France. But is his France as valuable as one's own Germany? And at the Last Judgment a strange miracle may occur. *The Strongest,* though thrown by an angelic hand, may fail to reach either pan of the scales for which it is destined. It will be too light, lighter than air; it will float in the final wind and be blown into limbo. The deeds of the novelist, the blood and the tears that he caused, the victories that he won for his country – they will remain, and by them he will be judged and assigned to his appropriate eternity. But when the search is extended to the central sanctum where he says to himself, 'I did this,' and also 'I am I,' nothing may be found in it except a pinch of dust.

[1920]

Georges Clemenceau, *The Strongest*

The School Feast

Together with other children, one seems to be seated again at a deal table in the Rectory Field, amid mugs of hot, weak tea and glistening planes of bread and butter and cakes and vases of limp, wild flowers, and flags of the Union Jack and of other nations, even of the German nation, for it was laid long ago, was that table, and the children who sat at it are now men. It is the School Feast. The site of our revels has previously been occupied by cows. The weather is appropriate to the event; not good, but not exactly bad, and not too many caterpillars fell off the oak trees into the jam.

At the head of the table lie a Bible and a dish of plums, and the schoolmistress stands above them and paws the air with ritual gesture to keep the wasps from settling. She is presently joined by a dignified and attractive figure, a little more than lay yet less than priest. 'The Reverend Stopford Brooke' some call him, but others say 'Mr Stopford Brooke'. He takes up the Bible, but does not open it, for some of the children may be atheists and he would alienate no one, and in glowing yet general terms he says a grace, and indicates the nature of our feast. 'It is the banquet of English Literature,' says he, and glibly enumerates the various cakes. Presently his eye lights on the dish of plums, and a confused but helpful metaphor results. Even as plums are eaten by children and wasps so can English Literature be put to good uses and bad, not but what wasps also have their good uses. The upshot is that we shall come to no harm even from Lord Byron. And we did not. It is only in retrospect that we grow critical. That school feast has, from the modern point of view, one great defect: all the delicacies tasted alike.

At the present day, immensely disillusioned, one does not go to literature for ethical sustenance. Stopford Brooke did.

He sought, like us, to connect literature with life, but he was a preacher, and a Victorian, and he looked in Crabbe, Blake, Wordsworth, and Shelley for sermons that would confirm his own. He thought that their text was 'Naturalism'; what 'Naturalism' was he did not so strictly think, and one seeks in vain in these republished Essays for a clear definition of it. It is seeing a flower as a flower, it is calling a spade a spade, it is country life, cosmopolitanism, realism, idealism, and the Divine vision. It was 'delivered from its swaddling clothes' by Wordsworth and Coleridge, it 'overstrained its manhood and breathed its last in Keats.' It left a child behind it, Naturalism No. 2, who 'for ten years or so grew in silence,' inspired Baily, Tennyson, Browning, and met its death in William Morris, we are not told how. Nor is this the end. This child has also left a child 'whose multitudinous efforts to express itself we hear hour by hour and day by day.' Do we? We thought we did at the School Feast. But today the whole metaphor seems no more alive than a bundle of sermon paper. It may be our fault; it may be the fault of the years through which we have passed, but a hardness has entered our hearts, and we feel towards the amiable orator and his Naturalisms much as Crabbe felt towards another clergyman:

> Circles in water as they wider flow
> The less conspicuous in their progress grow;
> And when at last they touch upon the shore
> Distinction ceases and they're viewed no more.
> His love, like that last circle, all embraced,
> But with effect that never could be traced.

Yet he had one advantage over any critic who can write to-day. He was nearer ethically to the poets whom he criticized. They, too, wished to 'do good', and though the immensity of their genius transplanted their wish to other realms, the moral hankering remained in them. Stopford Brooke was well qualified to examine such hankerings. He was, within limits, a good psychologist. He notes, for instance, Shelley's tendency 'to become emotionalized as he wrote, even by opinions with which he disagreed, if they happened to be noble or imaginative' and his remarks on Byron's conception of sin are weighty and profound.

It is when we come to the poetry that he fails us. Beauty was to him only the fact that gets the preacher going, and he could not realize that a poet's message is far greater than anything that he manages to say, that it is not information, but a quickening of the fellow poet who slumbers within the reader; that poetic activity must be stated in terms not of good and evil but of life and death. He would reply that the two categories are identical, that Life is good, that Death is evil. But they are not identical, anyway not for the twentieth century. We seek the vital from a complication of reasons; the nineteenth century the moral, and the great gulf between us is fixed mainly on these lines. The final essay (on Byron's 'Cain') is the best. Rhetoric and loose metaphors give way to more disciplined statement. Yet even here we are getting not at the life, but at a lesson (that if we do not sin ourselves others have to sin for us, so that we may know good as good) – and at a lesson that we find more vividly presented in Dostoevsky

It is, indeed, impossible to read the book without feeling a trifle superior. The banquet of literature, as the modern critic serves it, seems far more dainty and varied. Still, the good old School Feast had its points. It realized that literature, and poetry in particular, is of supreme importance, and that no man can flourish without partaking of it. By stressing the ethical importance it has passed out of date: but how soon, and for what reasons, will the criticisms of today suffer a like oblivion? Living as we do in the backrush and onrush of immeasurable tides, is it likely that any words we utter about the past will be durable? Stopford Brooke, whatever his limitations, was part of an ordered society. He could look back without interruption to Shelley, and a gap no wider than the French Revolution divided him from Pope. This gave him a certain advantage over ourselves: the spectacle of orderly development cannot have seemed to him so strange, and if the whole round earth is indeed bound by gold chains about the feet of God, he was in a better position to perceive it.

[1920]

Stopford A. Brooke, *Naturalism in English Poetry*

A Great History

It's no good humming and hawing; at least it is, but before the operation begins the following sentence must be penned: A great book. The writer tries to outline the history of the world, from the epoch of igneous gas to the establishment of Christianity; he succeeds, and it is the first duty of a reviewer to emphasize his success. Whatever he may do in his second volume he has achieved a masterpiece in his first, and one desires to offer him not only praise but thanks. Unconvincing as a Samurai or a bishop, he has surely come through as a historian. A great book; a possession for ever, for the ever of one's tiny life.

But now let us lower the voice a little, otherwise nothing gets said. What, after reading the book, is one's main sensation? Perhaps that it wasn't so much a book as a lecture, delivered by a vigorous, fair-minded and well-informed free lance. He was assisted by a lantern – its assistance was essential – and bright and clear upon the sheet he projected the misty beginnings of fact. The rocks bubbled and the sea smoked. Presently there was an inter-tidal scum: it was life, trying to move out of the warm water, and subsequent slides showed the various forms it took. A movement also became perceptible among the audience; one or two of the prehistoric experts, discontented at so much lucidity, withdrew. Man, Neanderthalian, Palæo- and Neo-Lithic; man in Mesopotamia and Egypt; nomad man; man in Judæa (more experts go out), in Greece (still more), in India (exeunt the theosophists), in China (murmurs of 'me no likee') and in Rome. Over Rome there is a serious disturbance; the Public School masters rise to protest against the caricature of Julius Cæsar, while the neo-Catholics denounce the belittlement of the Pax Romana and the Latin Thing, and lumber out to drink beer. The lecturer, undeterred by these secessions, describes the origins of Christianity and loses the Anglican section of his flock meanwhile, though the withdrawal is quieter in this case, and due more to bewilderment than wrath. Finally the lights are turned up, and the room seems as full as ever: one can't believe that a single person has left it. Immense applause. The lecturer thanks the lanternist. . .

In praising so large a work, one must presumably begin with its arrangement. Arrangement is a negative quality, but a great one: it is the faculty of not muddling the reader, and Wells possesses it in a high degree. He masses his facts together, kith with kin, yet they seldom overlap chronologically: there is a little confusion as one crosses from prehistory into history, but really this is all. How masterly, for example, is the arrangement of the Roman and the Chinese Empires! One knew that they were contemporary and alike menaced by 'barbarians', but here one sees China elbowing off the attack, and so generating a westerly movement with nomad tribes which is communicated across Asia and Europe, and finally overwhelms Rome. Maps and time-charts elucidate the process. How masterly again, and how necessary, is the emphasis laid upon the novelty of civilization! It is an episode, the latest in the career of Man, just as Man is only an episode in the career of the earth. 'Half the duration of human civilization and the keys to all its chief institutions are to be found *before* Sargon I.;' yet man is thousands of years older than the earliest institution, and millions of years before man there was life. With the help of time-diagrams this proportion is made clear: another triumph of arrangement. Arrangement seldom receives its due praise, though we suffer and whine as soon as it is absent. It is the oil that allows the machine to function. From it proceed the ease and the pleasure with which we read ahead.

Selection is of course a more controversial topic, and here the critics can get going if they think it worth while. Each of us can write two long lists: of facts that Wells might have left out, and of facts that he ought to have put in. Here is an item from the first list: The Scythian expedition of Darius occupies too much space: Wells has been seduced into garrulity by the companionship of Herodotus, and in his account of the crossing of the Danube he even inflicts 'imaginative' touches that are unwarranted by his original. And here is an item from the second list: the Sicilian expedition of Athens occupies only a sentence: yet it is in the opinion of other historians a fact of the highest importance – pivotal, not merely dramatic – and Wells should at least show cause to the contrary. So might one go on, even adding flourishes of scholarship such as 'Surely Pompey's Pillar at Alexandria wasn't meant for a sea mark.' But is there any point in going on? Listen to the experts! They are beginning to argue over their beer. They are saying to each other: 'It's only in *my* period he breaks down – he's quite sound in yours.' There is not a man alive who could have selected from those millions of years so well, and we had better acknowledge this handsomely, and give the writer 'good' again.

A third merit is the style. The surface of Wells' English is poor, and he does not improve its effect when he tints it purple. But it does do its job, as the following example will show. He is speaking of the nomads (and, by the way, his sympathy with outsiders contributes largely to the balance of his historical outlook). He is wanting to describe their migrations, which combined a steady advance with a north-and-south movement between winter and summer pasturage. So he says: 'They moved in annual swings, as the broom of a servant who is sweeping out a passage swishes from side to side as she advances.' You may complain that the sentence is journalistic rather than literary. But hasn't it 'got' the nomads for you, and so fulfilled the aim of the historian? Similarly with the refilling of the Mediterranean in 30,000 BC and with the disaster that overtook the Mesozoic reptiles; such events, hitherto somewhat academic, will be intimate in the future, because Wells has written of them racily.

Arrangement, selection, style: so these make up the case for his *Outline*, and it is an overwhelming case. Now let us attempt to state the other side.

[1920]

H. G. Wells, *The Outline of History*

A Great History II

We indicated last week the chief merits of Wells' *Outline.* Now for the defects, and the first of them is a serious one. Wells' lucidity, so satisfying when applied to peoples and periods, is somehow inadequate when individuals are thrown on to the screen. The outlines are as clear as ever, but they are not the outlines of living men. He seldom has created a character who lives (Kipps and the aunt in *Tono-Bungay* are the main exceptions); and a similar failure attends his historical evocations. He has occasion in this volume to sketch about thirty eminent humans, from Akhnaton to St Benedict, and only one of them sticks in one's mind. That one is Cato the Censor, and he is galvanized into life not so much by the author's insight as by his crossness. Cato is the type Wells cannot stand, and the result is a brilliant tirade such as might occur in the *New Machiavelli.* Of course he does not intend to produce a portrait gallery, and it is well that this is not his intention, for if it were his history would fail. As it is, the eminent humans appear as diagrams, lettered at their characteristic angles; the lecturer points to the lettering and then passes on. Often no harm is done; the case becomes serious when an individual has, so to speak, to be the epitome of his age, when he is required by the historian to focus all the unhappiness or joy or hope that surrounds him. Xerxes was such an individual at Salamis, as Æschylus and Herodotus both realized. But when Wells would also achieve this most necessary effect, he makes a disagreeable rattling noise and produces a passage like this:

> We can imagine something of the coming and going of messengers, the issuing of futile orders, the changes of plan, throughout the day. In the morning Xerxes had

> come out provided with tables to mark the most successful of the commanders for reward. In the gold of the sunset he beheld the sea power of Persia utterly scattered, sunken and destroyed, and the Greek fleet over against Salamis. . . .

Over against such a sunset the only possible comment is, 'Don't do it again; it isn't your line.' But he does it again. Observe how he dramatizes a sorrow even more representative than Xerxes':

> We are told that a great darkness fell upon the earth and that the veil of the temple was rent in twain; but if indeed these things occurred they produced not the slightest effect upon the minds of people in Jerusalem at that time. It is difficult to believe nowadays that the order of nature indulged in any such meaningless comments. Far more tremendous is it to suppose a world apparently indifferent to those three crosses in the red evening twilight, and to the little group of perplexed and desolated watchers. The darkness closed upon the hill; the distant city set about its preparations for the Passover; scarcely anyone but that knot of mourners on their way to their homes troubled whether Jesus of Nazareth was still dying or already dead. . . .

Over against such a red twilight the only possible comment is a coloured illustration, and the publishers have provided one. There we may see the three crosses, so far more tremendous than the fantasies of Tintoretto, and we may reflect on the nemesis that attends the non-Christian who would write sympathetically of Christ. Wells' failure on Golgotha, however, is due to the same cause as his failure at Salamis. He cannot create individuals, and when he would use one to epitomize a great contemporary emotion the result is a mess. Arrangement, selection, lucidity of style, no longer assist him. He often tells us that individuals ought to merge themselves in something greater, and he has practised what he preaches, for we come away with no knowledge of the faces and hearts of his thirty dead leaders.

Thus, though his history 'lives', it is in a peculiar way: by its fundamental soundness, expressed through brilliant parallels and metaphors; not by imaginative reconstructions of individual people or scenes. We see the nomads advancing into the Roman Empire like the housemaid's broom, but if Wells took one of the twigs of the broom and tried to describe its mentality he would at once become thin and sentimental. It is a history of movements, not of man. Nor is this its only weakness. As a rule the writer most admirably suppresses his personal likes and dislikes; there are none of the explosions that interrupt his fiction, and much dignity and coherence accrue. But in one direction he does break out. He has one little complaint against the past, which, try as he will, he cannot silence; he cannot pardon it for having been so ill-informed. Even in Mesozoic times ignorance is censured. He notes the uneducated tendencies of the reptiles, who might have averted extinction had they taken appropriate steps. He has, again and again, to deplore the incuriosity of Homo Sapiens, who will not study science, will not invent tippy labour-saving appliances. Man might have evolved the conditions of 1920 a thousand years earlier if only he had bucked up. The Chinese invented printing, but made no use of it owing to some mental blur. The Alexandrians had a library, but their books were shaped like pianola rolls, and consequently awkward to consult. 'One thinks at once of a simple and obvious little machine by which such a roll could have been quickly wound to and fro for reference, but nothing of the sort seems to have been used.' And the Romans were worst of all, ignorant of geography and economics, and not even developing the steam engine devised by Hiero; why, the legions might have rolled about in motor lorries! Irritability is better than reverence, but it does result in some absurdity and in a sort of Polytechnic glibness. Our curiosity is stimulated, our wonder never; the lecturer has no use for wonder. He doesn't know how life began, but there is nothing mysterious in its beginnings; he might know them and probably some day will, and the intertidal Palæozoic scum is no queerer than the beach at Southend; it is only less accessible to students. Compare such an attitude with that of Rémy de Gourmont in his essay 'Une Loi de constance intellectuelle'. The account of early man there given may not be as learned or as brilliant as Wells', but it shows an instinctive sympathy with the difficulties of invention. The conscious kindling of fire, according to de Gourmont, was the highest mental achievement of our race, and he can strip us of our clothes and match-boxes, and set us to watch the awakened blaze, while Wells would only be annoyed that it wasn't kindled earlier. He confuses information with wisdom, like most scientists, so his judgements are sometimes very naïf, and though his intelligence is both subtle and strong, it cannot quite supply his lack of imagination.

And what is it all about, anyhow? What is the meaning of this evolution from igneous gas, through scum and Christianity, to ourselves and mustard gas? De Gourmont had his answer: 'Evolution n'est pas progrès. L'évolution est un fait, et le progrès un sentiment.' And Dean Inge, though he adds a proviso in favour of Hope, as a clergyman must, makes the same answer. Wells does not agree. His hand holds a lecturer's castanet, but his heart is Victorian, with a quite Tennysonian trust in the To-be. To him evolution is progress, and though a few events (e.g. the Punic wars) are condemned as purely toxic, he is on the whole inclined to give a good mark to everything that happens, on the ground that it makes the past a little more like the present. What of the present? He will tell us in Vol. II, but we may be sure that he will condone it by pointing to the future. There is no collaring these optimists. They asked for science in 1914, they got it, and in 1920 they still ask for science. Nor would one wish to collar them, for it is only an optimist who could attempt a history of this planet. To the rest of us it is a planet full of scraps, many of which are noble and beautiful, but there seems not any proof that it progresses. 'Seek no proof,' says Orthodoxy, as she gazes up to heaven through the bottom of her beer mug, but Wells will not go as far as that. He has the air throughout of adducing facts, of arguing that Science will do the trick if only we have enough of her. He sees that humanity is creative. He cannot see that there may be an incurable defect in us, a poison sucked from the Palæozoic slime, that renders us incapable of putting to good use what we have created. When he approaches this problem his manner becomes episcopal, and he introduces that curious but not unfamiliar figure, his 'God':

> The history of our race and personal religious experience run so closely parallel as to seem to a modern observer almost the same thing; both tell of a being at first scattered and blind and utterly confused, feeling its way slowly to the serenity and salvation of an ordered and coherent purpose.

The religious experiences of Wells, like those of Mr Britling, have been little more than a visit to a looking-glass in whose area he has seen an image of himself which imitates his gestures and endorses his deficiencies; if he feels his way to a chair, no doubt his reflection sits down too. But it is hard to see what consolation the human race can derive from this, or what parallels it can supply. It has indeed had another experience, but one that the writer despises or ignores: the experience of mysticism. The neglect of mysticism is, from the psychological point of view, the chief defect in the book, for mysticism may be selfish or erroneous, but it dwells permanently in the human mind, whispering, when least we expect it, that education, information, action, and history itself, are an illusion. It can be explained away – part of our original malaise, perhaps; but it cannot be weeded out; it is as ineradicable as death. Christ had it occasionally; by 'the Kingdom of Heaven' he meant sometimes (though not always) a Kingdom in Heaven. Buddha had it often. And Wells, by pooh-poohing it, has made of his two chief characters mere spiritual and social revolutionaries. Men want to alter this planet, yet also believe that it is not worth altering and that behind it is something unalterable, and their perfect historian will be he who enters with equal sympathy into these contradictory desires.

Such are the defects of the book; but, as the previous

article indicated, they are entirely outweighed by its merits. A great book – a book to buy rather than to order from the library, and consequently one or two practical remarks may be in place. Price, moderate considering. Print and paper, excellent. Binding, strong but rather clumsy; in the copy under review the pages have been gashed by the fastenings. Coloured illustrations: tolerable when they reproduce photographs, vulgar when they attempt to be 'imaginative'; in the later instalments (not here reviewed) they are getting worse – there is an awful thing of the Crusades. Photographs: well selected, well reproduced – though here again there is a falling off in the later instalments, as regards number, size, clearness and appropriateness; it is to be hoped that the publishers are not going to skimp their enterprise as it proceeds. Time-charts, plans, maps, other drawings: these, by Mr J. F. Horrabin, are admirable and invaluable; the scholar as well as the draughtsman has been at work. All the same, there should have been fewer sketches, and more photographs of prehistoric implements, Greek vases, Indian gods, etc., because Mr Horrabin's method tends to uniformity. And there shouldn't have been any fig-leaves: they are contrary to the whole spirit of such a book.

[1920]

H. G. Wells, *The Outline of History*

Mr Wells' *Outline*

This Outline, like Dante's, ends with the word 'stars'. 'Life, for ever dying to be born afresh, for ever young and eager, will presently stand upon this earth as upon a footstool and stretch out its realm among the stars,' is the precise expression. Whether Love will succeed in moving such stars seems doubtful; they look unresponsive, and here and there they wink. It has been a great book, finely planned, well arranged, full of vivid historical sketches and of telling raps upon the knuckles and noses of the great, but as soon as it starts for the stars its charm decreases. We are beckoned towards a 'Community of Knowledge and Will', which will replace our present 'Communities of Obedience and Faith', and which will satisfy both our civic tendencies and also those nomad emotions that stir, especially at springtime, in the human breast. There are always to be Open Spaces. Why before such generous promises do we remain cold and a trifle frivolous? Why does the closing canto of the *Paradiso*, theology and all, seem more practical than this municipal millennium? That the *Paradiso* is great art is only half the answer; Dante's real advantage over Mr Wells as a prophet is that he believes in God. He who wishes to make a statement about the future that shall be these three things, complete, optimistic, convincing – he must believe in God. *News from Nowhere*, to take one example, is optimistic and convincing, but it is incomplete; it has to reject such human emotions as would clash with Eternal Life beside the Upper Thames. *L'Île des Pingouins*, on the other hand, rejects nothing and is wholly convincing; but its conclusions are pessimistic. While here is Mr Wells, complete, optimistic, but failing to convince. The globe he describes refuses to evolve into the footstool he anticipates. His method is scientific, his enthusiasms are for science, but his final deduction would only be credible if stated transcendentally:

> And our singing shall build
> In the void's loose field
> A world for the Spirit of Wisdom to wield.

Perhaps our singing will. But our acts and the observable acts of our neighbours will not. They build Civilization.

The author might reply to this, firstly, that he does believe in God; secondly, that there are, even in the civilization of to-day, hopeful symptoms. But his 'God' is only an italicizing of his own emotions; he despises mysticism; he regards Buddha and Christ as mere social revolutionaries, and the Neo-Platonists as nothing; his Invisible King is consequently but a Brocken Spectre who can never have a palace of his own. While as for the hopeful symptoms that he notes in contemporary civilization: they have appeared too often in the past to inspire much comfort. For instance, he prophesies that 'No European Government will ever get the same proportion of its people into the ranks and into its munition works again as the Governments of 1914–18 did.' One hopes this is so, but history suggests that the present movement against militarism is but the normal reaction after a war, and will not be transmitted to the following generation. No! Unless we can show a divine and increasing support of all that makes for righteousness, a sort of heavenly bonus on our better deeds, unless we can show with the Christian that a man shall see God, or with the Indian that he shall be God, the precious things on earth must obey the same stern and unsympathetic law that has ruled them in the past. Precious they are, and if an individual has the straight chance of dying for them and takes it, he has been lucky. But they are childless. That is their law. History reveals evolution, not progress.

If the last chapter of the *Outline* with its star-scraping is unsatisfactory, so for another reason is the last chapter but one. Its title is 'The International Catastrophe of 1914'. The chief events of the last six years have to be recorded, an impossible task, for no one yet knows what the chief events were. Our 'own' times, as they are ironically termed, are anything but ours; it is as though a dead object, huge and incomprehensible, had fallen across the page, which no historical arts can arrange, and which bewilders us as much by its shapelessness as by its size. The writer is intelligent, tender even, but how thin his voice sounds, as he comforts President Wilson or scolds Sir Edward Carson! Not now, not yet! The chapter is as it was bound to be, journalist jottings, which a new fact or reaction will erase. Nor is Mr Wells the best journalist obtainable. In 1914 he lost his head and wrote hysterical letters to the newspapers, and when he recovered, he never used his high position to expose the catchwords or moderate the passions of the mob. The instinct for safety (least amiable feature in his complex character) seems to have dominated him. Bernard Shaw, his intellectual and moral superior, lacks that instinct, and consequently Shaw to-day is discredited, while Wells has increased his popularity, and quite wiped out in *Mr Britling* any suspicions that were roused by *Ann Veronica.* Not out of such stuff is a reliable contemporary historian made. Throughout the chapter, we feel that for all his big words he is never ahead of the age, e.g., that he would not damn the Peace of Versailles unless the reception of Mr Keynes' book had indicated which way the wind is blowing.

The nine preceding chapters deal with the past, and continue the scheme and spirit of the first volume. That volume has already been favourably reviewed in *The Athenæum* (July 2 and 9 last), and there is no reason to modify the praise there given.

Here is a sympathetic account of Islam and of the great non-Christian empires that began to form in Asia in the thirteenth century and threatened Europe for three hundred years. The treatment of the Middle Ages and Renascence is perhaps less successful; and with the seventeenth century Mr Wells' personal objection to autocracy gets out of hand, so that a long series of monarchs are smacked in rather a monotonous way. An odious century, but corporal chastisement is unprofitable, and all through the eighteenth century (so much less odious) the sound of smacking continues. It is pleasant to sail for America, where the writer is again in harmony with his subject; with the American and French Republics a new hope enters Western society. After Napoleon (we will return to Napoleon in a moment) comes the finest and most thoughtful chapter in the book, 'The Realities and Imaginations of the Nineteenth Century'. The reality is the sudden growth of science, which politicians ignore, pursuing misty or antiquated aims, and neglecting the three problems confronting the new age, the problems of Property, Currency, and International Relationship. Autocracy has been scotched, but a new idol, the anthropomorphic nation, takes its place. Men are taught that England and Germany have feelings and even faces and feet; Mr Gladstone talks for three hours to Mr Darwin about the wrongs of Bulgaria. Each nation claims absolute sovereignty, and as Mr Wells points out, until that claim is modified there can be no security or liberty for the individual. Here he has certainly laid his finger on the most pernicious of our ideals; whether science will persuade us to abandon it is another question and one which he does not face. Science might be an educative force, but who is to educate our scientists? They have shown few signs of educating themselves. Though they hold the politicians in the hollow of their hands, and could cripple modern warfare by refusing to research into poison gas or explosives, they have hitherto acquiesced like prostitutes and recriminated like theologians, refusing nothing, and then erasing from their sacred books the names of the scientists who have been researching on the other side. Mr Wells fails to bring out this point. It is all very well to blame Mr Gladstone for his indifference to Darwin, but the indifference of scientists to Humanity is far more sinister. They come out of their laboratories as they went into them, uneducated, with neither the strength nor wish to say 'No' to a War Office and its beastly demands.

It is instructive to study his optimism when it reels under a shock, and a shock is provided by the career of Napoleon. Kings, educated in a bad tradition, he can understand, but Napoleon, educated by the Republic, yet subverting it, is more than he can bear, and he explodes with wrath. He greets the Emperor as 'this dark little archaic personage, hard, compact, capable, unscrupulous, imitative and neatly vulgar', who made the frontiers of Europe 'wave about like garments on a clothes-line on a windy day', and ends by 'prowling about a dismal hot island shooting birds'. His victories, his Code, are belittled. Twice we are told that his mother birched him, not once that his Egyptian adventure produced the *Description de l'Egypte*, a scientific cyclopædia which under other auspices would certainly have roused Wells' enthusiasm. Napoleon is a terrible irritant. He upset Tolstoy likewise, he unhinged Mr Walsingham in *Kipps*. But he was a great man; it is unfair to minimize him because he interrupts one's hopes for the development of mankind.

However, this article must conclude with praise, indeed with homage; the *Outline* as a whole is a wonderful achievement, and nothing in our generation is likely to supersede it. The inaccuracies of which experts complain, and the æsthetic blindness that distresses the cultured, are outweighed by the lucidity of the plan, the vitality of the execution, and the ceaseless pouncing intelligence of H. G. W. which brings something to the surface in every century, even if it isn't the most important thing. 'Standard Italian dates from Dante (1300).' This may be a hard saying for some of us, for it is the only reference to Dante in all the seven hundred pages! Mr Wells' ideas of what is supreme in human achievement can therefore never coincide with ours. But we must take what he can give us, and it is what no other historian has given – a survey of Life from the Palæozoic age to our own, which will help each, according to his vision, *a riveder le stelle.*

[1920]

H. G. Wells, *The Outline of History*

A Cautionary Tale

In his introduction Mr Belloc states his qualifications for writing a book about Europe. They are even more dramatic than one expected, for the chief of them is Intuition. In a deep and mystic sense, he is one with his subject-matter, and for this reason: because he is a member of the Roman Catholic Church. As a Catholic he has 'conscience', 'con-scientia', that intimate knowledge of Europe through identity that is denied to Protestants, Agnostics, Japanese, and Jews. 'The Faith is Europe and Europe is the Faith.' Only a Catholic can understand or write European history, for all others are outsiders, are detached, and are therefore predestined to error. Mr Belloc has consented to read some documents, but intuition comes first, information afterwards. He reads rather to confirm the documents than to be confirmed by them, and he would have realized Europe quite as fully if he had read nothing or if there was nothing to read. Thus he holds a unique position, at least among English historians. He is unable to make a mistake. Whatever he says is true, because he has the Faith. Others may argue or persuade, he announces, and however much he stoops to the normal methods of scholarship we must never forget that he is mystically Europe at bottom. It is difficult to criticize a writer who believes himself to be Europe: so difficult that the brain does a side-slip and falls on to the most irrelevant matters. Such as: How will Mr Belloc spend the money he gets for this book? (He cannot invest it because Capitalism is 'one of the major consequences of the Reformation'.) How did he spend the money he got for writing *The Bad Child's Book of Beasts*?

> The Lion, the Lion, he lives in the Waste,
> He has a large head and a very small Waist.

All most irrelevant and frivolous, but one needs a breather before starting on the analysis.

Europe and the Faith is a most clever and stimulating essay written with Mr Belloc's usual power, though not with his old charm. Its thesis is as follows. Rome: the source of European civilization. From Scotland to the Sahara, from Syria to Spain, Rome created a single State, the Roman Empire, whose citizens were often antagonistic to each other, but always antagonistic inside the State. To attack the Empire itself was inconceivable to them, because they knew it to be eternal. Outside the Empire were barbarians, few in number and contemptible in outfit. On to the Empire descended the Church. The Church, not Christianity: the word 'Christianity' is unhistorical and must never be used, for the Church was not an opinion or a habit, but a 'body corporate based on numerous exact doctrines'. The Church might have descended on any clime and at any time, but did, as a matter of fact, select the Roman Empire, and was accepted as official under Constantine (AD 300). Then came the so-called 'barbarian invasions', which were really neither invasions nor barbaric, but movements within the Empire of Romanized troops – e.g., Alaric (AD 400), though Goth by birth, was a Roman general by profession, who was annoyed with the central government because it had refused him promotion. There may have been a few raids by genuine barbarians from outside the pale, but they are negligible, except in one case: the case of Britain, which was severed from the Empire for about a hundred and fifty years, but permanently reunited to it by St Augustine (AD 600). Except for the episode of Britain, the Roman Empire (i.e., Europe) remained intact until the catastrophe of the Reformation. The 'kings' that arose in it were not kings in the ancient or in the modern sense, but descendants of Roman officers of the type of Alaric, subjects of the central power. And that central power, whatever its local seat, was dominated by the Church. The Church took up the reins as the secular authority dropped them, and guided Europe to the Middle Ages, 'the highest civilization our race has ever known'. Why did this civilization end? Mr Belloc is inclined to see here a definite victory of the

Devil. But he also notes certain mundane causes, such as the Black Death, the sudden enlargement of physical knowledge, the growth of absolutism among the 'kings', and the existence of 'Prussia', or its equivalent. It is through Northern Germany that the Reformation comes – the Germany that had never been part of the Empire. And the Reformation would have been snubbed like other barbarian impertinences, it would have died, as it had been born, in the outer darkness, but for a terrible and incalculable catastrophe: the defection of Britain. Domestic difficulties and the covetousness of his nobles led Henry VIII upon the path of crime, and the results are Protestantism, Capitalism, Industrialism, Atheism, Pessimism, Imperialism, and the War of 1914. Prussia is again the villain today – the insensate barbarian, who this time drags Austria after her and even puzzles the Pope. She has been foiled, but the danger remains so long as there is heresy. Europe must return to the Faith or she will perish. 'The Faith is Europe and Europe is the Faith.' With these words the cautionary tale concludes.

Against it the author sets the tale of the Protestant historians – Freeman, Green & Co. – who teach that the Roman Empire decayed, like other institutions, and was rejuvenated by invaders, many of whom were of Teutonic blood, that Chivalry, Romance, the Crusades, Parliaments were non-Roman, that the Reformation was a timely protest against Romish corruption. No words can express Mr Belloc's rage and violence against such historians; indeed the possession of Absolute Truth seems to be as bad for the deportment as the possession of absolute power. Yet his rage is misplaced. Freeman & Co. had limitations; and their neglect of the Latin element in Europe is rightly corrected, but they do come up honestly for judgment, they do not take refuge in intuition and mysticism when their conclusions are questioned. Whatever their defects, they are historians, whereas Mr Belloc with all his talents is a special pleader who is more occupied in tripping up his opponents than in speaking the truth. His tricks are numerous and at first impressive. He sets a quantity of little traps into which one duly falls – one or two of them shall be examined in a moment – but a thesis grows suspect when it is hedged by too many little traps, and one closes the brilliant book with the conviction it's a wrong 'un. For the Roman Empire is as dead as Dido: the reign of Justinian is the latest limit to which it can be reasonably extended. It influenced greatly its successors, just as a man may influence his descendants, but it is dead, if that word has any meaning. Its death was concealed by a fiction that Mr Belloc ignores: the *theory* of the Empire, which appealed to legalists and dreamers, and which ambitious monarchs, from Charlemagne to the ex-Kaiser, have found useful in their interested appeals. Dante, in the *De Monarchia*, tried to make that theory a noble reality. But where Dante failed Mr Belloc, seven hundred years later in time, is not likely to succeed. The Empire is dead, and even the theory of it is forgotten. While as for the Catholic Church, that, indeed, is alive, and did become the Imperial religion under Constantine, and a temporal power under the Popes when the Empire perished. But the Reformation continued what the Renaissance had begun, scepticism and science built on the work of both, and only intuition can assert today that the Catholic Church is Europe, or that the war from which we are emerging was a Catholic victory.

A few words must be added on Mr Belloc's methods. It is one of his claims that all readers – not merely Catholics – may and must endorse his conclusions, because the conclusions are not theological (which Catholics alone can endorse) but historical: he deals not with the doctrines of the Church, but with its career. This is an important claim, and he makes it importantly. He only excepts those readers who are biased against Catholicism, and one assents to the exception as a fair one. But in practice 'bias' excludes all Protestants, Prussians, Jews, and Mohammedans, and all who have been at non-Catholic universities, particularly at Oxford, in a word, all who have heard of the Faith and refused to accept it! Here is a device, a disingenuous trick, introduced to overawe the inexperienced. Observe it at work in the controversial question of Christian origins. (We have italicized the crucial words).

> We know that we have . . . documents proceeding from men who were contemporaries with the origin of the Christian religion. *Even modern scholarship with all its love of phantasy* is now clear upon so obvious a point . . . If I read in the four Gospels (not only the first three) of such and such a miracle . . . I am reading the account of a man who lived at the time. . . .

Does modern scholarship desert its fantasies to support this? One would like to see a list of the scholars. The Abbé Loisy would scarcely be among them! But Mr Belloc can exclude Loisy as 'biased', and Salomon Reinach on the same grounds. Instead of the words 'Even modern scholarship with all its love of fantasy,' he ought to have written 'Catholic scholarship'. For it is all that he means.

Another device. Too learned and too wise to make misstatements, he has nevertheless built up his case by an artful system of selection and rejection. When it is convenient to know nothing – as in the case of the tribes outside the Roman pale – he implies that nothing can be known. When he wants to know something – as in the case of Britain after the withdrawal of the Legions – he strains every resource of the historian's art. At one moment he is out for facts, but when he comes to the spurious 'Donation' of Constantine he writes: 'Nothing is more valuable to true history than legend,' which presumably means that Constantine would have made the Donation if he had thought of it. Moreover, he is an adept at forestalling our criticisms, not by an argument but a sneer, so that he may frighten us out of making them. He has a row of pigeon-holes painted with such unattractive titles as 'academic economists', 'oriental pagans', and 'empty internationalists', 'pedants mumbling about race', and into one or other of these we must go if we disagree with him. But we shall come out again all right on the other side, for the pigeon-holes have usually no bottoms: they are part of the author's bluff. And, finally, there is a general trap, into which all the others lead. Nothing would please him better than if, irritated by his devices, we were to exclaim: 'Behold the fruits of Catholicism', for then he could reply: 'Blasphemy. Exactly. Blasphemy and bias.' Not this shall be our concluding charge. The devices are rather inherent in Mr Belloc's own character. He would have been just as slippery as an Agnostic or a Protestant. His book is an example not of the strange effect of religion on the mind, but of the strange uses to which some men can put their religion.

[1920]

Hilaire Belloc, *Europe and the Faith*

Edward VII

This book is dead. Thousands and thousands of facts are presented, and facts need not kill a book, but these facts do, because they are trivial, disconnected, and presented with incredible pomposity. Sir Sidney Lee has many valuable qualities: he is accurate, learned, temperate, he never stoops to sycophancy. But as to the eternal importance of his theme he has no misgivings. He cannot be too serious or swell himself out too large when he mentions royalty, the least sentence he writes must be tumid, gravid, authoritative, apopletic, apocalyptic. Kings may do wrong like the Kaiser or come to grief like the Czar, but they may never be presented lightly – that is the sin against the Lord's Anointed – and when the House of Guelf is concerned, it becomes physically impossible to use too many words.

> Despite the restraints on boyish liberty and the educational discipline in which the paternal wisdom chiefly made itself visible to the son, the boyish faith in his dead father's exalted and disinterested motive lived on.

Such a sentence pops when trodden upon, like seaweed, yet it would be wrong to say it contains nothing. A diplomatic residuum survives – something gummy, something as subtle in its way as literature though it exudes from the opposite end of the pen. Read the sentence again, and do not try to find out whether the Prince liked his father or was cowed by him, whether he obeyed him or disobeyed, for these are not the points. Consider instead the repetition of the adjective 'boyish'. It is significant. In literature a repeated adjective does something, and it does something here too: it helps us to forget that we are reading about a boy. The five words 'boyish', 'paternal', 'son', 'boyish', 'father', are used with a sort of inverted art. They are so many nails in the coffin of reality. They are used without vision, without music, without feeling, and consequently they leave us with a deep sense of the abstract importance of royalty. To convey that importance is the aim of an official biographer, and the achievement of the volume under review. That's why the book's dead.

What of the facts themselves? It is the attempt to inflate them into national events that makes them trivial: they were not trivial to the Prince. It mattered very much to him in the summer of 1867 that the Sultan of Turkey should receive a proper decoration. 'I wish you would write to the Queen on the subject as soon as possible,' he told Lord Derby; 'as there is no time to be lost.' Lord Derby thought a G.C.S.I. sufficient, but the Sultan let it be known that only the K.G. would do, and the Prince warmly concurred, for he had pleasant memories of his own stay in Constantinople. But Queen Victoria had never been to Constantinople, did not mean to go, had not invited the Sultan to England, was disinclined to do anything that pleased her son, and, finally, did not think it right to confer the Garter, which is a Christian emblem, upon a Moslem ruler's leg. The Prince was in despair. His energy and tact were strained to their utmost, and, continuing to lose no time, he scarcely left the Sultan's side for ten days. All went well, thanks to his assiduity. The Queen relented, there was a lunch at Windsor, a reception at the India Office, and – triumph of triumphs! – the bestowal of the Garter on the deck of the Royal Yacht at Spithead during a howling storm. The Sultan shed tears of gratitude and joy. To him, as to his young host, it must have seemed that an event of international importance had occurred. But before many years had passed, the Sultan was assassinated, and even earlier the Prince turned from Turkey to Russia and was equally flurried over a colonelcy in a Russian regiment, which the Czar offered him and the Queen would not let him accept. 'We are more independent without all these foreign honours,' wrote the Queen. And so to Oberammergau, which made a 'serious impression'. He 'had never been so struck with anyone in his life' as with the peasant who played the part of Christ, and managed to have a talk with him before proceeding to military manoeuvres in Hampshire.

In this constant flittering – which forecasts the still swifter movements of his grandson – the Prince was not the least trivial or inconsistent from his own point of view. His life sprang straight out of his circumstances and character and we shall never think clearly on the urgent subject of royalty until we realize this. If we do sometimes get cynical during eight hundred pages, it is usually the fault of Sir Sidney Lee. He should not imply that trinkets and uniforms, lunches, launches, and railway trains have any value outside the purely human, nor should he state that the subject of his memoir is a 'great historic figure'.

The Prince was indeed anxious to be a figure, and always clamouring for work, real work. He belonged to the great army of the constitutional unemployed which thronged Europe in the nineteenth century and is only just beginning to thin. The royal families bred abundantly, and there were numerous restless sons. In the fifteenth century these young men would have become condottieri, but they were constitutional, so they had to represent something or other, they didn't much mind what. It is pathetic to see them in their crowded palaces, scanning the political horizons for some form of popular life, and asking to represent it. An Austrian goes to Mexico, a Dane to Greece, and the Prince of Wales, debarred from more distant quests, attempts to be identified with the island of Ireland. His mother refused. She felt – and perhaps rightly – that she was doing all the representing necessary to the Empire and all the work modern royalty can ever do: signing papers, seeing Ministers, opening special boxes. And she felt, too – and some other observers have agreed with her – that the Prince sought publicity rather than work, and was too impetuous and desultory to make a satisfactory Viceroy. At any rate, after playing with his hopes for a time, she refused, and Ireland joined the long series of snubs she administered to her son. For the first fifty years of his life he was scarcely allowed to do anything, or to go anywhere save in a social capacity, and it is therefore impossible that a book dealing with those years can have any historical importance. It is the domestic tragedy that stands out. As a mother, Queen Victoria behaved very badly. The boy was over-educated by elderly experts, and when his rather ordinary mind and very normal character did not respond, she put him on a shelf as a failure. He grew into a middle-aged man, but remained on the shelf – and woe betide him if the sound of breaking glass came to his mother's ears. It never occurred to her that the Mordaunt and the Baccarat cases and other forbidden sweets could be ascribed to enforced idleness; or that she herself could be indirectly responsible for them. She may have been right to shelve him, but she was also cruel and blind.

The last two hundred pages of the book are the best because there is here less disproportion between the facts and the gravity with which they are related. The squabbles between the Prince and the Kaiser increased the existing mistrust between England and Germany, so that the royal personages managed to represent something at last, and a little to accelerate the outbreak of an European war. Here is one momentous step towards the catastrophe:

> After a short call on the Duke of Gmünden, on leaving Homburg, the Prince on 10th September reached Vienna, where he donned for the first time the resplendent uniform of his new Austro-Hungarian regiment of Hussars – gold-frogged tunic, red breeches, Hessian boots and shako. From his host's lips he at once learnt to his mortification that his nephew had stipulated that no royal guest save himself should be present at the Viennese Court during his forthcoming stay. No doubt as to the Kaiser's meaning was permissible.

When you have assigned the 'his-es' to their proper owners, you will realize that here was indeed an insult. The Hessian boots had to be pulled off, the red breeches to follow them, and the outraged and denuded uncle withdrew entirely from Austrian soil, to seek refuge with the King and Queen of

Roumania. In his next volume Sir Sidney will deal with the progress of the feud, and with its pendent, King Edward's cultivation of a particular type of Frenchman. The volume will probably be more interesting than the present one, but it is sure to show the same deadness of outlook and of style. Sir Sidney is not stupid or uncritical, but officialism has destroyed his scale of values. He has taken neither of the courses open to a responsible biographer. Hessian boots, red breeches, Garters – they can be treated from two points of view: the scientific, when they vanish, and the sympathetic, when they are seen to be of genuine importance to their wearers. But they are not of importance to the universe or even to Europe; nothing, nothing matters there, except distinction of spirit, and this King Edward VII did not happen to possess.

[1925]

Sidney Lee, *King Edward VII*

Peeping at Elizabeth

Do you wish you had lived in the days of Queen Elizabeth? I am thankful to have escaped them. The noise, the hopefulness, the vitality, the cant about chastity – I should have found them hard to bear, nor would a Reformed Religion have consoled. Gone was the dear Pope, overseas, underground; gone the traditions that echoed out of the past and whispered of future unity, and in their place, closing every vista, stood a portentous figure shaped like a dinner-bell. The hard reverberations of this creature filled the air, her feet twinkled in a septuagenarian dance, she made progresses and rude, metallic jokes, she exploited a temper naturally violent, she was a public virgin – and all she did she did for the honour of England. Could one have psychoanalysed her, one would have obtained relief, but that was not yet to be. Spenser, Sidney, Raleigh – no, psycho-analysis did not occur to them; they accepted the dinner-bell as solid woman; they did not venture to think. There was very little thought in those spacious times, just as there was little unashamed or uncontorted passion. Socrates, Cleopatra – no, they do not occur. Continents were discovered, beards singed, bowls bowled, but for all its bravery life had retreated to the muscles and the will, and even Shakespeare, who could have contained so much, suffered from the surrounding impoverishment as he pegged away at his thirty-seven plays.

Nevertheless, viewed from a sufficient distance, the Elizabethan age has two great attractions – lyric beauty and quaintness. Much good they would have done us on the spot, for beauty is rare always, and requires perspective to thicken it into an atmosphere, and as for quaintness, it disappears entirely when we form part of it. Open this quaint little book.

It is so naïve and disarming that we are tempted to hail it as a masterpiece. It is nothing of the sort, as its able editor realizes, and is of genuine importance only to the antiquarian. But open its pages! Schoolboys and servants elbow with old-world angularity, we dine with square merchants or my domical Lady Ri Mellaine; we have the illusion of sharing the daily life of a sixteenth-century woodcut. Even the writing imposes itself and asks to be considered fine prose.

> 'You mayd, goe fetch the childes cradle, make his bed, where is his pillowe? Seek a cleane pillow-bere. Set on the coverlet, now put him in his cradle and rocke him till he sleepe, but bring him to me first that I may kisse him: God send thee good rest my little boykin. I pray you good Nurse have a care of him.'
>
> 'Dout not of it Madame with the grace of God.'
>
> 'Well then, God be with you till anon.'

It seems profoundly charming and tender, and because the arrangements of the words and the punctuation are unfamiliar, they assume the inevitability of art. But who wrote the words, and why? The author was a Huguenot schoolmaster, and his aim was not to touch our hearts or even to depict his times, but to assist his pupils and attract new ones. On the opposite page of the book was a French translation. So the effect produced on us is not simply quaint, it is doubly quaint. Two influences have to be discounted before we can peep at that far-off age.

> 'From whence come you good scholar? is it time to rise, and come to schole at nine? Where have you beene?'
>
> 'Maister, I met him by the way which did leape, did slide uppon the ice: which did cast snow: which fowght with his fist, and balles of snow: which did scorge his top: which played for pointes, pinnes, cherie stones, counters, dice, cardes.'
>
> 'Enter in galland, I will teach you a game which you know not.'

The delightful catalogue, 'pointes, pinnes', etc., is really an exercise in vocabulary, and the same need explains the enormous menu at the Lady Ri Mellaine's dinner. Beginning with oysters and grace, her guests tackle every variety of boiled and roast meat, game, salad, and fish, she urging them on with such hospitable cries as:

> 'Come on, let me give you some of this Quince pye, of this Tarte of Almonds, of that of Cherrie, of Gooseberries, of Prunes.'
>
> 'Certainly Madame, I know not how we should eat any more, unless we should borrowe other bellyes.'
>
> 'Take away then all this, And bring us the Fruite. Doe you loue Cheese? There is holland Cheese, Some Angelot, Auvergne cheese, Parmesan. Will you have some grated cheese with sage and Sugar? If you find the same too strong, take some of that Banbury cheese, For it is mileder in taste (to the mouth).'

Nine kinds of fruit follow, and the meal ends with an aggrieved 'Why have we no Chest-nuts?' A superb performance . . . but it has been no more real than a banquet in Ollendorff.

The origins of the volume are explained by the editor in his introduction. He has taken four of these curious French lesson-books – three by Hollyband, who taught in the late sixteenth century, and one by Erondell which was published in 1605 – he has made extracts from them, added notes, and served up with woodcuts taken from the Roxburghe Ballads. The result is a most entertaining little volume, solidly quaint, and sometimes charming. Is it good literature? No. Can it be read with profit? Probably not. But it has, in its minute, inoffensive fashion, the commanding quality we attribute to that age; it compels, we are obliged to read it with pleasure.

For the Elizabethans excelled at putting things across. There was a vigour and swagger about them which all must admire and which some would adore. England begins to splash and send ripples all over the world, and English literature makes its big splash too. Epics, treatises, hundreds of plays, thousands of sonnets bounce about and would overwhelm the critic by their copiousness, but most of them have proved less permanent than the British Empire. Oblivion engulfed them because they had not spiritual sincerity. Freshness and vitality were not enough. It is in their treatment of love that their falsity becomes most obvious, but the roots of the trouble lie far deeper. Quite what was amiss we can see when we come to a less confident age, and read the poems of Donne. Donne tried to be straight about love and about other things also: he attempted the process known as thought. And though thought may betray a man individually and bring Empires to ruin, it is nevertheless the only known preservative, the only earnest of immortality. The Elizabethans, even the greatest of them, plumped for the native hue of resolution, and are receiving their reward; they increased our political power and glorified our race, and are rightly commended on public occasions. But they were at once too violent and too hazy to contribute much towards the development of the human mind.

[1925]

M. St. Clair Byrne (ed.), *The Elizabethan Home*

Poverty's Challenge: The Terrible Tolstoy

No one who is really poor – poor in Tolstoy's sense – would spend twopence on the *New Leader*, and consequently no one who is really poor will read these remarks. I address them as a capitalist to capitalists, and we shall mean by 'poor' those people who have not enough money to buy themselves food or clothing. We capitalists have enough. What shall we do with our surplus? Shall we buy more food and more clothes, shall we accumulate possessions and servants until we expire in fatness? Or shall we give away our surplus to those who have nothing? I don't know what we ought to do, but I know what we do. We compromise. We spend more than is necessary on ourselves – buy the newspaper, for instance – and we also give something away. How much, how little, we give away, depends on circumstances and temperament, and there may come a time when society is so ordered that charity is unnecessary. But at present compromise is universal and inevitable. Everyone – from millionaire to miner – spends more on himself than he need, and gives away less than he could to alleviate poverty – part of his surplus, but never all.

Why don't we give away all?

This was the question that presented itself with appalling vividness to a Russian land-owner in the eighties of the last century. Tolstoy was a man of property, who had added to his income through literature and journalism. In the sixties he had written a great novel, *War and Peace*, in the seventies another great novel, *Anna Karenina*. And then the question presented itself – the question that ruined him as an artist and turned him into a reformer. He went to live in Moscow, was distressed by the spectacle of urban poverty – so much more dramatic than its rural counterpart – and determined to give away more of his surplus cash in the future. Being extremely conscientious, he investigated before he gave away, and in so doing he came up against two disconcerting facts: in the first place nearly every case of urgent need among the poor had already been met by those of their neighbours who were not quite so poor; and in the second place all the poor had been peasants, and had come to town because the rich, who had robbed them in the country, had also come to town, and they hoped to recapture some of their own. So, firstly, Tolstoy could find no one to give his money to, and, secondly, he and his class proved to be the very cause of the poverty he was trying to alleviate. The shock of this double discovery threw him back upon himself, and what had begun as philanthropy continued as introspection.

But is not the question more complicated? Is not Society an organism? Have not different men different functions? They have certainly different capacities. Tolstoy answered 'No'. He would not admit complications. To him there was only one function for man – labour and life on the land – and consequently only one healthy form for society – the agricultural. Industrialism, science, art, and priestly religion are all vicious, because they assign different functions, and as soon as difference of function is admitted, differences of income are condoned. He condemned all governments because they uphold differences and employ force – he would have disliked Soviet Russia quite as much as he disliked Czarism – in some ways he would have disliked it more. To him the only good and real thing on earth was the individual, but this belief did not result in what is generally termed individualism. The Tolstoyan individual is a curtailed, denuded, castrated creature who would have aroused the contempt and ridicule of the ancient Greeks. Wealth, learning, pleasure, personal cleanliness, are all wrong because (the world being what it is) they differentiate. No advance can be made until the poor have been helped, and no man can help them unless he is himself poor. With them the circle begins, in them it terminates. Civilization has no right to be complicated so long as poverty exists.

'What, then, must we do?' Our duty – as set out in this amazing and perturbing book – is perfectly clear. We must abandon our surplus wealth, settle on the land, do manual labour, nourish ourselves without the interposition of money, and understand poverty from within, even if we get covered with lice in the process. Then, and not till then, shall we be able to help our poor neighbours, then we shall save our souls. Are you going to do this? I am not, and it is one of the merits of the later works of Tolstoy that they cause one to say 'No' definitely, even at the risk of being damned. They are not like being in church; they are not like a sermon from the Dean of Durham.

When the Dean of Durham (officially representing the carpenter Jesus) enjoins poverty upon me, I answer readily enough, 'Yea, Dean, yea,' because I know that when his sermon is over the Dean will go back to an excellent lunch, and leave me free to do the same. It is a put-up job between us, a farce that has gone on century after century, ever since Christianity became respectable. But Tolstoy is not like that. He does not go off to his lunch. He, too, had his insincerities of action, but they were not of the suave organized sort promoted and practised by clergymen. The bulk of him is sincere; he demands a sincere response, and that is why he is so painful to read. He exacts (in my case) a definite refusal. I believe that he is right, that poverty has been caused by wealth, and that it is impossible to help the poor without becoming poor oneself. But I will not do it, I will not part with the whole of my surplus. Will you? If so, discontinue (among other things) your subscription to the *New Leader*. And if the proprietors of the *New Leader* will do it, let them discontinue publication.

It is no use us trying to dodge the terrible Tolstoy by asserting that humanity will benefit indirectly from our various activities and incomes: it is an argument that slips off his back because he values only direct benefit to the individual. And so his question, 'What, then, must we do?' most of us will reply, 'Not what you tell us to do, anyhow,' and it is better that we should make this reply than remain vague, self-satisfied, and unseeing.

Having shelved the title and main purpose of this remarkable book, can we profit by its minor aspects? Yes, indeed! Much of it is excellent reading – especially the earlier chapters which so vividly describe slum life at Moscow. A fine artist and psychologist, he shocks and surprises us again and again by the sureness of his insight. He notes, for instance, that if he gave money to a beggar in passing, the beggar was pleased: but that if he first talked with him sympathetically, he was discontented. Why? Because 'he no longer regards one merely as a passer-by, but sees what I want him to see in me – a kindly man. But if I am a kindly man, my kindness cannot stop at twenty kopecs, or at ten roubles, or at ten thousand. It is impossible to be good-natured only a little . . . If I draw back, I show that all I did, I did not because I was a kindly man, but because I wished to seem kindly in the beggar's eyes and in the eyes of others.' This is disquieting, for we capitalists like to think that sympathy with the poor will please and improve them, and that a dole accompanied by kind words will be surrounded by heavenly radiance. Useless – for the reason that we have provoked without satisfying them a fellow being's hopes in our character: we have promised to espouse poverty, but only to the extent of a half-a-crown or five hundred pounds. It is bad to chuck money at beggars: it is worse to delude them with the mirage of friendship. Tolstoy sees this with unpleasing clarity.

He sees also the bad effects of property upon the character. If there were no poor people in the world, if everyone had enough food and clothes, possessions would still be bad, because they clog the life of the individual. We can all confirm this from our own experience. Possessions, and in particular furniture and ornaments, are most wearisome forms of wealth – far more tiring than balances at the bank – and the man who is entangled by them always develops heaviness of outlook and sluggishness of movement. He cannot do without servants for one thing. They have to dust and guard the beastly vases and sofas, and once dependent on servants, it is impossible to be intimate with the poor or to enter the kingdom of heaven. 'Property is the root of all evil; and the division and safeguarding of property occupies the whole world.'

Of course, Tolstoy elsewhere goes further than this. He heads for asceticism, which thinks not only possession but use and enjoyment to be evil, and he would intensely resent our picking up incidental hints from his teaching when we reject that teaching as a whole: which is what we are doing and mean to do.

Such is the effect which the book is likely to have upon most modern readers. They will deny its central doctrine, but attend to its side issues. It will, throughout, compel them to be sincere with themselves, and that is in itself a great experience. They will read it with disapproval, yet with shame. For though it was written for agricultural Russia and we read it in industrial England, though its economic outlook is wilfully narrow and its conception of the individual also narrow, yet it does what few other books have done: it brings home to us the existence of the poor.

It achieves this not by realistic details, not by sentimentality, not by statistics: all these methods have been practised elsewhere. Its success is really more akin to poetry. A poet assimilates his subject matter so that it reappears not only in what he says but in the way he expresses himself, in the very rhythm and diction of his verse, and that is what Tolstoy has done here, though he is writing about the most sad and shameful aspect of our so-called civilization, and though he is writing in prose.

[1925]

Leo Tolstoy, *What Then Must We Do?*

Literature or Life?

Henry W. Nevinson: The Boy Who Never Stuck

I am an old Snobstonian, and when I was at school we had an anthem, a slow, undulating ditty, almost impossible to sing in tune. The local organist had composed it, the words were by one of the masters, and the head master himself, in the course of a sermon, would sometimes comment on the truths it contained.

> Choose we for life's battle harp or sword or pen,
> Perish every laggard, let us all be men.
> So shall Snobston flourish, so shall England be,
> Serving King and Country, ruling land and sea.

Thus the anthem ran, and, as the head master said, there was a great deal to be learnt from it. In the first place, we must choose a profession, and, in the second place, having chosen, we must stick. The sword is the noblest choice, because it might lead to the death of a fellow-creature; still, those boys (he always called them 'bies') who felt unequal to murder had other opportunities reserved to them. Only, 'bies' must stick. They must stick even if it was a case of harps. How depressed I used to feel! The pen was perhaps the best of the three evils presented, but I always imagined it as a quill, to whose squeaks I should be chained eternally. One was clearly going to be a prisoner throughout life's battle – unless, indeed, one had the courage to become a laggard or that equally contemptible creature the 'bi' who didn't know his own mind.

Nevinson did not have my advantage of being educated at Snobston – he was merely at Shrewsbury – but he, too, has been worried by this problem of choosing, and has wondered whether he ought to select literature or life, even going so far on one occasion as to consult George Meredith on the point. While he wondered the clock kept ticking, and something went by on irrevocable feet – the same thing that goes by me now as I try to review his book, the same thing that goes by you as you try to read. On went Time, without giving him time to decide. For he had his living to get, also suffering made him indignant, also he wanted to see the world and his friends, also he was a passionate laggard; and what with one thing and another, he never succeeded in labelling himself.

Others have labelled him. Permitting him access to both sword and pen, they have called him a knight-errant. But, as he rightly implies, this will not wash. For there is something intimidating about a knight-errant – he is not the sort of person one wants to meet. Whereas Nevinson manages to suggest that he is an ordinary affable person who has led a mildly successful life as a journalist – who has, at all events, done nothing that the reader couldn't. To carry greetings to the Russian Duma after it had been dissolved, to take active part in the militant suffrage movement, to discover a slave trade in tropical Africa, to return to England and announce to Christian merchants that their profits were based upon that trade, to get ten thousand slaves repatriated, to throw up good jobs for conscience' sake, to alienate all Governments (and in particular the British Foreign Office, Colonial Office, and Home Office) to suffer hunger, fever, and frost-bite, to be poisoned by aconite, to be riddled by jiggers and bitten by venomous ants, and to do all these things rather negligently and with none of the proper kit, so that the reader feels, 'Oh, well, I could have done them all, too, if I hadn't been so busy reading': that is the peculiar achievement of Nevinson.

Which has he chosen, literature or life? Who knows, and who cares? We only know that he enhances our own sense of power, and that, though the clock continues to tick, it gives out a different sound.

This volume has not the colour and charm of its predecessor, *Changes and Chances*. On the other hand, it is more exciting and more solid, for it deals with episodes of maturity, and one of these episodes – the Angola trip – the writer regards as the main enterprise of his life. *Harper's Monthly* offered him £1,000 if he would undertake 'an adventurous journey' on their behalf, so off he popped in the autumn of 1904, and selected Portuguese West Africa as a favourable district for discomfort. He found more than he bargained for; indeed, £1,000 may be regarded as cheap. For slavery was in full swing, although, of course, it was not called by that name. Our Portuguese allies captured natives on the mainland, and shipped them to the Islands of Hell, San Thomé and Principé, where they laboured on the cocoa plantations until death released them. Thank God, no Englishman would do such a thing as that! We merely buy the cocoa.

Having investigated the situation thoroughly both on the mainland and the islands, and having escaped death at the hands of the scandalized planters, Nevinson returned home, and bore the news to the firm of Cadbury, which got most of its supplies from the district. The Cadburys were so pious, and their factories at Bourneville were so model, that he expected they would receive his exposure with enthusiasm and immediately boycott all slave-grown stuff. They did not behave as he expected. 'I was met by that peculiar hesitation which often characterizes Quakers when action is called for.' They behaved correctly, but they took their time. Guidance had to be sought from Sir Edward Grey and other authorities; independent reports had to be received and even held back. Meanwhile, the clock ticked. Not until four years later was the boycott declared, and during that interval thousands of pounds had passed into the pockets of Christian shareholders and thousands of natives had died. Thank God, such things are impossible in these days, except, perhaps, in

Kenya, where landed interests demand them! Slavery is now put down wherever the hand of Great Britain stretches, with the possible exception of Shanghai, where it is imperative for our trade. Our dividends can be drawn with a good conscience now.

What else is to be said about the book, except to tell the public to read it, and the author to buy himself a top-hat at once? For, terrible to relate, he possesses no top-hat. When he was summoned to Buckingham Palace to give private information to King Edward about an impending Russian invasion of England, he was obliged to borrow someone else's, which perched upon his forehead like a thimble. Through corridor after corridor he went, hiding the hat in his hand and 'catching sight of water-colours and drawings, evidently the labour of the Great White Queen's unassisted talent'. When he approached the dread presence a reprieve awaited him, and he was shunted into an ante-chamber, while an equerry ran to and fro and maintained communications with Royalty. He could hear 'the guttural notes of the voice that rocked the Empire', but he could not see, he could not be seen. 'We have seen this Mr Nevinson,' remarked the editor of a Bombay paper; 'outwardly he has the appearance of a gentleman, but at heart he is no better than a Socialist.' Wiser still, King Edward refused the mutual perils of an interview. So all went well, and all went well in another sense also, for a fortnight later the Russian Army Corps was withdrawn from the Finnish frontier.

Yet will he go and buy that hat? I have my doubts. For in his preface, quoting a passage of Seneca, he exclaims, 'May I die *plebeius senex* – old, and a member of the Labour Party.' He was not born in that Party. Like many another's, his roots were in Liberalism, and he has had to transplant himself before he could flower. He has brought to the soil of his adoption something that transcends party – generosity, recklessness, a belief in conscience joined to a mistrust of principles.

Edward Carpenter once told me that, though he disliked

western civilization for many reasons, he disliked it most because it produced such horrible old men. Nevinson, if he lives long enough, will disprove that as completely as Carpenter himself has disproved it. *Plebeius senex!* He must die some time, though it seems incredible. How will he fare at the Last Prize Giving? My late head master of Snobston is sure to preside over that function – he was a universal presider – and he will, I fear, show small mercy to the Bi who never stuck. 'Which has it been, H.W. Nevinson, Literature or Life?' I foresee an embarrassed silence. But perhaps the culprit's own account may be correct. He looks forward to another tribunal, other rewards. 'When I come to die,' he writes, 'my deep regret at leaving this beautiful world may perhaps be tempered by a vision of ten thousand little black men and women dancing around my bed to the sound of elfin *ochisangis* or echoing *ochingufus*, and crying in grateful ecstasy: "He sent us home! He sent us home!"'

[1925]

Henry W. Nevinson, *More Changes, More Chances*

Mr D. H. Lawrence and Lord Brentford

It was a happy and indeed a witty thought of the publishers to induce the most remarkable of our novelists and our most notorious Home Secretary to write pamphlets on the subject of indecency. Needless to say, Mr Lawrence and Lord Brentford disagree. Yet they have two characteristics in common, and it is well to observe what these are before passing on to their differences.

The first common characteristic is an emotional uncertainty which threatens them whenever they generalize about the public. Most men and women have, to put it bluntly, no opinions at all about indecency, sex, pornography, the censorship, etc. They have habits, but no opinions. The expert cannot realize this. Definite himself, he ascribes opinions where they do not exist, and if he is a reformer as well as an expert he tends to divide the public into friends and foes, and to ask himself which section predominates. Unable to discover, he loses his aloofness, and feels that he is surrounded now by friends, now by foes, now he cries, 'He that is not against us is for us,' and now, 'He that is not with me is against me.' Lord Brentford, for instance, complains that there is an enormous demand for improper postcards in England, and then says that if the trade was suppressed not more than a hundred people would object. Both statements cannot be true. And Mr Lawrence, though he understands his own reactions and so steers a straighter course, is likewise swayed when he thinks of the mob, hates and loves it alternately, regards it as a villain, a dupe, a comrade, rolled into one. This instability is natural. When they think of the general public, both writers echo an emotional uncertainty which was voiced long ago on the shores of the lake of Galilee.

Their second common characteristic is that each of them detests indecency, and desires to suppress it. Lord Brentford's opinion is familiar, but it is Mr Lawrence, not he, who writes, 'I would censor genuine pornography, rigorously.' Of course, as soon as we try to define 'genuine pornography' the battle opens; still, both disputants feel that there is something in sex which ought to be prohibited. 'It would not be very difficult,' adds Mr Lawrence, but he has not yet been Home Secretary. Lord Brentford, who has, did not find it very easy.

What is this accursed and illegal thing?

Lord Brentford dare not tell us, because from his point of view to define filth is to advertise it. He is obliged to hint, or to say that when a thing is wrong it is wrong. We can only find out his meaning indirectly, and, proceeding thus, we discover that he considers everything relating to sex evil with one exception: marriage. An administrator rather than a psychologist, he does not ask himself what marriage is. Marriage is marriage. Any instinct which does not lead towards it, or which disturbs it after consummation, is suspect. It was ordained as a remedy against such instincts, and for the production of children. And we must further note that children occupy, in his eyes, a peculiarly sacred position, partly because of the emphasis laid on them by Christianity, partly because they are the marriageable of the future. He always has a child at the back of his mind, who must be shielded from impurity, and many of his antics can be traced to a high and genuine knight-errantry. At the time when the *Well of Loneliness* case was still *sub judice*, he informed the London Diocesan Council of Youth that he was determined to suppress all books which made 'one of the least of these little ones offend'. It was a curious speech, coming at such a moment and from a Minister of the Crown, but it rose naturally to his lips, because he specializes on the welfare or supposed welfare of the child, and is willing to turn any masterpiece that might deflect adolescence from its authorized course. Marriage, the children, the family – that is his conception of society. Everything outside them or inside them is questionable.

If we grant his promises – that everything in sex except marriage is evil, and that children must always be protected, whatever the cost to adults – then his conclusions follow, and he expresses them here in a clever, good-tempered way. He is not a fanatic. He would not, he assures us, impose his opinions unless they were shared by the electorate. He acquiesces in democracy. And democracy has decided on some sort of censorship, whether it be of actions, speech, drama, cinema, literature, or art, and whether it be exercised before or after the event – though when 'the people learn, not merely to disregard but to detest all forms of indecency . . . no censorship will be needed.' The people will learn, democracy has already learnt. On this confused and characteristic note the pamphlet closes. It is the work of a competent man of affairs, who has strong moral convictions and does not niggle about with logic, who believes that his actions are right, and genially defends them against the aspersions of critics, when he has nothing more important to do.

To turn from him to Mr Lawrence is to turn from darkness into light.

Into what sort of light? Many will say that it beats through the bars of hell. But even those who detest him most must admit that they can see what he is talking about, whereas with Lord Brentford they could not see, they could only infer. He can tell us straight out what he finds evil in sex, because from his point of view to define filth is to sterilize it. To him the one evil is 'self-enclosure', and under this definition he includes not merely the physical act of masturbation, but any emotional counterpart of it, any turning-inward upon itself of the spirit, any furtiveness and secrecy, any tendency to live in little private circles of excitement, rather than in the passionate outer life of personal interchange. Man has his solitary side, but if he embraces this kind of solitude, he is damned. 'To-day, practically everyone is self-conscious, and imprisoned in self-consciousness. It is the joyful result of the dirty little secret.' Here (he argues) is the only real indecency, here is the genuine pornography which he would rigorously censor, here is the harvest which men like Lord Brentford have sown.

Some readers will be shocked by his brutality, others deterred by his occasional mysticism, others again will feel that he is only inviting us to exchange one type of supervision for another, and that it is safer to be judged by Sir Chartres Biron than to fall into the hands of a writer of genius. But of the importance and novelty of his attack there is no question. He has dealt a blow at reformers who are obsessed by purity and cannot see that their obsession is impure. He arraigns civilization, because it is smeary and grey and degrades passion by pretending to safeguard it, and confuses purity with modesty, and lifts up pious eyes to heaven and cherishes dirt elsewhere. And lest this should sound like vague denunciation, he quotes a couple of poems, with devastating effect. They are famous poems. One of them is, 'My love is like a red, red rose'. Is this a pure poem? No; 'my love is like a red, red rose only when she's *not* like a pure, pure lily.' The second poem is 'Du bist wie eine Blume' – a pure poem and also an indecent one; the elderly gentleman is mumbling over the child and praying God to keep her pure, pure for ever, pure for the dreary little circle of his own thoughts. For Burns sends his emotions outwards to mingle with human beings and become passions, Heine shuts his up in the circle of self-enclosure, where they fester. And Heine, not Burns, is the modern man. He is a typical product of repression, and when he tires of mumbling, 'So hold und schön und rein,' he will go to the smoking-room, and tell, also in low tones, an improper story.

What, then, is our remedy? Free speech? Not altogether. To say, as has been said above, that by defining filth Mr Lawrence hopes to sterilize it, is not quite to express his attitude. He does not wholly believe in free speech, for the reason that it never leads further than Dr Marie Stopes. However much we speak out and denounce our repressors, we shall still be imprisoned in the circles of self-consciousness, we shall merely be the grey denouncing the grey. To escape into salvation and colour, something further is needed: freedom of feeling, and how is that to be attained?

He does not tell us, except by mystic hints which only the mystic can utilize, and in this direction his pamphlet comes to a standstill. But as a polemic it is remarkable. He has brought a definite accusation against Puritanism, and it will be interesting to see whether Puritanism will reply.

One might sum up the conflict by saying that Lord Brentford wants to suppress everything except marriage, and Mr Lawrence to suppress nothing except suppression; that the one sounds the trumpet of duty, the other the trumpet of passion, and that in the valley between them lie the inert forces of the general public. If a battle develops, we shall all of us have to get up and take sides; but need a battle develop? There has never been one in France. Is not a more reasonable issue possible? Is not the solution to be found not in the ringing clarion calls of either camp, but in the dull drone of tolerance, tolerance, tolerance? I hope so. Nor is tolerance quite as dull as its worthy followers suggest. Tolerance has its appropriate dangers, just as much as duty or passion. It, too, can lead to disaster and death. It can do harm, like everything else. It can, in the subject under discussion, sometimes injure the young, precisely as Lord Brentford contends. But it does less harm than anything else. It blights isolated individuals, it will never poison a nation. It is on the whole best. It is the principle which causes society the minimum of damage, because it admits that the people who constitute society are different. Unlike Mr Lawrence, I would tolerate everybody, even Nosey Parker and Peeping Tom. Let them peep and nose until they are sick – always providing that in the course of their investigations they do not invoke the support of the law.

[1930]

D. H. Lawrence, *Pornography and Obscenity*
Viscount Brentford, *Do We Need a Censor?*

The Cult of D. H. Lawrence

D. H. Lawrence made trouble wherever he went. He was lovable and could be absolutely charming, but he was quarrelsome, and his life was a series of storms in which all his friends were involved, and many of his friendships perished. It was no use turning the other cheek to him when he was angry. He smacked that also, and was so adroit that he appeared to be acting on the defensive. His friends quarrelled with one another too; he even possessed that uncanny power. He could not be discussed without over-emphasis and irritation. Voices rose or were unduly lowered. And if his unquiet genius has attained to Olympus its place will be between Eris and Eros, gods differing only by a letter, and it will look down with amusement upon the appropriate gestures of men. For the quarrelling still continues. The world cannot make up its mind about him. Was he divine? 'Certainly not, he will survive only in a few descriptive passages,' say some. 'Certainly he was,' retort others, 'you are shallow fools to deny him.' But though they denounce unbelief they do not agree upon orthodoxy. Bitter words pass between them, semi-theological words. They cannot decide how he ought to be worshipped, and if he retains anything of his old sense of humour this ought to entertain him.

Mr Middleton Murry, who knew him well at one time and has followed his career with care, here indicates the foundations of a cult. It is a cult on modern lines, where the deity comes in for some shrewd knocks, and only attains apotheosis under a running fire of criticism. Reverence, evenness, dignity, impersonality, all that constitute traditional religion, are absent, nevertheless the writer's attitude throughout is that of a priest. He desires to mediate rather than to interpret, he is slightly scared at what he is doing, and he attempts to communicate his alarm to the congregation. 'The ultimate incoherence, the ultimate agony. We feel that we have no right to be watching. But watch we must and listen we must. This is the agony of a great man.' Mr Murry's book contains sentences such as these. He even doubts whether he ought to have written it. But he pleads – very convincingly – that we can only find relief from certain painful emotions by writing them down and to one of his temperament there is no barrier between writing a thing down and offering it to the general public.

In *Son of Woman* he attempts, among other things, to analyse Lawrence's character. He is not concerned with his art – indeed he praises him for not being an artist, on the ground that genuine artists cannot exist in the present age. He even goes so far as to complain when his imagination 'puts a momentary spell upon us.' Most of us are thankful when it does. We read 'Elephants' – the superb poem to which he is here referring – not because it expresses some particular struggle or announces some particular doctrine, but because the poet's struggles and doctrines caused him to write magically. They were the liberating force. Without them his genius would never have flowered, and Mr Murry rightly condemns the shallow 'anthology' view of him, which admires him as the creator of a few beautiful descriptions, and refuses to recognize the force below. Whether he is equally right in ignoring the descriptions may be doubted. But Lawrence is an extraordinarily difficult writer. No one has yet succeeded in defining the relation between the flowers in him and the roots, and perhaps no one ever will succeed who has known him personally.

In analysing his character Mr Murry makes two most interesting suggestions. The first is that his passionate love for his mother unfitted him for intercourse with other women, and indeed for human relationships generally. The second is that he built up a dream image of himself, where his desires could be vicariously fulfilled. Plenty of evidence is offered on both points. We see how, in *Sons and Lovers*, he glorifies the mother, yet attempts to escape from her to the wife, and how in the later books the attempt to escape to a woman continues, and always fails. The bragging and bullying that so often repel us in his work – they are only confessions of his failure to be intimate either with woman or man. Which leads us on to the second point – the creation of a dream-image. Characters like Annabel in *The White Peacock*, Aaron in *Aaron's Rod*, Jack Grant in *The Boy in the Bush*, and Mellors in *Lady Chatterley's Lover* are, according to Mr Murry, portraits of Lawrence as he would have liked to be – the ruthless indomitable male. And Cyril in *The White Peacock*, Paul in *Sons and Lovers*, Lilly in *Aaron's Rod* and Somers in *Kangaroo*, represent Lawrence as he actually was – shrinking, sensitive, and exasperated. It is the type of analysis which Lawrence himself applied, with much less success, to the novels of Fenimore Cooper; applied to his own novels it gives good results, and Mr Murry convinces us that his male characters can be reduced to two types, while the female characters tend towards a single type, of which Miriam, in *Sons and Lovers*, is an early example.

But he hopes to convince us of much more, and it is at this point that all except the faithful must part company with him. Analysis is only one step in a grandiose drama of atonement, where love and hate contend or combine, and sins against the Holy Ghost can be committed with facility. Lawrence sinned. He denied Spirit, denied Love, shrank from the truth revealed to him in *Fantasia of the Unconscious* – which is, according to Mr Murry, his greatest book – played traitor to himself. Therefore he 'died' some time before writing *The Plumed Serpent*, and all his latest work is the utterance of a corpse. He died, he is doomed, yet centuries hence he will be understood and loved, and his only counterpart in the whole of creation is his opposite – Jesus. 'It was your destiny to fail us, as it was your destiny to fail yourself.' The words flow on in a menacing spate, and the mind of the unbeliever is carried away by them for a little. Then it withdraws, and tries to take stock. What underlies these lavish comminations and absolutions? Does Mr Murry feel that he himself and all of us are in a state of peril too? Yes, he feels this, and perhaps he is right. But he also feels – and here one dissents – a profound complacency in his plight. He relishes being scared and tries to infect others with his *malaise*. So might an adept, emerging from the shrine, hint that he has seen mysteries too terrible to mention, proceed just to mention them, and so send his disciples trembling away. And the love for Lawrence which he evidently felt but so emphatically announces only increases one's mistrust, for it enables him to dally with the most frightening of all *rôles,* the *rôle* of Judas. 'In this book have I betrayed you? Was it this, that I have done, of which you were afraid? There was nothing to fear. This betrayal was the one thing you lacked, the one thing I had to give, that you might shine forth among men as the thing of wonder that you were.' One wonders how Lawrence would respond to such a gift. A little coldly? Certainly he cannot complain of mystical threats and promises – he was prodigal in them himself. But he may now realize that they cut no ice either way, and that the desire to be disquieting may in the long run impair not only the critical faculty but the capacity for affection.

[1931]

J. Middleton Murry, *Son of Woman*

The Hat-Case

Years ago (it must be twenty-five years) I had the pleasure of meeting Mr Ford Madox Hueffer, as he then was, and he told an amusing anecdote which has epitomized some of his work for me since. It was about a gentleman who had a hat-case. He left the hat-case on the platform of a continental railway station, and went round the corner for a moment, and when he came back the case was still there. But when he took it up, it seemed to his shocked sense lighter than air. Up it flew. It had been gutted from below, and the hat was gone. Just such a shock sometimes awaits readers of Mr Ford's criticisms. Here, for example, is a hat-case, entitled *The English Novel from the Earliest Days to the Death of Joseph Conrad*, and presumably containing a hat. But lift it, and up it flies. We have been fooled, and since no one likes to be the victim of a practical joke, we are prone to complain that there is something wrong about Mr Ford, something gravely 'dicky', and to demand that a law shall be passed which shall prohibit for ever the leaving about of empty cases in public places. It is annoying, when one is an earnest seeker after truth and perhaps an examination candidate as well, to be told that ever since 1860 the *Pilgrim's Progress* and *Madame Bovary* have been among the four most popular books all the world over. It's untrue. They haven't been. And one's irritation is not diminished by being unable to say which have been. Anyhow, not those two. It's annoying, again, to be told that history has altered owing to the disuse of Plutarch, that Conrad, James and Crane are the three chief influences in contemporary fiction, that English fiction and fiction all the world over are identical, that Bach and Holbein are the world's two greatest artists, Anthony Trollope also running; that *Babbitt* was suggested by *Pamela*, that Our Lord and Tibullus used to be mentioned more frequently in conversation, and that Mr Ford himself has never known anyone who has known Miss Virginia Woolf. Why, he dedicates this very work to a friend in common! Surely we can catch him slipping at last. But no, we cannot; because there is no such person as Miss Virginia Woolf. She is Mrs Woolf. The statement is strictly accurate; two slips have made one slap, and this is annoying again.

The publishers, foreseeing our honourable scars, caution us upon the dust-cover that Mr Ford is not so much writing criticism as 'thinking aloud', and this certainly puts us wise if not exactly wiser. We are now astonished not when the hat-case is empty, but when it is full, and again and again, if one will but read him in this spirit, a gratifying weight tugs at one's arm. 'The function of the Arts in the State – apart from the consideration of aesthetics – is so to aerate the mind of the taxpayer as to make him less dull a boy.' How admirably this is put, and incidentally how it justifies the book itself! For Mr Ford does aerate us, and to repine because he is capricious or impertinent or because we disagree with him is wilfully to retreat into the depths of the Dunciad. I tested my own dullness over two passages. Not happening to like Scott, I read with joy: 'Obviously even the *Antiquary* is worth consideration if one had the time.' And happening to like Fielding I read with rage that 'although *Tom Jones* contains an immense amount of rather nauseous special-pleading, the author does pack most of it away into solid wads of hypocrisy at the headings of Parts or Chapters.' And having, beyond my likes and dislikes, the rudiments of a critical apparatus, I felt that both statements may be false in one universe and true in another, and that in Mr Ford's universe they are true.

What is his universe? It is not quite what he would have us think. It is composed of personal sensitiveness, of the quality that distinguishes him as a novelist, and that distinguished him as an editor when in days long past he so brilliantly conducted the *English Review* and so discerningly and generously helped his juniors. He himself would say that it is a more solid affair; that he holds certain principles – novelists oughtn't to preach, they ought to concentrate on the story, they oughtn't to caricature, and so on – and every now and then he alludes to these principles in a commanding way. But if he held opposing principles, it would make no difference, for the reason that his is not a nature that rests on generalities. His merit lies in his swiftness. At moments he turns sad, dignified and dynastic, and assumes the air of the repository of artistic traditions, and at such moments one cannot help smiling. But he must excuse our smiles; he has often enough had the laugh of us with his empty boxes, and he has written a fine little slap-dash book.

There is no dash and no slap about Dr Ernest Baker's *The History of the English Novel: Intellectual Realism, from Richardson to Sterne*, and no fineness about it either. Of course, unlike naughty Mr Ford, it delivers the goods. Here are the cases, labelled in sequence from Richardson to Sterne. The worst of it is one has no inclination to open them. For the book is dull, badly written, and conventional in its judgements despite its dalliance with modernity. It is, for instance, a convention to be arch over Richardson's life, so Dr Baker duly arches. It is the present convention to detract from Sterne's detractors, so, with all their original insensitiveness, he detracts. His work may contain original research (I am not qualified to say), but it has none of the other merits of scholarship; it cannot marshal facts plainly or discuss them philosophically, or give a straightforward account either of a novelist's life or of the contents of a novel:

> This brief summary of the events in Sterne's life bearing directly or indirectly on the genesis of the extraordinary book which he had launched upon the world may from this point be still briefer. By the middle of 1761, four more volumes of *Tristram Shandy* had been published. Sterne's health was steadily growing worse. He was told that the only way to save his life was to betake himself to a warmer climate; so in 1762 he went to Paris, in spite of difficulties due to our being at war with France.

That is a fair specimen of the style; it inclines us neither to hear about Sterne nor to read *Tristram Shandy*, and in places it becomes unintelligible (e.g., in the seventh sentence on page 13, where, owing to incompetence over the use of relative pronouns things get into a sorry mess). Were the book less pretentious, one would not be severe, but it sets out to be a 'history' not a manual, and it is the fourth of a series which is apparently trundling down the centuries to the present day. Richardson, Fielding, Smollett, and Sterne are the chief authors treated; Amory and others are discussed, and there are many references to Cervantes, Marivaux, etc. But they and all their works remain dead. It may be annoying when there are no hats in the cases, but it is worse when there are no heads in the hats, and we return with renewed appreciation to Mr Ford.

[1930]

Ford Madox Ford, *The English Novel*

Scenes and Portraits

I read *Scenes and Portraits* twenty years ago, and one of the stories in it, 'The King of Uruk', has never faded from my mind; perhaps it is the most exquisite short story of our century. And the other day I read *Her Privates We,* thought it the best of our war novels, and now learn that the two books are written by the same man.

Is there any connection between them? At the first glance they seem so different. One is so luscious and suave, the other all roughness and horror. One is a dream, the other reality. One leads us among philosophers and kings, the other among common soldiers who are covered with mud and vermin and fight rats and pilfer stores, and use unprintable words and die of unmentionable wounds, and are not even heroic according to civilian notions.

Yet there is a connection. Both books are the work of a man who has found the world a place of pain, but who believes that, owing to pain, love comes into being. *Her Privates We* was as much a love-story as a war-story – though it would not be so understood by any of the actors in it, nor was it so understood by many of its readers. It told of a comradeship that can only be born out of agony. It was a Nihilistic book, because the author had no faith in civilization; he regarded peace as an interlude, war the only reality – a reality through which alone man's deeper nature can be evoked.

I do not agree with Mr Manning's standards. I would rather see man's deeper nature destroyed for ever than have another war. But, while I read him, he made me feel that without pain love is impossible, and I feel this again while reading *Scenes and Portraits.* Here, too, man moves from sorrow to sorrow – from Uruk to Greece, from Florence to the shades; and neither the beauty of the world nor the beauty of his own words can comfort him. But sorrow brings compassion, and perhaps in his own image, perhaps through the eyes of a god, love looks up at him at last from the pool of his tears. The book is sceptical in tone, pagan in colouring, yet it distrusts happiness as profoundly as any mediæval monk; it finds the glories of our blood and state significant only because they will soon shrivel up in everlasting fire.

From the merely literary point of view, Mr Manning suggests Landor, Pater, Anatole France. He is urbane, drowsy, academic, ironical, and (with the exception of 'The King of Uruk') his stories are unlikely to interest a large public. They are discussions rather than stories. Socrates discourses with friends and enemies in the house of Euripides, a Roman describes St Paul amid the olives of Spain, Renan greets Pope Leo XIII in the Paradise that is reserved for the disillusioned. There is little action, and the disputations savour of the study.

But 'The King of Uruk' takes us into a world of movement and poetry. Working upon old Chaldean myths, it tells us of Merodach, who is seized with the terror of death; not only he will die, but the race of men; not only the race of men, but the stars. The high priest, to divert him, relates a recent adventure: in a valley near by he has found a man and woman who are naked, simple, and happy, and has learnt in their horoscope that they will be remembered as long as human life exists. At first Merodach fears for his kingdom, but the priest reassures him; their happiness will not last for long. The king now desires to visit these admirable barbarians; his queen and the little princess desire to come too and to see the great apple tree that stands in the midst of the valley, and the snake that coils in its branches. And so, with 'his wives and his concubines, his poets and his pastrycooks, his falconers, his flute-players and his players on the viol, his bow-men and his spearmen', Merodach went forth into Eden. What he found there, what the little princess found, what tradition of their visit survived into future ages, I must leave to Mr Manning to relate.

It is a perfect story, perfectly told. It might have been written by Anatole France but for one great difference: it substitutes compassion for tolerance. Mr Manning, when he has seen the cruelty and evil of existence, is never tempted to withdraw and contemplate. His sympathy is active, and that is why it has become an armour for him, and allowed him to endure the Great War and to write down afterwards the revelation the war gave him.

[1930?]

Frederic Manning, *Scenes and Portraits*

William Cowper, An Englishman

The bicentenary of Cowper's birth was celebrated last November with befitting mildness. Perhaps there have been too many anniversaries lately, perhaps the autumn of 1931 was an unfortunate period. At any rate, Cowper attracted little attention, as he himself would have expected. The professional men of letters made no noise, for the reason that their paeans had been anticipated by a perfect biography, Lord David Cecil's *The Stricken Deer.* And even if the men of letters had piped up, the public at large would have declined to listen. For who reads Cowper today? This is surely his last appearance upon the general stage. Wordsworth (to mention a spiritual kinsman) still keeps his place; in the great holocaust of literature that is approaching he will survive for a little. Cowper perishes. His magic is too flimsy to preserve him, and his knowledge of human nature is too much overshadowed by fears of personal damnation to radiate far down the centuries:

> Those twinkling tiny lustres of the land
> Drop one by one from Fame's neglecting hand.

he wrote, 'on observing some names of little note recorded in the *Biographia Britannica*,' and the epitaph might be his own. The London booksellers, who should know, say that the demand for his poems has not been stimulated by the recent modest ceremonies. There has been a slight increase of sales for his *Letters.* That is all.

It is not an unsuitable moment for him to perish, for England is perishing, and he was English. He was not British or enlightened or far-sighted or adaptable. He was English, and most so when he forgot his nationality and took a country walk. He had his conscious patriotic gestures, and some of them were effective; but there is a stay-at-home air about them which makes them rather ludicrous in our eyes; the poet defies or depreciates the foreigner from his study-chair, as did most patriotic poets before Rupert Brooke. It is only when he forgets his high mission that he touches our blood and speaks for our land. Out he steps – not forgetting an umbrella, for he understands the climate. Out he steps, accompanied by a lady when the clay is not too tenacious, and he walks over the weeds and under the elms, or across the empty hayfields, or, puffing healthily, he climbs a gentle ascent, from the top of which he can look back upon the River Ouse. None of the walks are very long; the scenery is neither flat nor hilly, the river is always the Ouse. Had it been the Severn or Thames the view would have been grander but less typical. The Ouse is the water of England. It belongs to our soil. We can scarcely imagine it ever leaving us to enter the sea. It is as near as could be a horizontal stream. And Cowper – who found in the placid trinity of Bucks, Beds and Hunts, such respite as the Furies allowed – is linked with their unostentatious river and with the fields that edge it. He saw the Ouse first at Huntingdon, when the clouds of his preliminary illness were lifting, and the Unwins received him into their affection. He dwelt by it at Olney and Weston Underwood, scenes of his happiness, tragedies and triumphs. And he bade farewell to it at St Neots, when all was lost, and he and Mrs Unwin, both of them insane, were carried away to end their days by the sea. How he mistrusted the sea! He could note its beauties, but it was too restless for him, and too large. And he was equally suspicious of mountains: 'I was a little daunted by the tremendous height of the Sussex hills,' and he compares himself to the athlete who could 'leap nowhere well except at Rhodes,' since he cannot write well, or even write at all, unless he is at Weston Underwood. As illness increases, the terror of exile from the Ouse grows more acute, and we find him crying from Norfolk as if it was Siberia: 'I shall never see Weston again. I have been tossed like a ball into a far country from which there is no rebound for me.'

Of course he was an invalid, and his attachment to local scenes can be discounted on that account. He had not enough vitality to seek new experiences, and never felt safe until habits had formed their cocoon round his sensitive mind. But inside the cocoon his life is genuine. He might dread the unknown, but he also loved what he knew; he felt steadily about familiar objects, and they have in his work something of the permanence they get in a sitting-room or in the kitchen garden. He does not greet them with surprise nor with any felicitous phrase. It is rather the instinctive acceptance which is part of rural life. Consequently, to read him is really to be in England, and the very triteness of his moralizing keeps us planted there. Brilliant descriptions and profound thoughts entail disadvantages when they are applied to scenery; they act too much as spot lights; they break the landscape up; they drill through it and come out at the antipodes; they focus too much upon what lies exactly in front. Cowper never does this. He knows that the country doesn't lie in front of us but all around. In front is an elm tree, but behind our backs there is probably another elm tree, and out of the corner of each eye we can see blurs that may represent a third elm and a fourth. And so with the country people, the ploughman or the postman, we may or may not meet them on our walk, but in either case they were somewhere. All this comes out in his work, and we get from it the conviction that we have a humble and inalienable heritage, country England, which no one covets, and which nothing can take away.

Alas, it is a conviction which finds no support whatever in facts. The country Cowper loved is precisely what is going to disappear. The grander scenery of England will probably be saved, owing to its importance in the tourist industry, but it will pay no one to preserve a stray elm, puddles full of ranunculus, or mole hills covered with thyme; and they, not the grandeur, are England. They will be swept aside by pylons and arterial roads, just as Cowper himself is being trodden underfoot by the gangs of modern writers who have been produced by universal education. Excellent writers, many of them. Writers of genius, some of them. But they leave no room for poor Cowper. He has no further part in our destinies. He belongs to the unadvertised, the unorganized, the unscheduled. He has no part in the enormous structure of steel girders and trade upon which Great Britain, like all other Powers, will have to base her culture in the future. That is why his bicentenary fell flat.

[1932]

Coleridge in His Letters

Goose, darling, genius, practical man! When shall we see Coleridge plainer? Our earlier view was simple: here was a poet who took drugs, and adorned literature and the copy books at the same time. What does genius avail if it cannot resist temptation? How unlike Lord Tennyson! Trouble began when it was realized that Coleridge was drugging himself heavily before he wrote any good poems, and that the poems themselves arise out of abnormal states. And there was further trouble when the period of his critical activity had to be considered; he ought, by rights, to have become a nervous wreck, yet he lectured and wrote energetically. It became obvious that there were two peaks in his achievement, the creative, in 1796–97, and the critical, some twenty years later. But even this was too simple: the critical period is an extended range of mountains rather than a peak, and the gulf between it and the creative is not an unrelieved abysm of despair.

He himself gave us all the help he could. He is one of the most explanatory of writers. But he is also one of the least revealing. The more he describes his health, his finances, his mental states and his personal relationships, the more muddled do we become. It is only when he fastens on an outside theme, such as Shakespeare or a voyage to the Antarctic, that he remains lucid. And all these fresh letters of his that have lately been published – they only heighten the contradictory lights, they do not round him off or allow us to say 'So that was Coleridge!' He will defeat the schoolmaster in us for ever. And if we have entered into his exalted view of human nature and the universe, there is something satisfactory in this. He has assailed our finite intelligences and suggested that the letter weight and the tape-measure are not the only measures conceivable, or even attainable.

However, let us leave all that for a moment and bring out our letter weight, and place some of these letters on it. What a thrilling collection! How well they have been edited by Professor Griggs, of Michigan University! How greatly the student of Coleridge is indebted to him, to Professor Lowes, and to American scholarship in general! There are four hundred letters, and they are either unknown, or have hitherto been published in mutilated forms.

They illustrate every aspect of Coleridge's long life, and we can argue that he comes out the better or the worse, as we please. Take, as an example, his relations with his wife. From this additional correspondence it seems clearer than it used to be both that she hooked him, and that he proved a troublesome fish. The origins of the union are well known. He and Southey had, in their undergraduate days, a scheme for emigrating and setting up an ideal community – the sort of scheme which fascinated D. H. Lawrence over a hundred years later. Wives were necessary, and several Miss Frickers were available. Southey picked a good one, Coleridge was less fortunate, and by the time the scheme was given up he would like to have disentangled himself from the lady too. But she pointed out that she had missed two matrimonial chances on his account, and annoyed her uncle, and she would be compelled to marry a man whom she disliked if he abandoned her. So, although he never felt anything for her beyond pity, and was in love with someone else, he married her, and made her unhappy. He now comes out as a typical male. His gallantry and sentimental idealism give place to an unseasonable display of reason, and the letters he writes eight years after their marriage must have been quite maddening. They are, at the same time, extraordinarily wise and extraordinarily silly letters. Only a masculine intelligence could have produced them:

> My dear Love, let me in the spirit of Love say two things. (1) I owe duties, and solemn ones, to you as my wife, but some equally solemn ones to Myself, to my children, to my

> friends and to society . . . When duties are at variance, dreadful as the case may be, there must be a choice . . . (2) Permit me, my dear Sara, without offence to you, as, Heaven knows, it is without any pride in myself, to say that, in six acquirements, and in the quantity and quality of natural endowments, whether of feeling or of intellect, you are the inferior. Therefore it would be preposterous to expect that I should see with your eyes and dismiss my friends from *my* heart . . . If you read this letter with half the tenderness with which it is written, it will do you and both of us *good*.

Here is the familiar situation of the big sweet-natured man tied to the small jealous wife, and every word that Coleridge says is true. But what a fool to say it! What insensitiveness! What a refinement of cruelty he achieves by the (1) and (2), and by the gentle tone! And if these did not drive the poor woman frantic, imagine her reaction to the final paragraph, which is: 'Write immediately, my dear Love, and direct to me – where? That's the puzzle – to be left at the Post Office, Carmarthen.' Yes! She is to write at once, although both the children have the worms, and he – he will possibly pick up her letter some time or other at Carmarthen, and probably never read it.

The relation of Coleridge to his wife occupies only a small part of the letters collected by Professor Griggs. They illustrate every period and topic, and constantly give us new lights. The quarrel with Wordsworth, for instance, is more violent than one had realized: 'even to have any thought of Wordsworth, while writing these lines, has, I feel, fluttered and disordered my whole Inside.' And the hallucinations are more terrible: 'Night is my Hell. Sleep my tormenting Angel. Three nights out of four I fall asleep, struggling to lie awake – and my frequent Night-screams have almost made me a nuisance in my own House. Dreams with me are no Shadows but the very substances and foot-thick Calamities of my Life.' Wherever we turn we get the sense of greater intensity and complexity, we are surer than before that Coleridge is one of the most important and interesting people who have ever lived in England. And we manage to see him, at moments, outside space and time, and thus catch sight of the new country to which he beckoned us, that country whose only proper language is poetry, yet it also speaks through the mouths of philosophers and the actions of ordinary men.

[1932]

Samuel Taylor Coleridge, *Unpublished Letters* (ed. E. L. Griggs)

Ancient and Modern

A. E. Housman has been well served by his executors. Both these books are good, they will delight his audience, and he himself should tolerate them. The posthumous poems appear with his acquiescence; the sketch, delicate and firm, gives to his character an outline which he could not resent and atones for any excursions into intimacy by two erudite appendices. His shade can ask no more. It certainly will not want a favourable review. Even that flimsy creature whom he so much despised, even a literary critic, is not tempted to over-praise. His lofty shade advances over our eulogies, warning us to be clear in our thinking, precise in our diction, accurate in our punctuation and discreet in our sentimentality.

The sentimentality – that perhaps is the main problem. The passionate broodings, the indignations and devotions, the emotional reconstructions of an actual or imagined past: these, which lie at the heart of the poet, what place did they occupy in the man? He was an unhappy fellow and not a very amiable one. To his friends he accorded the measured intimacy well described by Mr Gow, to his acquaintance he could be sardonic and (what was still more disconcerting) petty. Pettiness also disfigured his scholarship; his attacks on other Latinists in his prefaces to Manilius and to Juvenal are brilliant, scathing and sound, yet they are in the last analysis undignified, for dullness ought to be reprimanded dully. He was too small to see this. What is the relation between all these tiresomenesses and the burning desire to help another which is so moving in his poems – the outstretched hand, the lifted brow, the beating heart, the faithfulness that shatters the gates of hell. What connection can be established between the stilted, uncertain-tempered don and the writer of:

> Ho every one that thirsteth
> And hath the price to give,
> Come to the stolen waters,
> Drink and your soul shall live.
>
> Come to the stolen waters
> And leap the guarded pale,
> And pull the flower in season
> Before desire shall fail.

The two books under review help to answer this question – a question to which no mark of interrogation has here been appended, as the proof-reader beyond the grave will observe. The 'sketch' helps most. Like Housman himself, Mr Gow is interested in the truth, and, expounding it quietly, he brings his man alive.

> The critic in whose eyes 'high heaven and earth ail from the prime foundation', the rebel forced 'by man's bedevilment and God's' into unwilling conformity with standards which he condemned, was marked for a life of discontents, and they were reinforced by the antinomies of his mental outlook. That his desire for friendship has been overborne by fear of what friendship might hold in store, has already been suggested, and his desire for fame was similarly counter-balanced by fear of the honours which in most men would have gratified it.

In passages such as these, Mr Gow pulls Housman together, and connects his unamiability and his creative power. He emerges as a man who was difficult to meet but is not difficult to understand; the troubles of his angry dust are ours, though they took an unusual shape, and if we do care to give him a bad mark it is the mark which in one form or other stands to the discredit of us all: timidity.

The poems help, too. About half-a-dozen of them are

marvellous, and purists may wish that these alone had been printed. His editor, Mr Laurence Housman, has rightly taken another view, and has included several poems which are echoes, several which are imperfect, and a few weak ones. This is the proper way to edit a person who wrote living stuff. Fragments of what is merely scholarly or clever should be differently treated; they ought to be burned, and this indeed is the fate to which the Professor has consigned his prose remains. The poems, forty-nine in number, bring up the published total to a hundred and fifty-four, and one point which comes out in a general retrospect is the bizarre yet fertile alliance between the manner of them and the matter in them. The manner is scholarly and churchified; 'Ho every one that thirsteth': the dean might be giving out a hymn. The matter is blood-hot or death-cold. And the reader remains in an agreeable state of suspense and can never foretell how much he is going to feel. It is as if he took up a sampler to estimate its period-value and then observed, embroidered in it, some bitter and explosive truth. The sentiments mean more to him than if he had been prepared for them, as a result of which the whole sampler gains in importance. The 'antinomy' which Mr Gow regrets in Housman's life is thus the mainstay of his poetry. The hymnal framework, the polished antithetical style of writing, increase the passion of the theme, and give it much more force than could be achieved through ruggedness and verbal daring.

The theme, like that of Shakespeare's Sonnets, involves a story. But, here as there, it is impossible to figure the story out and discover through what mutations it passed before the writer clamped it into print. We shall never know the name and number of the soldier 'cheap to the King and dear to me' who haunts the three volumes in so many uniforms. We shall never know why the account of a murder and execution, read by chance in a local paper, produced the Terence group. A poet hides things up and pares them away, not because he is refined, but because his method requires it. The living fact which he experienced was entangled in dead stuff which did not interest him: he has to isolate it before he can express it passionately, and because it is isolated it changes and is unrecognizable to his biographer. Of its bones are coral made. Matthew Arnold's 'Margaret' poems and Meredith's 'Modern Love' are other examples of the process, and the true reader of poetry is he who can detect when a poem is the result of the process and when it is merely an exercise. The late Sir Sidney Lee thought the Sonnets were an Elizabethan exercise, and his arguments are unanswerable. And some admirers of Housman have presented him as a sort of serious Austin Dobson, whose inspiration was the classics: Epicureanism and Stoicism for the sentiments, Horace, the Greek Anthology, etc., for the images and turns of phrase. Certainly the classics abound in the present volume (Sappho, Callimachus and other sources have been pointed out), and he loved his old stuff. But that, too, suffers a sea change, and is subdued to the temper of his mind. The last verse of his translation of *Diffugere nives* imports a quality not to be found in the original, and when he summons the classical boat of Charon and the classical grammatical device of apposition, this is what he turns out:

> Crossing alone the nighted ferry
>   With the one coin for fee,
> Whom, on the wharf of Lethe waiting,
>   Count you to find? Not me.
>
> The brisk fond lackey to fetch and carry,
>   The true, sick-hearted slave,
> Expect him not in the just city
>   And free land of the grave.

Ancient has become modern. The tags and tricks of the past have been bent to his personal pain. He has written elsewhere that 'to transfuse emotion – not to transmit thought but to set up in the reader's sense a vibration corresponding to what was felt by the writer – is the peculiar function of poetry.' He practises what he preached. Whether the reader on his side vibrates accurately is another question, and the views put forward in this article may be queried. That his poems are *not* scholarly exercises; that is the only point on which one can dogmatize. They are what he says they are: the vibrations, the motions of his heart. There we must leave him.

Housman's handling of life – it is too sincere to be called a philosophy – is full of incongruities. He praised virtue, he praised licence, too. He both denied and denounced God, and why denounce what does not exist? He laboured to build himself an abiding monument in scholarship, yet he knew that every building stands upon sand. Incapable of illusions, he pursued phantoms; convinced of treachery, he dreamt of affection. Unlike most of us, he would not tolerate the second best, and so was threatened with shipwreck unless the seas kept miraculously calm. His intelligence and sensitiveness imperilled him, shocks disturbed him which were imperceptible to coarser chaps. Things might have been much worse: he found an adequate haven at Cambridge, he was fortunate in making a quiet circle of friends who understood him, and outside the college gates an appreciative public cackled, not always unwelcome or unheeded. He enjoyed a glass of port. That is something. One wishes he could have enjoyed the happy highways which he resigned in the body and possessed so painfully in the imagination, but he was not destined for vulgar pleasures. Perhaps he had a better time than the outsider supposes. Did he ever drink the stolen waters which he recommends so ardently to others? I hope so.

[1936]

A. E. Housman, *More Poems*
A. F. S. Gow, *A. E. Housman*

A Bedside Book

For such as have beds, and for such beds as have sides, this is an ideal bedside book. A few pages of it, occasionally read between sirens, may help us to keep our heads through the approaching winter. It is an unusual book. Sir Sydney Cockerell has had the good idea of publishing letters written to him in the course of his life, and he has had the good fortune to find in Miss Viola Meynell their perfect editor. Only a professional writer will appreciate the nature of Miss Meynell's achievement. She can easily give us interesting scraps, but she has done more than that; she has pulled the scraps into shape so that we get a series of facets of literary and æsthetic history during the last fifty years. Humped in our shelters, we peer at them while the rubbish explodes overhead. They gleam, they glow. They are the facets of a lost jewel.

Most of Sir Sydney's letters come from eminent people, and I cannot help smiling when I reflect what a very dim lot the friends of my own lifetime are by comparison. They would not provide a saleable volume or even a publishable one. However, that is by the way. His activities and enthusiasms have brought him into natural contact with some of the most interesting personalities of his age, and he has had the gift of eliciting their best from them by his sympathy, intelligence, and good sense. From Ruskin to Lawrence of Arabia, from Octavia Hill to Charlotte Mew, from Tolstoy to the Maltravers Herald, from Ouida to Professor York Powell – it is a varied assembly, but it is none the less a jewel, which a vanished state of affairs has deposited. All these people were civilized. They differed in outlook and genius, but they belonged to the same cultural stratum, they possessed or understood leisure.

> To me, in this my quiet time of somewhat sad reflection, it seems as if there was nothing for the miserable minority owning some common sense but to hide their injured feelings in the study of the ancient arts remaining to us, or we shall die daily – which is nothing less I fancy than the life in Hell.

Thus writes Philip Webb, architect and partner in the firm of Morris and Co. Ladysmith had been relieved, and the din of the celebrations vexed Philip Webb. We may laugh at the occasion of his letter but it rings true, and truer today than when he wrote it. He, and his fellow-correspondents, are in a sense an 'ancient art', and they are particularly precious to us, who can by the force of circumstances create nothing.

Sir Sydney was for nearly thirty years Director of the Fitzwilliam at Cambridge. He found it a dull second-rate collection, he raised it by his devotion and persistence to the position of a museum of national importance. (To be praised as a beggar by the late Lord Knutsford is praise indeed, and there is a letter according it.) His post, reinforced by his expert knowledge of mediaeval manuscripts, brought him into the artistic and the craftsmanly world: letters from Ricketts, Emery Walker, Lethaby, and many post-pre-Raphaelites result. For literature, he had an equally good line of approach, he was secretary first to William Morris and then to Wilfrid Blunt, and he was the friend and executor of Thomas Hardy. Hence many contacts – Henry James, Hale White, Conrad, Bridges, Yeats, etc.

The biggest batches of letters are from Ruskin, from Blunt, and from that fantastic figure Cobden-Sanderson. The Ruskin letters, which come early, are of great interest, and Sir Sydney has linked them together by a commentary, in which his youthful adoration of the prophet is analysed and confirmed. The Blunt letters detail a connection of his maturity. The interest of the Cobden-Sanderson batch is comic. It describes the Quest of the Book Beautiful, and, arising therefrom, the quarrel between Mr Cobden-Sanderson and Sir Emery Walker over the ownership of the type of the Doves Press, which Mr Cobden-Sanderson finally and illegally threw into the Thames at Hammersmith. Having done so, thus wrote he:

> And may the River, in its tides and flows, pass over them to and from the great sea for ever and ever or until its tides and flows for ever cease; then may they share the fates of all the worlds, and pass from change to change for ever upon the Tides of Time, untouched of other use.

Helpful, sane, and aware of the sacredness of property, Sir Sydney could not condone such a gesture. He reasoned with Mr Cobden-Sanderson, who was a barrister as well as an aesthete, and he did his best to patch up the quarrel between the two gifted artists. Indeed, so far as his personality comes out, it is as a harmonizer, a quiet intervener among the long-bearded bright-eyed geniuses. Sometimes their nerves go wrong, sometimes their finances. Doughty puts all his money into Rubber and Kent Coal: 'the last, bought at high prices, though geologically sound are worth nothing, and Rubber yields now nothing', and Sir Sydney organizes a fund for the purchase of his Arabian notebooks. Indeed the only correspondent whom he seems to ruffle for an instant is A. C. Benson, who turns fretful on the subject of lust.

But one could amble on and on over this welcome book. By its nature, it eludes criticism, or generalizing – except for the generality that it is civilized. I will end by mentioning two corresondents whose merits surprised me: Ouida and the second Mrs Thomas Hardy. Ouida I had been taught to regard as a figure of fun. I had no idea of the excellence of her English, or of her sincerity – she is apparently replying to a question:

> If you do not believe in the divinity of Christ, what remains? What of course was always there, a poor man of fine instincts sore troubled by the suffering and the injustice which trouble Tolstoy today. He drew the poor after him, naturally, by his assurances that the future would

compensate them for their painful labour. But I have never been able to understand how theories so crude, so illogical, so uneducated, and unsupported, could ever attract or satisfy intellectual minds.

'One must believe something,' I am told. Why? Why should one need a belief?

This is the language of a woman who knows what she wants to say. No hesitation, not a word out of place, the rhetoric rising naturally out of the emotion. And the same applies to Mrs Thomas Hardy, though what she wanted to say was very different. Self-effacing, and modest, Mrs Hardy cannot have realized how well she wrote. She was thinking only of her subject-matter, of her husband, of her correspondent:

> We had a very quiet Christmas, we two, alone, with Wessie – our only diversion being that T. H. *would* give Wessie goose and plum-pudding and the result was what might have been expected. . . . He saw a ghost in Stinsford Churchyard on Christmas Eve, and his sister Kate says it must have been their grandfather, upon whose grave T. H. had just placed a sprig of holly – the first time he had ever done so. The ghost said: 'A green Christmas'. T. H. replied, 'I like a green Christmas'. Then the ghost went into the church, and, being full of curiosity, T. followed, to see who this strange man in 18th century dress might be – and found no one. That is quite true – a real Christmas ghost story.

Here again what admirable English! The whole picture, with its attendant humour and mystery, is built up in a few words. And the final sentence, which a smart critic might reject as twaddle, is essential to the atmosphere. That is the kind of letter which Sir Sydney was lucky enough to get. We must thank him for allowing us to share it, and much else, with him; and we must thank Miss Meynell too.

[1940]

S. C. Cockerell, *Friends of a Lifetime*

George Crabbe: the Poet and the Man

To talk about Crabbe is to talk about England. He never left our shores and he only once ventured to cross the border into Scotland. He did not even go to London much, but lived in villages and small country towns. He was a clergyman of the English Church. His Christian name was George, the name of our national saint. More than that, his father was called George, and so was his grandfather, and he christened his eldest son George, and his grandson was called George also. Five generations of George Crabbes!

Our particular George Crabbe was born (in the year 1754) at Aldeburgh, on the coast of Suffolk. It is a bleak little place: not beautiful. It huddles round a flint-towered church and sprawls down to the North Sea – and what a wallop the sea makes as it pounds at the shingle! Near by is a quay, at the side of an estuary, and here the scenery becomes melancholy and flat; expanses of mud, saltish commons, the marsh-birds crying. Crabbe heard that sound and saw that melancholy, and they got into his verse. He worked as an unhappy little boy on the quay, rolling barrels about and storing them in a warehouse, under orders from his father. He hated it. His mother had died; his father was cross. Now and then he got hold of a book or looked at some prints, or chatted with a local worthy, but it was a hard life and they were in narrow circumstances. He grew up among poor people, and he has been called their poet. But he did not like the poor. When he started writing, it was the fashion to pretend that they were happy shepherds and sheperdesses, who were always dancing or anyhow had hearts of gold. But Crabbe knew the local almshouses and the hospital and the prison, and the sort of people who drift into them; he read in the parish registers the deaths of the unsuccessful, the marriages of the incompetent, and the births of the illegitimate. Though he notes occasional heroism, his general verdict on the working classes is unfavourable. And when he comes to the richer and more respectable inmates of the borough who can veil their defects behind money, he remains sardonic, and sees them as poor people who haven't been found out.

He escaped from Aldeburgh as soon as he could. His fortune improved, he took orders, married well, and ended his life in a comfortable west country parsonage. He did well for himself in fact. Yet he never escaped from Aldeburgh in the spirit, and it was the making of him as a poet. Even when he is writing of other things, there steals again and again into his verse the sea, the estuary, the flat Suffolk coast, and local meannesses, and an odour of brine and dirt – tempered occasionally with the scent of flowers. So remember Aldeburgh when you read this rather odd poet, for he belongs to the grim little place, and through it to England. And remember that though he is an Englishman, he is not a John Bull, and that though he is a clergyman, he is no means an 'old dear'.

His poems are easily described, and are easy to read. They are stories in rhymed couplets, and their subject is local scenes or people. One story will be about the almshouses, another about the Vicar, another about inns. A famous one is 'Peter Grimes': he was a savage fisherman who murdered his apprentices and was haunted by their ghosts; there was an actual original for Grimes. Another – a charming one – tells of a happy visit which a little boy once paid to a country mansion, and how the kind housekeeper showed him round the picture gallery, and gave him a lovely dinner in the servants' hall: Crabbe had himself been that humble little boy. He is not brilliant or cultivated, witty or townified. He is provincial; and I am using provincial as a word of high praise.

How good are these stories in verse? I will quote some extracts so that you can decide. Crabbe is a peculiar writer: some people like him, others don't and find him dull and even unpleasant. I like him and read him again and again: and his tartness, his acid humour, his honesty, his feeling for certain English types and certain kinds of English scenery, do appeal to me very much. On their account I excuse the absence in him of a warm heart, a vivid imagination and a grand style: for he has none of those great gifts.

The first extract is from 'Peter Grimes'. It shows how Crabbe looks at scenery, and how subtly he links the scene with the soul of the observer. The criminal Grimes is already suspected of murdering his apprentices, and no one will go fishing with him in his boat. He rows out alone into the estuary, and waits there – waits for what?

> When tides were neap, and in the sultry day,
> Through the tall bounding mud-banks made their
> way . . .
> There anchoring, Peter chose from man to hide,
> There hang his head and view the lazy tide
> In its hot, slimy channel slowly glide;
> Where the small eels that left the deeper way
> For the warm shore, within the shallows play;
> Where gaping muscles, left upon the mud,
> Slope their slow passage to the fallen flood.

How quiet this writing is: you might say how dreary. Yet how sure is its touch; and how vivid that estuary near Aldeburgh.

> Here dull and hopeless he'd lie down and trace
> How sidelong crabs had scrawl'd their crooked race;
> Or listen sadly to the tuneless cry
> Of fishing gull or clanging golden-eye;
> What time the sea-birds to the marsh would come,
> And the loud bittern, from the bull-rush home,
> Gave from the salt-ditch side the bellowing boom:
> He nursed the feelings these dull scenes produce,
> And loved to stop beside the opening sluice.

Not great poetry, by any means; but it convinces me that Crabbe and 'Peter Grimes' and myself do stop beside an opening sluice, and that we are looking at an actual English tideway, and not at some vague vast imaginary waterfall, which crashes from nowhere to nowhere.

My next quotation is a lighter one. It comes from his rather malicious poem about the Vicar of the Parish 'whose constant care was no man to offend'. He begins with a sympathetic description of Aldeburgh church, and its lichen-encrusted tower, and now he turns, with less sympathy, to the church's recent incumbent. Listen to his cruel account of the vicar's one and only love affair. He had been attracted to a young lady who lived with her mother; he called on them constantly, smiling all the time, but never saying what he was after: with the inevitable result that the damsel got tired of her 'tortoise', and gave her hand to a more ardent suitor. Thus ended the Vicar's sole excursion into the realm of passion.

> 'I am escaped', he said, when none pursued;
> When none attacked him, 'I am unsubdued';
> 'Oh pleasing pangs of love', he sang again,
> Cold to the joy, and stranger to the pain.
> Ev'n in his age would he address the young,
> 'I too have felt these fires, and they are strong';
> But from the time he left his favourite maid,
> To ancient females his devoirs were paid;
> And still they miss him after morning prayer.

He was always 'cheerful and in season gay', he gave the ladies presents of flowers from his garden with mottoes attached: he was fond of fishing, he organized charades, he valued friendship, but was not prepared to risk anything for it. One thing did upset him and that was innovation: if the Vicar discerned anything new, on either the theological or the social horizon, he grew hot – it was the only time he did get hot.

> Habit with him was all the test of truth,
> 'It must be right: I've done it from my youth'.
> Questions he answer'd in as brief a way,
> 'It must be wrong – it was of yesterday'.

Though mild benevolence our priest possess'd,
'Twas but by wishes or by words express'd:
Circles in water, as they wider flow,
They less conspicuous in their progress grow:
And when at last they touch upon the shore,
Distinction ceases, and they're view'd no more.
His love, like that last circle, all embraced,
But with effect which never could be traced.

The Vicar's fault is weakness, and the analysis and censure of weakness is a speciality of Crabbe's. His characters postpone marriage until passion has died: perhaps this was his own case, and why he was so bitter about it. Or they marry and passion dies because they are too trivial to sustain it. Or they drift into vice and do even that too late, so that they are too old to relish the tastiness of sin. Or like the Vicar they keep to the straight path because vice is more arduous than virtue. To all of them, and to their weaknesses, Crabbe extends a little pity, a little contempt, a little cynicism, and a much larger portion of reproof. The bitterness of his early experiences has eaten into his soul, and he does not love the human race, though he does not denounce it, nor despair of its ultimate redemption.

But we must get back to the Vicar, who is awaiting his final epitaph in some anxiety.

Now rests our Vicar. They who knew him best,
Proclaim his life t'have been entirely rest: . .
The rich approved, – of them in awe he stood;
The poor admired, – they all believed him good;
The old and serious of his habits spoke;
The frank and youthful loved his pleasant joke;
Mothers approved a safe contented guest,
And daughters one who back'd each small request: . . .
No trifles fail'd his yielding mind to please,
And all his passions sunk in early ease:
Nor one so old has left this world of sin,
More like the being that he enter'd in.

For the Vicar died as a child, who retains his innocence because he has never gained any experience.

Well, the above quotations from 'Peter Grimes' and from the Vicar, one about scenery, the other about character, should be enough for you to find out whether you have any taste for the story-poems of George Crabbe. Do not expect too much. He is not one of our great poets. But he is unusual, he is sincere, and he is entirely of this country. There is one other merit attaching to him. The George Crabbe who was his son wrote his life and it is one of the best biographies in our language, and gives a wonderful picture of provincial England at the close of the eighteenth century and the beginning of the nineteenth. Even if you are not attracted as much as I am by Crabbe's poetry, you may like to get hold of his life, and read how the poor little boy who rolled barrels on the quay at Aldeburgh made good.

[1941]

The Mint by T. E. Lawrence

I saw a good deal of T. E. Lawrence while he was writing *The Mint.* He was not in the Air Force at the time – he had been driven out of it by a newspaper stunt and was hiding away amongst the Tanks instead – but he managed to get back there and on April 16, 1928, he wrote to me from Karachi, referring to 'some notes on life in the ranks . . . crude unsparing faithful stuff; very metallic and uncomfortable.' These notes turned into *The Mint.* I read it in typescript. Letters passed between us and later on we talked, and later still, after his death, I was lent a copy of the privately printed edition. So I have been in and out of the book from its early days and in that way I am well qualified to talk about it.

In another way I am ill qualified. I know nothing whatsoever of the life it describes. I have known servicemen of course – at Lawrence's own retreat of Clouds Hill, for instance, where I met friends of his with whom I still keep in touch. But I have always known them off duty, I have never seen them at work, still less worked with them. I have never shared any of Lawrence's experiences, so I cannot interpret them except by guessing at them and I cannot check his statements. Is he telling the truth? He did not always, and he will always bewilder those excellent people who identify telling the truth and being true. True he was, but he loved fantasy and leg-pulling and covering up his own tracks, and he threw up a great deal of verbal dust, which bewilders the earnest researcher.

Why ever did he join up? Well may you ask. Why break off a brilliant career and plunge into the squalor of an R.A.F. depot when nobody wanted him to, when indeed a good many officials were inconvenienced by his insistence? Why exchange comfort and distinction for fatigues and the square? It was partly the desire to abase himself, to crash from the heights of commanding to the depths of obedience, it was partly the desire to hide, partly the itch for adventure. But believing him, as I do, to be true, I believe there was a deeper motive than these. He joined up because he wanted to get into touch with people, and felt he could only do this by doing the work they did, and by sharing their lives. He is very difficult to understand and probably did not understand himself, but throughout his complexities there is one constant quality – namely, compassion. It showed itself in little things, in ordinary kindnesses – such as I and most of his friends experienced. It showed itself also in the deeper, the literal sense, of the word compassion; in his desire to share experience with people and if necessary to suffer with them.

The Mint is a good book – better technically than the straddling *Seven Pillars.* It is soundly constructed: three sections which connect with one another to make a coherent whole. The first two sections deal with the Uxbridge depot, the third with the Cadet College at Cranwell in Lincolnshire, to which he was posted as an aircraftman. The atmosphere of the three sections varies but there is always the idea of training: one might paraphrase them as The Misery of not being trained; The Misery of being trained; and The Joy of having been trained. The conceptions of training and of loyalty dominate *The Mint. Per ardua ad astra.* Or as one of his own mates put it, 'Per ardua ad asbestos'. For loyalty changes its objective. At the depot it is the loyalty of the down-trodden trainees to one another, it is the fellowship of the Insulted and Injured. In the third section it is loyalty to the air and to the R.A.F. whom he regards as its sole conqueror. I will try to think about this later on. Just now, whatever the ethical appropriateness here of training and of loyalty, we may agree that they bind the book together excellently and make it a well made book.

It is also a well written book. Lawrence's style, though slow-moving and mannered, can convey a great variety of actions and attitudes, scenery and scenes, to do which is a main function of style. He can do you a repartee, a rough house, a sprained ankle, a garbage bin, the slow passing across windows of the moon, troops in church, himself at Marlborough House, bird cries, bacon and eggs, and can capture for you one after another the impressions that have impinged upon his unusual mind. He only fails when he tries to examine the workings of the mind, when he becomes introspective or even merely philosophic. Then the slow motion of the style generates stickiness and its mannerisms crack into self-consciousness, and he conveys nothing to us except that he is a good deal worried, which we have already guessed. There are not many of these introspective passages in *The Mint.* If there were more, its compactness might suffer. It is made up of sixty-nine vivid, short chapters, each easy to read and all geared into the general scheme of training and of loyalty. It is the work of a man who had much to put across and knew how to put it.

Before I go further, I would like to emphasize that the general edition now on sale is almost exactly the same as the original privately printed edition of 1936. I did not think it would be. I thought there would be bowdlerizing and cuts, especially in view of the book prosecutions which have been so prevalent lately. One scatological passage has been omitted, so have 'the coarse words automatic in barrack-room speech' (there are about half-a-dozen such words and nearly everyone knows what they are). And there are some slight textual variants, due to collation of manuscripts. That is all. Otherwise it is exactly the same as the original edition, and the editor, his brother (Professor A. W. Lawrence), and the publishers are to be congratulated on it. They have also issued a small unexpurgated edition for subscribers.

Now to tackle the Uxbridge depot. Here is a grim story. The misery experienced there, both before and during training, could have been avoided, he thinks. It was caused by the officers being too few and too aloof and the N.C.O.s being too numerous and too uncontrolled. Having too little to do, they fall upon the hapless recruits and put them through the mill, dealing out punishments and fatigues indiscriminately and sometimes reducing them to nervous pulp. A chapter about a garbage cart – to give it a bowdlerized name – passes belief, and even more fantastic are some sacks, full of grease and maggots, which the recruits have to boil up and get clean for the butcher, the result being a stinking soup which had to be thrown away, sacks and all. There's a morning's work for the Royal Air Force! And when they pass from the chaos of not being trained to the rigours of being trained, they encounter the same wastage and cynicism, plus physical distress: they encounter Stiffy, the drill adjutant, an ex-guardsman who is incapable of seeing anything beyond drill, punishments and drill. The portrait of Stiffy is delicately drawn and there is a clever turn at the end of it when he makes an ingratiating speech to his victims as they are leaving and advertises himself not such a bad fellow after all: whereupon they despise him.

Professor Lawrence in his introduction says that his brother did not write *The Mint* as propaganda for alleviating recruits' hardships. It is clear, however, that he thought they should be alleviated and that unless they were alleviated R.A.F. morale would suffer. Here is the passage where he expressed this view.

> They have put us into maudlin fear, to moral abasement. A little longer . . . and we're hospital cases. Five have slunk there already; or rather three have slunk and two decent lads were carried in.
>
> I have been before at depots and have seen or overseen the training of many men, but this our treatment is rank cruelty. While my mouth is yet hot with it I want to record that some of those who day by day exercise their authority upon us, do it in the lust of cruelty. There is a glitter in their faces when we sob for breath . . . which betrays that we are being hurt not for our own good but to gratify a passion. Alone of the hut, I've energy at this moment to protest. . . . I am not frightened of our instructors, nor of their over-driving. To comprehend why we are their victims is to rise above them. Yet despite my background of achievement and understanding, despite my willingness . . . that the R.A.F. should bray me and remould me after its pattern: still I want to cry out that this our long-drawn punishing can subserve neither beauty nor use.

The R.A.F., like other organizations, evidently believed in breaking down individuals so that it might build them up again in more serviceable shapes: before the metal could be minted it had to be melted. If you want an extreme example of such breaking down and building up, read Orwell's *1984*: there you get *The Mint* in excelsis. Whether the Uxbridge depot went too far in its breaking down process as Lawrence thought, whether depots today are different, I do not know, though some of you may. I will turn to the pleasanter side of his picture: to Hut 4, to the mutual loyalty of the recruits who were being broken. He shared a hut with fifty others who came from different places and classes. In three days all were friendly and (as he shrewdly observes) never became any friendlier. What they wanted from personal relationship was solidarity, mutual support against the over-harsh discipline of training, and as soon as they got it they felt safe. The N.C.O. in charge of the hut was decent, and when they were not too exhausted by P.T. – oh the noise they made:

> The key of Hut 4 remains laughter; the laughter of shallow water. Everywhere there is the noise of games, tricks, back chat, advices, helps, councils, confidences, complaints: and laughs behind the gravest of these. The noise is infernal. Our jazz band is very posh of its kind, because Madden leads it with his mandoline. He is supported by two coal-pans, the fire buckets, five tissued combs, two shovels, the stove doors, fire boiler lids and vocal incidents. The louder it is the louder they sing, the more they leap about their beds, strike half-arm balances, do hand-springs and neck-rolls, or wrestle doggily over the floors and iron-bound boxes. There's hardly a night without its mirthful accident of blood letting.

There is plenty of this gay and good tempered stuff in *The Mint.* Much of it is lively reading, 'Give him a gob of your toffology', they cry, when they want him to answer the sergeant back. And he gives it. And the sergeant is struck dumb.

Outside these contrary principles of the Square and the

Hut, Discipline and Loyalty, stands Church Parade, professing to reconcile them and to represent the principle of Love. Lawrence watched its efforts with detachment. A bare, over-restored fourteenth-century church gave him convenient opportunities for reflection.

> Worship seemed due from us on so sunny a morning. So perforce I heard another unreal service and again its misapplication stung me, preached as it was over the serried ranks of those healthy irks I knew from the skins upward. Now they were alike – dressed and all singing 'The King of Love my Shepherd Is' with the voice and the pagan enjoyment of their everyday blasphemy. Nor did their minds see any contradiction between their worship and their life. Neither their clean words nor their dirty words had any significance. Words were like our boots, dirty on the fields, clean indoors; a daily convention, no index of the fellows' minds. They had not learned to speak. The blind padre was still labouring to draw a response from the dumb. The truckling humility of his general confession, his tremendous pretence of absolution, jarred across the congregation – as stridently as would one of our oaths across a hushed church. Simply there was no contact between these worlds.

There is much else to discuss in the Uxbridge sections. But we must move on – as did he.

Here is a cheerful account of him as he leaves the depot and starts his journey to Cranwell.

> At the station gate they threw on my shoulders (knocking my cap off) the kit bag of all my spare goods: only eighty more pounds. The trip slowly convinced me that this military equipment was not designed for peace-time trains. I had become too wide to advance frontally through any carriage door. In each queue or press I jabbed the next man with a buckle in the mouth, or browned the next woman with my equipment's clay. The old lady next to me in the Underground wore a flippant skirt, all doo-dahs. My

> scabbard chafe enlarged one of these. She rose up and went, more fretted even than the skirt. I bulged with relief into her extra space, but my water-bottle tilted nose-down on the arm-rest and filled the vacant seat with a secret lake.

The third section of *The Mint* – the one I have labelled 'The Joy of having been trained' – is a complete contrast to its predecessors and is intended to contrast. It shows the positive, idealistic side of the R.A.F., it celebrates its conquest of the air and it is foreshadowed by a quaint barrack-room eulogy of Lord Trenchard. Pleasant, airy reading it makes; full of summer sun and Lincolnshire wind, and huge hangars where officers and men co-operate; full, too, of common sense and informality and service loyalty to a common cause, and the trustfulness of men who have all been trained and can consequently trust each other. There is no longer the split between loyalty and training that made Uxbridge so tragic and so fascinating. All is accord. At the end there is a thrilling set-piece in honour of speed: he on his motor-bicycle, his Boanerges, races a Bristol fighter, close above him in the air. The last words of all are: 'Everywhere a relationship: no loneliness any more.' Relationship is *through* the R.A.F. Not the relationship a civilian calls 'personal'.

I was never easy about this third section and sometimes discussed it with him. I told him that he might have been happy at Cranwell but he had not succeeded in communicating his happiness to me, that he had plunged me into a sort of comforting bathwater where I sat contented and surprised but not convinced that I was being cleansed. I wanted something more detergent than bathwater after Hell. I also complained that he was being fair minded and had thought it his duty to emphasize the pleasanter side of the R.A.F. before laying down his pen. Against this he defended himself mildly. As regards happiness, we agreed that it is of all emotions the most difficult to convey, and that perhaps he had been happy although he had not said so.

Re-reading this third part today I still feel dissatisfied although it contains some brilliant chapters. It is too insipid a conclusion for such a serious work. Moreover, time has been unkind to it. The conquest of the air, for which he romantically yearned, has been all too thoroughly achieved. From sixty to seventy countries are now flying about in the stuff, and some of them own hydrogen bombs. Romance must look further afield than the air – or perhaps nearer at home in the unexplored tracts of the heart. And the eulogy of speed rings unacceptably when one thinks of the nature of his death. 'Per ardua ad asbestos'.

I sometimes speculate whether he will ever become a national hero. He has few of our national characteristics but that is no obstacle. He is no more alien to our stodginess than Nelson was to the stodgy court of George III. He nearly made the hero grade in the early twenties amid the splendours of his Arabian reputation, and again in the mid-thirties after his dramatic death. Then oblivion and criticism thickened and now he is in the limelight again and once more the subject of a newspaper stunt. I do not expect the press will be further interested in him. That part is over. But he had mystery about him, and power, and the power to inspire affection and to create legends, and there are moments when I see him, smiling rather wryly, in the British Valhalla, at the same time glad and not glad to be there.

[1955]

T. E. Lawrence, *The Mint*

The Charm and Strength of Mrs Gaskell

My personal link with the late Mrs Gaskell is slight, but I should like to evoke it before approaching her work.

It occurred when I was in my early teens. My aunt took me to a garden-party in Surrey, driving in her own victoria but with hired horses, as she thought it might be too far for her own horse. A friend of hers also attended the party, taking guests in a wagonette. For the return journey the two ladies decided that it would be 'more festive' to exchange their guests, and thus it was that I drove back in the wagonette. The victoria followed behind us and to our horror its horses ran away. We whipped up ours to escape them, they only ran faster, and pursued and pursuer were soon hurtling down the leafy lanes. The victoria began to break up. Objects flew out of it in increasing order of weight – first the wraps, then the cushions, then a thin lady, then my aunt, then a stout lady, then the coachman fell off the box, the equipage overturned, and the horses, which had climbed a bank as if to get a better view, looked down upon the chaos critically. No one was hurt. And nothing was damaged except the coachman's coat, which tore up the back: 'It was man against 'orse,' he kept chanting, 'and one or the other was bound to go.'

That evening, over our champagne – for my aunt always called for champagne at a crisis – we discussed the accident, and she told me that the stout lady, the one who had fallen out last, was a Miss Meta Gaskell, and that she was the daughter of the Mrs Gaskell who had written that sweetly pretty book, *Cranford*. Another daughter, Miss Julia Gaskell, had been in the wagonette with me, and had been the agonized spectator of her sister's peril. Thus, and only to this extent, am I linked with a great Victorian novelist. For a great novelist Mrs Gaskell assuredly is, though not on the achievement of *Cranford*.

Cranford cannot be called a neglected book. Its sweetness and prettiness have attracted a swarm of appreciative insects who have hummed over it and buzzed about it and carried its savour far and wide. It has the charm of smallness and unpretentiousness. It has a steady vein of humanity, and almost too steady a vein of humour. Now and then nobility is touched – as when Miss Matty insists on changing the countryman's note for gold, though she has been warned that the note is worthless – but as a rule pathos and weepy-weepy do duty for tragedy. Perhaps because we live in strenuous days, the drama seems over-quiet. A carriage accident, such as I witnessed, would be inappropriate. If the Honourable Mrs Jamieson's equipage upset, and threw her and Miss Matty and Miss Pole and Mrs Forrester and Mr Mulliner out on to the Drumble road, the noise would be excessive, it would crack Miss Smith's eardrums.

Cranford conveys too tame an impression of Mrs Gaskell's genius. It is unfair that her reputation should have been tethered to twitterings.

With their sounds in our ears, let us attack the following paragraph from *Sylvia's Lovers*:

> 'But there's heat too, i' some places,' said Kinraid, 'I was once on a voyage i' an American. They goes for th' most part south, to where you come round to th' cold again . . . Well, we were i' th' southern seas a-seeking for a good whaling ground, and close on our larboard beam there were a great wall o' ice, as much as sixty feet high. And says our captain – as were a dare-devil if ever a man were – "There'll be an opening in yon grey wall and into that I'll sail, if I coast along it till th' day o' judgement." But for all our sailing we never seemed to come nearer to th' opening. The waters were rocking beneath us, and the sky was steady above us; and th' ice rose out o' the waters, and seemed to reach up into the sky. We sailed on, and we sailed on, for more days nor I could count. Our captain

> were a strange, wild man, but once he looked a little pale when he came upo' deck after his turn-in, and saw the green-grey ice going straight up on our beam . . . All at once, th' man as were on watch gave a cry; he saw a break in the ice, as we'd begun to think were everlasting; and we all gathered towards the bows, and the captain called to th' man at the helm to keep her course, and cocked his head, and began to walk the quarter-deck jaunty again. And we came to a great cleft in th's long weary rock of ice: and the sides o' the cleft were not jagged, but went straight sharp down into th' foaming waters. But we took but one look at what lay inside, for our captain, with a loud cry to God, bade the helmsman steer nor'ards away fra' th' mouth o' Hell. We all saw wi' our own eyes, inside that fearsome wall o' ice – seventy miles long, as we could swear to – inside that grey, cold ice, came leaping flames, all red and yellow wi' heat o' some unearthly kind, out o' th' very waters o' the sea; making our eyes dazzle wi' their scarlet blaze, that shot up as high, nay, higher than th' ice around, yet never so much as a shred on 't was melted. They did say that some beside our captain saw the black devils dart hither and thither, quicker than the very flames themselves; anyhow, *he* saw them, and he just dwined away, and we hadn't taken but one whale afore our captain died, and first mate took th' command. It were a prosperous voyage, but, for all that, I'll never sail those seas again, nor ever take wage aboard an American again.'

Thus speaks Charley Kinraid, young, handsome, warm blooded and tough, and the lovely Sylvia, Desdemona to his Othello, is soon clasped in his honest if not altogether innocent arms. His speech need not be overpraised: the dialect – supposed to be Yorkshire – is perfunctory, and the imagination displayed cannot approach Melville's, who is strangely foreshadowed. But what a wide world the speech introduces! How it reveals to us that Mrs Gaskell's kingdom extends beyond leafy lanes and small drawing rooms! And much else in *Sylvia's Lovers* confirms this. The characterization of Sylvia and her parents is unfussy and unpatronizing. The atmosphere of an eighteenth-century fishing port is deftly conveyed, and it is difficult to realize that it was inspired by a fortnight's holiday in Whitby with Meta and Julia.

It is a fine novel, and would be finer but for Mrs Gaskell's misfortunes over Sylvia's other lover, Phillip. Phillip is everything Charley isn't – high principled, studious, unattractive, cold as an iceberg on the surface, murkily volcanic, and capable of dastardly conduct for the loftiest reasons. For a time his creator handles him with commendable firmness – Mrs Gaskell can be pretty relentless in her quiet way. But he sins; and as soon as he sins her hand falters. Having sinned, Phillip must suffer, he must repent, he must atone, he must work out his salvation in fear and trembling and at great length. And throughout the last ten chapters of the book she works away like a housekeeper, trying to cleanse the repulsive figure whom her genius has effectively befouled. From her correspondence with her publisher, it looks as if there may be a technical as well as a moral reason for Phillip's extended martyrdom: *Sylvia's Lovers* was planned to appear in three volumes, and threatened not to be long enough. Anyhow she spoilt it.

Her masterpiece is *Wives and Daughters.* Written at the very end of her life, it is not quite finished.

Here are a few facts about her life. Elizabeth Cleghorn Stevenson was born at Chelsea in 1810, died in 1865: and during that period she produced six novels (*Mary Barton, Cranford, Ruth, North and South, Sylvia's Lovers, Wives and Daughters*), about forty short stories (of which 'Cousin Phillis' is the best), a *Life of Charlotte Brontë,* and a quantity of journalism – reviews, etc. Writing was her profession, though her circumstances and her natural benevolence led her into philanthropic work amongst the poor. As a child she went to live with an aunt at Knutsford, in Cheshire, and happy memories of it remained vivid through her life, and supplied the main element in her comedy. Knutsford appears not only as Cranford, but as Hollingford in *Wives and Daughters,* as Eltham in 'Cousin Phillis', etc. It is her faithful and cheerful little companion. Whenever we meet spinster ladies, quaint and perhaps tiresome, we may be sure it is not far away.

In 1832 she married the Rev. William Gaskell, a Unitarian Minister in Manchester, and got into closer touch with the industrial north. The marriage was happy – though the Minister may have felt a little over-shadowed by his successful wife. With the success of *Mary Barton*, her literary horizon began to expand, and by the time she was writing *Wives and Daughters* she was a leading novelist, a close friend of Charles Dickens, friendly with George Eliot, etc., and the object of acidity on the part of Mrs Carlyle. Amiable and competent and devoid of jealousy, she made few enemies, and is not a juicy subject for a biographer. She is buried at Knutsford. No scandal about her survives, for Meta went through her mother's papers shortly before her own death, and destroyed nearly all of them – Meta, whom with the capriciousness of memory I see eternally falling out of my aunt's victoria.

Wives and Daughters is a comedy. Girl gets Boy. But with what care, with what reservations and postponements must the word 'comedy' be employed! It is a long, subtle, undulating book, composed of sections that connect up with each other but slightly, yet contribute to the final effect. Up-to-date people who think it was written by Miss Ivy Compton-Burnett (and I have heard this adorable brick dropped) are not so completely wrong, for there are plenty of the masterly muddles and the semi-quarrels and the shifting of positions which are essential to comedy and which can only be contrived by novelists of delicacy and resource.

Wives and Daughters is however inspired by something more vital than disillusionment. It believes in the goodness of human nature, and by stating its belief implicitly it helps some readers to shelter a flickering flame. Mrs Gaskell was a good woman, who had experienced and caused happiness, but she was no fool and knew that the world contains sharks. A shark is her villain here: though he lacks the full complement of teeth. She also employs a scheming stepmother, who causes abundant pain, but as the story unfolds the scheming softens into selfishness and the selfishness into silliness, so that we are sorry when the stepmother departs, which she does, with the following words – they happen to be the last words in the unfinished manuscript:

> Molly, you should learn to understand the wishes of other people. Still, on the whole, you are a dear sweet girl and I only wish – well I know what I wish: only dear papa does not like it to be talked about. And now cover me up close, and let me go to sleep, and dream about my dear Cynthia and my new shawl. . . .

Molly Gibson is our heroine, and I prefer her company to that of any fictional maiden of her century. In the first place I know what she looks like, which is always a relief. She is rather short, brown face, level brow, straight-gazing, plentiful black hair that insists on crinkling. She does not dress well – as a country-doctor's daughter she has so much to do – but she enjoys finery when she can get it and has good taste. Towards the end of the book, when Boy approaches Girl, Mrs Gaskell yields to the temptation to elongate Molly and to equip her with interesting diseases, but throughout most of it she retains her sturdiness. She has need of it. For upon her, in a natural way, descends plenty of trouble. Her father's remarriage is the first and the worst and she has scarcely got over the loss of his company and confidence when Cynthia arrives (her stepmother's dubious, exquisite daughter), to cause in the long run much more pain than pleasure.

Molly's outlook upon life is naïve, but she quickly learns from experience – quicker than any Jane Austen heroine, and much quicker than her gasping Victorian contemporaries. She expects the best from everyone she meets: seldom finds it: reassesses and gives the benefit of such doubts as remain. Her devotion to Cynthia survives disillusionment. She learns to judge strangers shrewdly, and can say of a brilliant barrister 'I think he is very nice in all his bits but rather dull on the whole.' How often has one felt this about brilliant barristers! She can dismiss the well-meant consolations of an inexperienced young man who informs her that her father's remarriage will not seem so disastrous some day: that may well be, she replies, and it may not seem disastrous to the angels, but she herself has to live here, has to live now. She is brave and can take risks and face scandal. What she wants is affection, simplicity, straightforwardness, and in the end she gets them.

Associated with Molly are her father, her stepmother, and her step-sister, and the four of them carry the book. Mr Gibson is a triumph – hard-working, intelligent, caustic: and unobservant. He is so much occupied with his job that he does not notice what is happening inside himself and others, and so lands himself with a goose for a spouse. His discovery of his mistake is tragi-comic. Of the goose no more need be said. But Cynthia is another triumph of the novelist's art. It would have been so easy to harden Cynthia into a Becky Sharp. Mrs Gaskell never forgets that she is complex, never empties on her the vials of moral indignation, or requires her to atone. The preachiness that marred *Sylvia's Lovers* has worked itself out, or only survives as increased sensitivity.

How I could go on about this book! It had a great reception when it came out in 1866: Henry James reviewed it enthusiastically and perceptively in a New York paper. But it is largely forgotten here today, and appears to be completely forgotten in America. Among its merits are its pleasant descriptions of the countryside and the width of its social canvas. Let us end with the Earl and the Countess talking: they have not been so much as mentioned hitherto:

> 'Very good – very good indeed! Clare to join you at the Towers! Capital! I could not have planned it better myself! I shall go down with you on Wednesday in time for the jollification on Thursday. I always enjoy that day; they are such nice, friendly people, those good Hollingford ladies. Then I'll have a day with Sheepshanks, and perhaps I may ride over to Ashcombe and see Preston. Brown Jess can do it in a day, eighteen miles – to be sure! But there's back again to the Towers! – how much is twice eighteen – thirty?'
>
> 'Thirty-six,' said Lady Cumnor, sharply.
>
> 'So it is: you're always right my dear. Preston's a clever, sharp fellow.'
>
> 'I don't like him,' said my lady.
>
> 'He takes looking after, but he's a sharp fellow. He is such a good-looking man, too. I wonder you don't like him.'
>
> 'I never think whether a land agent is handsome or not.

They do not belong to the class of people whose appearance I notice.'

'To be sure not. But he is a handsome fellow: and what should make you like him is the interest he takes in Clare and her prospects.'

'How old is he?' said Lady Cumnor with a faint suspicion of motives in her mind.

'About twenty-seven, I should think. Ah, I see what is in your ladyship's head. No, no, he's too young for that. You must look out for some middle-aged man if you want to get poor Clare married: Preston won't do. I'm beginning to think she'll never get on as a schoolmistress: I say, my lady, what do you think of Gibson? He would be just the right age – widower – lives near the Towers?'

And Gibson it is, as Molly presently discovers. And Preston it is who will cause her and Cynthia so much trouble and vexation.

[1957]

Fog Over Ferney

'Voltaire thou should'st be living at this hour'. How right the poet was! But if he was living at this hour what influence would he have and would he be interested? I have concocted a little fantasy – it does not merit the name of an article – to discuss these two questions, and I will begin by transporting myself to Paris on May 30, 1778, when he died, aged eighty-four.

His last moments were notorious: a clergyman had asked him whether he recognized the divinity of Christ, to which he had replied 'For God's sake don't talk to me any more about that man.' 'You see, he's not quite himself,' the clergyman skilfully remarked to a colleague. Their enemy, the arch-mocker, whom they could not help liking, then died and was confusedly buried. Midnight struck. On the twelfth stroke Voltaire sat up in his coffin; and my fantasy begins.

He was feeling extremely well. He had had enough of Paris and its adulation, and levitated himself back to Ferney, his country estate on the borders of France and Switzerland. He now sat up in his bed. He rang a bell and Mme Denis came in. She was his mistress as well as his niece, as everyone knew, and after appropriate dalliance he asked her what the date was. She said it was the morning of May 31, but added that the year was 1958. Voltaire had lain in his tomb or been thrown out of it for 180 years. He was not much surprised. The universe is full of exceptions and he prepared to continue his career with unimpaired vigour. His first demand was for a substantial meal and plenty of coffee; his second for writing materials, so that he could communicate his recent experience to one of the crowned heads of Europe. He proposed to be witty and philosophic and just a little blasphemous on the subject of resurrection. It should give pleasure.

Before deciding which crowned head he would address, he inspected Ferney. Several people whom he had known seemed to have moved in. There was an appalling smell of burnt vegetables from one room – Mme du Chatelet was weighing fire – and excruciating noises from another: Frederick the Great at his flute. He had always kept open house, and again he was not surprised. But Ferney puzzled him. It was smaller than he remembered, and it was dimmer. The charming theatre where his friends had acted his tragedies and also those of subsidiary dramatists like Racine – it was so cramped. And the church he had built near the front door and so civilly dedicated to the Almighty – *Deo erexit Voltaire* – seemed no larger than a chapel. And even stranger than the smallness was the dimness. The gracious white house still proclaimed: Humanity, Civilization, Enjoyment, but the whiteness no longer radiated. Was it the fault of the trees, which had certainly grown since he planted them in the eighteenth century? Not entirely. The real miscreant – he might have guessed it – was on high. A Fog had descended from heaven. There was a Fog over Ferney. It no longer shone forth as a beacon. It had declined to a glimmer. Candide, intending to revisit it, had missed the turning in the obscurity and had arrived at Lourdes or Billy Grahamland instead. This was unexpected. Never mind. Something else to write about. He sat down in his study with his writing materials before him, only to discover with amazement that there was not a single crowned head who would wish to receive a letter from him.

He went through the list. Elizabeth II of England? So charming, so estimable, but no philosopher. With Catherine of Russia no comparison, no. The Queen of the Netherlands? A serious reader, yes, but deflected from rationalism by a female faith-healer. The King of Greece – none of whose subjects could possess civil rights unless they had been baptized into the Orthodox Church? No. The King of Iraq? A lively lad but too restless to concentrate. The Emperor – for there *was* an Emperor but he was neither Roman nor Holy, and of Abyssinia? No. And when he turned from the crowned heads to the helmeted ones, that is to say the generals who by their personal prowess or by some other means had become heads of their respective states, he found the same lack of response: General de Gaulle, General Mao, General Franco, General Eisenhower, General Ayub, General Abboud, Marshal Tito, Field-Marshal Bulganin, Generalissimo Chiang Kai-shek, vanished generals who were never mentioned by any decent diplomat, like General Neguib: all manifested the same indifference, and so did the colonels from Nasser to Perón. Even the states which professed to have a civilian government like Switzerland or Portugal, had shown themselves recalcitrant to his spirit – Switzerland who had forbidden an anti-nuclear conference to be held on her soil; Portugal who had forbidden a British statesman to set foot on hers. And Ireland with her censorship and Australia with her savage customs houses and New Zealand who allowed no work of art to approach her insipid shores: no. Always no. Only one head of a state would welcome a letter from him, and that was President Nehru of India. With an exclamation of delight he took up his pen.

At that moment Mme Denis brought in his chocolate, looked over his shoulder, and observed he was writing in French. French, she reminded him, was no longer the universal language, and Frenchmen no longer everybody. This perplexed Voltaire even more than the absence of crowned heads. French not eternal? He laid down his pen and tried to think the paradox out with many a resentful grimace. English, Spanish and, most extraordinary of all, Russian were surpassing French as media of world-communication. Presently he hit upon an explanation, and it is a plausible one. French had spread in 1798 because of the greatness of its literature, but by 1958 the interest in literature was declining. It was not only Ferney that was smaller – France had shrunk too. There was fog not only over Ferney but in *La Ville Lumière* herself.

Where then was there light? In Magnetogorsk perhaps, or Coventry, or Essen, or Pittsburg, but it was not the sort of light by which one can see to read. It was the light of applied science. Voltaire was not a good-tempered old man nor a very nice one, but there is this to say for him, he never whined like his neighbour Rousseau. Pulling himself together he composed his letter to President Nehru in French, apologizing as he did so for the barbarity of the tongue, and putting as he did so his tongue in his cheek. He omitted any reference to Kashmir, for he did not wish to alienate his one influential friend.

The letter was despatched and is said to have given pleasure in New Delhi. Voltaire was thinking to whom he should write next or what instance of cruelty he could denounce (cruelty had spread while he was in his grave, for the reason that there were many more people to be cruel to each other) when Mme Denis waddled in again in a state of great excitement. She had heard an extraordinary noise in the passage. She imitated the noise – errmph-err. She was an indifferent mimic and irritated her uncle, who struck at her with his cane and went to see what the noise was for himself. It was the telephone. It invited him to broadcast. He accepted.

He broadcast very well, said exactly what he liked, was obscene, subversive, blasphemous, and did not discover for some time that he was speaking to a tape-recorder and that nothing was allowed on the air that might disturb the Establishment. '*La voix de Ferney*', as it was called, provided platitudinous compliments to liberty and humanitarianism, mild deism, inexplosive tolerance, and innocuous jokes. It might have been the voice of Rousseau – Rousseau who denounced plays lest they corrupted his fellow hypocrites at Geneva. Still, even after he discovered the deception, he continued to broadcast – publicity is something – and this brings me to the end of the first and longer part of my fantasy.

What I have tried to suggest is that Voltaire, had he been living at this hour, would have been a pretty dim figure, and not nearly as influential as Bertrand Russell. Though learned, he was desultory and amateurish, his science was haphazard – think of how he cut off the heads of snails and slugs – and he readily turned an experiment into a joke. His temperament was literary and the mid-twentieth century is not a period in which literature is influential. Literature is enjoyable, it may promote individual salvation – it has promoted mine, and since I am only four years younger than Voltaire, I venture to interpolate this – but the time is gone when it awed Top People. The last time that the British nation reacted to a merely literary event was at the funeral of Thomas Hardy in 1928. That was thirty years ago. Today, those who influence others on the Voltairean scale must possess precise knowledge, organizing power and the willingness to suffer. It counts that Bertrand Russell was deprived of his fellowship at Cambridge and was imprisoned in Wandsworth gaol.

Voltaire also went to prison. Nevertheless Ferney cannot shine far. It is too small. It sparkled on the crest of a wave which has broken. His influence on our present world would be negligible.

But would he have found our world interesting? Answer – yes. The work of Freud and of Einstein would have fascinated him however superficial his comprehension of it. He would have popularized Einstein as he did Newton, and used Freud to discredit Pascal. The knowledge that the physical universe can destroy the human race and that the human race is actually encouraging it to do so would have accorded with his cynicism and provided him with a further example of our imbecility. Perhaps it might have inspired him to write another brilliant *conte*. The spectacle of Mr Dulles, Mr K. Field-Marshal Montgomery, and other contemporary giants demarcating planetary space and proceeding to eliminate their own planet from bases on Venus or Ganymede might have given even richer results than anything he had obtained from Maupertuis at Potsdam. To his lively and resilient mind the destruction of humanity would seem more than ever inevitable but his compassion for individuals would not have ceased, nor would his curiosity. Curiosity is his message to us. Curiosity cannot avert doom, but it can act as an inoculation against fear. The marvellous universe into which we have been born and where we may be contriving our death has developed one more marvel, namely the enquiring human mind.

What else can I add? In writing of Voltaire an anti-climax must always be sought. Several are available. I will choose the economic anti-climax. He was a shocking gold-digger. Mme

Denis was another, who spent much of her life in digging away from under him the gold he had dug. So she recognized rapacity in him. When he had inspected Ferney and written some letters and broadcast, he set to work to get rich, and found it easy, thanks to his astuteness and to the intricate flaws in our civilization. He surrounded himself with advisers and other crooks who knew how to dodge the income tax and import and export regulations, and to run up the expense accounts. He employed Public Relations Officers to say how upright he was, and lawyers to threaten proceedings if anyone disagreed. He invested in commercial television, and aerial advertising, he bought up good newspapers cheap and turned them into bad ones that sold, he became one of those barons who advance their fortunes under the slogan of National Trade and adored being photographed amongst them on the *Queen Mary*. Yes, he was thankful to have been re-born into a century which kow-tows increasingly to Big Business, and he was thankful to have slumbered through the nineteenth century where the deceitfulness of riches was still sometimes denounced and the parable of the Needle's Eye not entirely ignored.

That ends the anti-climax to my fantasy. Had Voltaire possessed our sanitary advantages, he would have compared it to pulling a plug.

[1958]

The Prince's Tale

In 1954 there was a small conference of Italian writers at San Pellegrino, the place where the mineral waters come from. It was enlivened by the arrival of three strangers from Sicily – a poet, a prince, and their servant. The poet introduced the prince, who had no known connection with literature: Prince Giuseppe Tomasi di Lampedusa was his name. He was dressed in good black clothes of an unfashionable cut, supported himself on a thick stick, and if spoken to bowed courteously and retired. He was of enormous size. The servant never left him – equally huge and blackened by the sun – and the strange trio moved through the conference as a single entity during their brief stay.

Another visitor was Signor Giorgio Bassani, a man of letters, and a few years later he heard of the manuscript of a novel written by a Sicilian nobleman. He got hold of it, recognized its value and realized that it was the work of the gigantic prince, who apparently had started to write it immediately after his return from the conference and had scarcely completed it at his death. He introduced it to the publishing firm of Feltrinelli, which had already made a scoop over *Dr Zhivago*, and was now to scoop again. For the sales of *Il Gattopardo* have been enormous, both in Italy and in France, and now it arrives in a good English dress to try its luck here.

It is a novel based on, or rather inspired by, family papers and family tradition. The House of Lampedusa had long been established in the island, and the novelist's great-grandfather had witnessed the arrival of Garibaldi in 1860, and like the hero of the novel had been a passionate astronomer. This family and personal element is stamped on the book. It is not a historical novel. It is a novel which happens to take place in history. Only once does a historical character intrude – King Bomba – and he is rapidly reduced to domestic proportions.

We first meet the hero, Prince Fabrizio, in his Palermo palace – a small one, the great palace is inland at Donnafugata. He is engaged in his daily recital of the Rosary, and as he finishes his anxieties return. Some are appropriate to the times, others to his character. Outwardly he is alarming and arrogant, and the family tremble, for he is in a bad temper this morning – the imminence of Garibaldi worries and confuses him, also coffee has been spilt. Inwardly he is honourable, intelligent, generous, sensuous and idle, and his anxieties are not ignoble for he is trying to sort out what is good in the approaching changes from what is bad. He cannot take the easy, aristocratic line that everything new is bad. Leaving his cowed children and accompanied by Bendico, his floundering and adorable dog, he goes out into the garden which is scented almost to decay with the contending violence of flowers. (Bendico makes short work of these.) And there are other troubles. A soldier has been found dead in the garden – no one could explain it, fighting for his king and country presumably, but he was dead and his guts came out. The Prince is disgusted, is compassionate, worries. It is an epic of worry rather than of high tragedy, and this gives it its peculiar power; serious worry; the personal and political issues are important and they can only be resolved in the night sky, by the stars. The army of unalterable law (for the stars were mistaken for that in the nineteenth century) continues invincible while kingdom and family fall, while the shield of the Leopard crumbles, while the Princely House trembles and contracts into Concetta, an old spinster, who, half a century later, throws away the mummy of a dog. Up in his observatory with his faithful Jesuit, the Prince can endure the present and the future, and can find the greatness he would have liked to establish in his daily life.

The first six chapters deal with the uneasy submission of all concerned to the House of Savoy. The scene is transferred to Donnafugata, the inland palace, where the Leopard seems to re-establish his failing power. The migration to Donnafugata, the merciless sun, the ubiquitous sand, the wails of the French governess, together with more subtle forebodings, are marvellously described, and here, amidst new intricacies, we get to know the second most important character in the book, the Prince's nephew, Tancredi. Tancredi is a fascinating study. He is almost a very fine young man – brave, resourceful, charming, energetic, kind, pleasingly ironical, and he loves his uncle who loves him. But there is something wrong about the lad, though it is difficult to say what, something shoddy and sly: he is not exactly treacherous, but he is capable of treachery. He marries the rapacious daughter of a dubious mayor, for lust. Yet was she unsuitable? Was he not well matched? Would he have done better with Concetta, his magnificent cousin, the youthful pride of their house, whose heart he broke?

Tancredi had fought for the new order and does well out of it. He tries to work the old Prince in, and urges him to become a senator – other aristocrats have. But partly through grandeur, partly through indecision, the Prince refuses. He will acquiesce, he will even be courteous, but he will not co-operate. He bows and withdraws. Consequently his fortunes decline, and were the novel written by the heavy hand of Balzac we should leave him in utter destitution. We do not. We are concerned with worries, not with tragedy, and we leave him in 1881, dying in such comfort as a capable doctor and a tolerable hotel can provide, and in the midst of his family so far as it survives. He has a series of strokes, and as the final one overwhelms him:

> Suddenly amid the group appeared a young woman: slim, in brown travelling dress and wide bustle, with a straw hat trimmed with a speckled veil which could not hide the sly charm of her face. She slid a little suede-gloved hand between one elbow and another of the weeping kneelers, apologized, drew closer. It was she, the creature for ever yearned for, coming to fetch him; strange that one so young should yield to him; the time for the train's departure must be very close. When she was face to face with

> him she raised her veil, and there, modest, but ready to be possessed, she looked lovelier than she ever had when glimpsed in stellar space.

This *giovane signora* is only a recollection of a passenger whom he had seen on the train coming south. What genius, on the novelist's part, to introduce her, at this supreme moment, and not some character already docketed and staled!

What a tribute to the urbanity of death! The whole chapter scintillates with power and with a tenderness that is untroubled by pity. There is no summing up, no moral balancing, though before his consciousness weakens the dying man thinks what has happened to him and employs himself in separating the good moments from the bad: Bendico had been a good moment. He dies his own death, and if we ask 'Was he a success or a failure?' we are using irrelevant words.

Whether he is based on the novelist himself or on the novelist's great-grandfather, the Prince Fabrizio lives on his own account. See him out hunting and killing minute animals in an enormous landscape. Observe him with his Princess whom he bullies and who adores him.

I first read this noble book in Italian, but my knowledge of the language is too slight to enable me to judge Mr Archibald Colquhoun's translation. It does not flow and glow like the original – how should it? – but it is sensitive and scholarly, and the passage quoted above was a pleasure to transcribe. The difficulties of translation must have been considerable. For instance the Prince has a mistress, a peasant girl to whom he repairs when he is cross with his wife, and in a moment of intimacy she exclaims '*Principone!*' combining the feudal with the erotic in a way that amuses him. But how can '*Principone*' be translated? We are given 'My Prince', and no doubt this is the best that can be done. And '*Zione*', which is what Tancredi calls him? It has to be 'Nuncle'.

The translation is prefaced by a useful historical note about the Risorgimento. Having read it the reader should go easily forward. Let him, however, not forget the stars. Fixed – as they are not today – in the black Sicilian sky, they look down upon the fortunes of men, and offer to those who can look up at them not only escape but majesty.

[1960]

Giuseppe di Lampedusa, *The Leopard*

The Arts in General

Tate versus Chantrey

Since the beginning of the war few of us have taken much interest in Art. Literature is different; literature lies closer to our daily life, and can, like music, open doors that lead out of it, and be a positive support against anxiety and pain. But pictures and statues seem curiously remote at such times as this. Rightly or wrongly, most of us regard them as luxuries, only to be enjoyed in holiday mood, and their every mention evokes a sneer. For this reason the Report of the National Gallery Committee – a most important and entertaining document, which would at other times have kept the Press busy for weeks – is likely to fall to the ground unnoticed. It is a pity that this should be so. There will be a world after the war, a world in which pictures and even statues must figure; and if the Committee's recommendations are adopted they are likely to figure less discreditably than they have in the past.

This Report deals in part with the leakage of masterpieces out of this country during past years into America and Germany, but the most interesting section is concerned with the Chantrey Bequest. This Bequest (£2,100 per annum) was made by Sir Francis Chantrey to secure for the nation whatever was best in contemporary British Art. His intentions are beyond dispute – the best, wherever obtainable; but unfortunately he appointed as administrators the President and Council of the Royal Academy, with results that are common knowledge. The Royal Academy – an institution neither officially nor actually representative of British Art – has regarded the bequest as its own perquisite, and has spent it almost exclusively on the works of Academicians. These works it flings annually at the nation, to be housed at the national expense. There was a Committee of Inquiry some ten years ago, but nothing resulted. The Academy has the money and sticks to it, and the unlucky Tate Gallery is – at first sight – in its power, being legally compelled to nourish the Chantrey brood.

What a brood it is! What a spectacle are the rooms at Millbank that shelter it! There are a few works of merit, of genius even, but the rest are Costume Pieces, or examples of the Kiss-mammy and Wave-to-daddy schools. It is right that such pictures should be painted, for they give many people genuine pleasure, but it is not right they should cost so much, it is not right that they should be bought for the nation. Chantrey art, say its defenders, is popular, to which the reply is that popular art is never permanent: its place is consequently in a Christmas number, not in a national collection. The Kiss-mammy of one generation is invariably nauseous to the next; daddy, who once wore corduroys and whiskers, wears khaki and a blob-moustache now; and ten years hence will have to wear something else if he is to maintain his emotional appeal. He is obviously a bad investment, even as a popular investment, but what is the Tate to do? The Chantrey dumps him, year after year. He is not only bad in himself, but – as the Report points out – he harms the Gallery by making it ridiculous. The funds of the Tate are so small that each year the Chantrey pictures must bulk larger in proportion to the rest. The standard they set is so low that artists or owners of modern masterpieces fight shy of a collection that includes them, and cannot be induced to present their pictures or 'to sell at modest prices for the honour of being represented in the Collection as is frequently done in France'. British painters 'whose works are eagerly bought for Continental galleries', are unrepresented in their own country, while a 'double standard of admission is set up', and the Tate sometimes refuses 'pictures superior in artistic merit to those which are simultaneously purchased under the Chantrey Bequest'.

What can free the poor Tate? In the first place, legislation. Parliament can put the Chantrey on a proper basis, and the Committee recommends that it should be asked to do this; the wishes of the testator will then be carried into effect, and his money purchase whatever is best in contemporary art. But, failing legislation, the Tate still has a powerful weapon. It is compelled to receive the Chantrey brood, but by a happy and Gilbertian chance is not compelled to exhibit it. It has the right to send it straight into the cellars, and the Committee recommends it should exercise this right – a right which was even admitted by the President of the Royal Academy, one of the witnesses called. The arrangement would not be ideal. The nation would be no nearer getting pictorial value for its £2,100, and the Daddies and Costume Pieces would be debarred from their very real sphere of usefulness elsewhere. But it would be better than nothing. The Gallery would cease to be grotesque. It would begin, however feebly, to represent contemporary art. And the Royal Academicians would have to retreat from an untenable position and admit the right of a national collection to decide how a nation's bequest shall be spent. That they will retreat without such pressure is improbable, because they do honestly think that the Burlington brand is the best, and that they would not be doing their duty if they recommended any other. One cannot blame them. It is right they should believe in the tradition that has formed them, it is natural they should believe that old tired men are the best judges of beauty, it is inevitable that, thus believing, they should select for this year's Chantrey a nude statue – not a naked statue like M. Rombeaux's, which would be not quite nice, but a dead decent studio nude: a small Kiss-mammy, and a View. These are the nation's latest acquisitions. It remains to be seen what the Tate will do when they arrive.

[1915]

Report of the National Gallery Committee on Matters Connected with the National Arts Collections

The Extreme Case

'He sacrificed everything to his art.'

The words might occur, and probably do, in the works of the widows of Royal Academicians: 'Spending every autumn in Italy or our Berkshire home, Sir William sacrificed everything to his art. Art is an exacting mistress, as he would often inform young aspirants who had come to ask his advice on this all-important subject, frequently asking them to stop on to lunch, so that it was quite a toss-up whom some great lady or other would find herself sitting next to. But my husband was quite indifferent to such contretemps, and I think never happier than when . . .' The words flow on until they carry Sir William to his last resting-place in the Abbey.

Paul Gauguin was not young when he made this sacrifice. A middle-aged bourgeois, for eleven years he had worked in a Paris bank, and been a model husband and father at home. Heaven knows why he made it. He began to paint as a pupil of Pissarro, first on Sundays, then 'tous les jours'; then gave up his bank and his family, and drifted to Tahiti; then, going further still, went native in the Marquesas Islands; to die at fifty-five of worry, of poverty, and of a mixture of tropical and Parisian diseases. He left nothing behind him there except some canvases, an armful of bastards, and a little carving. Here is a case more extreme than that which was in Sir William's widow's mind, and, like all extreme cases, it must be examined carefully: it may throw light upon a most complex and reputable person – oneself. Just as the extremist St Catherine of Siena elucidates our religious impulses, and the extreme abstraction of the Economic Man elucidates our economic, so may Gauguin elucidate the impulse to 'sacrifice everything for art', which is as widespread as the desire for God or Mammon, and which beats, though with seemly feebleness, in the breasts of us all.

Not even in Michelangelo did the impulse appear in purer form. Though Michelangelo sacrificed everything, he was distracted by other claims: he minded about his nephew, he fell into hate or love. Gauguin contains no such alloy – no unselfishness or generosity or dignity, not even much intelligence or wit. There are moments when he is 'decent' or 'interesting', but they are exceptional. From the worlds of morality and intellect he beckons us equally away. Nothing matters to him except pictures, and all he asks from us is brushes, canvas, tubes, and food, so that he could produce them. We refused – one could not be sure that the pictures would sell; Sir William, usually so encouraging, had characterized them as an 'insult'. And in consequence Gauguin lacked money, and his letters to de Monfreid from the South Seas are mainly a whine about francs:

> Chaudet depuis 4 mois ne m'a pas écrit un mot . . . S'il était fâché vous le sauriez. Tous les mois le cafetier doit lui donner 150fr. Je les aurais que cela m'aiderait toujours un peu, ainsi que les 200fr. que vous dîtes rester à mon avoir. Ne serait-ce que 25fr., il faut me les envoyer. . . . Dire que je ne peux gagner 2,500fr. par an régulièrement: tandis que D——— en gagne 10,000.

Or again:

> Pendant mon dernier séjour en France j'ai été aussi gracieux que possible pour les W——; toujours ma bourse à la main. D'eux, point de lettres. J'ai chargé W—— de recouvrer en mai 800fr. qui m'étaient dus pour cette époque; (pas un mot: pas d'argent) . . . Tandis que l'Etat achète 300 francs sur sa demande à titre de fonctionnaire une toile de Z . . .

These extracts – each of them with its fretful 'tandis que' – are typical. It is not that Gauguin was a misanthrope: he was too unphilosophic to condemn humanity. He was merely annoyed that D. and Z. should have what he hadn't. In easier circumstances he would not have written about them to de Monfreid, nor indeed have written to de Monfreid at all. He could do without sympathy. But de Monfreid might send him paints, dahlia tubers, mandolin strings, and above all francs. Consequently he wrote – queer savage begging letters: the Extreme Case needs money from his fellows, nothing else, and offers nothing in return, not even a theory of life.

Gauguin was, however, a normal being physically, and the fact that he happened to have a body led him to some generalizations that must not be too seriously taken. 'Maison du Jouir' was carved on his hut in the Marquesas, and inside were two texts addressed to ladies only, one of them announcing 'Soyez amoureuses et vous serez heureuses,' and the other, 'Soyez mystérieuses et vous serez heureuses.' M. Segalen, in his eloquent and fascinating introduction, preaches a little on these texts, but surely the less said about them the better: they throw no light upon the artist's mind. It is true that Gauguin had women to live with him when sufficient francs arrived; that he felt, sometimes for six months, an interest in his latest child, and that he wrote, 'L'animalité qui est en nous n'est pas tant à mépriser qu'on veut bien le dire.' But he also wrote, 'Laissons ces sales bourgeois – même s'ils sont nos enfants – à leur sale place, et continuons l'œuvre commencée'; and this – this, and nothing else – is his philosophy. He was not a limner of Polynesian beauty, as M. Segalen, anxious to celebrate *la femme*, suggests. Nor could he have painted indecently, as the missionaries asserted, for the reason that he gave up all for his art, and such a man, even if he tries to be indecent, is seduced during the attempt by something yet more fascinating. Viewed in the light of this temperament, how feeble do 'Soyez amoureuses' and its pendant become! In the Marquesas, on the walls of the hut, they meant much, because pictures by Gauguin attended them to lend felicity. So can the text 'Gloria, gloria, gloria' borrow from an Italian altarpiece a glory not its own. But the actual words teach us no more about life than does the doxology: they proceed from the duller parts of the painter's mind.

What, then, was this 'œuvre commencée' for which he sacrificed his wife, family, friends, income, personal cleanliness and life? The present reviewer is not competent to say. A series of photographs should conclude the article, but in their absence we may listen to what Gauguin says himself – always bearing in mind that words are not his medium and that he may be misleading us.

His account of the process of creation reads convincingly enough. He thinks that there is a moment 'où des sentiments extrêmes sont en fusion au plus profond de l'être,' suddenly to burst forth in the lava-stream of creative thought: much may have gone on previously, but this is the first moment of which the artist is aware; reason had nothing to do with it, and he should not correct its products by the light of reason, saying afterwards, 'I have got that arm too long.' (Michelangelo knew a similar process.) And, as we should expect, it leads away from the realistic imitation of nature: if the picture bears the impress of that supreme moment all is well, and the distortion justified. Is or is not the arm too long?

> Oui et non. Non, surtout attendu qu'à mesure que vous l'allongez, vous sortez de la vraisemblance pour arriver à la fable. . . . Si Bouguereau faisait un bras trop long, ah oui! que lui resterait-il, puisque sa vision n'est que là, a cette précision stupide qui nous rive à la chaine de la réalité matérielle.

This theory may lead to Symbolism, but it did not in Gauguin's case. Symbolism had attracted him in Paris, but he soon broke away. 'Une croix, des flammes . . . V'lan, ça y est, le Symbolisme.' Though he distorted Nature, he dared not abandon her, and when he painted his masterpiece (as he terms it) men are men, the idol an idol, and trees, trees.

The title of this masterpiece is 'D'où venons-nous, que sommes-nous, où allons-nous?', its theme is human destiny, the canvas five yards by two, the tone 'bleu et vert Véronèse,' against which the nudes stand out boldly. Birth is to the right, Death to the left – not represented directly, but by figures near to those states; in the centre a huge Polynesian plucks fruit. Behind are the Vanity of speculation and the Certainty of some other existence, though it may be an existence that annihilates this. 'Tout se passe au bord d'un ruisseau sous bois. Dans le fond, la mer, puis les montagnes de l'île voisine.' Such is Gauguin's description, and it should be read attentively by all who would understand themselves, for as soon as the picture was finished he tried to commit suicide: he had been in extreme misery throughout.

> N'ayant rien reçu de Chaudet, ma santé tout à coup presque rétablie, c'est-à-dire sans plus de chance de mourir naturellement, j'ai voulu me tuer. Je suis parti me cacher dans la montagne où mon cadavre aurait été dévoré par les fourmis. Je n'avais pas de revolver, mais j'avais de l'arsenic que j'avais thésaurisé durant ma maladie d'eczéma: est-ce la dose qui était trop forte, ou bien le fait des vomissements qui ont annulé l'action du poison en le rejetant, je ne sais. Enfin, après une nuit de terribles souffrances, je suis rentré au logis.

Seven hundred francs then arrived from Chaudet, also 150 from Mauffra, and he painted five years longer. His end, when it did come, was less characteristic: it was tarnished by an unselfish act. He had reported a gendarme for selling native women off the Marquesas. The facts were undisputed, but the local magistrate upheld the gendarme and sentenced Gauguin to three months' imprisonment and a fine of 1,000 francs. He had to appeal. 'Toutes ces préoccupations *me tuent*,' he wrote, and they did: in the spring of 1903 the Extreme Case passed away, and his effects were disposed of by auction.

'Où va-t-il?' The missionaries whom M. Segalen interviewed did not know. It is difficult to think of him in any well-constructed heaven, or climbing the rungs of any astral ladder. On earth he was at once everything and nothing, and what place have such in a Beyond? He might be sent to Hell, of course, or he might be told that his sins were forgiven him because his pictures were so good. But both of these judgements feel unsatisfactory, and it is simpler to suppose that annihilation, absolute and eternal, closes such a career as this. He sacrificed everything to his art, remember – and no one who does remember will ever dare to write the phrase again – and in that sacrifice he would gladly have included whatever experience the life beyond death may provide. Perhaps he made an agreement to this effect with Lucifer, Son of the Morning, whose statue, crumbling and obese, M. Segalen half thinks he may have found, enthroned in a shed between the Maison du Jouir and the sea.

[1919]

Paul Gauguin, *Lettres de Paul Gauguin à G.-D. de Monfried*

Revolution at Bayreuth

I first heard 'The Ring' exactly fifty years ago at Dresden. I still have the old programmes and I took them with me to Bayreuth when I heard it again this summer. It and I have changed a good deal in the course of half a century and it has changed even more than I have. At Dresden we were still in the full flood of realism. The scenery imitated nature as best it could. The Rhine Maidens swam as only sopranos can. Brünnhilde had a real horse, Siegfried a practicable bear, and Fricka was drawn on to the stage by artificial goats whose sides panted in and out like concertinas to indicate the urgency of her visit. Realism minimizes production and the name of the producer does not occur on these old programmes – he was of no importance – nor was the conductor. But the singers receive their due, and the voice of one of them, Frau Wittich, still resounds in my ears across two world wars. She is the most glorious Brünnhilde I have ever heard. She and Herr Burrian, a great Siegfried, are now silent, and the Opera House where they triumphed is now in the Russian zone. So farewell to Dresden, where the most expensive seat cost 8s.; and all hail to Bayreuth, where the cheapest seat costs £2.3s., and where – well, you shall hear.

My season was most enjoyable. I took 'The Ring', *Parsifal*, and *Lohengrin*, giving *Tannhäuser* a miss. I stayed not in the town, but fifteen miles out in a tiny country hamlet. There I could walk in any direction through meadows and cornfields and up into woods. There were streams and familiar flowers. There were no poles, no wires, no aeroplanes, no advertisements, and I was often reminded of what the English countryside used to be before it was ruined. Large rural areas, such as still remain in Germany or France, can survive the impact of industrialism. A small area like England is inevitably pocked and scarred. From this homely paradise I drove in of an afternoon to Bayreuth, there to confront the problematical, there to be impressed to be sure, and even delighted, but there also to be irritated.

The famous theatre disconcerted me. It is an odd shape outside. Inside it is neither stark nor smart, and I had somehow expected starkness. What were those ornate corinthian capitals doing? What was that criss-cross pattern on the ceiling? Also I was disappointed with my seat. I bought the cheapest in the belief that every seat at Bayreuth commands a perfect view of the stage. This is not so. I was too far to the left. I never once saw Klingsor. However, all regrets vanished as soon as the music started. For the theatre is constructed entirely of wood inside, and owing to that and to its happy proportions it reverberates to sound as if it was itself a musical instrument. A lack of brilliancy has been diagnosed, but there is any amount of the sumptuousness that Wagner requires. I shall not be speaking about the music, so let me here emphasize how magnificently it sounded, how finely the orchestra played and most of the singers sang. Hans Hotter as Wotan and as Amfortas was superb. Also Martha Mödl as Kundry: I found her a little too elegant for Brünnhilde. And Birgit Nilsson as Elsa.

The Festival is now run by the composer's grandsons, Herr Wieland and Herr Wolfgang Wagner. They are young men of talent and determination, and they have restored Bayreuth to a pre-eminence which long may it retain. They are theorists – Herr Wieland Wagner in particular. They respect their grandfather's libretto and music, and admit no variant from either. But his stage directions they neglect, and indeed seem to contradict from an inverted sense of duty. If their grandfather directs a character to sit – like Hagen before the Gibichung Hall – the grandsons make him stand. If he gives a character a hat, they take it off. If he provides for transitional scenery – scenery which can easily be done with modern appliances and is excellently done at Covent Garden – they drop an old-fashioned curtain instead. Above all, when he indicates brightness, they install half-lights and gloom. Bayreuth hates light, hates colour, mistrusts movement, and identifies mysticism with mist. It is trying to get away from the realism of Dresden, and to evoke the wonder of the world rather than its prosaic and contradictory details. That is a worthy aim but it is not achieved by smothering all the details in murk. On the eyes alone the effect was unpleasant, and so were the tiresome spotlights which had to be used to show who was singing. So I did sometimes get irritated and sometimes worse than irritated – namely, insecure. I could not always feel certain that these innovations were sincere. I feared that they were sometimes introduced not from conviction, not even for experimental reasons, but in order to show off and to shock. This feeling of insecurity was not continuous. It came and it went and when it came I could always shut my eyes and listen to the music, but I don't like shutting my eyes.

Let me get rid of the worst at once. The worst was assuredly the third act of *Parsifal* – particularly the part of it which is accompanied by the Good Friday music. Wagner instructs Parsifal to wear black armour. Consequently he came in dressed in a grey boiler suit. In the centre of the stage was a round, raised area resembling a crumpet, which had indeed lain there throughout the drama. Into this he stuck his spear. He then proceeded to talk with Gurnemanz, who was similarly dressed and the effect became incredibly comic: two polar explorers had succeeded in installing an aerial. Around them stretched, or were supposed to stretch, flowery meadows, such as I had seen and enjoyed in the country that very morning. How were these represented? By smears, by expanses of gooseberry fool. The whole thing was so ugly and so silly that one departed with deep misgivings to the Temple of the Grail. Here the prospect was anyhow forceful. At the close, Parsifal held up the Grail alone into a universe of gutta-percha grey. All human life had vanished but on the walls of the Temple what looked like a motor-tyre became visible as the curtain fell.

That seemed to me innovation at its most suspect, and I was not reassured by a pompous article in my programme, or by an esoteric diagram encouraging me to look still deeper into Wagnerian truth. In particular, the dresses were so vexatious – as they were elsewhere: poor Parsifal was only one in a gallery of guys: Hunding looked like a Roman senator, Siegfried a gym instructor or a hiker, the Valkyries high-class governesses, and Wotan wore no hat. Wagner instructs him to wear one, and Siegfried when being rude to him says, in effect, 'Where did you get that hat?' – but sings it softly with his back to the audience, in the hope it will not be heard. With the exception of Loge and one or two other supernaturals, misdressing was persistent.

But enough of that. I will turn to the successes. They were many. Finest of all was the end of *Götterdämmerung*, which I will leave to the end of my talk. Fine was the opening scene of *Rhinegold*. Here the darkness quivers and flows, blurs of light in it are the Rhine Maidens high up in it, deep down in it, and Alberich joins them in it, an iridescent toad. The sun strikes the gold which is shown as a tablet. A veined surround is born, a sort of medusa, and towards it from the right drifts in more gold, a circular blur. When Alberich advanced on the tablet and wrenched it from beneath innocent hands, I knew that here was a producer who knew what he wanted to do, and could do it.

Another triumph was the forging of the sword in *Siegfried*. Acting was permitted once in a way, and wisely, for without acting the physical excitement of that scene cannot be conveyed. It is a heroic romp. Siegfried in a patch of ruddy light, Mime in a greenish patch, did their bests, hiss went the blade, crash the anvil, topple the pot, and there stood the dubious hero armed. It does not do to think earnestly about Siegfried. Bayreuth started him off with a rush and a crash and stopped one thinking. I have never objected to him less. It is essential to one's enjoyment of 'The Ring' that Siegfried should be bearable, that his caddishness should be accepted as boyishness and his infidelity as hallucination. He is an awkward customer, but he got pulled through. And the scene on the Valkyries' rock went well enough, though it was dangerously unadorned – no tree, no helmet, no horse, only a curved horizon with an opposing curve melting into the sky.

Odd as the scenery looked, it was odder still when one was

on the stage with it. One morning I had the chance of going behind the scenes – a fascinating tour, though beset with many physical perils. They showed us the orchestra first, and I climbed up wooden steps of varying heights into the conductor's seat. Down below me, confusedly disposed as it seemed, were the desks of the performers, over one hundred and twenty in number, and behind me, hiding us all from the audience, stretched an incurved shell of wood. I could not see the stage until I bent a little, ever so little, forward, and then the whole of it slid into view. Descending, I saw upon the desks the scores of the opera that had last been performed – namely, *Siegfried.* The scores were not printed but in manuscript, beautifully written. They were old, some of them perhaps dating back to the 'seventies when the opera was first performed, and each performer who had played from then had signed his name on the opening page. These names, stretching back through so many seasons, are the Bayreuth tradition for me.

If the orchestra spoke of the past, the stage into which we now clambered proclaimed the future. It was occupied by a large round object, shaped like a muffin, six feet thick (I stood against it) and about twenty-five feet across, and tilted sharply towards the auditorium. This was the Valkyries' rock. Here Brünnhilde had been laid to sleep and Siegfried had awakened her at his own risk. I advanced over this object with precaution. It creaked at each step, my toes or my heels ran into my shoes, and all around me stretched a nasty drop. This muffin was permanent to 'The Ring', as the crumpet had been to *Parsifal,* but more skilfully disposed and disguised: many fine effects had been built on it. Behind it, towards the back of the stage, was the cyclorama, and at the very back a most unexpected inmate: Siegfried's dragon. This belonged to the old world of realism and of Dresden. It was exactly what a man in the street expects a dragon to be, though it had not thus appeared during the performance, when it was smothered in smoke and cloud. An expanse of corrugated iron behind the dragon closed the prospect. A door opened in this and we were back in the open air.

The theatre was full throughout. In the intervals the

audience ate in the well-managed restaurant or strolled about the gardens and avenues and even into a rustic cornfield. It was a mixed audience and varied on its feminine side from ladies in brown tweeds to ladies with blue hair. It was international. It was also unexpectedly young: a large percentage of it must have been under thirty. Near me sat an R.A.F. boy who had scarcely heard Wagner before but had come all the way from the British zone to find out what 'The Ring' was like, and was getting on with it better and better, he said. His pleasure and the general enthusiasm have set me thinking on the vexed subject of Wagner's popularity. I understand why young creative musicians should detest him. They are trying to produce something different – something clean and crackly upon a rigid substructure – and they cannot stand the thick orchestration, the woolliness, the emotionalism, the slow motion, the heavy nineteenth-century furniture and the occasional vulgarity of the Master. Others, who are not doing creative work, follow their lead. In purist circles Wagner is taboo, and when I said I was going to Bayreuth I encountered such remarks as 'I am afraid I am for Mozart', a slight pause being made between the *Mo* and the *zart* which had the subtle effect of a reprimand. Why an outsider like myself and why other outsiders should not be both for Wagner and Mozart I do not know. We are not composers. We have no creative obligations. And I believe that the coming generation, when left to itself, does like them both, and that consequently Wagner will endure. If he does not the human race loses.

So I came away from Bayreuth full of gratitude, though I do not expect to go there again, though I was sometimes irritated, and though I regret the inevitable expensiveness that restricts it to devotees who can raise a bit of cash. Oh for Dresden! But Bayreuth is a fortress. Long may it stand, and may no one ever drop a lighted match into it. The interior being entirely of wood, it would blaze up like Valhalla, to be replaced by some scientific building where all the sounds fall dead, as they do in our Festival Hall.

The last act of *Götterdämmerung* was the Festival's greatest achievement. By the end of 'The Ring' Wagner's hands were very full, and, great juggler though he was, he sometimes let an item drop. One of these items is the freedom of humanity through love. It was stated at the outset of the cycle by Alberich, when he renounced love, and it is reaffirmed at the close by Brünnhilde, but not as fully as might have been expected, and oddly enough there is a long passage in the libretto of Brünnhilde's final song which Wagner never set to music. Contrast her brevity with the amplitude of Isolde. His hands were too full, worlds were crashing, gods and heroes coming to grief, and perhaps the only permanent thing on earth is the Rhine.

That, I think, is the item seized by the Bayreuth producer. Both scenes of the act are dominated by the eternal river: in the first, Siegfried plays with the maidens in a chasm of glacier green and sits on a shimmering rock for his final narrative: in the second, the river fills the stage from below, while high above murky flames seize the pinnacle that is Valhalla. The spectacle, the flood of music, united into a single sensation, the whole universe was divided between water and fire; and only afterwards did one remember that not one single human being was shown on the stage, and that the freedom of humanity through love had been lost in the shuffle. I do not criticize the producer for this; in a supreme effect like the end of *Götterdämmerung* it is more important to be passionate than to be logical. He overwhelmed his audience and they cannot expect more.

It was strange after this terrific, this cosmic, close to 'The Ring', to drive out into the night and into the most dramatic thunderstorm I had ever encountered. Nature had felt herself challenged by art and summoned all her resources. They were considerable. There were several storms in the distance, lighting up the dark pine-woods that crept from the tops of the hills and differentiating their stems, and the mild Teutonic landscape became alive. It was a fascinating spectacle and suddenly it was no longer a spectacle but an action in which the car became an actor. For a special storm burst exactly over the car – there was forked lightning, there were torrents of rain, and then a deafening noise as hailstones as big as lumps of sugar peppered the roof. Where was the

Festspielhaus now? Where its scenic effects? The car staggered to a standstill in the heart of a wood. It could not make headway against the slipperiness and the wind. It cherished the hope that not all the trees in the wood would be struck by lightning and that those which had not been struck would hold up those which had been, and there it waited while Donner and Fafner and whatever else was about prowled and hissed. Then came the abatement – if it had not come I should not be here; nothing was as bad as it had been; less wind, smaller hailstones, fewer flashes, still less wind. The night subsided into an ordinary rough night, and the car got back safely from *Götterdämmerung.*

[1954]

Diversions

Diana's Dilemma

All the past week at the tram-station, a cinema advertisement of the usual extraordinary appeal has displayed itself upon a hoarding. The advertisement is in French, but having been educated at an English public school I cannot only read that language but can translate it for those who cannot. Rendered into our Northern idiom it runs as follows.

> Diana – it is thus that the name herself the heroine of this rich film – will die according to the opinion of the doctors who tend her. She is happy about it for, otherwise she would have to avow her shady past to him whom she has not the right to wed. Meanwhile sincere love, sunshine and the beautiful sky of the blue lake of Como heal her, and her lover who ignores that Diana has lived the worst adventures wishes to conduct her to the altar. She is not worthy of it, she thinks, and when the almond trees are in the flower she precipitates herself into the lake to seek oblivion. Diana is saved and her marriage will have place.

It has had place for ought I care or know. Having followed the Dilemmas of Myra the week before, and of Lyda the week before that, and of Juliette, Scava, Silvia and Grazia in previous weeks, I somehow felt that Diana's would land me in nothing new. There would be the same situation, the same motorcars, the same greyhound; the telegram would be handed on the same silver salver. The trees and shrubs would be agitated by the same old wind, there would be the same illness, the same escritoire, the same worst adventures, the same palm lounge, the same light woman among the same heavy furniture. Not that there was the least danger of impropriety. Oh no! The film censor would take care that the same kiss did not last for longer than the regulation ten feet, and that the same minimum of drapery shrouded ankles, wrist and throat. There would be nothing improper, but there would be nothing new – except the scenery, the management having evidently determined to present an Italian lake. No doubt it was the 'turn' of an Italian lake to be presented just as when D'Annunzio's *La Gioconda* was given here; it was the 'turn' of Rome, and that exquisite tragedy which was written for Florence, and whose every line breathes the Florentine Renaissance, was brutally transferred from Tuscany to an alien atmosphere, an alien scene. Heroines have their preferences. Diana if consulted might have preferred to precipitate herself into Windermere or Niagara. But no! It is the turn of Como and into Como she, or rather the doll that is substituted for her, must jump. Her marriage will then have place, will it? I think not. As soon as the doll has been dried Diana will take a train to Venice, there to recline, as Cora, in a gondola upon the Grand Canal, or to climb, as Laura up some tottering Campanile.

The scenery is of course the best part of the film, and he would indeed be perverse who did not enjoy the series of very pretty photographs that are jerked up and down before his eyes. But beyond the photograph what is there; what in the name of art, or life, or beauty, or fun? If people took the cinema frivolously one could understand its appeal. But they take it seriously. They attend, they do not talk. They talk at plays or concerts or operas, but during a cinema they are quite silent, and if one looks at them in the semi-darkness one sees they are all staring wrapt at the screen. Perhaps their attention is physiological not psychological. In other words, perhaps they are not attending really, but are mesmerized like rabbits by the bright flickering head of a snake. When the lights are turned up there is a sigh, a curious stir. Some moralists affirm that the audience has been educated. I doubt it. Other moralists complain that they have been holding one another's hands. I doubt this too. They have received nothing and conveyed nothing. Vacuity has gazed at vacuity. Scrappiness at scraps; the human mind has, like Diana, precipitated itself into the lake to seek oblivion.

After one of these entertainments I returned in pensive mood to the tram. Our heroine – I think she was Scava – had only just died on a costly carpet. We had seen her as a full length, as a bust and finally as an immense face which had filled the horizon, like some big pale whale. The mobility of that face was as remarkable as the size. Eyelids, heavier than quilts had slipped to and fro over the eyes, in which tears larger than a balloon had glistened, while another aperture, yet vaster and more exquisitely formed, opened below to disclose an impeccable colonnade of teeth. Here was nature at its greatest, surely. Yet I was not content. And even when the face faded and we were switched back to a lovely romantic gorge which had played I forget which part in Scava's earlier undoing, I found it not as lovely or romantic as the commonplace street down which I was waiting to tram. It was now night, certainly, and night knows a magic beyond the reach of art or day. Yet the whole world of ordinary experiences seemed crying: 'the diversion mankind seeks is not to be found in any cinema it is here, here'. A fruit shop was opposite: it ran from the darkness as a square of light, no larger than a cinema-screen, but oranges and cucumbers, bananas and apricots glowed in it, like jewels, or piled in the foreground stood in black relief against the radiance, where an Arab moved like a magician. The name of this shop in Greek, is, 'The Garden of the Hesperides' and the fruiterer, his grasp of French not being equal to mine, has translated it as 'Le Jardin des Soirées'. He may call it what he will, he has reminded one customer that life can be more beautiful and amusing than art – an agreeable reminder. Diana's dilemma is so dull. That is its greatest defect. It is duller than life. It is incidentally false but fundamentally dull. A fruit shop beats it as poetry, just as the sea murmuring against the embankment opposite, tells of more passion than all the waters of Como, sacred though they be to expensive and adulterous love.

But those are the remarks of one who, where the cinema is concerned, is irredeemably a prig. He does even agree with his fellow prigs, who sometimes declare from platforms that a film can be a great educational force, and build up the character of the young citizens.

[1917]

Sunday Music

Every Sunday at eleven the Casino of San Stefano presents an animated scene. The audience is arriving for the quarter-to-eleven concert and the performers are arriving also. The great hall is filling. See the pretty dresses! See the hats! See the Berberines loaded with ices and beer! See the dear little children flitting hither and thither with modish gesture, while their mothers form many a chatty group at the tables and rattle the chair legs with their parasols! See the conductor too! He raises his baton, as one who would conduct. See the performers! They propose to respond. They move their mouths and arms, and one of them, as if pursuing some private enquiry, beats upon a drum. See! see! But do not expect to hear. Sunday music at San Stefano is for the eye.

There was once upon a time another Sunday concert. The period was twelve years, the place Munich, the scene a Bier-Halle – a building, almost as large as San Stefano, whose architecture curiously combined an Early Christian Basilica and a Railway Station. Such blends are not infrequent at Munich. Up in the Sanctuary if you think of that building as a church (otherwise up by the Booking Office) sat the band from the Kaiser's Imperial Yacht, performing with sailory precision the Fire Music from *The Valkyrie*, and down in the auditorium sat squadron after squadron of awe-struck Germans, masticating silently, and among them sat I. Yes! The hand that now wields this pen once raised in its trembling fingers a mug of lager beer. And just as the mug reached my lips something went wrong with the lid. I don't know what. I touched the beastly thing or something. Anyhow it rose up on end, hit my nose, and fell back upon the beer with a slight noise like 'plob'. I might as well have dropped a bomb. Hisses broke out, scowls, exclamations of horror and rage. I had insulted Germany's Kaiser, her Navy, and her Art. Crimson, I replaced my mug, and that day drank no more.

It is better to be inattentive with Latins and Levantines than to attend with Teutons, and San Stefano, whatever its defects, is not a censorious place. As the concert proceeds the children gather force, and during a Beethoven Symphony I have counted as many as seven of our little ones running about in single file. Their leader I named the Syrian little girl, her followers the French, Jewish, Italian, Armenian, Royalist and Venizelist little girls respectively. The Syrian was a truly lively creature who from time to time would bound past the notice that prohibited her from entering the Club Enclosure, to execute a merry rat-tat upon its boards. The others did the same, and then general conversation ensued, and those who had mothers butted them in the chest out of civility. When they were rested the leader gave the signal and away they flew, all ribbons and lace and spectacles and curls. Meanwhile another child (I dubbed him a Copt) had actually got on to the platform and, very witty, had been imitating the conductor and his father had been scolding him not for this, but lest he should fall. And Beethoven, like another child, had done what he had to do, and had sent up the fountain of his sound, though no one could hear it.

There are seasons of fair weather even at San Stefano, and during those it has seemed to me that fine music was being finely played up in that little shell. But was ever art more for art's sake! Except the performers, who there has heard every note in a performance? Not I, and the noise is sometimes so great that I doubt the performers hearing either. If, by a series of coincidences, the children are tired and the Berberines absent and the mothers reading novels by Henri Bordeaux, then profiting by the unusual lull, the sparrows start. See the sparrows too! Did ever sparrows chatter like the San Stefanese? A sparrow in a German concert-hall betrays no emotion except fear, but the sparrow here lives and loves and nests and fights close above a sixty-man-power orchestra. The ancient Romans would not have minded this. Find in that what consolation you can. They were curiously tender to sparrows, were the ancient Romans, even shedding tears when they died. They saw in them the birds of the Goddess Venus and heard in their flight the approach of her car. And Antony and Cleopatra who once commanded music (this is certain) not far from San Stefano, and who felt on their foreheads the same sea-breeze that rattles its windows today, must also have raised their eyes to such feathered dalliance, and smiled indulgently each to each, a great king to a great queen. Antony and Cleopatra are gone, gone is their luxury which has scandalized so many generations of historians and contrasts so unfavourably with the home life of modern monarchs. Antony and Cleopatra will never again drink pearls or catch salt fish or wear each other's robes; their music, unheeded or heeded, will never again ring out between temples and palaces of marble, the very city they admired is indistinguishable. Nothing of the Alexandria they knew survives except sea, sand, and little birds: remembering which, be tolerant if you can of that exasperating twitter, which has drowned whatever is still audible in the Beethoven Sympathy.

But hush! our sight-seeing is over. The concert is at an end. The audience applauds, the mammas shut their books, the children, ever generous to a defeated competitor block up the gang ways and clap their little gloved hands. People rise to go. Why, in the face of such approbation do the performers continue to move their mouths and fingers? What more do they want? The conductor, why does he move his baton still? And now a dispute breaks out in the audience itself. Those who are nearer begin to argue with the more remote, and gradually prove that the Symphony is still going on. The orchestra has not finished really. It was only traversing a soft passage . . . And there comes into my mind the soft passage at the end of *The Valkyrie* as it was performed twelve years ago by the band from the Kaiser's Yacht. There, the conditions and the execution were flawless. Brünnhilde swung into slumber like a well-oiled gun. One heard every note, and when the pianissimo had died away one broke into respectful applause, and ordered a nourishing sausage, and was permitted, with complete freedom from any punishment, to talk. Yet something was wrong. Some item was lacking which Sunday Music at San Stefano, for all its exasperating mis-management, does provide. A single item but an important one. Antony and Cleopatra were very keen on it. Enjoyment.

[1917]

Higher Aspects

On all sides, as is usual, stretched the horizon. Overhead, much as usual was the sky. But below, things were very unusual indeed. They were so far off in the first place – 5000 feet – and so large in the second, comprising the entire city of Alexandria, the lakes of Hadra and Mariut, plentiful helpings of the delta, the desert, and the Mediterranean, and one or two clouds. I looked down upon these assorted objects with complacency. They were too far off to be frightening: one might as well be frightened of an Atlas. Sometimes I sat upon a leather music stool, sometimes got down and sidled about the enclosure in which it stood. The wind howled and tried to blow my mouth out of my face, but conditions were comfortable otherwise: half motorcar half yacht. A few strings ran along the walls of the well, and the pilot's well displayed some fanciful watches and clocks. Sometimes he folded his arms to indicate his superfluity which I had never doubted. And this was flying, this was what scientists had aimed at and poets dreamed of for centuries. Even Shelley never flew.

Now that the great event had come off, the overwhelming fact in it was the beauty of the Earth. And it was beauty of a new kind. Scenery has beauty, so has a map; what one saw from this height was an unexpected combination of the two. There were myriads of fields, like green dominoes, varied with an occasional red one: they stretched away, their tints growing fainter, until they merged into the haze of the south. Into their order impinged the curves of the two lakes. Mariut was grey, Hadra a saucerful of olive brown. The sea edged the land with blue, green, purple and white. Further out it was untroubled blue. And all this suggested a map, carefully coloured, but as soon as one had accepted the suggestion one realized with a delightful shock that the map was alive. It did not merely unroll beneath us. It was alive in itself. The white of the sea moved, pumped up from below. The clouds moved, and so, more solid than themselves, did their shadows. When we passed above sand we could see our own shadow, following like a little dog. And here and there were alterations more subtle – they might be men or trains or the waving of palm trees – but they were a continual reminder that the crust of the earth is alive, and I shall always think – though the thought is unphilosophic – that this is what the earth 'really' looks like, a being neither scenery nor map.

Of the works of man I must speak with less enthusiasm. The houses of Alexandria – alas that I should have lived to say so – looked like decayed teeth. Resorts of the influential, such as San Stefano, figured worst, for they resembled what is known in dental parlance as a 'bridge', stumps and gaps being connected by slabs of compo. But all the buildings are quite ugly enough to be pulled up by the roots and flung into the sea. Nor does the city atone by any distinction of outline. Her mouth, to continue the metaphor, needs drastic remodelling. It sags at one end and is congested at the other – a nasty sight. Of course to blame her would be unfair. She did not expect to be examined from above, and the architects of the future will – (if we regain the leisure and inclination to build beautifully) – remedy this, and will design houses that look beautiful from the air and cities that blend with the land. Flying hitherto is purely destructive. Except gun powder, no invention has been made so exclusively for death. But it has another side which if developed will give new delights to mankind.

Meanwhile somewhere in the void a little ghost was coughing, kokka, kokka. That was me. Aviation is no cure for a snuffling cold. And the pilot would occasionally lift his glove to his face and twitter. No other noise reached me through the steady yell of the wind. Alexandria, as far as sound went, might have lain on the moon. I was soon to be punished, though, for thinking of her slightingly. A dreadful thing happened. She rose without the least warning, and looked in at my right eye. I faced the horrid vision and it fled – only to peep in at my left with the sea on top. Then she got round at the back of my head. It was too much, and I steadied myself on my music stool, like the old lady when the Margate steamer tilts. This righted Alexandria, and we were soon traversing her as pleasantly as before, though in the reverse direction. I shouted I wasn't exactly frightened. The pilot nodded and replied 'side slip'. And side slip wasn't what had happened – it was what was going to happen. Next moment we fell – so I afterwards learnt – 1000 feet to the right, then headed over and fell 800 to the left. I was exactly frightened now and closed my eyes. When I opened them Alexandria had regained her proper level. But she had not done with me. At the command of 'zoom' she stood up on end like a target and grew perceptibly larger. We must be rushing towards her teeth and for the first time muscular, as apart from aesthetic, sensations occurred. We and not the universe were moving. We might even hit something. And we did. Not Alexandria, but a solid lump of air which Providence interposes at the end of every zoom. My legs went cold. Out flew my stomach. It quivered on the edge of the well . . . then slipped back in to position and life went on as before, with myriads of sunlit fields, and waters, and radiant sky. A zoom, you see, is an aerial toboggan, and reproduces on a gigantic scale the emotions of that pastime. Afterwards it is nicer than tobogganing because you have not fallen out on your head. At the time, I scarcely knew.

Such is flying as it strikes an innocent passenger. Moments of funk divided by a vision so glorious that one forgets them instantly. No other generation has seen that vision with the sensual eye, though the poets have guessed it through their imaginations. Dante guessed better than Shelley, I find – no doubt because he had a saner conception of space. It is Dante in whom one afterwards notes parallels. Like him, we had looked down on the little spot of earth that makes us so fierce – in this case on Alexandria with its rival Pâtisseries. We too had beheld 'l'alto trionfo del regno verace', the triumphant exhibition of reality, of the reality that is neither scenery nor map. And we shared a problem that troubled Dante even in the Empyrean. How is it possible to describe that reality to people who have never left the earth? I think it is not possible. There is nothing mystic in aviation, but no earthly pleasure resembles it. It has opened a new kingdom of material beauty, to inherit which one must simply go up into the air.

[1918]

The Fiction Factory

The poor, dear novel! The poor, poor, little thing! Who would have thought that a Mr Clayton Hamilton, instigated by Mr Brander Matthews, had been scanning it narrowly from on high! It ran about so happily, like an inoffensive hen, and scratching in the dust and the grass of life it routed out so many objects, some valuable, some not. And lo! suddenly down swoops the American eagle. Not that the eagle is the least unkind or rough. He merely lays the hen on her back and tells her what she has been doing. And if she squawks faintly that she didn't know she was doing anything particular at all, the eagle screams his acquiescence and notes, for the benefit of future hens, the importance of the subconscious element in fictional art. Here it all is. A revised and enlarged edition, too. Here is the 'necessary triple process' through which every novelist must pass (namely, scientific discovery, philosophic understanding and artistic expression). Here are the three merits he must aim at (namely, momentous material, masterly method and important personality). Here are the nine ways in which he may make use of the weather. 'Although the weather,' we are told, 'is a subject upon everybody's tongue, there are very few people who are capable of talking about it with intelligence and art.' When they write novels their incapacity is further illustrated. Let them, therefore, study the weather in theory and practice, at the same time memorizing the following rules and examples.

For the weather may be, firstly, 'non-existent, as in a nursery tale'. Then it may be 'decorative' (Pierre Loti). 'Utilitarian' (*The Mill on the Floss*). 'Illustrative' (*The Egoist*). 'Planned in pre-established harmony' 'Fiona Macleod'. 'In emotional contrast' (*Master of Ballantrae*). 'Determinative of action' (in a Kipling story a man proposes to the wrong girl, owing to a sand storm). 'A controlling influence' (*Richard Feverel*). And, ninthly, it may be itself a hero (Vesuvius in *The Last Days of Pompeii*). The hen rises. Now she is wise. But I do not think she will ever feel up to laying an egg again.

The truth is that good writing can only be learnt from good writing. Mr Hamilton glibly agrees, and at the end of each chapter he says 'Suggested Reading. Read the most important works of fiction mentioned in this chapter.' But what he doesn't see (at least he doesn't put it in this edition, though he may tabulate it in the next) is that we learn not from studying a book, but from enjoying it, and that in consequence there is nothing to be learnt from his. He has read widely and he is clear and he is catholic, desolatingly catholic, but he has neither emotion nor taste, and so cannot provoke those qualities in others. 'Of course not. They are innate,' he smiles. Of course. But his book denies this truth in spirit, though it may affirm it in words, and if it fell into the hands of a young writer would certainly do him harm rather than good, and lead him to believe that fiction can be manufactured by attention to externals. A machine-made article may be better or worse made, but it remains a machine-made article, and however tippy the processes, it can never have individual distinction. It may have the coherence of logic, it will never have the coherence of life. 'La vérité en toute chose étant extremèment délicate et fugitive, ce n'est pas à la dialectique qu'il est donné de l'atteindre,' says Renan, and no amount of tabulating or conscientious reading can help a writer who would be creative, while the writer who is not creative will be helped by them only too much. Never again, for instance, will he get muddled over the Point of View. For it may be:

Class I - External
 (i) Point of View of leading actor
 (ii) Of subsidiary actor
 (iii) Of different actors
 (iv) Epistolary

Class II - Internal
(i) Omniscient
(ii) Limited
(iii) Rigidly restricted

He will be enabled, with fatal ease, to turn out seven different kinds of novels, and if in each he adopts a different attitude towards the weather, he will total sixty-three. Oh yes, and there are two 'tones'. Impersonal and Personal. A hundred and twenty-six. But I retire from the roar and the clanking. The poor dear novel! The poor, poor little thing!

[1919]

Clayton Hamilton, *Materials and Methods of Fiction*
Ernest A. Baker, *The History of the English Novel*

Green Pastures and Piccadilly

What should we do without sin? – in the theatre, that is to say! In life, quite a number of people *se fichent d'elle*, but the stage, deprived of her loyal co-operation, would collapse at once. Without sin there can be no suffering or remorse, no broadmindedness, and consequently no play. Plays are not all the same because there are fortunately two sorts of sin – irregular unions based upon love and irregular unions based upon money – and also two sorts of saints, the unco' guid, and the 'real' saints, who comprehend the sinners of the first class and utter dark economic redes that condone the existence of the second. Variety in plays is, therefore, possible, though the central figure should always be a man about town, weak and pleasure-loving, but good at bottom and capable of abrupt and permanent reform. The title of *Green Pastures and Piccadilly* makes everything so plain that it seemed scarcely necessary that the curtain should go up. When it did, there they all were in the Rectory drawing-room – the dear old vicar who will prove to be so human as well as such a saint; his wife; an unco' guid; their innocent daughter, arranging flowers, but capable of announcing 'a clean woman demands a clean man' before the evening ends; Jack, madly in love with her, yet uneasy about something; and Jack's father, a rich blunt manufacturer, same class as the vicar. One's only doubt was about the sin. Which sort was it going to be? and here I must own that the author misled me, chiefly by means of a black-and-white sofa cushion, very brazen, which figured among the furniture of the sinner's flat. And behind the sofa cushion hung a piece of canvas painted to represent Piccadilly, and bringing that terrible place even nearer to us than it is to the Ambassadors Theatre. All this was misleading. Daisy belonged to the first class, and Jack should have installed her more appropriately. But Jack always did blunder. He put off telling Daisy about his marriage until the very day before it took place, thus creating the maximum of irritation and suspicion at both ends. One realizes his difficulty. He was obliged to mismanage everything, or there would have been no dénouement; and he was obliged to take a flat in Piccadilly, or there would have been no title. Still he was his own master about sofa cushions, and he really might have shut the window.

But perhaps Daisy bought the cushion to please Maudie. Maudie (class two) was reckless and loud, though her heart was of gold. It was Maudie who cried 'Revenge!' and flew down to the Rectory in the third act, to interrupt the wedding. 'Madam, you have made some mistake,' said the dear old vicar, and his wife said 'These persons!' But Maudie didn't care. She gave them all what for, and just then the door opened again and the parlour-maid announced 'Miss Daisy Bird.' The Rectory was the last place that Daisy had meant to come to when she left the flat. Badly as Jack had treated her, she loved him deeply, and would have died sooner than create a scandal. She had only come away in order to stop Maudie, but you know what happens when you do that on the stage. You can stop neither Maudie nor yourself. And if anyone tries to stop you the same fate overtakes him; he too is hurled into the burly until the characters are all collected for the final scene. At all events so it was in Daisy's case, and the vicar's wife, generally so censorious, seemed to understand her difficulty and quite accepted the above excuse. Then the actors classed themselves by word of mouth – rather quickly, for they had evidently performed the operation for a good many years. The manufacturer said with deep respect, 'And if ever you need money . . .'; the vicar said with deep respect, 'I shall think of you . . . often . . . .' Daisy left, sobbing but strengthened, and Jack and his future bride ran through their reconciliation scene. Down went the curtain; up it went showing everyone in a row; down it went, and away one flew to Piccadilly to scramble for the

Tube. Squashed in a lift, in a mass of other respectable people, one thought: 'Why are such plays written, why produced? Has ''John Walton'' ever for one moment thought clearly or felt deeply upon this subject of irregular unions? Has she (or he) ever conceived of sin except as something that makes the stage go round?'

> Amor, che al cor gentil ratto s'apprende
>   prese costui della bella persona
> che mi fu tolta, e il modo ancor m'offende.
>
> Amor, che a nullo amato amar perdona,
>   mi prese del costui piacer si forte
> che, come vede, ancor non m'abbandona.
>
> Amor condusse noi ad una morte . . .

It can be done! But it has to be done differently.

[1919]

The Sitters

What can we get out of this book? for we shall certainly never get into it. It is a book about great people. There they sat, scattered all over the world. Some of them sat in their offices, others in their snuggeries, others in French *châteaux* behind the firing line. They sat on high chairs, low chairs, rocking chairs, easy chairs, swivel chairs, sofas, chesterfields, camp-stools, poufs, or in a row at tables, but they all sat; that seems to be the one characteristic that great people have in common. Resting their main weight upon a certain portion of their bodies (one is obliged to paraphrase) and resting their feet upon the ground, General Foch, Sir Edward Carson, Prince Lvoff, Lord French, Lord Milner, Lord Kitchener, Miss Edna May and Mr Hugh Walpole all sat, occupied in being great, when the door bell or something gave a ring, and a card came in upon a silver salver. 'Isaac F. Marcosson.'

'Not a bit of it' or 'Show the gentleman up,' replied the great person, in accordance with his temperament, but, whatever the reply, it rewarded Mr Marcosson richly. If he got in he learnt something, if he was hoofed out he learnt as much. For it is too wonderful how great people differ. Some want interviews, others don't; some need tempting, others bluffing, others expose themselves by refusing. Ah, what a life! A different technique each time. Mr Marcosson will never lead that life with me nor probably with you. Still, that's no reason why we, too, shouldn't have our bit of fun.

If we feel in a social vein, why not flit with the author through palm lounges and hear the brilliant talk? The sitters are fencing with rapiers of steel. You can listen to the 'most effective retort' he ever heard made. It was made to a lady by Mr Israel Zangwill. She asked him his Christian name, and he replied, 'I have none.' Or you can assist at the following duel of wits:

> The cleverest of the Frohman epigrams was inspired by Chambers. They made an irresistible team. When writing a note the playwright once asked his friend:
>
> 'Do you spell high-ball with a hyphen?'
>
> 'No, with a siphon,' replied Frohman.
>
> It was give and take like this all the time.

But more often you will be in serious mood, and seek the council chambers where the destinies of nations are planned and the battlefields where they are executed. The author will take you there, too. In his early days he had a difficulty, because there is a tradition in some quarters of 'rubber-soled diplomacy', which had to be overcome. Sometimes no one answered the bell, and if he did get in the inmate, more often than not, 'shut up like a clam'. He trumpeted his failures exultantly, but one cannot live for ever off clams and nothing else. Gradually he learnt his trade and induced his celebrities to be less coy. He studied their vanities, appealed to their interests. He convinced them that, as a business proposition, an interview would pay them. They must keep in touch with the public, and he knew what the public wanted. The great people acquiesced, and though the generals remained seated, as befitted their profession, the politicians and newspaper proprietors rose in increasing numbers and walked towards him. They introduced him to one another, too, seemed positively anxious to hand him on, Lord Northcliffe being particularly kind over this, and, indeed, it appears that if once you 'get in' with great people you need never stop; you accumulate letters in unstuck envelopes and scribbled visiting cards like a snowball, and roll, an increasing portent, from end to end of the habitable world. The doors fly open, the servants rush about. Mr Marcosson with a letter from Mr Lloyd George, Mr Marcosson with Lord Beaverbrook's autograph photograph, Mr Marcosson to interview Mr Galsworthy, Miss Alice Hegan Rice and General Nivelle. Telegram from Signor d'Annunzio to Signor Marconi: Mr Marcosson to interview it. Sir Eric Geddes late for an appointment with Admiral Beatty: Mr Marcosson the reason. Oh, it is marvellous! But as he himself points out it is a miracle that could not have happened in normal times. His success is due to that painful yet apposite catastrophe of a European war. The Germans dehumanized war but the Allies humanized it (the thought is his own), and the main outcome of the humanization is the interviewer. Without an interviewer great people scarcely exist. He creates the necessary bustle round them and thus dissipates the sense of *ennui* that too often creeps over the public when fighting has continued for three years; he reminds us that great men are on high, communicating with each other over our heads. He tells us the little things they say. For instance, Lord Haig said, 'It is a war of youth,' and he said it 'not without sadness'; it was 'a flash of that tender inner thing which strong men so often hide behind a grim or stern exterior,' but from Mr Marcosson it was not hidden. It is quite overwhelming when a great man has an ordinary decent emotion like this. One scarcely knows which way to look. Again, Lord Northcliffe loves his mother. Too amazing! 'Every day that he is in England he calls her up on the telephone. When he is out of England he sends her a telegram. This daily message from her firstborn is as much a part of her daily life as food.' Haig and Northcliffe are the greatest of all great, because one of them represents war and the other journalism. They stand on the twin summits of human achievement. Yet there is room for greatness in other walks also, and social reformers, ventriloquists and poets are admitted to these pages provided they have come to the top. Everyone gets in except Lenin and the 'Kaiser That Was'. Mr Marcosson tried to meet them but failed, to his eternal glory: 'I should have looked upon each adventure as an excursion into crime.' His luck did not desert him even here.

An interviewer's career has two aspects. In his sublimer moments, Mr Marcosson speaks of himself as a salesman, in his more modest, as an artist. He has a line of goods that he has got to push, but he is also a combination of novelist, historian, and poet. The passage in which he states this aspect is too long to quote in full, but the following extracts will give some idea of it:

> In the last analysis all fiction is merely a transparent record of human desire, progress, and inspiration done in terms of the larger journalism. So close is the relation between journalism and literature these days, that much fiction is unconscious fact, and *vice versa* . . .
>
> Nothing is more imposing than history. Yet when all is said and done, Mommsen, Gibbon, and John Richard Green were simply vicarious reporters, sitting in the secluded ease and comfort of libraries, cataloguing the past . . .
>
> Poetry is full mate to history. Keats was nothing more than a reporter of his emotions. Wordsworth reflected nature in terms of verse. Byron was the realistic and rhythmic depicter of passion and desire.
>
> Of course, there are two kinds of reporters. One is the type of man who becomes a sort of chronic reproducer of bald facts as he finds them. He remains an ordinary chronicler of events. In a word he is the photographer.
>
> On the other hand you have the reporter who transmutes facts through the alchemy of his own personality. He becomes the maker of literature. This is art.

It is worth pondering over the above passage, for it throws light upon the type of mind that comes to the top, in a war. Mr Marcosson is (or was) at the top. Of that there is no question. He is ten thousand times more influential than you or I. He convinced the great people that he was what they wanted, and his propaganda efforts were largely responsible for the entry of America into the conflict. While others suffered and starved he went about ringing bells, and over-emphasizing the replies. A natural indignation rises in us, but it is an indignation that should be directed against ourselves. Where there is ignorance and passion there will the 'interviewer' flourish, where there is education, real education, he disappears, he takes to travelling in scent or sewing machines instead of in human beings.

[1920]

Isaac F. Marcosson, *Adventures in Interviewing*

Places

Rostock and Wismar

The heart does not beat quicker at the names of Rostock and Wismar, nor does the finger find them instinctively on the map. They slumber in one of Europe's backwaters – too far east, or north, or something – where even Baedeker gets drowsy, and sows imaginary tram lines along the deserted streets. The lover of the Baltic style of architecture will visit them; and so will he who studies the rise and fall of the Hanseatic League. But the really nice person will only take them on the way to Stralsund; and why should he go there? The country is flat, the sea shallow, the fourth-class railway carriages far from comfortable; and the Baltic style itself has been compared in fretful moments to a Gruyère cheese.

Rostock, with a reputation for bustle, lies eight miles from the mouth of the Warnow. It is a test town. If the tourist is happy here, and can love its huge pallid churches he will be happy elsewhere. The centre of interest is the Neumarkt, every house in which has a gable. Here is the inn of *The Sun* (admirable), the inn of *The Moon* (almost too quaint), the inn of *Russia* (fashionable but dear; three marks for a bed), the decadent art-shop full of Toteninsels, the manly art-shop, full of prancing Majesties, and, loitering in front of these, undergraduates, for Rostock is a University town. The gable gains by repetition: two go for nothing, ten for very little. But the Neumarkt must contain dozens; and therefore, grey as it is, prosaic as are its details, it is picturesque.

Either art-shop sells picture post-cards of the Grand Duke of Mecklenburg-Schwerin, whose palace is hard by. His chest is broad, but not as broad as Majesty's; his medals and his moustache will never come as thick, nor his war horse prance so perpendicularly. All this is as it should be; but it makes the young fellow look headachy and sad. He would like to be first in his own town. He would like to have a nicer palace. He would rather it did not carry you back to the Westbourne Grove. He is grieved when you hurry away from it to the margarine factory and exclaim: 'Now here is something worth seeing at last.' For the pigs of Rostock become margarine in a fair patrician mansion, pleasingly proportioned, delicately carved, and adorned with *Vigila et Ora*, and other wise remarks. Do not censure them for this. They had to go somewhere; and in Rostock you find an old house quicker than a new one. Moreover, margarine is a Hanseatic article – or would be if the Hansa League still existed. Those Baltic merchants loved pigs, and herrings, and beer, and all that stoutens man's body, or makes his heart glad in a northern way. They ate, and grew fat, and were not ashamed. They knocked the King of Denmark over when he tried to catch their herrings. The Holy Roman Emperor strolled northward; and they knocked him over too. And at last, outside their pew in the church of St Nicolas at Stralsund, instead of carving *Vigila et Ora*, they carved this:

> He who's no merchant, stop without,
> Or else I'll hit him on the snout.

Ponder these things, and consider which is incongruous: the Grand Duke or the margarine.

Sentiment is vindicated; but the fact remains that there is very little to see in Rostock – much that is old, but little that is beautiful. When the merchants made a great conscious effort (as at Lübeck, where they were determined to go one better than the bishop, and built the Marien Kirche in consequence) – they succeeded. But they never builded better than they knew. They never strayed into immortality, like the Italians. They ate their dinners and won their battles. But they were seldom anxious over beauty, and never stumbled on it unawares.

Perhaps there was more anxiety at Wismar. There is certainly more charm. It has not the pleasant situation of Rostock, nor has it the same profusion of old houses. But the churches are splendid; and even the absence of water is a gain, for it leads to water-works. Water-works are common enough. But they were not so common in the sixteenth century; and that is the date of the Wismar building. It is quite small, and, standing as it does in the corner of the market place, might easily be ignored, or mistaken for a newspaper kiosk. The core of it consists of a mysterious mass, ribbed and twisted – presumably the cistern, but such a cistern as no plumber saw in his wildest dreams. This is encircled by an arcade and gratings, with Renaissance sculpture at the angles, and a long Latin poem for a frieze. How the cistern worked, if at all, and how many gallons, if any, it contained, are interesting questions for the enquiring mind. The Latin poem does not attack them, being occupied with the sanitary authorities and their pursuit of the reluctant nymph. The situation is quite Ovidian. First this went wrong, then that: it seemed as if they would never catch her, or only catch her muddy. Towards the last couplet she yields, and the 'Wismarii Patres'.

> Bring (with the help of God) fresh water that is not brackish,
> Bring it in quite little pipes, all from the lake of Schwerin.

These water-works are nicely seen from the *Old Swede*, a fifteenth-century restaurant hard by. Or one can eat round the corner, in the *Wädekin Hotel*, whose gable dates from 1363. After a heavy dinner, one moves across the market place to look at the splendid group of buildings that adjoins it on the west. This group contains two churches of cathedral size, a palace in the style of the Italian Renaissance, and, most wonderful of all, the Alte Schule. Here is a pageant of warm colour which shifts from ruddy brown to pink, a frank avowal of material in which the very restorations have dignity. Crude new bricks, the bricks of our Surrey suburbs, look strangely beautiful when set in the midst of bricks that were crude and new some hundreds of years ago. There is no nicety of contour: a tower will try to be a spire, and then blunder back into a tower again. There is no hint of the city's personality, of her Presiding Genius; one town, if sensible, is very like another; and it is not likely that a Wismarian father of twenty stone was severed by any spiritual gulf from a father of the same weight in Rostock. There is only brick. But, whereas the Rostock brick was pallid, and built churches the colour of King's Cross station, the brick of Wismar is red, and builds her into glory that is everlasting, because it can be for ever renewed.

The palace (not of brick) would, after all, be better in Italy; and as for the churches, there are finer in Lübeck, though even Lübeck does not mass them in such splendour. But the Alte Schule is unique.

Mathematically described, the Alte Schule is a rhomboidal parallelopiped of black and red bricks; irreverently described, it is like a long narrow cardboard box, which a naughty child has sat squashy at the corners; reverently described, it is a hollow slice of fairy land, wherein should pace a queen, looking out through fairy windows upon a dull, rectangular world. It has the strange distinction of fantasy – stranger than ever in the midst of so many solid churches, solid houses, and four-square jokes – a fantasy which no restoration can destroy, for it depends, not on humoursome details, but on the building's very ground plan. Long, narrow, askew, with frequent windows on either side, and a tiny, stair-like gable at the end, it is as dainty as a jest in the music of Mozart, and as impossible to describe in writing. The Baltic stylist at Wismar, or it may be the spirit that presided over the trend of Wismar's streets, has produced a thing of beauty that is just a little unlike any other beautiful thing in the world.

From Wismar the railway, following the course of the quite little pipes, goes southward to Schwerin. But Schwerin is no bourgeois town; and its glories are another, and possibly a greater matter.

[1906]

A Birth in the Desert

On the fringe of the Libyan Desert, forty miles west from Alexandria and two miles south of the sea, some remarkable buildings are standing – so remarkable that tourists have been known to approach them, to sit down in their shadows, and to look them up in a guide-book. The Libyan Desert is here composed of delicate limestone ridges, clothed with flowers and separated by little fields of barley in the spring, and bare at all other seasons, awaiting the next spring. It is not the desert of fiction, where all save the heroine is sin and sand; and though a few Bedouin sheikhs move about, they, like their surroundings, keep quite quiet. In harmony with the scenery and its inhabitants rise these puzzling buildings, abrupt, visible for miles, yet spiritually at home. Who built them? The guide-book does not say. What is their date? What style are they in? Egyptian? Not exactly, but then we are not exactly in Egypt; Egypt starts with the irrigation a few miles behind; Egypt was the river Nile. Are they Tunisian, Algerian, southern Spanish? Not exactly, again. Did the Bedouins put them up? Impossible, Bedouins don't build, they are nomads; look at their tents there, almost Mongolian in outline, and harmonizing with the low ridges of the hills. Then whence came this austere beautiful town, with its unfinished walls, solemn market place, court-house, antique memorial column? Whence the great building outside it – basilica or factory? – with its long roof and arcaded tower? Our last conjecture was, indeed, the nearest to the truth. Bedouins don't build. But if they did, they would build like this. Something has evidently happened, some influence has passed over the desert, and the latent architectural capabilities of a race have been stirred.

Burg el Arab is in no guide-book because it only dates

from 1918. It began under the Great War, when everyone, Bedouins especially, ought to have been intent on bloodshed; and it even grew with the connivance of the British Military Authorities. When the Last Judgement comes and the generals – ranged apart as befits their rank – are asked each of them to say what he did for God, one will proudly reply, 'I bombed Rheims,' another 'I spoilt a few Tiepolos at Venice,' and so on; but some general or other out of Egypt will hang his head because he created or permitted creation. Imagination and humanity broke loose here in the heart of horror, and after the Senussi were checked and pacified a curious experiment was made, of which we see only the unfinished shell. It was hoped – and part of the hope found fulfilment – that the district could be held not by force, through mounted police, but by interesting itself in its own affairs. The Bedouins needed a store-house, a court of justice, and a market place, and, above all, some centre in which they could take a pride, some visible symbol of their dry, enduring civilization. Burg el Arab tried to supply this, and the enthusiasm they brought to its making suggested that the experiment was sound. It was not to be a town in a residential sense – only a seat of government and an occasional place of social intercourse and trade. It was to be quite small (about 400 yards by 200), but a mosque would have been added, also a library for genealogies and other tribal records, also a 'castle' – we shall see in a moment for whom.

The scheme rested on an economic idea. Bedouins and Egyptians don't mix well, and fusion is for the present deemed impossible, yet they might be useful to each other and so acquire mutual respect. Now the trade with the west – such as it is – is in the hands of Cairo and Alexandria merchants. It would be greatly increased if there was an adequate transport system – and here the Bedouin would come in. He would not trade to any extent on his own account, but he would be the carrier between Egypt and Central Africa, and Burg el Arab (which is close to the Alexandria-Hammam railway) would be the starting-place of his caravans. Such was the practical, as apart from the spiritual, side of the experiment. There was also a carpet factory, which was transferred from the neighbouring town of Amrieh, and which employed 400 Bedouin women and produced excellent though somewhat expensive rugs. But the factory (though superb architecturally) is incidental; the place could never be an industrial centre – only a stronghold for the imagination and a depot for the African carrying trade.

While the scheme was developing (with the sympathy of both English and Egyptian friends), a great and sudden change took place away on the Nile, which altered the whole political perspective. Great Britain fulfilled the promises that she had been making since 1882, and virtually left Egypt her independence. The effect upon Burg el Arab was disastrous. Young Egypt could not look with any sympathy upon a small Bedouin town, sticking like a pimple on its new-born flank. It condemned the experiment as unpatriotic, superfluous, and absurd, and began to throw various Oriental difficulties in its way. Ministers said they would help, couldn't, funds were cut off – and in the end the official mainly responsible for the scheme (an Englishman) has resigned; work has stopped, and the exquisite buildings are likely to join the past and become one with their neighbours, the ruins of Abumna and of Abusir. The Nationalists are not to be blamed. Old countries can't learn their lesson, so how should young ones? Egypt for the Egyptians, Britain for the British, France for the French! No country has seen that nationalism leads to discomfort within and disaster without, so it was not to be expected that the Cairo Government would favour a subject race who were traditionally Egypt's enemies. Inevitable, but sad. There is so little public beauty in the world. It is nearly always personal and subterranean, seldom rising to the surface in the form of a town, seldom allied to a hope. When it seeks not its own but the good of ordinary men, and strives to express what is latent in their minds – then its frustration has something tragic about it.

To state in an article without illustrations that Burg el Arab is 'beautiful' means, indeed, nothing; a series of photographs and plans should follow at this point. But even photographs and plans could not convey the landscape, the quality of the soil and the sky, and it is in conjunction with them that the town establishes its claim. Like them, it seems harsh at the first sight, but it has latent gentleness – even as they, once a year, give birth to delicately scented flowers. It is one of the few creations of an epoch that gloried in degradation and destruction; one of the few proofs then forthcoming that the life of man, like the life of plants, refused to lie buried in ugliness and muddle for ever. Buildings and flowers! Near the town is the small tomb of a saint. He used to be both nameless and mute, but during the war he was roofed over with copper, and the attention stimulated him. 'Mohammed of the Copper Dome' he was now called, and simultaneously he began to speak. 'Some day there will be large buildings near me,' he used to say, and he used to come out of his tomb at night and sit by his dome (which had been made from the air-tight boxes put into small boats to lend them seaworthiness after submarining), with the result that in the morning the masons on their way to work were greeted by a most delicious smell. They were not surprised. 'Just as the cold earth throws up the beautiful flowers and their perfume,' they said, 'so occasionally it throws up Mohammed and his.' Both seemed to them equal births of a benign power, which the seasons may retard but cannot destroy.

Since Egyptian nationalism – for quite comprehensible reasons – will not encourage the scheme, is it doomed to extinction? There remains one other factor: the Egyptian King: The dynasty has a slight traditional connection with the district: the ex-Khedive Abbas concerned himself with it when he built the railway. And King Fuad himself has taken some interest in the building, realizing perhaps that it is desirable for a modern monarch not only to express nationalism, but to supplement it, to represent the minorities in his kingdom as well as the majority. Burg el Arab was planned in this expectation. It anticipated a personal overlordship, and in the middle of the town a big house or 'castle' was to arise, which was to symbolize royalty and be its occasional residence. There was to be a small annual ceremony. The sheikhs were to assemble and render up the key of the town to the King, who, before giving it back, would review the events of the past year, and receive the Bedouin oath of allegiance. Whether the King is sufficiently attracted by the scheme to take personal action has yet to be seen, but he is certainly its only hope, and he himself would probably find in it a source of strength rather than of weakness. There is no question of British influence, which would naturally be resented. Burg el Arab lies silent and empty. King Fuad (though Egypt is his main concern) might do worse than attach this unique little ornament to the hem of his robe.

[1924]

The Eyes of Sibiu

It never occurred to me that when the Pied Piper of Hamelin led his little charges through the mountain they would emerge in Roumania. Nor did it occur to Browning either, for in those robust days of his Roumania scarcely existed and Hungary, if anything, was the exit which he conceived. But here they were, his fair-haired and blue-eyed German children, clean, friendly and a little dull, and here they grew into broad-shouldered men, and here, behind them, were the crinkled green hills, anti-macassared with trees and picked out here and there with white threads of snow. Their old home had been over those hills. History, stranger than poetry, had brought them half across Europe without the help of a tunnel, and had planted them out to resist the eastern invaders, and to build fortified churches and towns.

This was one of their towns. Sibiu which they called Hermannstadt, and standing in its lovely square I thought – well, I thought of nothing appropriate, one never does when sightseeing, only it was a most lovely square, and what so took me were the elongated eye-shaped openings in the roofs of the houses. It was as if the heavy dark red tiles had parted to produce a wink. And this fancy can be substantiated, for (a) the openings were the exact shape of eyes, this lay beyond argument; (b) in the centre of each was a window resembling a retina; (c) a pigeon, with the thoroughness one recognizes as German, would frequently perch in the window and, glancing this way and that, act the part of a pupil. The pigeons sometimes overdid their parts to be sure, for they would perch in pairs and so generate a squint. One recognized the tendency to over-emphasis. But the broad lines of the scheme were admirable, and, watched by these amiable flickering eyes the great square slumbered in the sun. A statue of St John Nepomuck stood in the middle. He is a saint usually confined to bridges and, as if astonished by his surroundings he had gone into baroque. Among the onlookers were two churches and the great Brukenthal palace, once the residence of the governor. The rest were private houses.

Sibiu then turned its square the other way round; that is to say, passing through an archway, one encountered a new and much more dramatic arrangement. Everything proved to be on the summit of a hill, and the buildings began curving and sheltered a vegetable market in their sweep. As I descended and looked back, a fresh factor entered – a church with a spire, which grew the farther one got from it, until its size was stupendous. This was Sibiu from the outsider's point of view, piled up threateningly, and though again I thought of nothing appropriate it strikes me now that when the easterners saw it they must have halted.

The Germans in Transylvania are said to be more German than they are in Germany; the Hungarians there claim to be the original Hungarians; the Roumanians there despise the Roumanians of the Old Kingdom. It is a country of mosaic, not of delicate shadings; the races are splintered and composed in their charming surroundings uneasily. Only in their architecture does one find rest. Buildings that have stood long enough have a tendency to shake off history and become part of the scenery, and though some of the villages round Sibiu are German, and have fortified churches and strongholds where the communal bacon is hung, and others are Roumanian with accessible blue verandahs, they are all mixed up among the same trees and flowers and mud. There is everywhere – at least to my ear – an international undertone, however little we may attend to it in our daily lives. It seems to have no practical significance, but it is a comment that never ceases, and is sounded rather strongly among these hills.

I climbed back into the town. It was now late in the afternoon. All was still tidy and Teuton. The ramparts had been converted into a promenade where a string band played Johann Strauss with a charm and a dignity that our English orchestras have lost for ever. It was night. More miscellaneous music came from the restaurants, the pigeons went to sleep, great eyes looked at one another without winking and looked at the stars. I came across eyes again at Brashov, but they were not elongated, and the windows in the middle of them were bare and square. Indeed, had I not been to Sibiu, I should not have recognized them for eyes. It is a town which I am never likely to forget, partly owing to the kindnesses I received there; and even Browning's Pied Piper (a character of whom I was never fond) gesticulates less tiresomely when he comes out of his tunnel and turns into that statue of St John Nepomuck.

[1932]

India

Iron Horses in India

When the European enters his first Indian railway carriage, he feels himself in a moving palace, so many are the luxuries that surround him. There are sofa-beds, racks, hooks, washing apparatus, electric lights, a white lincrusta ceiling from which electric fans depend, and there are windows of which no Westerner has ever dreamed – shutters to keep out the glare, wire screens to keep out the flies, blue-grey glass to keep out everything. Meals are served on the train, or else the train stops while they can be eaten, gay little time-tables and maps of India hang framed in the embossed wall-paper. Housed in such comfort, might one not travel for ever?

First impressions wear off, and there are few who keep this whole-hearted enthusiasm. For one thing, no place is a palace when filled too full of furniture, and – except at Bombay, where it is not to be done without bribing the ticket inspectors – every passenger brings all his luggage into the carriage. The tourist is the worst sinner in this respect, but an old-fashioned Indian gentleman well on the travel, or a large Eurasian family each with a plant in a pot, can give even the tourist points. A trunk is a trunk, an object of known dimensions, but what of a bundle of bedding which, when undone, swells to twice its previous size and cannot be done up again? Or who can cope with a round little brass vase which turns over at a jolt of the train and deluges the floor with water? Or with fourteen rolling melons? All day and all night the luggage piles up, and the journey that began in a palace is apt to end in a box-room.

Nor do the appliances always work. The windows jam, the tap sends an empty sigh instead of water into the washing-basin, and the sofas grow strangely rigid when one tries to sleep on them. There are usually four – two each side of the compartment, running parallel to the windows, and two above these, which are unhooked at will from the wall. It is a choice between evils. The lower sofas are easier to get into, but the upper are less easy to fall out of, because the chains that secure them to the ceiling also secure one's prostrate form from jolting over the edge. The lower are out of reach of the electric light, while the upper can't open the windows. In the lower, people may wake you through sitting on you by mistake, but if you are in the upper they may, equally by mistake, remove your luggage without waking you at all. It is difficult; but in no case should one choose the fifth sofa that is provided in some second class carriages, midway between the lower two, and that combines all the evils of upper and lower – away from the lights and the windows and the racks, short, insecure, exposed to every avalanche of luggage and inrush of dust.

There is furthermore the trial of unpunctuality. One must censure lightly here: no Indian train rivals the South Eastern. But it is unpunctual, and in a way peculiarly its own. It starts up to time, and is generally up to time at the terminus. But between whiles all sorts of things happen. Sometimes it is detained by matters of State: the local rajah who was going to join it has not turned up, and it waits half-an-hour for him; or an important sahib is talking to another sahib on the platform: he doesn't see why he should be punctual when the rajah wasn't, and the train waits for him too. Or passengers forget to get in, or those who are in forget to get out, and the train stops again while they alight screaming; or it stops for social reasons, so that the guard may chat with his friends, or the engine driver wash his face in the fountain. Later and later it gets, missing all the connections at wayside junctions. What does it care? It will arrive at its terminus punctually. When three-quarters of its course are over, it leaps forward, heedless of sharp curves or of monkeys and pariah dogs sitting on the lines; heedless of passengers who are trying to sleep inside. On it rushes, dashing down hill in the dawn, and the Company note with pleasure in their Way Book that the Ujjain-Bhopal Mixed was again up to time.

There are four classes in the Indian Railways. First class

passengers are usually Europeans: Indians who travel first generally engaging a special carriage. The second class is patronized by both Europeans and Indians, and it is here that occur the 'unpleasantnesses' of which one hears so much, and which are, happily, so infrequent. Much has been written on this subject; but it has been written round a few cases and worked up by the Press; as a rule the two races travel together in a harmony which it requires fools on both sides to disturb.

Between second and third classes comes the 'intermediate', frequented by Eurasians, and only attached to a few trains.

The backbone of the railway system in India, as in England, is the third class. It is the only class that pays: first is run at a loss. Since first class fares are double second, and six or eight times as much as third, it may be surmised that the third class traffic, to pay, must be enormous. And it is. The waiting room – a large open shed – is packed before the arrival of every train. The door is unlocked, out the passengers rush, their luggage on their heads and their babies on their hips, and they storm into the long carriages, which are full already; sometimes they are repulsed: the compartment can hold no more. The train goes on without them, every window gesticulating. After a few laments they go back to the shed to wait for the next.

It was said that the Indian would not travel; that he was timid, conservative, and that he would be defiled by associating with passengers of lower caste. But caste, in some ways so stubborn, is pliable in others, and timidity has yielded to the desire for excitement and a little fun. When a certain branch line in the United Provinces was being constructed, it was at first possible to procure labour without paying any wages at all; the coolies were carried up free in trucks to the rail-head, and this contented them. They worked all day, were carried back to their villages in the evening and recounted their treat to relatives round the fire all night. Even now this enthusiasm survives; the third class carriage, though crowded, is happy; the passengers are as happy as if they were in a museum; families walk through them hand in hand, not looking at anything in particular, but pleased with the atmosphere of wonders that surrounds them. And a train is even more wonderful than a museum, because it moves.

Some observers declare that in the end the Railway system will break down caste. It is true that the Hindu often relaxes a little; he should buy all his food at a special refreshment room – such as is provided at some stations – but he is inclined to consider that fried sweets are not really food and may on a journey be bought anywhere, and that a bottle of soda water may be quickly quaffed without grievous sin. All the same, it may be argued that the Railways will do more for Hinduism than they will against it. They have greatly increased the popularity of the religious fairs. Formerly pilgrims walked to the holy places, or even measured their length along the roads. Now they go in the comparative comfort of a cattle truck, and their numbers grow yearly. Of the two and a half million souls who converged on Allahabad for the bathing fair of 1912, nearly all must have come by train. What are bottles of soda water compared to this?

And as the Indian train goes forward, traversing an immense monotony and bearing every variety of class, race and creed within its sun-baked walls, it may serve as a symbol of India herself. She jolts and jars and puts the brake on, but, roused from her ancient stillness by science, she does move, and though one must not press the simile – (for the train arrives ultimately, whereas India has not arrived so far nor even learnt the name of her destination) – there is nevertheless truth in it. The first class – white skinned and aloof – the second and intermediate where the two races mingle – the third class many-coloured, brightly-clothed, and innumerable as the sand – the train has brought them together after so many centuries and is dragging them towards one goal. Palace and box-room and truck have this in common: they do move.

[1913]

The Gods of India

Religion, in Protestant England, is mainly concerned with conduct. It is an ethical code – a code with a divine sanction it is true, but applicable to daily life. We are to love our brother, whom we can see. We are to hurt no one, by word, or deed. We are to be pitiful, pure minded, honest in our business, reliable, tolerant, brave. These precepts are not incidental. They lie at the heart of the Protestant faith, and no accuracy in theology is held to excuse any neglect of them. The man, however orthodox, whose life is bad, is described by his fellows as 'not really a religious man', as 'a hypocrite by whom God at all events will not be deceived'.

The code is so spiritual and lofty, and contains such frequent references to the Unseen, that few of its adherents realize it only expresses half of the religious idea. The other half is expressed in the creed of the Hindus. The Hindu is concerned not with conduct, but with vision. To realize what God is seems more important than to do what God wants. He has a constant sense of the unseen – of the powers around if he is a peasant, of the power behind if he is a philosopher, and he feels that this tangible world, with its chatter of right and wrong, subserves the intangible. He can point to a Heaven where virtue is rewarded, and to a Hell where vice is punished, but he points without enthusiasm; to realize or not to realize, that is the question that interests him. Hinduism can pull itself to supply the human demand for Morality just as Protestantism at a pinch can meet the human desire for the infinite and the incomprehensible. But the effort is in neither case congenial. Left to itself each lapses – the one into mysticism, the other into ethics.

If the above distinction be correct, it will follow that the two creeds can never hope to understand one another, and certainly that is the impression one gets from Mr Martin's book. His subject is Indian mythology, and he handles it well; no better guide for the beginner could be imagined; in turn he surveys Vedic, Puranic, and local deities, quoting freely from sacred books and modern authorities, and illustrating his remarks by photographs. But, naturally enough, he comments. Being a missionary he could scarcely do otherwise, and though anxious to be fair to 'the gods and goddesses', his comments are naturally scathing. Deity after deity is summoned before the tribunal of Wesleyanism, and dismissed with no uncertain voice. Krishna stole butter as a baby, and worse later. Jagganath is a goggle-eyed log. Brahma 'has an unenviable moral record', and his head was once cut off by the thumbnail of Siva's left hand. 'What a scene is this for the wonder of the world!' Mr Martin cries. Some goddesses are Satanic, like Kali, others corrupt, like Radha. And as are the deities, so are some of their followers: lustful, cruel.

Is this the Hindu religion? Is it really this trayful of naughty dolls? Well, in a sense it is. One can dispute isolated points with Mr Martin. His wholesale condemnation of Krishna worship (p.142) is surely monstrous. His quotation from Lyall (p.311) has been wrested to bear false witness. But, details apart, he makes his case: Hinduism is not what he can regard as 'really religion', and his hatred of it is inevitable. Good and evil are blurred. The benevolent wife of Siva assumes, as Durga, the name of the demon she conquers, and, as Kali, his attributes. Demons, by their holiness and austerities, can acquire power over the gods, and are only kept out of heaven by a trick. Sex is worshipped – symbolically in Saivism and actually in some Sakti-rites. The divine is so confounded with the earthly that anyone or anything is part of God. In this chaos, where shall a man find guidance? What promise does he receive?

Guidance there is, but not towards a goal that has ever seemed important to the Westerner. And the promise is not that a man shall see God, but that he shall be God. He is God already, but imperfectly grasps the mystery. He will realize the universe as soon as he realizes himself, and pity, courage, reliability, &c., may help him or may hinder him in his quest; it depends. The deities may help him, or they may mislead, like the shows of earth; it depends, depends on the step he has taken just before.

> Is that God or a King that comes?
>   Both are evil, and both are strong;
> With women and worshipping, dancing and drums,
>   Carry your Gods and your Kings along.
>
> When shall these phantoms flicker away
>   Like the smoke of the guns on the wind-swept hill,
> Like the sounds and colours of yesterday,
>   And the soul have rest and the air be still?

For outside the 'trayful of dolls' are the hands that hold the tray, and occasionally tilt it and present the worshipper with emptiness. Krishna and Siva slither into the void. Nothing is more remarkable than the way in which Hinduism will suddenly dethrone its highest conceptions, nor is anything more natural, because it is athirst for the inconceivable. Whatever can be stated must be temporary. 'The gods and goddesses,' writes Mr Martin, 'are largely self-condemned,' and so, in a very profound sense, they are. They are steps towards the eternal. To a Protestant, such an arrangement seems scandalous, and since Mr Martin has misapplied Lyall, one may perhaps apply him. 'It is idle,' he writes, 'to think of ingrafting the rigid and simple faith of the Saxons upon the Hindus.'

The present reviewer has been reminded of a picture that a Holy Man once explained to him at Benares. It showed the human frame, strangely partitioned. God was in the brain, the heart was a folded flower. Yoga unfolded the flower, and then the soul could set out on its quest of God. Two roads lay open to it. It could either proceed directly, by the spinal cord, or indirectly through one of the Hindu deities who were dispersed about the body. When asked which road was the best, the Holy Man replied 'That by the spinal cord is quicker, but those who take it see nothing, hear nothing, feel nothing of the world. Whereas those who proceed through some deity can profit by—' he pointed to the river, the temples, the sky, and added, 'That is why I worship Siva.' But Siva was not the goal.

[1914]

E. O. Martin, *The Gods of India*

The Temple

'Ought we not to start? The elephants must be waiting.'

'There is no necessity. Elephants sometimes wait four hours.'

'But the Temple is far.'

'Oh no, there are thirty of them.'

'Thirty temples! Are they far?'

'No, no, no, not at all – fifteen really, but much jungle; fifteen to come and fifteen to go.'

'Fifteen of what?'

'Fifteen all.'

After such preparations, and in such a spirit, the Temple used to be attacked; and came off victorious. Whether it was one or fifteen or thirty, or thirty miles off, or thirty miles of temples, was never proved, because the elephant misunderstood, or plans changed, or tiffin was too delicious. Evening fell, and the pale blue dome of the sky was corniced with purple where it touched the trees. 'It will now be too late for the Temple.' So it keeps its secret in some stony gorge or field of tough grass, or, more triumphant still, in the land beyond either, where a mile and an elephant are identical and everything is nothing.

There are signs, however, that the elusive building has been brought to book at last. English parish churches and American wooden houses have been classified and obliged to state where they are and when they were built. Why should the Temple be exempt? Anglo-Indian officials, such as will stand no nonsense, have penetrated the jungle and demanded plain answers to plain questions; and reluctantly, and giving all the trouble they can, the Temples have replied. Prevarication is useless. It is no use saying: 'I am a temple no longer. No man, not even a god, has visited me for a thousand million years.' Once a temple, always a temple; and in any case the statement is unhistorical. Pointing with his switch, the official mutters: 'Clear away those custard apples so that we can have a look at the beastly thing . . . seventeenth-century Vaishnavite! Exactly. And I was told it was Jain. . . . And look here: the women are not to pat cow-dung on it. If they do they'll get fined.' He rides on, and the Temple is cleaned up, and is photographed, looking sulky and spruce, and information such as the following is collected:

> To the north of Navilkuriki is a fine *mastikal* containing figures of husband and wife, the latter holding a mirror in the left hand and a lime between the thumb and forefinger of the right hand. In some cases flames are shown as issuing from the head of the female figure, and the couple are represented as dancing as an indication of their joy after coming together in Heaven. A well executed *mastikal* was also found in Nanjappa's back yard. The bottom panel has a standing couple, the female figure holding a mirror in the left hand and a lime between the thumb and forefinger of the right hand. On both sides of the couple is a female figure on horseback holding a mirror and a lime.

And so on until myriads of monuments thoughout the peninsula have uttered their little secrets. Some there are – perhaps the majority – who can speak no more except with the general voice of the earth. They have become dust again, or a pathway, or new temples. From others sanctity has ebbed; outwardly perfect, they have been deserted through some weariness or terror that they inspired. Others are dying; a priest still plays with a few holy toys on the floor, but above him are darkness and whirling bats. A few are alive and bang gongs, which grieve the missionaries and irritate the Club ('There's that Temple again at its puja – something up if one only knew it'). And over all of them archaeology now presides – Pallas Athene, as patient and as dignified as ever, yet somehow not looking her best. It is difficult to say what is amiss with our goddess. Perhaps she has encountered one of the Indian deities – Krishna, for instance – and they did not get on. At all events, as one reads these Reports, one does miss the high consecrated fervour that inspires similar publications about Egypt and Greece. The Anglo-Indian officials seem to set their teeth and get through the mirrors and limes in Nanjappa's back yard as quick as they can. It's a job that's got to be done, like any other job. And their Indian collaborators, though more leisurely, have likewise the air of pursuing a profession instead of a passion.

One ought perhaps to except Mr Narasimhachar, Director of Archaeology for the State of Mysore. His Report – which is much more interesting than either of those that come from British India – is lightened by flashes of enthusiasm. He describes terrible climbs and tremendous views, and alludes to an inscription about 'A European lady named Ellen', who died of cholera in 1846 in Sira, and to a Fakir who did penance until he became an ant-hill. But the other writers, even when they are describing buildings as interesting as the Buddhist monasteries at Nalanda and the Jain temples in the Deogarh Fort, work doggedly and almost unsympathetically. One can scarcely blame them for this, for, as already indicated, the general deportment of the Temple is odious. It is unaccommodating, it rejects every human grace, its jokes are ill-bred, its fair ladies are fat, it ministers neither to the sense of beauty nor to the sense of time, and it is discontented with its own material. No one could love such a building. Yet no one can forget it. It remains in the mind when fairer types have faded, and sometimes seems to be the only type that has any significance. When we tire of being pleased and of being improved, and of the other gymnastics of the West, and care, or think we care, for Truth alone; then the Indian Temple exerts its power, and beckons down absurd or detestable vistas to an exit unknown to the Parthenon. We say 'Here is truth,' and as soon as we have said the words the exit – if it was one – closes, and we fly back to our old habits again. So must it have been in the case of the Curator of the Muttra Museum, who fled from his exhibits to assist the Great War. He did not go in person, but he sent a grand total of over 100 recruits, and the Assistant Recruiting Officer wrote to him in consequence. The letter is quoted. It thanks the Curator for 'any your cheerful optimistic vieds' – mysterious praise of which we can only be sure that it implies a reaction from transcendentalism – a reaction which, in other forms, comes out clearly enough in most pages of these Reports.

At the end of each Report is a long list of photographs for sale. But is one allowed to buy them? The question is less idle than it sounds. Some years ago the present reviewer was in India and tried to buy photographs. Down many a jungle path he tracked them, but in vain, and only after several weeks was the appropriate Anglo-Indian official found and a meeting arranged by a mutual friend. 'Yes,' said the official bleakly. 'The negatives are certainly there. But it is scarcely the Government of India's business to cater for the stray globe-trotter.' It was rather rude of him, but it was something else besides: he was expressing, though unintentionally, the wishes of the Temple itself. What does it matter if everything is known provided nobody knows it? The Temple has never resented the omniscience of God. An infinite number of negatives locked up for eternity in a box belonging to the Government of India – the conception appeals to the religious sense, it renders even archaeology bearable, and it is significant that this particular Anglo-Indian should still figure as a prominent official in one of the publications under review – there is no occasion to specify in which.

[1919]

Annual Reports: Hindu and Buddhist Monuments; Northern Circle: Archaeological Survey, Eastern Circle, Mysore Archaeological Department

Jehovah, Buddha and the Greeks

It is unlikely that Jehovah and Buddha have ever met, too diverse are their habits. Not even their common interest in law approximates them, because to one of them Law means a Table, and to the other it means a Wheel. The utmost we can say is that once they experienced the same event, and that their reactions to it are interesting. The event was the invasion of Alexander the Great. Those who kept the Ten Commandments and those who followed the Eightfold Path became abruptly and simultaneously aware of that energetic young man. His active mind and still more active body hurried over the ancient world, flattening out its prejudices and boundaries before it had time to exclaim, 'What's this?' and leaving some considerable hollows into which, after his departure, new influences began to trickle. Three hundred curious years ensued. A little troupe of gods, moderate in size and human in shape, advanced inland and confronted the Asiatic deities, and carried with it such portable luggage as the plays of Euripides and the Socratic method. The feelings of Jehovah, when the troupe ascended his Holy Hill, are notorious; we may read in Maccabees how he prohibited all gymnastic exercises in Jerusalem, and refused to bind his brows with Bacchic ivy. The feelings of Buddha are uncertain; but we may see in the Gandhara sculptures that he has permitted classical motives to engarland his legends and to drape his own person, and we may draw our conclusions. Anger on the one side, benign indifference on the other: such apparently were the attitudes of the two living religions of the day when Greece impinged upon them.

To say that Jehovah was an-angered is, however, to state

the situation too simply. The Jewish people were at this time in a complicated position. They were disappearing into the Gentile world, and while the parent stock in Palestine remained orthodox, the Dispersal adopted the Greek speech and dallied with Greek thought. At Alexandria an important Graeco-Judaean civilization sprang up, which produced the monumental translation of the Septuagint, the beautiful poem of The Wisdom of Solomon, and the interesting philosophic system of Philo. The Jews who remained in Palestine produced nothing as notable, and partly for this reason posterity has censured them. Mr Norman Bentwich (he is a prominent Zionist) takes a different view; in his judgement the Jews of Alexandria and elsewhere were entering upon a dangerous path, and the authentic voice of Jehovah continued to peal from Mount Moriah as formerly. He supports his view with learning and moderation, and by two main arguments. In the first place (he says) Greek culture was by now on the decline; it had degenerated into a 'confused amalgam with a low moral standard, declining intellectual grasp and vague cosmopolitan professions', and had, therefore, little to offer that was good. And in the second place the temper of the age was opposed to monotheism and to the reasonable worship and contemplation of God; it yearned for redemption, expiation, atonement, aeons, emanations, logoi; once admitted into the Holy of Holies, it played the traitor and opened the doors to a thousand extravagances, and in particular to Christianity. The Palestinian Jews, he would have us note, remained on their guard.

The Rabbis instinctively recognized a canker in this medley . . . It was not Pharisaic narrowness on their part, but a clear intuition of the essence of Judaism and of the overpowering necessity of preserving its outlook uncontaminated, which led them to set up fences against foreign incursion. They were opposed not to freedom of thought, but to free play for demoralizing influences; and if their attitude was one-sided at the moment, one-sidedness was necessary to sanity.

But who is to decide when an influence is demoralizing? It is at this point that the average Gentile must part company with Mr Bentwich and must note that beneath his moderate words the weapons of intolerance may lie concealed. One-sidedness always is necessary at the moment; it is always today rather than tomorrow that we have felt it our duty to be unreasonable, as the inquisitions and censorships testify throughout history. The point is important, for Mr Bentwich's book, though it does not allude to present events in Palestine, has a close bearing on them. It is Zionism at its best, but that best seems not quite good enough for the future peace of the world. One does not wish to see Jehovah re-established on Mount Moriah and gradually subjecting beneath his yoke the Jews of the Dispersal – those very Jews who have done so much for civilization during the last two thousand years. Jehovah would never have allowed Philo to speculate, nor Spinoza, nor Einstein; it would never have been the moment. The Rabbis would instinctively have recognized a canker, as they recognized it in Christ, and have taken action accordingly. In other ways Mr Bentwich is a sound guide who gives a vivid account of the contests and compromises of a fascinating time. His estimate of Hellenistic culture is on the whole just, though he forgets its science: one cannot speak of the 'declining intellectual grasp' of an age which measured the earth and invented conic sections. And his account of the Palestinian traditions should be carefully studied, for he has made the subject his own. The upshot is that the Greeks, in their subtle advance against Jehovah, met with general success and one rebuff. They enforced their language and much of their culture upon the Jews of the Dispersal, but recoiled, as did their inheritors the Romans, from the uplands of Palestine.

Now let us see how they fared further East, in the other citadel of religious vitality, in India.

The problem here is more obscure, for there is no literature. The Indian genius, never historical, produced not even a Josephus to record the collision of ideals, and we are thrown back on archaeology. A number of objects have been unearthed, from Afghanistan southward to the Jumna, which show Greek influence and are sometimes Greek in effect. To select from the examples given by Mr Bannerjee: a coin with a nautch girl on the reverse, but a Greek costume; representations of Pallas Athene and Ganymede. It is clear that the successors of Alexander the Great were playing the same game in the Punjab as in the Levant, and were fostering a Graeco-Buddhist civilization, contemporary with the Graeco-Jewish civilization of Alexandria. Did they encounter a similar opposition? Apparently not. It is priests who sharpen the edges of our souls, and the priestly period had not yet begun for India. There is so far nothing corresponding to the Palestinian rabbi, with his instinctive recognition of cankers. Buddha, already on friendly terms with the Hindu Pantheon, could behave with perfect politeness to the new troupe from Greece. Pessimistic, and inclined to cynicism despite his compassionate heart, he knew that religion is not a reality but a habit of the mind, superior to most habits, but like them to be abandoned before we escape from the Wheel – to be lived down, in fact, although the process may extend over a thousand of our lives. Whether men gained good or evil from gymnastic exercises would depend on their own predispositions; it could have nothing to do with the origin of gymnasiums. Such was the spirit of India, as powerful as the conscious national spirit of the Jews, as the sequel shows. For in a few generations the Hellenic influences died out, not through persecution, but because their day was ended. Poseidon becomes Siva on the coins, Artemis a wild Apsara, and the Greek types of Gandhara are lost in the sculptured jungles of Amaravati. There is a break in Indian records about 400 AD, when a mediaeval darkness descends. But before that break come the Greeks and their ideals have disappeared.

In modern times this episode has produced a controversy. Some critics have declared that Alexander the Great is the true begetter of Indian civilization, and that Indian art in particular could never have arisen without the assistance of Europe. A shallow and impudent theory; it is now discredited, and we are in more danger from the critics of the opposing school, who assert that Greek influence, so far as it existed, is bad, and that all Graeco-Buddhist statues are inartistic and mechanical. Mr Bannerjee, in his excellent book, goes carefully into the question. He is a patriot, but he also cares to get at the truth, and his verdict is that the influence of Greece in India, though slight, was stimulating, and revived parts of an organism which were lying dormant or tending to decay. He does not indulge in rhetoric or generalities; the verdict is built up from considered cases, and we feel at the end that though he has not the mental push of Mr Bentwich, he has more of the Historical spirit.

The passage of time has almost expelled both Jehovah and Buddha from their holy places; almost, but not quite – the parallel is curious here. The glory is gone from Mount Moriah, but the rock where Abraham offered Isaac remains, and the Dome of the Rock covers it, a provocative extinguisher, which Zionists would probably remove. The glory is also gone from Boddh-Gaya, where Buddha obtained enlightenment, but a small temple exists, where he is adored by favour of the British Government in a half-hearted fashion. Boddh-Gaya is a sunken area; standing on its edge, one looks down on a tangle of paths and votive bells. No Indians worship there, for Buddhism has died out of India, in accordance with its own law. But pilgrims from Thibet sometimes light lamps so that the floor of the temple looks like a lake of fire and streams of hot air agitate the dirty banners above the image. Behind the temple is a neglected tree, descendant of the Bo tree where Buddha sat and struggled with evil until 'the different regions of the sky grew clear, the moon shone forth, showers of flowers fell down from the sky upon the earth, and the night gleamed like a spotless maiden.' Where are those flowers? 'Rams and righteousness!' thunders Jehovah. Where is that righteousness? 'Nothing in excess,' murmured Athene to them both, and disappeared more completely than either .... And amid the contradictory echoes humanity moves forward, stumbling and jibbing upon its own painful road, and obstinately refusing to accept salvation.

[1920]

Norman Bentwich, *Hellenism*
Gauranga Nath Bannerjee, *Hellenism in Ancient India*

Missionaries

The Missionary enterprise of the nineteenth century still awaits its impartial historian. Heroism and trivialities, martyrdoms and raffles, breadth and narrow-mindedness, alliance with and protests against the economic exploitation of the natives: what a tangle! The hour for an examination is approaching, perhaps, for there is no doubt that the era of Missionary expansion draws to a close. Missions in England began with the industrial revolution. Thanks to the development of machinery, a pious and leisured middle class came into existence who, mindful of the Gospel injunction, prepared to evangelize the heathen. There had been missionaries before their day, but they had been isolated idealists like St Francis, or had held the sword of the State like Cortes and Pizarro. Middle-class Englishmen shunned either alternative. They did not want to be murdered nor to murder, but to convert, and being business men, they knew that nothing can be done without money. Subscription lists swelled; and in particular did elderly and childless women find comfort in the movement and would sometimes leave it all their wealth. Much unselfishness and heroism went to the growth of Missions, but they also met a home need. There was surplus money in England, seeking a sentimental outlet. Some societies would have endowed art and literature with the surplus: our middle class spent theirs in trying to alter the opinions and habits of people whom they had not seen.

But the surplus could not exist for ever. The industrial revolution, which created it, also created the abyss that has swallowed it up. The factories, as the century progressed, produced more and more guns and ammunition. The Gospel of Peace was preached to all nations, but the countries that preached it most meanwhile perfected the sinews of war. In 1914 there was an explosion at the heart of Christendom whose effects are incalculable; but among them we may predict the decay of foreign Missions. It is not only that the heathen have shown themselves puzzled and cynical, so that Chinese who have served in France raise eyebrows when cargoes of Bibles arrive in China. It is that there is less money to pay for the Bibles. Missions must mainly depend on private enterprise. No Imperial Government dare subsidize them in its own territories, or it risks a religious mutiny. And private enterprise, taxed without, and ravaged by agnosticism within, grows less and less inclined to foot the bill.

When we pass from the subscribers to their agents, we enter a finer country. Missionaries have their faults (Mr Tyndale-Biscoe's incredible little book will exhibit them), and there are bad missionaries. But for the most part they are Christians of integrity, and fine fellows, too, who try not merely to alter the heathen, but to understand him. It is the missionary rather than the Government official who is in touch with native opinion. The official need only learn how people can be governed. The missionary, since he wants to alter them, must learn what they are. He often seems to be, and sometimes he is, the ideal student of human nature, passionate after facts, and moving through analysis towards sympathy. (We shall find such a missionary in Mr Pollard.) He has largely abandoned 'direct preaching', and tries to win converts by showing Christ in his life. Having gained a man's affection and helped him materially, he will say in effect: 'You like me, and I have done things for you that your countrymen have not done. Christ is the cause of my character and conduct: will you too not declare for Christ, since you appreciate His gifts?' A conversion of this type is a very secure one, since it is based on friendship and trust, and the missionary may legitimately rejoice.

Yet some natives are obdurate even here. They suspect, and not without reason, a spiritual flaw. Why should an Englishman sail all these miles to be kind to someone whom he'd never heard of? Could he find no one to be kind to at home? Their attitude is well put by a missionary who writes from Tripoli, and whom Mr Gairdner quotes:

> It is difficult to love a Moslem, because he is not very loveable, and also because he usually resents a too near approach to him until in some way his confidence has been won. When acts of kindness and love are done to him he is sure to suspect that I am doing it, not for his sake and because of simple disinterested love, but for some reason of self-interest known perhaps only to myself . . . At best I am doing it in order to win him from Mohammed to Jesus Christ, and even this is perceived to be an interested motive.

The suspicion is merited because sooner or later the plea for Christianity will be made. The acts of kindness are not really disinterested, though the missionary may pretend to himself that they are. He may not perform them in order to convert, but having performed them he will find conversion easier, and of this he will take full advantage. He will in the long run try to alter the other man's opinions – and indeed it is to do this that he is paid by the old ladies at home. Disinterested love is the finest thing in the world, but it does not act thus; it does not cause one to accept a ticket to Tripoli on the chance of some unknown Tripolitan needing one's help. Only the love of propaganda can do this, and the new type of missionary is here less frank than his predecessor who stepped ashore Bible in hand. Among primitive faiths he will have greater success, but he will fail even more completely against a fully-developed and conscious creed. The Moslem, like everyone else, can appreciate disinterested love, but he must be assured that his friend does not by a mental reservation identify that love with the cause of Christ, and, of course, the missionary does and must identify the two; it is the central mystery of his faith, and the doctrine of the Redemption rests on it.

These are the burrowings of psychology. On the surface are beneficent schools and hospitals, work in the zenanas, etc., a various and varying interference with the habits of Oriental peoples, particularly with their sexual habits, an occasional alliance with economic Imperialism (as in Uganda in 1892), and an occasional protest against the same (such as was made by the Bishop of Zanzibar a few weeks ago). To add up all these activities into 'bad' or 'good' will be the historian's task; all that one can say now is that they are European in origin, and financed by a class of people whose incomes are decreasing. Of the four writers under review, Mr Pollard assuredly did 'good' to the tribes of Western China, for he has the most charming and sympathetic personality; Mr Gairdner and Miss Burton, tactful, well-informed and devoted, should do good rather than harm; while Mr Tyndale-Biscoe gives us his own assurance that he has done good and nothing but good, and the assurance of Sir Robert Baden-Powell that he 'has succeeded in the delicate operation of strengthening the moral backbone of large numbers of boys in Kashmir.' But could any of the four – even Mr Pollard – have executed their mission twenty years later? They come at the end of an epoch, when the industrial West is still able to subsidize its religions and the agricultural East still willing to accept them. There will always be missionaries so long as there is Faith, but, in the future, they will tend to be isolated enthusiasts, like St Francis and Raymond Lulli in the past.

It is in the missions to the Jews and to the Mohammedans that the retreat will first be sounded, for here are the most intractable fields. Islam (with which Mr Gairdner's convenient manual deals) never responded, and, except to the eye of faith, the thousands of pounds here spent by provincial England seem utterly to have been lost. As Mr Gairdner says: 'When Islam once takes hold it becomes almost impossible, humanly speaking, to dislodge it,' and though his book ends on a clarion note, he relies on exclamation marks and capital letters rather than on argument. Why, indeed, should a Mohammedan turn Christian? He cannot be persuaded logically to exchange his one God for a God who is both one and three: the doctrine of the Trinity (though Mr Gairdner does not mention it) is a permanent stumbling-block. And his difficulties are more than philosophic. The central mysteries of Christianity are actively repulsive to him. It is a question of emotion, almost of taste. Take a text that seems so beautiful, not only to Christians, but to all who have grown up in Christian surroundings: 'For God so loved the world that he gave his only begotten Son.' This text will give three separate shocks to an orthodox Moslem, so alien to his sentiments is it that God should love a world, that he should be a Father, and that he should allow his Son to die. The door that sometimes swings open between Christianity and Hinduism gives no entrance into Islam, and in the race for Africa Islam has indeed beaten Christianity.

No such problems need trouble Mr Pollard among the Nosu, a wild tribe on the upper waters of the Yang-tse. He did, it is true, sing them a hymn in Chinese on arrival, but they did not understand Chinese, and when the hymn was translated into Nosu they laughed, and Mr Pollard seems to have laughed also. He calls himself a 'pioneer', and perhaps this is what a missionary should always be, free to indulge his noble and tender impulses, but exempted from connecting them with theology. Such impulses, when interwoven with romance, make a most attractive book, and *In Unknown China* can be warmly recommended to all classes of readers. It is full of splendid descriptions of scenery and customs. Here and there it rises to heroic level. The story of the glorious young chief who sickens of leprosy and kills himself shows that Mr Pollard can soar far above the humorous sympathy where most of his confrères stick; he is capable of unabashed reverence, he can move to tears. The Nosu loved him, and no wonder. They offered him a wife, an agreeable girl who wore coral beads. We know that he did not marry her because he says he did not, and missionaries always tell the truth; but he has certainly left his heart among those savage hills, and the heart of many a reader should hasten thither after it. Were one discussing travel-books and not mission-books, one would be able to speak at greater length of this charming writer, and of the wild and lovely world that he reveals.

But now it is time, yea, it is high time, to turn to the Rev. C. E. Tyndale-Biscoe, M.A., headmaster of the C.M.S. School at Srinagar, and to the deeds for the Empire and Christianity that he has wrought in that city. There is no rubbish about sympathy now. Take the Kashmiri by the scruff of his neck; that is the only way you can strengthen his backbone. Kick him about until he has learned Boy Scout methods. Srinagar was a cesspool, moral and physical, when Mr Tyndale-Biscoe arrived – Brahmanism and corruption, early marriages, cruelty to animals, nor did the population wash. Not 'boys' were his pupils, but 'jelly-fish': he can only call them 'jelly-fish,' bundles of dirty linen; and he started their education by throwing them into the river Jhelum, then he caned and fined them and bullied them into breaking caste, and mocked their religious observances, also thwarting and insulting their parents whenever an opportunity occurred, for he knew that whatever Indians think right is bound to be wrong, and that the British Raj exists in order that missionaries may drive this home. Two quotations will indicate his spiritual scope:

> If you wish a boy to stay at your school, do not be too kind to him or visit him when he is ill or in trouble (though of course you will do so, notwithstanding, knowing that right will prevail in the end), but be hard on him; and if you have occasion to punish him, then punish him severely, and he will love and follow you like a spaniel:
>
> A wife, a dog, and a walnut tree
> The more you beat them the better they be,
> But truer still of the Kashmiri;

and again:

> God in His love has allowed us to know and accept Christ as our Saviour, and the least we can do is to pass on His knowledge to others.

Mr Biscoe's success in passing on his knowledge is immense. Srinagar totters under his blows: he tells us so, and missionaries always tell the truth, especially when they are schoolmasters. And even if he exaggerated, his book remains valuable, for it indicates the sort of person who is still trotting about in India. The Indian climate has much to answer for, but it can seldom have produced anything quite as odd as *Character Building in Kashmir* – anything quite so noisy, meddlesome and self-righteous, so heartless and brainless, so full of racial and religious 'swank'. What is the aim of such a book? As the Rev. C. E. Tyndale-Biscoe, M.A., himself puts it, 'Qui bono?' And why has the Church Missionary Society published it? For it is bound to create grave prejudices against their other workers in the Foreign Field.

Amid such varied efforts does the labour go forward, the labour of imposing a single religion upon the terrestrial globe. It is an extraordinary ideal, whatever one's personal sympathies, and it will bulk more largely than we realize in our history, when that history comes to be written. To what extent Christians still hope for their universal harvest, it is not easy to say. They think it right not to give up hope, but that is rather different. They can scarcely ignore the double blow that the war has dealt to Missions – cutting off their funds and discrediting the Gospel of Peace at its source. And even if they ignore it, the heathen does not. As an Egyptian remarked to a well-wisher in a moment of exasperation: 'But for what you want to visit my country for? Visit England, Scotland, Ireland first; yes, and Wales.'

[1920]

S. Pollard, *In Unknown China*
W. H. T. Gairdner, *The Rebuke of Islam*
M. E. Burton, *Women Workers of the Orient*
C. E. Tyndale-Biscoe, *Character Building in Kashmir*

Reflections in India

I – Too Late?

Once upon a time an Indian whom I know undertook a railway journey in his own country. He had lain down to sleep when the door of the carriage opened and an Englishman entered and greeted him as follows: 'Here, get out of that!' The greeting was instinctive. The Englishman meant no harm by it. It was the sort of thing one had to say to a native whom one found sprawling in a first-class compartment, or what would happen to the British Raj? 'Do you want your head knocked off?' the Indian retorted. A dust-up seemed imminent, but no, the threat was just what the Englishman understood. He said, 'I say, I'm awfully sorry, I didn't know you were that sort of person,' and they settled down together amicably. Argument, apologies, appeals to the station-master or the courts, would have been useless; the Indian had taken the only possible course, and saved the situation.

Ten years passed and the same man went for another railway journey. It was he who entered the carriage this time, while an Englishman, an officer, was in occupation. The latter sprang up with *empressement* and began to shift his kit. 'Here, take my berth, it's the best; I'm getting out soon.' 'No, why should I?' 'Oh, no, take it, man, that's all right; this is your country, not mine.' The Indian remarked grimly: 'Don't do this sort of thing, please. We don't appreciate it any more than the old sort. We know you have been told you must do it.' The unfortunate officer was silent. It was so. Orders had come down from Headquarters enjoining courtesy, and in his attempt to save the British Raj he had exceeded them.

This hasty and ungraceful change of position is typical of

Anglo-India today. Something like a stampede can be observed. Some officials have changed out of policy; they know that they can no longer trust their superiors to back them up if they are rude or overbearing – even the Collector of B——, whose woes I will presently relate, has probably learnt his lesson by this time. Others have undergone a genuine change of heart. They respect the Indian because he has proved himself a man. They allude to the present crisis less with bitterness than with a wistful melancholy. They dread the reforms, but propose to work them. 'Yes, it's all up with us,' is their attitude. 'Sooner or later the Indians will tell us to go. I hope they'll tell us nicely. I expect they will – they're always very nice to me.' One can't call such an attitude cowardly. It is a recognition, though a muddle-headed one, of past mistakes. The decent Anglo-Indian of today realizes that the great blunder of the past is neither political nor economic nor educational, but social; that he was associated with a system that supported rudeness in railway carriages, and is paying the penalty.

The penalty is inevitable. The mischief has been done, and though friendships between individuals will continue and courtesies between high officials increase, there is little hope now of spontaneous intercourse between the two races. The Indian has taken up a new attitude. Ten or fifteen years ago he would have welcomed attention, not only because the Englishman in India had power, but because the etiquette and customs of the West, his inevitable destiny, were new to him and he needed a sympathetic introducer. He has never been introduced to the West in the social sense, as to a possible friend. We have thrown grammars and neckties at him, and smiled when he put them on wrongly – that is all. For a time he suffered, and it was with shame and resentment that he found himself excluded from our clubs. He was sensitive and affectionate; he had a traditional respect for authority, and longer than was quite dignified he courted us, and we, quick to note servility, smiled at one another again, and remarked that we ought never to have given him education, since it only made him unhappy. Today he has ceased to suffer. He has learnt to put on neckties the right way, or his own way, or whatever one is supposed to do with a necktie. He has painfully woven, without our assistance, a new social fabric, and, as he proceeds with it, he has grown less curious about the texture of ours. The other day, travelling in the districts of a great native State, I reached a remote town which had only 12,000 inhabitants, and was over 80 miles from a railway station. The scenery was magnificent, the antiquities superb – but that is another story; we are concerned with the local club, which had a membership of sixty, and to which the officials and other residents repaired every evening. No Englishman had helped them – none existed – and few of them knew English, but they had provided themselves with the usual appliances – a tennis-court, a billiard-table, cards, chess (which they played in the wrong, or Oriental, fashion, allowing the king to move like a knight); they had taken what they wanted from the West, and were using it instead of being used by it. A club of officials is nowhere a thing of beauty, and this one was architecturally the sole blot on the town. But there it was, created and alive. It proved to those lonely uplands that modern India is socially independent of the Englishman at last, and does not care how Englishmen amuse themselves, nor whether they are amused. The problem has been solved. But at the expense of greater problems elsewhere.

'Oh, but their womenfolk!' That parrot-cry still arises, though less shrilly than formerly. 'My husband says he doesn't see why he should let an Indian see his wife when the Indian won't let him see his wife.' The *purdah* difficulty, a real one, has been seized upon by Anglo-India, and has been emphasized and exaggerated, and even made an excuse for official discourtesy. It is useless to point out that *purdah* in India is not impenetrable, that the Parsis do not observe it, and the Marattas only in modified form; that even Islam moves towards a change. One expected that Englishwomen would be sympathetic; but no: the eyes and voice hardened, and 'My husband says he doesn't see why,' again rent the air. And if one said that one had actually shared in Indian family life, both Mohammedan and Hindu, been motor drives, sat on chairs or the floor as the case might be, the eyes grew incredulous, and the voice changed the conversation as improper. If the Englishman might have helped the Indian socially, how much more might the Englishwoman have helped! But she has done nothing, or worse than nothing. She deserves, as a class, all that the satirists have said about her, for she has instigated the follies of her male when she might have calmed them and set him on the sane course. There has been an English as well as an Indian *purdah*, and it has done greater harm because it was aggressive. Instead of retiring quietly behind the curtain it flaunted itself as a necessity, and proclaimed racial purity across a live wire. Things are better today. There are institutions like the Willingdon Club at Bombay, where men and women of both races can meet. And the lady who said to me eight years ago, 'Never forget that you're superior to every native in India except the Rajas, and they're on an equality,' is now a silent, if not an extinct, species. But she has lived her life, and she has done her work.

This social friction (it is sometimes said) only affects the educated classes, and we need not consider their feelings, since they did not help to win the war and would run away if the Afghans invaded. This argument ignores – among other points – all the uneducated Indians who collide with uneducated Englishmen. There is a great 'Second Society' where the disasters of club-land are enacted in a cruder form, and beneath 'Second Society' lie other strata, all echoing the footfalls from the top. Here is the sepoy, back from France, failing to see why the Tommy should have servants and *punkahs* when he has none. And here is the European chauffeur who drives through the streets shouting at the pedestrians and scattering them; the looks of hatred they cast back at him show how deep the trouble goes. India is not Westernized yet, but she is more closely knit than she used to be, and an impact by the West on one part of her frame is transmitted to others. When the Collector of B—— fined a pleader two hundred rupees for appearing before him in a Gandhi cap, he thought, no doubt, that the matter would stop where it was. He told the pleader to come back again in two hours' time; who did, still wearing the cap, and was fined two hundred more rupees. The pleader appealed; the case was tried locally, by an English Judge, and decided against the Collector; and the population of B——, which had hitherto worn any old thing on its head, at once trotted into Gandhi caps and escorted the Collector with shouts of 'Mahatma Gandhi ki jai' whenever he went out for a ride on his not very good motor-bicycle. The population ought to have weighed the illegality and insolence of the Collector against the fairness of the judge, and to have given the British Raj the benefit of the doubt. But the mind of a mob doesn't work thus. The attack on an educated Indian reacted in thousands of uneducated veins, and swelled the cause of Nationalism.

India today is a chopping sea, and this social question is only one of its currents. There are Mohammedans and Hindus; there is Labour and Capital; there are the native princes and the constitutionalists. Where the sea will break, what wave will uprise, no man can say; perhaps in the immediate future the chief issue will not be racial, after all. But isolating the question, one must say this: firstly, that responsible Englishmen are far politer to Indians now than they were ten years ago, but it is too late because Indians no longer require their social support; and, secondly, that never in history did ill-breeding contribute so much towards the dissolution of an Empire.

[1922]

Reflections in India

II – The Prince's Progress

It is easy to be wise after the event, but in this case nearly everyone was wise before it also. With the exception of the contractors and the extremists, scarcely anyone in India wished the Prince of Wales to come. The Army did not want him, nor did the Civil Service outside Simla, nor did the responsible merchants in Bombay and elsewhere, nor did the Native Rulers, whose finances are scarcely recovering from the visit of his great-uncle, nor did the educated Indians, whether friendly or hostile to the Government, nor did the people. All agreed, whatever their politics or rank, that now is not the time for a solemn and delicate ceremonial, that the existence of the tie between England and India should not be emphasized at the moment it is under revision, that the ancient troubles and complicated sorrows of a continent cannot be soothed by sending a pleasant young man about in railway trains, all handshakes and jollity, and proclaiming in his graver moments that he is 'anxious to learn'. No doubt the Prince is anxious, and no doubt he will learn, but it will be at the expense of other people. While his visit has intensified existing problems, it has also created problems of its own. His safety has to be secured, and the unfortunate Government, afflicted with Moplahs and the Diarchy and other genuine difficulties, has in addition to persuade hundreds of millions of people not to be rude. All this was foreseen, and, though apparently avoidable, has come to pass. Fate did not conceal what was written in her scroll.

Imperial pride and the will of a Viceroy are the agents

through which Fate has worked. It was unseemly to our weavers of Empire that a royal progress should be twice postponed; it would look as if they doubted India's enthusiasm; it would look what it was, in fact. Prestige can only be maintained by pretending it has not been questioned. And this high logic was confirmed by the considered conclusions of Lord Reading. Whom the Viceroy consulted it is difficult to say; I am told, on good authority, that in inviting the Prince he acted against the advice of his provincial Governors, who reported public opinion as everywhere hostile, and in accordance with the assurances of his Indian counsellors, Pandit Malaviya and others, who promised adequate success. Which account, if true, shows how little eminent Indians can know about their own countrymen; but anyhow, it is easier to believe than another account, which says that the Prince has come to India because he wanted to come. A few people argued that he came in order to announce some dramatic boon, such as was conferred by his father at Delhi – an acceptable settlement with Turkey, perhaps; but the Viceroy has pointed out that any such announcement would be unconstitutional, and that we must expect nothing from this visit but the honour of it.

It is in Calcutta that the new trouble started. The Bombay riots, terrible to the victims, did not harm the Government, because they provoked a reaction in the visitor's favour, and placed Mr Gandhi in a difficult position. The reception at Bombay was not bad, and after it the Prince disappeared into the deserts of Rajputana, dining with the Maharajah of Rutlam, staying with the Maharana of Udaipur, who is descended from the sun, &c., all of which is easy and safe. But when he reappeared in British India, at Allahabad, a changed atmosphere awaited him, because, during his tour in the Native States, the Government had taken to repression. The day of his landing (November 17th) had, in Calcutta, been observed as a *Hartal* and as a full-dress rehearsal of the reception intended for him. Eye-witnesses – awed Englishmen – bring amazing accounts. They say that the volunteer organization was perfect, with police and permits complete, and displayed a calm enthusiasm that was very impressive, and an efficiency that could only come from careful preparation. The discovery that Indians can run a great city without European assistance filled the Calcutta merchants with dismay, and they appealed to Lord Ronaldshay. The volunteer organizations were declared illegal, and extensive arrests followed, both in Bengal and elsewhere in British India.

As a result of this firm policy the Prince, when he reached Allahabad, was greeted by five miles of deserted streets, and by scarcely any bunting. He is said to have resented the insult, and if so, it shows how completely he has been secluded from reality, for he ought to have known that such an insult was possible at any moment of the tour. The spirit of self-sacrifice in Indians is often spasmodic and temporary, but while it lasts it is supreme, nothing can stand against it, and at the moment of writing most of the educated population is ready to go to jail. The Moderates are deserting the Government because their protests against the arrests have been ignored. Important Indian officials resign their posts, often under pressure from the zenana. The wife and daughters of a member of the U.P. Government go on hunger-strike, and his withdrawal from public life can only be a matter of hours. A man whose brother has been arrested condoles with the sister-in-law; she, and his own sisters, repulse him indignantly; there is nothing to mourn here, they say, it is those who have not gone to jail who should feel sorrow and shame. Another lady, whose husband expects arrest, tries to learn how to carry on his *Swaraj* work in his absence, although unsympathetic to *Swaraj*, and prefers to remain unguarded, when he leaves her, rather than return to the comfort of her family. These three instances (all with names attached) happened to come to my notice; there must be thousands more, proving that the women as well as the men are desperate. Heroism is common in no country, and few Indians could share, with Mr Gandhi, a martyrdom deliberate, long-drawn, and obscure. But any Government can create heroism by foolish edicts, as Rome found when she directed the Early Christians to worship the Emperor, and the Government of India is finding in consequence of its semi-mystical parade of the Prince of Wales.

Fresh-featured and smiling, the Prince has, of course, certain human assets, and the students of Benares University are said to have been delighted with his appearance, and to have cheered when a turban was put on his head. But it is doubtful whether his jolly, democratic manner, so welcome to our colonies, will suit a land which was once the nursery, and is still the lumber-room, of kings. If royalty is to go down in India it must go down strong. The Prince's *naïf* hesitations, his diffidence, his friendly avowals of ignorance, do not produce the effect intended. Indians wish he was having a nicer time, and could have come privately for some sport; but his royal aspect is not discussed, nor has he revealed it himself in any of his public utterances. What he does or is they do not discuss; they are not interested, because he represents no tradition which they can recognize – not Alamgir's, nor Sivaji's, nor even Queen Victoria's. He belongs to the chatty, handy type of monarch which the West is producing rather against time, and of which the King of the Belgians is the leading example. It is a type that can have no future in India. If it crowned another work, if the subordinate Englishmen in the country had also been *naïf* and genial, if the subalterns and Tommies and European engineers and schoolmasters and policemen and magistrates had likewise taken their stand upon a common humanity instead of the pedestal of race – then the foundation of a democratic empire might have been well and truly laid. But the good-fellowship cannot begin at the top; there it will neither impress the old-fashioned Indian who thinks a Prince should not be a fellow, nor conciliate the Oxford-educated Indian who is excluded from the local Club. It will be interpreted as a device of the Government to gain time, and as an evidence of fear. Until the unimportant Englishmen here condescend to hold out their hands to 'natives', it is waste of money to display the affabilities of the House of Windsor.

By the time these remarks are printed the progress will be nearly over. Mr Gandhi enjoins politeness, but his conception of politeness is not that held by Royalty, who will scarcely be appeased by deserted thoroughfares and closed shops.

Direct protests are unlikely, because the idea of abstention has entered deeply into the Indian mind. On the other hand, the methods of Non-Co-operation pass inevitably into violence; the line between persuasion and compulsion is difficult to draw; and there will be endless obscure tussles between the shopkeepers who have closed and those who want to remain open, tussles in which the authorities glady intervene: 'To protect law-abiding citizens and to enforce order.' The formula and the result are both familiar. It is sad that the pleasure of a young man should be spoilt, but it is sadder that hundreds of other young men should be in prison on account of his visit to their country. What one may call the general Indian trouble exists in any case, and is deeply and complexly rooted in the past. But this particular trouble seems the needless decision of a day, unless indeed we suppose that Fate and not volition rules the Empire, and that a rapid darkening of our stage has been decreed.

[1922]

Woodlanders on Devi

Eighteen years ago, in a palace in India, I read Hardy's *Woodlanders*. The palace was in course of construction. Three sides of the quadrangle were under the Office of Works, the fourth side, which was semi-sacred, was under the Commander-in-Chief. He was a simple, affable officer, who did not trouble himself with his army; indeed how could he, when they had no uniforms? His main duties were social: he drank port with us, he joined in a card-game called Jubbu, sitting on a carpet in the quadrangle while the coolies clanged and the dust fell and the cards were dealt anti-clockwise with the happiest results. He was full of little courtesies, and drove up one evening clasping a live fish in a towel; he hoped it would do for my supper. Rooted in reality, he did not trouble himself with the building; his side of the quadrangle rose but slowly, and never reached the stage of having floors. This did not signify, since it was intended as a memorial to the late Maharajah, rather than for residence; a few workmen hit at it, and contended with the superior hordes of the Office of Works, and saved his honour.

It is impossible to be too intricate on the subject of India, and it would never do to go on to Thomas Hardy without mentioning a third functionary connected with the building operations. His name was 'Eighteen Offices'. Eighteen Offices was bad tempered. He seldom appeared, and was never invited to play cards. He had certain vague rights over the material and the area and at times he would emerge from the city (which lay about a mile behind us), and would shout, lecture, contradict and interfere, kick up the shavings, and point angrily at the puddles of cement. He was understood to be asserting his honour, so the extra confusion he caused was not resented. 'Eighteen Offices has arrived; we can but do little today.' The Commissioner of Works and the Commander-in-Chief disputed with him, and with one another in his presence, but not acrimoniously. All three were drawing salaries, and remembered them.

If I turned from the confusion inside the palace I looked over the palace garden. This too was in course of construction, and caused me much anxiety, for I was in charge of it. It covered acres and acres, and before I arrived some grandiose scheme had been evolved of which I never got the hang. I begged for a plan, a memorandum. None was forthcoming. Ignorant of the language, or rather of both languages – for they talked Mahratti inside the palace and Urdu in the fields – I should have cut a silly figure had cuteness been the order of the day. Four lotus ponds, eighty-three semi-circular flowerbeds, each measuring fifteen feet by seven and a half, nineteen rows of pits for mango trees, lemon-pits, an extension to the Electric House, two colossal terraces and a pergola – which was which, and which ought to be finished first? All one had to go by was dells and dumps. Cows got in, attracted by the stray tufts of vegetation, and I ran about chasing them. Large blocks of masonry lay in the way or in what seemed to be the way. I suggested moving them, but no, they belonged to Eighteen Offices, they had better be left. Expenditure was encouraged, and I bought bags upon bags of flower seeds: the desert should at all events blossom like an annual.

Just as the weather grew hot and the soil cracked, I made a tragic discovery. There was no water. There was plenty of provision for water – abundance of pipes, and a standard tap stood over each semi-circular bed, and everything connected with a raised cistern, a magnificent mass of metal which stood on four legs and dominated the country for miles. But there the sequence ended. The cistern was empty, nor could it ever be filled. The gardeners did their watering from two small wells which dried up in May. I lamented loudly, and went from colleague to colleague, asking for help. All agreed that it was very disheartening; what good to plant trees or sow seeds when they die? Suddenly the Commissioner of Works thought of the solution. 'Oh!' he cried, 'there is the Water that Speaks.' 'The Water that Speaks? What is that?' 'A never quenchless well, ever running. We should have thought of it for your garden before.' Others cried, 'Yes, yes, the Water that Speaks.' As soon as the day cooled we set out to inspect this marvel. It lay in a deep hole on the farther side of the raised chaussée. We scrambled down to it over rubble, warning one another against a huge black snake which was said to live close by. 'It is beautiful water, but I don't see how we can use it for the garden,' I said – all had waited for me to express an opinion. 'The road is in the way for one thing. We can't pump it up in the cistern, and we can't carry it across in skins.' 'No we can't, we can't, it has been a mistake,' agreed the others pleasantly. We returned to the palace in a pensive and friendly mood. They had shown me a kindness, and I had had the sense to see it when shown. I could then just realize – and I always realize it now – that these people were civilized, they were in accord with their surroundings, they were not struggling to adjust themselves against time, like the doomed westerner. I give their untidiness a good mark too. For the last ten years have taught me that tidy streets, spotless railway stations and penalties for rubbish are often the outward signs of clean-ups and cruelty.

So the garden died, as gardens in India do, and just at the same time the building of the palace stopped in all its sections. The coolies trooped off to the Deccan, the Sikhs who were putting up the electric light went back to their firms, leaving wires hanging from the ceiling for the flies, and extra holes in the walls for the squirrels and birds. Economy was the reason: the State had suddenly decided it could afford no more. However, there were plenty of rooms to live in, and much less dust on the move and much more peace, and at last I began to read *The Woodlanders*.

Trees, trees, undergrowth, English trees! How that book rustles with them! I read it looking out over my bumpy burnt-up garden. Beyond the garden, on the farther side of the chaussée, rose Devi, a burnt-up bump of a hill. Devi was sacred, and odd to look at, for it was topped by an outcrop of rock, which tilted jauntily, like a messenger boy's cap. It was brown like the garden, dusty like the palace, but not depressing, not dead. One day, as I raised my eyes to it, the trees I had been reading about transplanted themselves to its slopes and hung for a moment in a film of green. Not a vision, only a literary fancy, but a very pleasing one. The magic of Hardy had projected itself into this leafless spot, and, with no feeling of nostalgia, I saw the beeches and ashes and oaks of Wessex waving. The magic passed, Devi reappeared unclothed. Beneath the outcrop at its summit I could detect the cave which contained an unobtrusive god.

[1939]

The Art and Architecture of India

One hundred and ten years ago, Lord Macaulay made a speech in the House of Commons. Here are some of his remarks:

> The great majority of the population of India consists of idolators, blindly attached to doctrines and rites which are in the highest degree pernicious. The Brahminical religion is so absurd that it necessarily debases every mind which receives it as truth: and with this absurd mythology is bound up an absurd system of physics, an absurd geography, an absurd astronomy. Nor is this form of Paganism more favourable to art than to science. Through the whole Hindu Pantheon you will look in vain for anything resembling those beautiful and majestic forms which stood in the shrines of Ancient Greece. All is hideous and grotesque and ignoble. As this superstition is of all superstitions the most irrational and of all superstitions the most inelegant, so it is of all superstitions the most immoral.

Thus spoke Lord Macaulay, together with much else, in the year 1843. We are now in 1953, and here is a large and learned book about the 'inelegant superstitions' he so forcibly condemned containing no less than 190 plates in which the inelegancies are illustrated, and numerous ground plans and elevations of the idolatrous temples that so roused his ire. It is true that few of the illustrations resemble the shrines of Ancient Greece. He was right there. But it does so happen that Greece and India are different places, seeking different goals, which trifling fact escaped him. Macaulay was a great man, and when a subject was congenial to him he could be sensitive as well as forcible. But he was not good at making the preliminary imaginative jump; he never thought of learning from India, he only thought of improving her, and since Indian art did not strike him as improving, it had to be destroyed.

A good deal of it was destroyed; and the residue was insulted; only in my own lifetime has it been recognized as a precious possession of the whole human race, and its presentation and classification attempted, and aesthetic appreciation accorded to it. Indian art is not easy – one cannot pretend that about it; it seldom appeals right away to the westerner, or else he catches on to it and then falls off it and has to try again: this has been my experience, and here is one of my reasons for being grateful to Professor Rowland of Harvard for his helpful book. I will try to summarize its contents.

The curtain rises over 4,000 years ago. The scene is the valley of the Indus. Here the remains of two great cities have been excavated. Their discovery caused great excitement, but we discovered very little about them. We do not know who planned them or what gods they worshipped. We cannot decipher their script. They seem to have been trading cities connecting on to Mesopotamia and they may have originated the Indian civilization we know. They flourished for over 1,000 years and then vanished. Perhaps they were swallowed up by the sand; perhaps they were destroyed by invaders from the north. We do not know. The curtain falls. Those two cities on the Indus form the prelude to our drama.

The next scene takes place much later, about 400 BC. As the curtain rises again we see that the invaders from the north have established themselves and are practising a religion akin to Hinduism. When it has fully risen we witness the establishment of Buddhism. And now the main drama begins. The connection between Hinduism and Buddhism is complicated. They are not rival sects: nothing so clear-cut as that. They both started in India and you can still see there – I have seen it and have picked a leaf – a descendant of the sacred tree under which Buddha sat when he attained enlightenment. They both taught, or usually taught, that this life is an illusion, and they both sometimes emphasized and sometimes ignored the unity of God. And both of them were entangled in local folklore. You cannot draw any definite line between Buddhism and Hinduism. Their real point of issue is social: they took up different attitudes towards the caste-system. Buddhism condemned caste and consequently is exported easily and became a missionary religion abroad. Hinduism was rooted in caste, and it tended to stay at home.

Professor Rowland is enthusiastic about Buddhism, and much of his book – almost a quarter of it – is occupied in following Buddhist exports outside India. He follows them north to Afghanistan and Turkestan, eastward to Nepal, southward to Ceylon and Java, Burma and Siam. My own interests are passionately Indian so I shall confine myself more strictly than he does to the Indian sub-continent.

Buddhism, I was saying, developed there about 400 years before Christ, when Ancient Greece was powerful. In time it produced two schools of art – one of them was the Graeco-Indian or Roman-Indian school up by the northern frontier, the other was a native Indian school further south, on the banks of the Ganges. The two sprang up under the same dynasty. The northern school used to be greatly praised by critics, especially by those who inherited Lord Macaulay's attitude, and felt that Indian art which had been influenced by Greece or Rome would not be as bad as art which was merely Indian. That was the attitude of Kipling; he gives a charming account of the statues which Kim saw in the Wonder House at Lahore: they were Graeco-Indian statues and I am not decrying them. But the southern stuff, the art which developed by the banks of the Ganges, is preferred by more detached critics, and Professor Rowland gives good reasons for the preference. Some of it is in London; you will find on the main staircase of the British Museum reliefs from a great Buddhist shrine.

Now drop the curtain again: I am sorry to keep on with this curtain but I cannot manage without it: it helps to arrest the sense of flux which paralyses us when we contemplate through so many centuries a civilization that is always flowing: it imposes upon India the semblance of form. Drop the curtain again, then, and raise it about the year AD 400: about the time when the Roman Empire is falling to pieces. What do you see now? You see Indian art at its highest. You see the beginning of the famous Gupta period. It was so called after one of the dynasties which reigned during it. Professor Rowland says:

> Seldom in the history of people do we find a period in which the national genius is so fully and typically expressed in all the arts as in Gupta India. The Gupta period may well be described as a 'classic' in the sense of the word describing a norm or degree of perfection never established before or since, and in the perfect balance and harmony of all elements stylistic and iconographic – elements inseparable in importance.

He proceeds to describe and to illustrate some of the masterpieces of that period: the caves, hollowed out into churches for the congregational worship of Buddha: the isolated statues of Buddha – for it is the religion that still dominates. Hinduism persists and the two Indian gods who are most worshipped today, Siva and Krishna, receive their shrines.

Somewhere about the year 800 – my figures are very rough: I pick on 800 because it was the year when Charlemagne was crowned in Rome and started, for that tiny place Europe, the Holy Roman Empire – the Gupta civilization came to an end and its curtain falls. Our next scene – and it will be our final scene – contains our major surprise. Buddhism has disappeared. Hinduism, dormant through so many centuries, becomes rampant and prevails. It had already modified Buddhism and complicated it. Now it manages to expel it; the caste system is reaffirmed, the elaborate Hindu temples arise with their towers that are not quite spires, their spires that just fail to be towers, their mushrooms and sun-hats, their gateways and gates, their colonnades, platforms and courtyards, their writhing sculpture – and the sculpture is sometimes obscene. All is being prepared for the displeasure of Lord Macaulay. And minds more sympathetic to India than his, minds less aggressively western, have also recoiled from the Hindu temple and regretted the expulsion of Buddhism. The late Lowes Dickinson had such a mind. My first visit to India was in his company, and I remember how he used to cower away from those huge architectural masses, those polluting forms, as if a wind blew off them which might wither the soul. This was not the Parthenon at Athens; no, it most certainly was not; and those gods with six arms or a hundred heads and blue faces were far from the gods of Greece.

I became easier with the Indian temple as soon as I realized, or rather as soon as I was taught, that there often exists inside its complexity a tiny cavity, a central cell, where the individual may be alone with his god. There is a temple-group in the middle of India, once well known to me, which adopts this arrangement. The exterior of each temple represents the world-mountain, the Himalayas. Its top-most summit, the Everest of later days, is crowned by the sun, and round its flanks run all the complexity of life – people dying, dancing, fighting, loving – and creatures who are not human at all, or even earthly. That is the exterior. The interior is small, simple. It is only a cell where the worshipper can for a moment face what he believes. He worships at the heart of the world-mountain, inside the exterior complexity. And he is alone. Hinduism, unlike Christianity and Buddhism and Islam, does not invite him to meet his god congregationally; and this commends it to me.

The name of this temple-group is the Khajraho group. There are twenty temples standing out of an original eighty-five and all of them are deserted. They rise like mountains of buff in the jungle. They were built shortly before William the Conqueror was born. They belong, according to Professor Rowland's classification, to the final period of Indian art – the period which began when Buddhism was driven from the land of its birth, and which peters out amongst the nineteenth-century Rajput miniatures.

I must allude in passing to the 190 illustrations already

mentioned. They are rather a disappointment. They have been intelligently selected, they range widely, some of them come off, but they do not on the whole give an adequate idea of the marvellous architecture and sculpture of India. 'What could?' you may say, and you are right. But photographs of the same subjects, which I bought out there, are certainly less inadequate. I have been doing some comparing, and my photographs win. Possibly the method of reproduction is at fault; I do not know; but here is a weakness in an otherwise admirable work, and I hope it may be remedied in future volumes of the series.

So much for my summary. I have lugged you, rather than led you, through the book, omitting much and patting into shape much that was amorphous. I have not discussed any of the non-Indian chapters, and one of them – about Cambodia – I have not even mentioned. Instead of these remote exports, I would rather have heard more about monuments native to the Indian soil: more about the Elephanta Caves, for instance; they are dismissed in under two pages. However, that is a personal preference. Moslem art is naturally omitted: it is a separate subject. But, just in passing, in order to emphasize the complexity of India, I would like to mention that Hindu and Moslem art do occasionally blend there. One example is the work of the Emperor Akbar. Another – a striking one – is the architecture of Ahmedabad, where the mosques, though correct ritually, are compounded in the Hindu style and waver aesthetically into temples. And there is a third example in a Moslem tomb outside Golconda, in the south. Eating my lunch there – one does, or did, eat one's lunch at Moslem tombs: it was part of their graciousness and courtesy – I could admire two styles of architecture on a single little building. I like to record these bastards of Moslem and Hindu, though they may not be congenial to contemporary politicians. The past is never as cut and dried as the present would like it to be. And the present, with its insistence on purity and its fanatical faith in the racial or religious 100 per cent, needs a reminder of this.

I will end by reminiscing about one of the monuments which I have seen and enjoyed. I will choose the Elephanta

Caves, just mentioned. They are well known, being on an island near Bombay, and those who have seen them may think that 'enjoyment' is the wrong word to employ. Certainly nothing more solemn, more remote from the pleasures of daily life, can be imagined. I would not picnic in an Elephanta Cave. I last went there on a steamy December afternoon, nearly eight years ago. The waters of the harbour were very calm, and close to the island they became shallow and muddy. A mangrove swamp was starting. 'Up to no good' is always one's reaction when mangrove swamps are mentioned, but they are not sinister to look at. Their bright little green noses pushed up on either side of the slippery landing stage. There was a climb up a couple of hundred feet, through brushwood, ticket-taking, and close ahead, over a level space, the chief cave. It showed as a dark gash in the cliff wall. It has been terribly damaged. The Portuguese, when they discovered it in the sixteenth century, did what they could to destroy the shrine. They, too, despised the religion and art of India.

The cave is dedicated to Siva. Enormous sculptures of him loom, and the light, filtering into the main chamber from several directions, picks out his limbs unexpectedly or illuminates the magnificent giants who guard his shrine. Above is the living rock, supported by pillars hewn out of it and meriting the title of 'living', for vegetation springs from its cracks. Elephanta is not one of those caves in which one exchanges light for darkness steadily. It is broad, it does not dig far into the mountain, and one's impulse is to wander in and out of it through the various gaps, always finding new effects and unexpected drama. The eight giants round the sacred sentry box impressed me most. They were not doing anything, as Siva was in the niches at the side. They were not dancing on the world or treading down demons, or slaughtering, or getting married against a background of air-borne imps. They were merely guarding the symbol of generation, and they had guarded it for 1,000 years. Elsewhere Siva predominated. He was everywhere. He was the male sex and the female also; all life came from him and returned to him. I like the idea – grave scholars have entertained it – that his wife got tired of this, that constant unity with the deity bored her, and that on one of the Elephanta reliefs she is depicted as losing her temper.

I do not remember much else about that gracious and enviable day – only the haziness and the stillness outside and a road which curved left round the hill towards some other caves. Our small party had the good luck to be on Elephanta alone, and no doubt that has recommended it to me. It is certainly unique. I have regretted that Professor Rowland has not said more about it, but what he does say is stimulating, and I will quote him:

> The colossal panels of Elephanta suggest spectacular presentations on a stage, their dramatic effectiveness enhanced by the bold conception in terms of light and shade. Probably such a resemblance to the unreal world of the theatre is not entirely accidental; for in Indian art, as in Indian philosophy, all life, even the life of the gods, is an illusion or play set against the background of eternity.

[1953]

Benjamin Rowland, *The Art and Architecture of India*

The English Scene

The Ceremony of Being a Gentleman

The English are still a good-tempered race, and they do not mind being abused by foreigners. They feel that a foreigner must cheer himself up somehow, considering what he is and where he comes from, and they regard his abuse as involuntary flattery. 'Our two good friends, Fritz and 'Ans, will now oblige with the "'Im of 'Ate,"' said the sergeant-major at the classical concert party; and a couple of German prisoners, trembling with terror, were duly led on to the platform and forced to perform before our troops, who roared with delight, joined in the chorus, and loaded them with chocolates and cigarettes. English humour! So exquisite if one happens to be English! But if one isn't, if one is Fritz or Hans or Dr Renier even, then one may feel that there is something rather uncanny in this armour of constant laughter, something almost perverse. Being English, I have written, 'almost perverse'. Dr Renier would write 'perverse'. 'You may fight such a people. You may trade with them. But what an undertaking to try and live among them!'

He himself is from Holland. He is a historian and journalist who has lived for seventeen years in this country and seen a good deal of middle-class society and a little of the working class. 'With a continental shrug of the shoulders, I hold up my distorted mirror to Narcissus,' he says, and many surprising facts are reflected in these pages. He has written an excellent book, acute and witty, yet one hesitates to smother it with the usual reviewer's sweet-sauce, for the reason that it contains something besides wit and acuteness; there is an astringent quality in it, and no one who reads it carefully will be left with a very pleasant taste afterwards in his or her mouth. He is not anti-English – far from it, and if he were we should ignore him. But he does not chaff us agreeably, like M. André Maurois and others of the *débonnaire* school. He finds us just a little inhuman, just slightly unpleasing, and to be thought slightly anything is always galling: one's armour gets pierced at last. If Fritz and Hans had been more moderate in their blame, they would have received fewer cigarettes. It is so jolly to be hated out and out. It makes one feel all of a piece.

Dr Renier's dissection takes two forms. First, drawing on his personal impressions, he analyses in turn our self-complacency, our altruism, our sense of humour, our charm, our readiness to give money, our 'sexual repression with its attendant disorders of pruriency and animal worship,' &c. These qualities compose between them what he calls the 'ritualistic conception of life', which is the conception held by the average public school man today. He then attempts a second analysis, by means of history. He observes that during the seventeenth and eighteenth centuries and as late as the reign of George IV, another and a more spontaneous attitude to life prevailed. How and when did the change to 'ritualism' occur? He goes into the problem, and, in his closing chapter, suggests that the change is only temporary, and that the English are about to become human again, whether they like it or not.

By our 'ritualistic conception of life' he means what shallower observers have called our hypocrisy. He finds that between a stimulus and an Englishman's reaction to it a hidden process takes place, 'which makes the resulting response differ from what an unprepared foreign student would expect it to be,' so that we are always saying and doing things not because they have any meaning, but because they are supposed to be 'right'. 'How do you do?' says Mr A., on being introduced, but Mr B. must not reply, 'Quite well, thank you,' or, 'My asthma has been a little tiresome.' He, too, must say, 'How do you do?' And this small social formula has its parallels in the wider spheres of conduct and action, indeed, all through the English universe. There is a ritual, often cheerful (one may even make jokes on a cricket field), but always obligatory and usually meaningless, and it is a ritual peculiar to the upper middle classes of England; neither the Irish, the Scots, the Welsh, the colonials, nor the wage-earning classes have adopted it; it is the endless ceremony of being a gentleman.

Now the gentleman, Dr Renier argues, came in when the aristocrat went out. If we are to give him a date, it is 1832, the year of the Reform Bill. The traditional rulers of England were then in a state of panic. They saw their privileges usurped by an unknown class who turned out to be grocers and bankers, but who seemed at the time far more terrifying than the Clydesiders of today. In their despair they turned to education. Would it not be possible to pare the claws off these monsters while one was teaching them to wash their hands? And the monsters, equally terrified, agreed; would it not be possible for them, once their hands were washed, to say 'How do you do?' to the aristocracy? The compact was struck – unconsciously on both sides, but none the less firmly, and out of it was developed the public school system as we know it today. At first that system represented the homage paid by virtue to vice. Then Arnold of Rugby appeared, and vice paid homage to virtue. Dr Renier gives an interesting and sympathetic account of Arnold, as of another great Victorian schoolmaster, Edward Bowen of Harrow. Arnold tried to make his boys Christian, manly, and enlightened, although by his own showing he could not, since he held the nature of a boy to be fundamentally evil. What he could do was to give them an 'officer' outlook, and instil in them respect for qualities they could never possess. He succeeded in doing that, and it has become 'ritual', and still dominates England. Born of a political crisis, it has evolved into a moral code. But it has no natural roots in our character, and the Gentleman will scarcely celebrate his centenary. What with the rise of women, what with the rise of the non-English English-speaking races, what with the Zeit-Geist, and (I would add) what with our approaching national poverty, the queer interlude cannot continue. The worried, inhibited gentleman is about to pass away and Dr Renier does not regret him, or see any reason why self-restraint should disappear when self-repression goes.

Such is his main argument, and a brief analysis of his concluding chapters. The earlier chapters are the more amusing, and I particularly commend them to men who pride themselves on their sense of humour and to women who prefer animals to men. The chief defect of the book is an infelicity of style which occasionally obliges a reader to go through a sentence twice before he can be sure whether it is meant literally or sarcastically. And though Dr Renier's knowledge of our idiom is good, it is not quite perfect; 'I fear we have no telephone' does not mean 'I think we have no telephone' so much as 'I am sorry we have none.' But these are incidental drawbacks, and anyone who is interested in a first-hand account of our national character will ignore them. At times the writing is full of charm and insight. Listen to him on the subject of conversation. It might be assumed (he says) that English talk is boring; well, like most assumptions about the English, this is wrong:

> The Englishman is a being of delicate shades and distinctions. Behind his serene face and reserved manner he hides the reactions of an appreciative mind. He may not utter them directly, but he loves to pour himself out by implication. Oh the strange charm of two English people seeking one another, and finding one another through the barrier of conventional talk! No brutal searchlight, as between continentals, to set out the other person in clear-cut outline. There is a pleasant game without set rules, thoughts are thrown out that dance like fairies on the thrilling air of a hot summer's noon, meeting and joining hands for a dance that defies the laws of gravity. An allusion to a half-forgotten admission, a hint that is thrown out, caught up without seeming effort, memories that rustle, dull chords that faintly vibrate. Echoes re-echo, minds open and admit a new notion which is silently stored up. It is the greatest and finest game the English play – and do they even know that it exists?

For the ritualistic conception of life does not, in his opinion, make us either dolts, knaves or fools. But it does make us contorted and uncanny, particularly as regards sex, and he would like us better, and thinks we should like one another better, if it were abandoned.

[1931]

G. J. Renier, *The English: Are they Human?*

Breaking Up

It is the end of the school year, and the period when those who are in authority tend to address the young. The young cannot otherwise. Row behind row, their faces bright and polite, they sit or stand to the remotest corner of the hall, while the wave of eloquence washes slowly over them from the platform, breaks, withdraws, advances again, withdraws again over the shingle of smooth round little heads and the limpet-encrusted parents. What are the wild waves saying? Nothing particular, nothing that disturbs the delicious silliness of one's private dream. The eminent men on the platforms are speaking of character, character is the burden of their song, character, always necessary in the past will be even more so in the future, character, more character, most character. General Sir Archibald Montgomery-Massingberd at Cheltenham, prefers character to educational excellence as a means of preparing for the next war. Character, something out of Dickens. The Reverend J.D. Day, Headmaster of Stamford, gives five marks for character and five for capacity, and thirteen fellows get double firsts. Character, what mother got with the cook. A perfect character must be school chapel, unless it equals a perfect scream.

So did the chap on the platform with the wart showing through his moustache say 'scream' or did he say 'screen'? Never mind. Couldn't hear. It is the end of the school year. And at the end of the year a jaw means even less than usual for it immediately vanishes into the gulf of the summer holidays.

Unconscious of all this, or cynically indifferent to it, the platform talks on, and gets a certain satisfaction from the reflux of its own eloquence. Swish goes the wave against the opposite wall of the Hall, and bouf it comes back. Refreshed by their own spray, the eminent visitors continue to address the boys and the headmaster his bies on the supreme importance of character. I hesitate to introduce this subject again. They do not. They return to it as the eighteenth century returned to Nature and the thirteenth to God. Nature today is discredited – nudism, fads – and when it comes to religion we find the Headmaster of Rossall becomes distinctly wary in his references. 'Much had been said lately of Public School religion,' he is reported as saying, 'but perhaps the truest words were those of the Headmaster of Westminster, who said he found nothing to differentiate Public School religion from religion elsewhere.' It is chivalrous of one headmaster to ascribe such an epigram to another, and this brings us back to the subject of character again. Character is built up. It also builds. So can it have anything to do with my kid brother's box of meccano? Wrong again . . . chap on the platform with an eye like an egg is saying 'Character never becomes mechanical.'

Sometimes the waves are deflected, and instead of washing over the audience are turned through a hose-pipe upon the invisible public. There has been criticism of our schools in recent years, particularly on the ground that they turn out a standardized article, which goes well enough with other articles of the same brand, but which is not very adequate otherwise. They are charged with monotony, and this year several headmasters retort in chorus that this is not so, and that snobbery – another of the charges – is really to be found in the home. But on the whole it is the boys themselves who are addressed, and who are summoned into a world which, as far as my own notions go, has very little connection with reality, a world where everyone is either managing or being managed, and where the British Empire has been appointed to the post of general manager. Of internationality – little; of the non-white peoples – nothing; and even the peevish civilities which used to be extended to the League of Nations on these occasions seem to have ceased.

The arts are seldom mentioned except at the girls' schools (where, by the way, the speeches tend to be much more genuine and fresh). At Eastbourne, the Headmaster commended the Bayeux Tapestry, a copy of which the boys have painted round the school hall. But Lord Goschen, the guest of honour, who spoke next, declined the bait and remarked that 'Neither magnificent pageantry nor news of great feats had made him so proud of being an Englishman as when he visited a small band of Englishmen who without thought for self were keeping the peace so far as possible among the wild tribes of the North West Frontier.' Air bombing should make him still prouder. It is a relief to turn from this to Wellington, where there were four days extra holidays because Lord Derby's horse won a race and no nonsense about it, or to Leatherhead County School, where sensible remarks were made about Press propaganda. But the greatest relief is a speech at Rydal School, by Mr Hugh Walpole, which appears like a spring of fresh water in the midst of all the brine. Here, for a moment, we catch a glimpse of real people on a real earth. 'You will have to learn how to be individuals,' Mr Walpole told the boys. 'But when you have got your individuality you will have to use it for a common good. In the same way you must be patriots, but you must see that your patriotism helps the world and not only your own country.' This is easier said than done, but it is something to get it said. His speech is an example of genuine as opposed to pedagogic seriousness and of sensitiveness as opposed to Lord Goschen's deadening sentimentality. This is one of the few occasions when one hopes that the audience was awake.

Yet even Mr Walpole does not make the speech I want to hear. If the impossible ever happens and I am asked to help break up a school what I shall say is this: 'Ladies and gentlemen, boys and bies: School was the unhappiest time of my life, and the worst trick it played me was to pretend that it was the world in miniature. For it hindered me from discovering how lovely and delightful and kind the world can be, and how much of it is intelligible. From this platform of middle age, this throne of experience, this altar of wisdom, this scaffold of character, this beacon of hope, this threshold of decay, my last words to you are: There's a better time coming.' And then that school would break up.

[1933]

The Old School

Suppose me a schoolmaster, called (say) Mr Herbert Pembroke, and I have a boarding-house in the imaginary public school of Sawston. My day's work is over, my boys (whom I call bies) are safe in their cubicles and I take up a new book, as I still sometimes do, entitled *The Old School.* The title placates. It suggests caps with tassels, and photogravures in oak, and the words of the school anthem which I myself have composed flit pleasantly through my mind:

> Perish each sluggard! Let it not be said
> That Sawston such within her walls hath bred!

But as I read I turn purple in the face, then pale, then petrified, and finally open the study door and burst out to my sister, who does the matroning for me: 'Agnes! Agnes! Pray what is the meaning of this?'

Agnes is used to being asked what things mean and she does not immediately come. When she does I exclaim that here is the most disgraceful, ill-conditioned, unnecessary book ever published, and I cannot trust myself to speak about it.

She composes herself to listen.

'Here is a collection of reminiscences by boys who seem recently to have left their schools, and one would like to know under what circumstances. Here is the sorriest set of sluggards ever collected. Here are fine nincompoops. Come! They shirk games and the O.T.C., they have no notion of *esprit de corps,* they do not even work. And their names! E. Arnot Robertson! What a name for a boy! And Sean O'Faoláin! Scarcely a name at all! This personage writes of

Cork, if you please, and pray whoever heard of Cork as a school?'

'Well, if the boys do not come from proper schools it is naturally not a proper book,' says Agnes, who is adding up the washing under the rim of the study table where she thinks I cannot see it. 'I don't think you ought to worry – (one pound three and two) – over that, Herbert.'

'I am far from worrying, but I really must observe that Winchester, Malvern and Rugby are among the national institutions vilified.'

'Does Sawston come in?'

'Sawston! Certainly not. How could it? I should be very mortified indeed if any of our old—'

'Thirty-seven pillow cases. Might I look at this queer book now for a moment?'

'Yes, but omit the chapter on St Paul's.'

My sister glances about, opines that though E. Arnot Robertson went to Sherborne he was a girl, and then hands the volume back with that bright smile of hers which both sustains and irritates me. 'Oh, there's nothing to take any notice of,' she says. 'They turn out to be only authors – not people who matter – they are just writing to one another about how they didn't get on at their schools. We must remind the library to choose more sensibly for us next time. And talking of choosing – what, Herbert, oh, what about a fresh laundry? Do you agree to us trying the Snow White at Michaelmas?'

'I am far from supposing that the Snow White. . . .'

And far from supposing, far from imagining, Mr Herbert Pembroke and his sister fade away into ghosts. They have been evoked for a moment from a forgotten novel in which, nearly thirty years back, I tried to write about this same topic of one's old school. I did not like mine. I felt towards it what most of the contributors to this volume feel towards theirs, and the Pembrokes were what is now called a compensation-device. I invented them in order to get back a bit of my own.

> So shall Sawston flourish, so shall manhood be
> Serving God and Country, ruling land and sea.

I actually had to sing that. It seems incredible.

All the same, this book is not easy to review. It is rather scrappy. Here are eighteen men and women who have mostly been educated on public-school lines and have mostly disliked it, but not all of them have disliked it nor have they all been to public schools. Nor do they approach their immaturities in the same spirit. Some of them gossip sedately, others are charming, others do a raspberry, others use personal experience as a basis for some theory of education. The editor, Mr Graham Greene (Berkhamsted), shovels everything together as well as he can, but the book could, I think, have cohered better if he had either kept his selection strictly to public schools or else had worked to a much bigger plan and included a great many other educational models instead of merely a few – thus giving a real cross-section of adolescent England.

The contribution I have enjoyed most is Mr O'Faoláin's. He was educated by some gentle muddled monks at Cork, who taught him that there are twelve minerals, that combustion is due to phlogiston, and that circumcision is a small circle cut out on the forehead of Jewish children. He acquired this knowledge with an open book balanced upon his head, in order to protect it from the showers of broken glass which fell on occasion from the roof. The protection was adequate, and out of the cold and the smells of that huge crumbling room in that vanished school he has constructed a faery world of affection and beauty. The point of Cork is that there was *esprit de corps*, though it was never mentioned and could not have been pronounced. The monks and the boys worked together as a family, and conspired to defeat the Board of Education. One of the inspectors urged scholars to clean their teeth and supervise their hair, &c., and when he had gone, Brother Josephus 'swept us together into his bosom for ever and ever in one wave of indignation by saying in contempt of all inspectors "Boys! He thinks ye're filth." That *was* education, and if one thinks of the washing and washing and washing at Winchester – which as far as my information goes is the most bleached of our Big Five – one realizes the humanizing power of a little dirt, and the limitations of laundries, even when they are snow-white. There was superstition and ignorance at Cork, but these are evils which can be rectified. They have not the paralysing permanency of good form.

Except for Mr O'Faoláin, and Miss Elizabeth Bowen, who gives a calming and charming account of Downe House, and Mr Stephen Spender, who liked his time as a day boy at University College School, and Mr William Plomer, who, though he did not like Rugby finely eulogizes his late head-master – except for these and for some scattered praises and happinesses, the general tone of the collection is vinegary. My own tone. If it seems a little monotonous, a little too much like Mrs Gamp's salad, it is surely a needful change after so much oil. The amount of praise lavished on our public schools both by themselves and by sentimental foreign visitors has been preposterous and has led to unendurable complacency. So as for 'Honour', read Mr W.H. Auden's devastating analysis of its workings at Holt. As for Imperial training see Mr Derek Verschoyle on Malvern. The boarding-house system, fagging, the uneasy attitude of the authorities towards sex, the snobbery – see *passim.* No longer can Mr Pembroke and his sister lead the massed choirs in:

> Lo the flag of Sawston lifted high appears,
> Bravely hath it waved for twice two hundred years.

For the flag is getting torn, and according to Mr Greene, the entire system is doomed for economic reasons.

[1934]

Graham Greene (ed.) *The Old School*

The Political Thirties

Notes on the Way

Last week, in place of watching a new Mickey Mouse, I ought to have gone to the knockabout at Olympia instead. I should not have found it funny, and that would have been a good thing. For our English sense of humour, about which we are so stupidly conceited, is leading us into some nasty messes. Sir Oswald Mosley is, on the face of it, a figure of fun. He is the Wicked Baronet of melodrama, who has gone from party to party to make trouble, and slunk away from each with the cry of 'foiled': he belongs to the world of *Sweeney Tod* and *East Lynne.* He even wears black, and as a final absurdity, he is opposed by a second Wicked Baronet in red. Here is a promising entertainment for little Mr and Mrs Everyman, who have installed a sense of humour with their wireless and electric light, and are quite prepared to laugh the villain down. But the villain is stronger than they expected, blood is shed, teeth are broken, an old man is hit on the head, another man is thrown naked into the street, women slap and scratch, blacks and reds crawl along the girders like a scene from the Insect Play. Mr and Mrs Everyman become alarmed and want to leave the meeting but when they rise to their feet Fascists rush at them because they are creating a disturbance. They cannot get away and the *Daily News* correspondent is gripped by a burly steward and told to show up what he has written. The Fascists treat Olympia, which they have hired for the evening, like the Castle of St Angelo. They improvise a torture chamber, and Mr Gerald Barry, who looks into it, sees ten of them kicking a single victim. On another occasion the police see them savaging two Communists in the vestibule and dash in to save the men, although technically without jurisdiction inside the building. Elsewhere they have aeroplanes, and Major Yeats Brown, the mystic, has explained that they need armoured cars in which to attend meetings. The rest of us can walk to meetings or can take a taxi, and is all very ridiculous. But it is something else.

For the citizen who stayed away, the significant fact of that disgusting evening is not the violence but the criticisms passed afterwards by Sir Oswald on the police for their handling of the situation outside the building. The police, he said, should either have kept order outside Olympia or should have allowed him to keep it. He had given his instructions to the Commissioner of Police several days beforehand, through his chief of staff: no Communists were to approach. His instructions had been ignored and rioting had resulted, for which he was not responsible. Inside Olympia, Fascists did keep order, and their methods have been further described in a letter to *The Times* signed by Mr T. J. O'Connor and two other horrified M.P.s. These methods Sir Oswald would extend to our London streets. He would control the ordinary citizen throughout the area in which he holds a meeting by means of his private army. It simply takes one's breath away. To blame the police is one thing – we all blame them on occasion, for instance a magistrate has just censored them for being short with motorists. But to say to the police, 'Do as I tell you or else I shall do it!' My hat! Is the Commissioner going to sit down under this? The rank and file certainly will not. If they regard the Communists as an enemy and a cursed nuisance, they will regard the Fascist as the sort of friend who says: 'Yes, yes, Robert, you are a fine fellow and you want to help me down the Reds, but you don't quite know how to do it, you haven't been continentally trained as I have, also, though we won't rub it in, you're working class, so stand back, please!'

Meanwhile I sat in my cinema a couple of miles off looking not only at Mickey but at the Aran Island film, which I saw for the second time. It is the severest picture ever screened and often tedious, for there is no intimacy in it and much repetition, and it does not fit too well into its framework of Man versus Sea. However, there the sea was and the unfenced rocks, and the direct contact with simple facts which we all long for and do not know how to effect except artificially. There was the antique beauty. And I thought of another Irish island which I have visited and which is in some ways even more primitive than the Aran. There beauty is softened at moments into grace. When the day's work is done and the weather calm, the boys and girls go to the edge of the cliff and dance on the cliff in the dusk, the boys dance, the girls have both to dance and hum the tune. They are able to do this, because there is no priest on that island. I walked up and down – for it was very cold – watching them and listening to the gaspy little sounds which blended so sweetly with the whisper of the sea. I thought – well, of nothing, naturally one doesn't think, but in retrospect this and the Aran Island picture drift like a solemn mist through Olympia and its bloody little actualities. The antique beauty which is not eternal! No cunning in our civilization seems able to catch it and to give it to the men and women for their very own. Life bores them, and they turn from the dance to the drill hall.

It is the strength of Sir Oswald Mosley and his fellow-practitioners that they have managed to utilize this boredom, and more particularly the boredom which devastates people who are not quite sure that they are gentlemen. He possesses what is referred to in awestruck tones as 'personal magnetism' – a quality which has no necessary connection with nobility, decency, kindliness, intelligence, or constructive power. He magnetizes the bank clerks and little typists who don't know how to enliven life, gives them uniforms, grades and a cause and foe, and sends them forth as Samurai and Amazons to slosh the Reds. The optimist will look in here and say that if only the capacity for self-sacrifice which he exploits could be turned in other directions, we should have our better world. Yes! If only! But corporate self-sacrifice seems so seldom directed aright. It is run by people who feel nothing and understand nothing.

Three paths lie before us, I suppose, at the present moment, and Fascism is infinitely the worst. Firstly, there is the present order, which I prefer, because I have been brought up in it. I like Parliament and democracy. I should like England and Europe to muddle on as they are, without the international explosion which would end them, and it is just possible that this may occur, not through the spread of pacifism but because the militarists may be too muddled to pull the trigger. They may miss their Sarajevo. In the second place, there is Communism, an alternative which will destroy all I care for and could only be reached through violence, yet it might mean a new order where younger people could be happy and the head and the heart have a chance to grow. There, and on no other horizon, the boys and girls might return to the cliff and dance. If my own world smashes, Communism is what I would like in its place, but I shall not bless it until I die. And, thirdly, there is Fascism, leading only into the blackness which it has chosen as its symbol, into smartness and yapping out of orders, and self-righteous brutality, into social as well as international war. It means change without hope. Our immediate duty – in that tinkering which is the only useful form of action in our leaky old tub – our immediate duty is to stop it, and perhaps we can best do that by convincing Sir Oswald's backers that it will not pay. What does Lord Lloyd think of the Olympia business? What – if it is not too unkind a question to put to the kindest of men – does Sir J.C. Squire think? And those others whose names we are not permitted to learn – what do the financial backers of Sir Oswald think? He tells us, and no doubt correctly, that there is Russian money behind Communism. What secret money lies behind him, and what view does it take of his offer to supersede the police?

So much for the matter in hand. And now here is my span of Notes still unachieved, and I have already said what I really want to say. The rest must be padding. What could be more suitable as padding than the recent Honours List? I keep reading through this list and discovering in some corner of it or other the name of a friend. When this happens, or when I think of recipients whom I also would like to honour (such as Professor Elliott Smith or Mr. A.R. Powis, the secretary of the Society for the Preservation of Ancient Buildings), it seems to me an excellent list, and His Majesty wisely inspired.

Then I reach tracts of the unknown or spots of the despised and become frivolous and angular.

> Honours the Queen can give
> Honour she can't,
> Honours without Honour,
> Is but a Barren Grant,

So they wrote in those free Victorian times, poking fun at matters which are now become a little solemn, and Baron Grant wittily riposted by putting up a statue to Shakespeare in Leicester Square. In the present list the most obvious target for Mr and Mrs Everyman's mirth is a gentleman at Chislehurst who wrote an election poem called 'Stanley Boy'. He has been knighted, and why not? One ought not really to comment on an Honours List at all, for it is and has to be a blend of four distinct classes: public officials, supporters of the political party in power, philanthropists, and persons of distinction in their own right. All four classes get 'honoured', and when the honour takes the shape of a handle, will have to watch their step and their tradesmen's bills, but no principle is at work – in fact the only possible principle is that which a devastating friend of mine has laid down: he thinks that anyone should be granted an honour who asks for it. 'What would you like – knighthood, coronet, O.B.E., V.C.? Very well, here it is and do take it away with you.' So might an enlightened monarch address his great children's party. He would hand out Stars of India by the lakh, snip off Garters by the yard, and every reasonable person would be happy; there would be no aching hearts in quiet provincial towns, no tightened lips in college common rooms, no embittered hospital nurses, no unsuccessful business men, and our old aristocracy would be happy too, since it would spend its time in despising later creations. The only people who could not be cheered under such an arrangement are those cranks who concentrate on their work and find their reward in doing it, and these are past human aid. Such was my friend's vision, which remains unfulfilled like other hopes, and, needless to say, he has never been in an

Honours List himself. One does not cherish such a vision as soon as one has got anything.

Honours belong to the antique beauty. In that Irish island I mentioned there was a king. He died before my visit and was by profession the postman, but his daughters are still called princesses, and this mixture of nicknames and poetry carries more magic than any title which can be conferred through the recommendation of a Prime Minister. Our lives are getting too mechanized and our minds too sophisticated for us to find any lasting satisfaction in machine-made gifts. We want something honourable with which we are not naturally in contact, such as the rocks and the sea. And if one were not part of the human race one could look down on it with much pity at this moment of its history. It needs romance and does not know how to find it. Menaced externally by the results of its scientific research in the shape of New War, it makes trouble for itself within by requiring excitement and loveliness. This brings me back to Olympia and its brutalized young Blackshirts. They would not have been captured by Fascism unless they felt they were getting something fine and jolly. And they will not be released until they are offered a substitute. What is it to be? Morris Dancing? The cliffs grow darker, the night colder, the sea whispers 'Never no, never no,' as it slides on the pebbles, and I am left with one hard ugly little thought – that on the night of Thursday, June 7th, Sir Oswald Mosley tried to rule London from Addison Road to Hammersmith Broadway and that he will try again.

[1934]

Notes on the Way

Italy, Abyssinia, the League, the election. The notes for the month must begin with this sinister text, but I am too much muddled to elucidate it, muddled as well as worried, and hope to pass on next week to matters nearer my competence. My own notion, such as it's worth, is that the League was the best hope for peace, and that the British Government is now enthusiastic for it, but that our enthusiasm has only taken a practical form because Abyssinia neighbours Kenya and the Sudan, and because Italy is a Mediterranean power. If the trouble had occurred in a part of the world where we have no interests, we should not have weighed in. When the Italians call us hypocrites they are in this sense right, though not in any other. Sanctions are not unconnected with sanctimoniousness – a great pity. I think furthermore that we may have weighed in too late, and that France is going to leave us with the baby, and may go Fascist, and I think that our government, by snapping an election at such a moment as this, are behaving like a set of swine. This is a cloudy mucky view of the situation. Other people's heads may be clearer, and anyhow they will be able to support Mr Baldwin and Mr Harry Pollitt on the one hand, or Sir Oswald Mosley and Mr Lansbury on the other without my guidance. How shall we vote? It's one thing to endorse the Government's League policy, and I have already done that, with millions of others, by filling in the Peace Ballot. It's another thing to vote for men who, if they return to office, may announce that the League has failed, and are anyhow pledged to an armament ramp. Decent politicians would have postponed this election until the latest possible date, on the chance of the issue before the electorate becoming clearer. But is any politician decent when it comes to a question of retaining power?

World politics are indeed unruly; if the League fails they may become unmanageable, civilization may be destroyed by flames and bacteria, and the historian of the future may look back to 1935 as the date on which the human race finally collapsed under its own inventions. The odd thing is that, in spite of all the disorder, our private lives often remain happy and docile. We are washed about like jelly-fish in the rising storm, and yet each of us may preserve his personal radiance and inward poise. It's a matter of luck. Some of us are already going to pieces, and accord with the chaos outside. Others can't help enjoying themselves, though the moralist blames them. They are not insensitive, they realize what is going on in Abyssinia and elsewhere and they know that they themselves will soon be dashed dead on the beach. Yet the desire to create, to organize, to make friends, to help neighbours, to listen to music, to dig in the garden, to eat nice food and have a good drink, is so strong in them that they go on being happy in patches until the end. Constant happiness is only for the obtuse, but patchy happiness seems to be a possibility for all well-developed men and women, and perhaps it is their fate. And I think that's what puzzles us when we look at the state of the world today and try to sum it up. It's ghastly, and all the decent people who are struggling about in it know that it's ghastly. Yet when they get the chance they can't help having a pleasant time. There seems to be a profound division between our private and our public outlook – a division which goes deeper than the will, and which the psychologist rather than the moralist must be allowed to probe.

The other day I went to a concert and met in the interval a political worker of great ability and selflessness. He rather upset me, however, by bleating out apologetically: 'I've come in here for a little out of the battle.' Well, hundreds of other people had done likewise, we all knew things were pretty dicky outside. I didn't know what to reply, 'so you have' sounded tepid, 'so have I' pert, and I was reduced to silent sympathy. I went all uncomfortable, for the reason that his patches of happiness hadn't coincided with my own. His were shorter – they didn't bridge the interval between the two halves of the concert. Mine formed a single expanse – or would have done so but for his reminder. I felt ashamed, and my thoughts reverted to their round of worry: the League, the election, Italy, Abyssinia. What is a fellow to do? Utter, O someone, the word that shall reconcile outer and inner! In the realm of public battle a man is bound to lose his balance; in the private life he may keep it, but at the cost of becoming isolated. This disharmony has sounded all through human history, there is nothing new about it, we can hear it in Lucretius, St Augustine, Donne, Matthew Arnold, but it is loudest at times like the present when the ramparts of the world threaten to give way with a rush and to let loose upon the individual too much of the unknown at once. 'Give us Time in our time, O Lord' – I think that's my own prayer. Give us Time to adjust ourselves to the inventions of science. Broadcasting and aviation for example – if they had taken two hundred years to develop instead of twenty; we should have had some chance of using them properly. Give us Time, and we might achieve Peace!

Meanwhile the Italians advance, our election is in a fortnight, and – more agitating than either – a Fascist rising is expected in France before the end of the month. Newspapers convey so little, even when they are wishing to talk straight, and perhaps only those who have French correspondents can realize the tension felt. 'Nous sommes ici pour tout voire' writes a friend quoting a Provençal saying. He thinks that the long expected crisis is at hand. The Croix de Feu, the most powerful of the Fascist organizations, is believed to have completed its plans, and some of the newspapers have even published details of its proposed attack on Paris. The leader of the Croix de Feu, Colonel de la Rocque, is a mystic as well as a militarist. He appears to possess that deplorable quality known as 'personal magnetism', a quality which is always referred to in such awe-struck and respectful tones, and which always produces bloodshed if the magnetizer is allowed to get hold of a gun. The Colonel's advice to his followers is typical: 'Voyez net. Pensez simple. Soyez des réalisateurs, non des rhéteurs' – the type of advice already followed in Italy as the Abyssinians well realize, and in Germany as has been realized by the Jews. Whether 'Pensez simple' will go down in France remains to be seen. The French are rather peculiar. They believe in the intellect, and though this does not necessarily mean that they are more intelligent than other nations, it does enable them to combine for the protection of thought. In the face of the Fascist menace a remarkable organization has sprung up called 'Vigilance'. Its membership is entirely composed of intellectuals (professors, writers, scientists, school-teachers, etc.), and at present numbers over eight thousand, distributed throughout eighty centres in France and Algiers. Its political affinities lie towards the Left. It contains many names of distinction: Professor Rivet is the president, the vice-presidents are Alain the writer and Professor Langevin of the Collège de France. 'Vigilance' operates largely through pamphlets – the method of Voltaire, which always recurs in seasons of disturbance – and if its statistics are to be trusted, about 150,000 of these have been sold. It is also hoping to organize a week-end congress in Paris very shortly.

Now this is not just 'Foreign News'. It touches us all. If the Croix de Feu and other Fascist organizations succeed in France, we in England shall feel the impact at once, and Geneva will feel it also. We shall be isolated and our government will pile up armaments with increased complacency in Liberty's name. For the moment, no organization like 'Vigilance' exists in this country, and a very good thing too, for it is much better that writers and so forth should not organize or accept a political complexion until the last possible moment; they lose most of their bloom and distinction as soon as this happens, and they turn away from their proper job, that of creation. But the moment may arrive, it has arrived in France, and the appeal which 'Vigilance' makes to English sympathizers for general co-operation seems to me a reasonable one, so I will give its address: 18, Boulevard Magenta, Paris X. Any intellectual who cares to communicate with it will receive fuller information, and if anyone thinks 'intellectual' is a dreary sort of word, I most emphatically agree, but these are dreary times.

Trying to escape from them and to unmuddle myself a little, I put one or two of Hugo Wolf's songs upon the gramophone before concluding these notes. There, sure enough, was our problem, transferred into terms of music, and solved. There was the contest – not indeed between outer and inner, public and private, but between two distinct sorts of sounds: piano-sounds and voice-sounds. Hugo Wolf is the only song-writer I know who allows each sort of sound to go its own way. In many musicians (Schubert for instance) the piano accompanies the voice, in others it echoes the voice (e.g. Schumann's 'Nussbaum'), in others it alternates. Wolf alone seems able to create two independent and continuous streams of music, whose true relation is not revealed until the close. The piano generally goes on longest. The final bars of the piano in 'Nun wandre Maria' or 'Anacreon's Grave' or 'Ganymede' have a retrospective value which bears no relation to the notes struck. They throw back to the beginning and make the two streams into one. And this, it seems to me, is what great art does in these worrying times. It solves none of our bothers, personal or political, but it reveals a world where they might have been solved. Nor is this the end of the mystery; instead of being tantalized and irritated by such elusiveness and unpracticability, we are actually comforted, and return to what we choose to call 'actual life' with a better heart.

[1935]

The Long Run

Dying for a cause in which he believed, the late Christopher St John Sprigg would not desire to be reviewed with any posthumous tenderness. These essays (published under the pseudonym of Christopher Caudwell) were written by him shortly before he was killed in Spain, they hit hard, and no one who reads them will feel that a Communist makes a comfortable neighbour. They are never abusive, and are often cogent and brilliant, but they are always fanatical. They riddle the bourgeois' arguments and would like to riddle his body, for Caudwell believed that everyone who has not joined the Third International is wrong and must be doing wrong, and is consequently better out of the way. He had faith; and, as has often been pointed out, these modern political creeds have borrowed the passion and the ruthlessness which have hitherto been confined to religion. Regarded as propaganda, the book is surely a mistake. A wise and persuasive writer like Mr John Strachey may well make converts to his cause, and so may a warm-hearted, matey writer of the type of Mr Jack Common. But Christopher Caudwell is what has been called in Bolshevik diplomatic circles 'an error in exportation'. He ought not to be read outside the fold. He will only cause unbelievers to clutch at their pocket-books and thank their God that Mr Chamberlain and Herr Hitler excluded the Reds from Munich.

Some of us think that our pocket-books will be lost in any case, indeed, that everything is now lost except personal affection, the variety of human conduct, and the importance of truth. If we feel like this, we can read Caudwell with pleasure. We are bound to read him with admiration, for he is a sincere man and an able critic.

In the first part of the book he is concerned with some of his erring seniors – Shaw, the two Lawrences, Wells, Freud. He points out, quite rightly, that they all of them feel uneasy; whether they are scientific, amusing, poetical or practical, they are worried, and whether they confess or conceal their worry, their plight persists. He ascribes their uneasiness to their refusal to recognize the trend of the society into which they have been born – that trend being, of course, towards Communism. Bernard Shaw, though more satisfactory than his fellow thinkers because he has read Marx, clings to the bourgeois illusion that man is naturally free; he will not accept man's dependence upon society, he remains 'a brilliant medicine man, theorising about life', and rejecting the discoveries of science when they get in his way. T.E. Lawrence freed the Arabs, it is true, but freed them for what? to participate in the diseased French or British political systems; half-aware of the infection he had communicated, Lawrence escaped in remorse into the ranks of the army, where he found 'a kind of Arabian desert in the heart of the vulgar luxury of bourgeoisdom, a stunted version of his ideal, barren of fulfilment, but at least free from dishonour'. D.H. Lawrence and H.G. Wells are also crippled, one of them because he cannot do without class or the dark past, the other because he cannot do without cash. They are all 'pathetic' figures, pathetic being an expression of contempt; Caudwell gives them a little genuine sympathy and much platform-pity, and dismisses them as failures.

He handles his case so well that he leaves us feeling that there is nothing else to say. But there is something. All intelligent and sensitive people today are worried – there's no question about that and Caudwell may account for their worry correctly. But have not these worried people sometimes written readable books? And may not the malaise, the lack of adjustment, be the speck of grit which causes the oyster to secrete the pearl? His answer to this would be that in the Classless State we shall have no specks of grit, and that if maladjustment causes art, art must go; a valid answer from his standpoint, but he has not faced the fact that books do give pleasure; he has not discussed art at all, and he is prohibited from discussing it, although he possesses plenty of aesthetic reactions. He dare discuss nothing except opinions. For him, a book is only good if it stands in a sound social relation to its age, and consequently no book can be good today unless it is communist. *Kipps, The Plumed Serpent, The Seven Pillars* need rewriting, and what matter if, when rewritten, they are unreadable? Literature has nothing to do with enjoyment.

Through all these essays, and linking them together runs the idea of Liberty. Liberty is a leaky word, and it is surprising that Communists should venture on board of it. Fascists prudently keep away; they have promulgated that the individual must be enslaved to the state, and thus they avoid many difficulties, both practical and argumentative. But Communism is less sound than Fascism because it is more human; it does care about ultimate happiness, its final aims are thoroughly decent, and so it gets entangled in some of the difficulties which it diagnoses in democracy. Liberty is the most tiresome of these. So long as Caudwell attacks the bourgeois conception of liberty, he goes on gaily enough. It is in the first place indefinable. In the second place, although some people are comparatively free they cannot if they are decent enjoy their freedom while their less fortunate brethren are suffering. Both these points are incontestable, and Caudwell goes on to argue that the more the 'free' assert their 'freedom' the more will they enslave the unfortunate: 'bourgeoisdom crucifies liberty upon a cross of gold, and if you ask in whose name it does this replies, "In the name of personal freedom."' Our great mistake, he says, is the mistake of Rousseau: the belief that freedom is an escape *from* society instead of something which must be realized *through* society.

Something? Well, what thing? We now look for the positive, the communist, definition of freedom, and Mr Strachey in his introduction promises us that we are going to get it. 'One can only find salvation for oneself by finding it for all others at the same time,' says Caudwell – sound mysticism, but is it sound dialectic materialism, too? 'Somehow,' says Mr Strachey (observe the semi-mystical 'somehow') 'we must make men understand that they can find liberty not in the jungle, which is the most miserably coercive place in the world, but in the highest possible degree of social co-operation.' The first step towards this has to be the dictatorship of the proletariat. The dictatorship must presumably work through a bureaucracy, as it does in Russia, but the bureaucracy will not establish itself as a bourgeoisie – oh no! In some unexplained way the dictatorship will one day 'wither', and Karl Marx will turn into Father Christmas, and present humanity with the Classless State. This idealism and warm-heartedness is the inspiring force in Communism, the quality that distinguishes it from Fascism eternally. But what has happened to its logic? Just as we reach the summit of the exposition, and, our bourgeois illusions demolished, are expecting a positive goal, the exposition collapses. This collapse occurs in all religions – first the careful reasoning, the analysis of existing ills, and then the desperate jump to glory. Communism, like Christianity, jumps. And the shock is the bigger because of its previous aridity, its harsh technical arguments, economic and psychological, its contempt for all that is pleasant, wayward and soft. On we move, through the dictatorship of the proletariat to the full consciousness of the causality of society – and then we get a surprise-stocking. We open it: to discover that liberty means doing what is best for everybody else.

Talking with Communists makes me realize the weakness of my own position and the badness of the twentieth century society in which I live. I contribute to the badness without wanting to. My investments increase the general misery, and so may my charities. And I realize, too, that many Communists are finer people than myself – they are braver and less selfish, and some of them have gone into danger although they were cowards, which seems to me finest of all. Yet, if I contribute to the badness of contemporary society so do they; Caudwell's book, like my review of it, is printed upon bourgeois-produced paper by bourgeois printers, and profits the economic system which he condemns. And though they may be better individuals than I, they are none the less individuals; they emphasize the very category against which they protest. And as for their argument for revolution – the argument that we must do evil now so that good may come in the long run – it seems to me to have nothing in it. Not because I am too nice to do evil, but because I don't believe the Communists know what leads to what. They say they know because they are becoming conscious of 'the causality of society'. I say they don't know, and my counsel for 1938–9 conduct is rather: Do good, and possibly good may come from it. Be soft even if you stand to get squashed. Beware of the long run. Seek understanding dispassionately, and not in accordance with a theory. Counsels of despair, no doubt. But there is nothing disgraceful in despair. In 1938–9 the more despair a man can take on board without sinking the more completely is he alive.

[1938]

Christopher Caudwell, *Studies in a Dying Culture*

Trees – and Peace

A personal view? What about an impersonal view for a change? What about a few remarks on the subject of trees?

Trees are a change from politics, anyway, and they are so lovely to look at and so fascinating to think about, especially if one has watched them over a period of several years, and noticed their individual troubles and habits.

They have a career of their own which scarcely touches human events. They belong to no country – only to the soil where they grow. What a relief that is, and what a contrast to ourselves!

Of course one cannot retreat into trees, or hide from the enemy aeroplanes under the covering of their leaves, yet what a relief to remember them at odd moments, and to realize that for thousands of years they are likely to continue – weary at times, but not with our weariness, not vexed by our problems, not warped by our ideals.

Here, for instance, as I turn into the wood out of the public path, stand a little birch tree and a little elder. Each of them is about three feet high. They didn't exist a couple of years back; they have sown themselves, much too close for their own comfort, amongst the bracken and bramble of southern England, and are rising towards the sky face to face.

The grey squirrels and the rabbits, who nibble the bark of nearly everything in this destructive age, have not noticed them so far – the self-sown and the humble do sometimes escape.

Above them gesticulates a beech, drawing them up and inciting them to race against each other, and by the time the year 1940 is reached there will be a rare muddle on this particular spot.

Birch and elder will be cramping one another's limbs and tearing one another's skins, and they will also be vexing the beech, which is supposed to be superior, and was planted specially inside a collarette of wire to protect its bark.

It is lovely to watch the pretty pair and to reflect that they have no value, and only grow because it occurred to them to do so. They are older than the Spanish crisis, but not as old as the Abyssinian, and they may outlast crises here, and keep growing when the houses around them lie flat. Their shallow roots go deep down into peace.

Farther down the slope lies a packet of mixed stuff, some of it thirty feet high or more: mountain ash, more birches and beeches, a wild cherry and a poplar, a couple of oaks and a couple of horse-chestnuts, all muddled up with gorse and broom. Scarcely a surprise packet, but a very acceptable one.

Most of them – for this is a twentieth-century wood – are likewise protected by collarettes of wire, though nothing can save the berries of the mountain ash from the blackbirds. They are eaten, with hideous squawks, long before they turn crimson.

Half a mile away, on another slope, the mountain ash berries don't get eaten at all – the blackbirds don't recognize them; and a couple of miles off, on the other side of the hill, the rabbits don't even nibble down the undergrowth, and life is much simpler and easier. For there is no generalizing in the woodland, and those who do generalize don't observe.

There, as in cities, Fate chooses a restricted area for her operations, and sprays destruction irregularly.

'Some of us will die, others won't, our type will probably go on,' seems to be the message of the trees, and it isn't a bad message, though it takes no account of our dreams or of what we term 'civilization'.

On their own lines terrible things can happen to the poor creatures. Their buds can get frozen brown two springs running, with the result that the outer twigs die back, and the sap retreats to the trunk, there to form a few sparse and inelegant leaves.

A young beech, nipped like this, gets no better chance than an out-of-work lad in a slum; the pulse of existence never gets into it; it never knows what it is to be young; it sees life only as disease and dole; and when it's only a beech it had better be cut down.

Farther along the slope are two other plantations, one of sweet chestnut, one of larch.

The chestnuts stand knee-deep in gorse and toe-deep in the green of tiny seedling foxgloves. They grow rather weedily, lolling in summer under the heavy canopy of their leaves, like drunken parasols, but they are strengthening and improving, and in the autumn they shed their leaves impressively and with decision, and lay them like long oblong visiting cards upon the mould.

They, too, are quite young; by 2000, if nothing happens to them, they will be dropping their burrs upon somebody's grandchildren, and in their old age they may get that wonderful spiral twist on the bark which looks like strength, but is actually weakness.

Below the sweet chestnuts come the larches – only a dozen of them, and variously judged. Up they shoot, most of them, but two or three have lost their leader-shoots through the trivial malice of some insect, and a larch without a leader takes to strange ways; one of them spreads sideways into a bush; another undulates like the neck of a swan, and ripples year after year more faintly until it regains the lost straight line, and looks as good as its fellows, except to the eyes of the timber merchant.

An enormous sycamore dominates these larches – enormous, that is to say, in the southern sense, lush, squashy, quick springing, but with none of the grandeur and decision that ennobles a sycamore in the north, a sycamore, say, upon a Northumbrian farm.

What a jumble. And what nonsense to call the trees I have mentioned 'English'! Some of them come from the Mediterranean, others from Central Europe, and their enemy, the grey squirrel, is Canadian.

Englishmen are used to looking at them, that is all, and fasten upon them the transient label of a nationality.

If they have any relationship with human beings it is with all human beings; if they have function beyond the utilitarian, it is to remind us that we, like them, have been born and must die.

Meanwhile an aeroplane, drilling and droning away at the hollow tooth of the sky, suggests that the pace is quickening and the world, as we have understood it, will die, too. Agony is surely at hand. Things can't go on month after month without a smash.

But the trees, intent on their own business make no comment on this, and here is another reason for loving them.

[1938]

Memoirs

Recollections of Nassenheide

Please open this book [*Elizabeth of the German Garden* by Leslie de Charms] on page 128. There you will see a photograph of me. I am a slim youth, for the photograph is over half a century old, and I am standing beside another and more solid young man. His name is Herr Steinweg and he is a German tutor. I am an English tutor. In front of us sit two governesses, in white blouses, white aprons, long thick skirts and stout boots. One of them is German – Fräulein Backe – the other French, Mademoiselle Auger de Balben. And the photograph is entitled 'The teaching staff at Nassenheide in 1905'. There we are in the garden, in the pre-war summer sunshine, the sunshine that expected shadow but had no conception of disintegration. And there behind us lies Nassenheide, supposed to be a Schloss, but really a charming low grey country house, in the depths of Pomerania. Somewhere inside it, or perhaps in her summerhouse, writing one of her novels, is our employer, the Countess von Arnim, and somewhere else again must be our three little pupils.

Let me explain how I got out there. I wanted to learn some German and do some writing, and a Cambridge friend put me in touch with his aunt. She was English (born in Australia actually) and she had married an aristocratic Pomeranian landowner. She was, furthermore, a well-known and gifted authoress, who wrote under the name of Elizabeth. Her *Elizabeth and her German Garden* was widely read, and her three eldest girls had become household words in many a British household. I am not discussing her books, but they are much neglected today, and I hope that this excellent biography of her will bring them back to prominence. I was one of a series of tutors – Hugh Walpole himself was to succeed me – and I was to pick up in exchange what German I could. At first I feared I should not get the job, for I met none of her requirements: refused to come permanently, could not give all my time, could not teach mathematics or anything except English. But the more difficulties I raised the warmer grew Elizabeth's letters. She begged me to come when I liked and as I liked. She trusted I should not find Nassenheide dull, and she asked me to be so good as to bring her from London a packet of orris root.

My arrival occurred on April 4, 1905. Never shall I forget it. I took the express from Berlin to Stettin, and there had to change into the light railway for Nassenheide. When I arrived there it was dark. We drew up in the middle of a farmyard. Heaps of manure, with water between them, could be seen in the light that fell from the carriage windows, but of the Countess von Arnim not a sign. The guard shouted. There was no reply. He got off the train and plunged into the night, presently re-emerging with a farm labourer who was to carry my bag and show me where the Schloss was. Heavy luggage remained in the manure. We slipped and splashed through an atmosphere now heavily charged with romance, and in God's good time came to the long low building I was presently to know under sunlight. The bell pealed, a hound bayed, and a half-dressed underservant unlocked the hall door and asked me what I wanted. I replied, 'I want to live here.'

The hall was white and vaulted and decorated with the heads of birds and small animals, and with admonitory mottoes in black paint. The hound continued to bay. Presently the German tutor was aroused, the cordial and intelligent Herr Steinweg, who explained that I had not been expected so soon. He showed me my room, also my bed, but I could not occupy the latter for the reason that the outgoing English tutor had not yet vacated it. It was settled that I had better sleep in the nobler part of the house, in the best spare room itself. The cold was appalling in the spare room, the wallpaper excruciatingly pink and green, the sound of a pump from the farmyard where my luggage lay was ceaseless and ghostly. Came the dawn and came breakfast, and with it all possible kindness from my colleagues. And presently I stood in the presence of the Countess herself.

Elizabeth of the German Garden proved to be small and graceful, vivid and vivacious. She was also capricious and a merciless tease. The discomforts of my arrival seemed to have lowered me in her opinion: indeed I lost all the ground I had gained through refusing to come. Glancing up at my tired and peaked face, she said in her rather grating voice, 'How d'ye do, Mr Forster. We confused you with the new housemaid. . . . Can you teach the children, do you think? They are very difficult . . . oh yes Mr Forster, very difficult, they'll laugh at you, you know. You'll have to be stern or it'll end as it did with Mr Stokoe.' I gave her the packet of orris root, which she accepted as only her due, and the interview ended.

Subsequently our relations became easy and she told me that she had nearly sent me straight back to England there and then, since I was wearing a particularly ugly tie. I do not believe her. I was not. She had no respect for what may be called the lower forms of truth. Then we spoke of some friends of hers whom I had met in Dresden. 'They don't like me,' she said. I replied: 'So I saw.' This gave her a jump.

So my arrival was on the tough side. Still all went well, and all around us stretched the German countryside, which is my main theme. When I began to look about me I was filled with delight. The German Garden itself, about which Elizabeth had so amusingly written, did not make much impression. Later in the summer some flowers – mainly pansies, tulips, roses, salpiglossis – came into bloom, and there were endless lupins which the Count was drilling for agricultural purposes. But there was nothing of a show and Nassenheide appeared to be surrounded by paddocks and shrubberies. The garden merged into the park, which was sylvan in character and had a field in it over whose long grass at the end of July a canopy of butterflies kept waving.

It was the country, the flat agricultural surround, that so ravished me. When I arrived in April the air was ugly and came from the east. A few kingcups were out along the edges of the dykes, also some willow-catkins, no leaves. The lanes and the paths were of black sand; the sky, lead. The chaussée, white and embanked, divided the desolate fields, cranes flew overhead, crying 'ho hee toe, ho hee toe' as if they were declining the Greek definite article. Then they shrieked and ceased, as if it was too difficult. Storks followed the cranes. Over the immense dark plough galloped the deer to disappear into the cliffs of a forest. Presently the spring broke, slow, thematic, teutonic, the birch trees forming the main melody.

You cannot imagine the radiance that descended upon that flat iron-coloured land in May. The birches lined the dykes and strayed into the fields, mistletoe hung from them, some of them formed an islet in the midst of a field of rye, joined to the edge by a birchen isthmus. I would go to this islet on warm afternoons with my German grammar. At first the rye was low, later on it hid the galloping deer. Herr Steinweg and I, both friendly to Nature, took many short walks and he recited poetry. Sometimes we got into the forests. There was a track not far from the house that covered undulating ground and had not been planted too regularly and one evening the light flooded a gallery through it with golden beer upon whose substance a solitary leaf floated motionless. By chance I was myself also full of beer, and encountering the miraculous leaf I thought it might be an illusion. But I pointed it out to Steinweg, who was the soul of sobriety, and he saw it too, which proves its existence, doesn't it?

Steinweg and I had our rooms at the end of the long low annex that ran from the main building. I had a little room which got the morning sun, so that I could sit in my bath and be shone upon. He had a larger room where we harmoniously breakfasted, usually upon plovers' eggs. He had a passion for cleanliness, and would daily lift off the lid of the tea-pot to see whether it was coated, as had happened on one occasion, with jam, and it was owing to him that our stoves generally burnt, and that ashes did not sift too thickly over our possessions. He was a delightful companion, always cheerful and considerate, and most intelligent from the theological point of view. I only shocked him once, and if I tell you how I shall shock you: I let out to him that I thought telephone wires were hollow and that one spoke down them! He could not imagine such mental incompetence any more than you can and he was silent and cold for a little time afterwards. His pleasant temper, his good sense, and his slight inclination to autocracy made him the natural leader of us menials, and it is to him that the teaching staff at Nassenheide owed its most agreeable summer. Later on he became a pastor in the Lutheran Church. We kept in touch, he came to stay with me in England; indeed, our friendship survived two world wars.

The third member of our quartet was the French lady Mademoiselle Auger de Balben, a charming and child-like soul. Externally she looked a termagant, and well suited for the post of guarding little girls: she always sat in the schoolroom when Steinweg or I taught them. But her nutcracker-face, spectacles, grey locks, and rounded shoulders accompanied a delightful personality. She was always helping someone or making something – making I cannot remember what: paper boxes inside which you found a filigree rabbit or a pig made out of shavings: that gives the idea. I kept for many years the papier-mâché snake that she gave me when I left Nassenheide, together with its inscription '*C'est le grand serpent Boa, quand il mord ceux qu'il mord sont morts.*' (Herr Steinweg – he gave me *Faust.*) She was almost totally uneducated and had read fewer books and acquired less information than I should have thought possible. 'If I had been educated I might have become a famous woman like Madame de Sévigné,' she once remarked gaily. She could, however, play upon the zither and once when her bracelet caught in the strings of that unusual instrument and fixed her to it immovably, it took the combined efforts of her colleagues and her pupils to set her free. She could run like the wind. Everyone loved her. So did all animals and like a character in a book she would catch them, catch wild animals from the wood and birds in the garden, pet them for a little and let them go. I don't know what became of her.

Fräulein Backe – often called Teppi – was less happily

placed. The Countess had recently made her housekeeper as well as German governess, and she was overworked. The rest of us were probably underworked. I was certainly. My teaching duties were only an hour a day. I had abundant leisure for my German and my writing and was most considerately treated if I asked for leave. But Fräulein Backe was always on the run. The Countess called 'Teppi' at all places and hours. The children leapt on her back. The Count stormed because she had not provided potatoes; it was to her that Steinweg complained of the jam in our tea-pot; the servants cheeked her. She had not asked life to be thus. She was a tall, sentimental maiden and it was her secret ambition to 'live in art'. She sang when allowed to do so but so out of tune that permission was seldom accorded. Mademoiselle's zither was preferred. She loved discussing operas, particularly Strauss's *Salome*, and would dramatize its tenser moments. At times she would attempt fantasy, appearing as an Easter Hare in the garden amidst piles of coloured eggs, or giving at the Schiller centenary a comic performance of *Der Alte Moor* which was not thought amusing.

Dumb devotion bound her to the Countess and the family: her other passion was for the Inspector of Forests, a large, taciturn, handsome, married man; she would become lyrical about the stillness and beauty of his life in the woods. I met her again a few years later, during an amusing caravan tour which the Countess organized in Kent, and recently I had news of her death. It seems that her devotion persisted and that she remained the mainstay of the family through the tensions and tragedies that were to befall it. She died greatly beloved. Sometimes I apply the epitaph of Housman to her – the one about 'the brisk fond lackey to fetch and carry, the true, sick-hearted slave' – but it does not really apply, for Fräulein Backe has had the reward of gratitude even in this life.

So there we are in that photograph, the four of us immortalized. I do not intend to stray outside it and speak of our pupils, delightful and original and easy as they were, or of their mother, delightful and original and occasionally difficult though she was. I am not reviewing this biography, only reminiscing round the pages in it I know best. I will keep to Nassenheide, and to a couple of extracts from my Journal there.

> *May 28, 1905.* A 12 hours expedition to the Oderberge. (Herr Steinweg, Fräulein, Mademoiselle, self, 3 girls.) Straggling villages full of people who looked fairly happy. But never a comfortable effect, in spite of cleanliness and flowers. The roads are so broad and sandy, the houses are set so aimlessly in their surroundings, and there is no attempt to conceal or group the outhouses. A very pleasant day has happened too recently to write about it. The hills had a mountain stream running down them although they were only 300 feet high. The woods were full of bicyclists' paths. We had a second lunch and played skittles with a most rickety return-gallery for the balls, and saw a black bull calf, a very clean scullery, and a tall lady-artist in flowing white piquet. Then through woods of spindly oaks to Falkendorf, where I saw two most beautiful things: bathers running naked under sun-pierced foliage, and a most enormous beech, standing in the village like a god. A villager was proud of it. More woods with lilies-of-the-valley in them, and close to this house two lovers asleep by the road, face downwards, their arms over each other. They looked as ugly and ill-shaped as humanity can be, but I merely felt grateful.

The seven of us came back safe from the great Oderberge outing, although Fräulein Backe got 'bubbles' on her feet. When I wrote *Howards End* I brought in the Oderberge and other Pomeranian recollections.

The next extract is more meditative; and covers ground already indicated.

> *July 14.* At 8.00 this evening the east and zenith were full of huge saffron clouds. The moon showing at times between them. In the west the sun setting in clear sky with a few golden bars above it. The light from the trees fell marvellously on the moving hay carts and on the shoeless

> Poles. Would also remember the sun of last Sunday, into whose light we ascended in the dip ups of the birch woods. After beer it looked like a stream of beer, and its last reflections, together with those of the crescent-moon, were reflected in the Thur See. The magic change – I noted yesterday – comes at 6.15, now. Everything turns bright and coloured. Back from picnic with children. Smeared with blaubeeren, butter, milk coffee, dust and gooseberries.

It is curious that Germany, a country which I do not know well or instinctively embrace, should twice have seduced me through her countryside. I have described the first occasion. The second was half a century later when I stayed in a remote hamlet in Franconia. The scenery was more scenic than in Pomerania. There were swelling green hills rising into woodlands. There were picturesque castles and distant views. But the two districts resembled each other in their vastness and openness and in their freedom from industrialism. They were free from smoke and wires, and masts and placards, and they were full of living air: they remind me of what our own countryside used to be before it was ruined.

The tragedy of England is that she is too small to become a modern state and yet to retain her freshness. The freshness has to go. Even when there is a National Park it has to be mucked up. Germany is anyhow larger, and thanks to her superior size she may preserve the rural heritage that smaller national units have had to scrap – the heritage which I used to see from my own doorstep in Hertfordshire when I was a child, and which has failed to outlast me.

[1959]

Leslie de Charms, *Elizabeth of the German Garden*

How I Lost My Faith

A Presidential Address to the Cambridge Humanists – Summer 1959

Even a Presidential address must have a subject. I have chosen a very small one. I didn't want to exhort you, though to do so is the prerogative of Presidents, and I didn't want to remind you how important we all are, though they sometimes spend their time doing that too. I would have liked to have contributed something specific to the problems with which we are concerned – something about education for instance, or about crime, or about the nature of the universe – but I am not qualified, and I must keep to my small subject.

I propose then to tell you in a discursive way how I lost my faith. It will be rather a tame tale. Some humanists are born enlightened, others have striven towards the light, but in my case the gas got slowly turned up. Please don't expect either the heights of Heaven or the depths of Hell or even the choking fogs of doubt in my undramatic adventure.

To begin it at the beginning.

I am more or less middle-class. My father (the son of a clergyman) died early, and my mother retired with me into the country and provided me with a sheltered and happy childhood. Religion had its place: we were Church of England and she read morning prayers to the two maids and me, but she was never intense, and I suspect not very attentive. Her interests lay elsewhere: in helping her neighbours: in running her little house and garden: in district visiting: and in criticizing Queen Victoria's Jubilee. The middle classes kow-towed to Royalty much less than they do now.

They were not under the continuously dripping tap of the B.B.C. which has done so much to sodden rebellion. My mother, generally so retiring, once rose up at a public meeting where it was suggested that everyone, however poor, should give the dear Queen one penny, and said she wouldn't.

We went to morning church on Sunday, when the mud was not too bad, but I remember no religious instruction there, and our rector, the Rev. William Jowitt, was not one to inflict it. He was a pleasant out of doors parson, scholarly and idle, who rode to hounds and played chess, and whose stock of sermons was scanty. Every now and then we got the one about Esau and Jacob. Esau he secretly admired, Jacob he detested and had to make the best of. ('Esau was a grand man, he was a huntsman. He was a splendid fellow. But we must never forget that Jacob was the chosen of God.') Mr Jowitt produced nine daughters and after them, one son, and when you recollect that the son grew up to be Lord Chancellor, you will realize that the rectory was no place for the Soul's Awakening.

Nor was my home.

Dispiriting books got into it of course – *Line upon Line* was one of a scripture series which included *Precept upon Precept* and *Lines left Out*, and there was *Agatha and Jessica's First Prayer*, and *Baxter's Second Innings*. Baxter was bound in red and white and had a crest on him like a cricket blazer; he may have embittered me against the noblest of games. But I tended to read the *Swiss Family Robinson*, or about history or the stars.

At the age of eleven I was sent to a preparatory school at Eastbourne, kept by the Rev. Hutchinson, but as far as religion was concerned, things went on as before. It was about this time that the Japanese were considering whether they should abandon their own creed and adopt someone else's and they sent a mission of enquiry to Europe who reported favourably on the Church of England on the ground that it aroused no enthusiasm. They might well have visited Mr Hutchinson's school. Not that he was unaware of the dangers surrounding us; he once told us with popping eyes that in the very next road there lived a man who did not believe in God called Mr Huxley. The information meant nothing to us, we wondered whether the house of anyone so inconceivable would have a special shape, and when it had not, let the matter drop.

I was a pious child – that goes without saying – and I could be easily upset. The other day, going through old papers, I turned up a letter I wrote home from the school. It is dated Good Friday, 1891, and it is about a little boy called Henson. My mother had urged me to be kind to Henson since nobody liked him, and since nobody liked me much either, this suited the rest of the school, and he and I were left a great deal in each other's insipid company. I thought however that he was improving, thanks to my example and happier thanks to my personality. But this Good Friday he disappointed me.

> All the others went to church, but Henson and I had colds, so I thought I would speak to him about Good Friday. I asked him if he knew why they had gone to church and he did not. I explained to him and then told him about Easter and Ascension Day. He had never heard of them and he knew nothing about Jesus. He would say that Christ could not have died long ago if he had only been born last Christmas. I was very much shocked.

From the company of Henson, I went as a day boy to a public school, where the spiritual shallows continued – complicated rather than deepened by confirmation and by adolescence. And at eighteen I went on to Cambridge (King's), immature, uninteresting, and unphilosophic, but seriously disposed, and something akin to development began.

At that date compulsory morning chapel had just been abolished and an alternative offered: it was permissible to sign in at the Porters' Lodge before 8 a.m. instead. This proved the undoing of many an earnest child: the Porters' Lodge was more central than the chapel and one had not to dress up so much for it, one could run through the streets, in pyjamas and a dressing gown. My lodgings were where the

Guild Hall now stands and I could daily be seen rushing up St Edward's Passage to mingle with the larger flood which surged from the College itself. The day started with secular levity and contributed to our indifference to the chapel. (It is curious how little in those days the overwhelming building entered into the consciousness even of the devout. Today it is much more integrated with the College.)

In my second year I moved into college where my Christianity quietly and quickly disappeared, partly through my friendship with Hugh Meredith, who already disbelieved, and partly because of the general spirit of questioning that is associated with the name of G.E. Moore. I did not receive Moore's influence direct – I was not up to that and have never read *Principia Ethica.* It came to me at a remove, through those who knew the Master. The seed fell on fertile, if inferior, soil, and I began to think for myself – that most precious experience of youth which is far from universal, and is often discouraged. I thought first about the Trinity and found it very odd. I tried to defend it in accordance with my inherited tenets, but it kept falling apart like an unmanageable toy, and I decided to scrap it, and to retain the main edifice. I did not realize that it was a question of all or none, and that the removal of the Trinity had jeopardized the stability of the Incarnation. I began to think about that. The idea of a god becoming a man to help men is overwhelming to anyone possessed of a heart. Even at that age I was aware that this world needs help. But I never had much sense of sin and when I realized that the main aim of the Incarnation was not to stop war or pain or poverty, but to free us from sin I became less interested and ended by scrapping it too. My attitude towards the personality of Christ helped to hasten the general collapse – I'll touch on that later on. And so by the end of my third year I disbelieved much as I do now. To adopt a famous local phrase: the debunking of Christianity was effected with comparatively little fuss.

And then King's suddenly blew up. It was the famous row over the College Mission. The Mission was a quiet affair down in some London slum. A similar affair had been attached to my old school and I thought nothing about it –

money sent, probably a gymnasium, all very vague. But our leading atheists took alarm. They approved of a Mission, they disapproved of Christianity, and much to the discomfort of the authorities they called a meeting to protest. Their aim was to set up a counter-mission of an agnostic type. The difficulties of this they had scarcely faced but they were an intelligent and reasonable group. Maynard Keynes was one of them, Hugh Meredith another – he has kept it up – and so until his death did George Barger, afterwards Professor of Chemistry at Glasgow. They were sincere and bellicose and the orthodox soon became distressed not only with their opinions but with their impertinence in holding any. The then Provost, the Rev. Augustus Austen Leigh, a worried and just man, took the chair, and more worried still was the clergyman who was running the Mission, working very honourably according to his lights and unable to grasp what was happening.

Early in the dispute, the orthodox got into rough water. One of their younger champions unfortunately employed the expression 'non conformists and such', meaning that men who had not been at Eton, which he had, or didn't belong to the Established Church, as he did, were nevertheless not negligible. This spread dissension in the Christian ranks. Varieties of opinion, and even of social standing began to appear. The atheists on the other hand were exultant. They accepted with glee the appellation of 'such', it gave them a touch of colour to relieve their drabness, and they formed themselves into the 'such' party. 'Come along, aren't you going to join the suches, be a such,' and so on. And this suddenly bursting out of gaiety had importance, for it connected disbelief with daily life. The controversy continued long after the Provost had closed the meeting and since disbelief had a freshness it cannot claim today, there was widespread excitement. All that I contributed myself to the hullaballoo was a poem, composed in the rhymed couplets that were held to be so stinging at the time, and taking the form of a travesty of the proceedings. It was never published but I can remember a few lines. The various religious bodies stated what they proposed to do for the poor;

they then quarrelled and then the chairman dismissed them with politeness.

> Thank you, sir, thank you, thank you very much,
> We now will hear the policy of Such.

Such then rose, and appeared most conciliatory.

> My policy is simple, just and true
> I'm willing to help you, sir, you, and you.

But alarm spread when he explained that, forestalling Communist technique, he proposed to insinuate himself into the vitals of all parties, and destroy them and their work from within:

> Till children, sniggering back from Sunday school,
> Know twenty ways of proving you a fool,
> Till hooligans have Hegel for their teacher
> And every navvy owns his pocket Nietzsche.

The poem ended with the hooligans themselves erupting from the back of the Hall, and wrecking the proceedings, equally exasperated with belief and with unbelief. I intended them to typify the human heart. My friends enjoyed the poem, but felt it did not contribute to enlightenment and I destroyed it.

Meanwhile, another undergraduate, a serious minded, athletic and popular New Zealander, was busy writing something of a very different type. He was deeply stirred by the College Mission controversy, and it woke up the fanatic in him. He realized that he was right and that everyone else was wrong, and in danger of Hell Fire, from which he must save them. The pamphlet, which was of the C.I.C.C.U. [Cambridge Inter-Collegiate Christian Union] type, was published at his own expense. It was well written, its sincerity burnt, and it made the most impression on those who agreed least with it, like Hugh Meredith. It helped in its tense way, like 'Such' in its gay way, to connect private speculations with daily life. The whole affair woke us up outwardly as well as inwardly. That is my excuse for talking at such lengths about the far-off undergraduate flare up. (Harrod's Life of Lord Keynes contains a description of it.)

As for the College Mission – there is not much to add. A second meeting was held, the Provost again in the chair with delegates from all parties, and it was decided that secular work should be done in connection with Cambridge House. Whether anyone went and did it and how the hooligans reacted, I do not know. I didn't do any myself, though I was stimulated to do some teaching at the Working Men's College, and there made one of the most permanent of my friends.

By this time I was sure of myself, and announced that I had lost my faith rather pompously to my family. It so happened, though I did not know it, that my father had lost his about 30 years previously and had recovered it after a short interval. My family assumed that I should follow the paternal pattern. They did not worry, and when time went on they got used to my having no faith, and so it has gone on since. I have been spared the trials of Ernest in *The Way of All Flesh.*

I now come to the only original part of my Presidential address: namely my attitude towards the character of Christ as the Gospels present it. I am unsympathetic towards it. This is unusual. Christians, of course, are sympathetic – and non-Christians generally agree, and often preface their attacks on his claims to divinity by eulogizing him as a man. So I have to defend myself against all parties. The Christ we know is what the gospels tell us he was, we cannot see behind them or discount the misrepresentations they may contain and even in the Gospels there is much that Christ says and does that I do like and often think about – the parable of the hidden talent, for instance, and the parable of the husbandmen with its generous defence of unfairness, and the preference of Mary to Martha which so annoyed Rudyard Kipling, and the marriage at Cana, and the reminder that adultery is an aspect of sex and that precious objects must sometimes be spilt recklessly and not sold for charity – and the blasting of that sterile fig tree – in fact all the sayings and doings that move away from worldliness towards warmth. And I am touched by the birth stories, and overwhelmed by the death story. But there is so much on the other side, so much moving away from worldliness towards preaching and threats, so much emphasis on followers, on an élite, so little intellectual power (as opposed to insight), such an absence of humour and fun that my blood's chilled. I would on the whole rather not meet the speaker, either at an Eliot cocktail party or for a quick Quaker talk, and the fact that my rejection is not vehement does not save it from being tenacious. It may seem absurd to turn from Christ to Krishna, that vulgar blue-faced boy with his romps and butter-pats: Krishna is usually a trivial figure. But he does admit pleasure and fun and jokes and their connection with love. And in one of his aspects, that of charioteer to Arjuna, he manages to produce the most famous of the Indian's utterances.

Perhaps my greatest barrier to approaching Christ has been Christian art. Having moved away from the antique hero in the catacombs and perhaps from the Nordic hero in the *Song of the Rood*, it creates a Christ who is nearly always in pain or with premonitions of pain, or with recollections of pain. The sufferings, we are told, are undergone for our sake, and the effect can be tremendous emotionally and aesthetically – Tintoretto's *Crucifixion in Venice*, Titian's *Entombment* in the same city come into my mind – but when the emotion recedes I think, 'I hope none of this has been undertaken for my sake, for I don't know what it's about.' And I believe that if I had lived BC instead of AD I should have exactly the same chances of salvation, if there is such a thing as salvation.

But as I'm on pictures there's one more I want to mention – not a well known one, but it is a very satisfactory picture from my point of view – a fresco of the Last Supper by Andrea del Castagno at Florence. It is satisfactory because the head of Christ is intellectual, as well as compassionate, and the void I have just now criticized gets filled.

Looking at the complications and omissions of the Christ Figure, I understand why in the Middle Ages Christendom turned to the Virgin Mary. The mother gave birth to the child, saw him grow up and saw him killed. Here is something immediately comprehensible to which we can accord heartfelt pity, and the fact that Mary seldom said or did anything notable on her own account only makes her the better medium between mankind and the incomprehensible. Her seven sorrows were her own, anyhow until the theologians got hold of her, and they were not entangled with the notion of atonement.

Needless to say I have got out of my depth in the above. So let me restate my main point, namely that I don't desire to meet Christ personally, and, since personal relations mean everything to me, this has helped me to cool off from Christianity. If the religion of my fathers (i.e. C. of E.) had provided me with a more satisfactory father-figure, brother-figure, friend, what you will, I might have been more tempted to stay in it. It contained much that I respected and respect, but too little that I could care for.

I may add that my indifference towards Christ did not prevent me from usurping his position myself in my childish daydream. All I had to do was to walk about the countryside while my disciples followed me. They listened. I talked. I liked that. And in my other childhood daydream – that of living with savages – I always converted them to Christianity before we launched our canoes or sat round our cooking pots. I cannot think at this distance of time why I did this, but it was soon over, and the savages never objected.

One further note on the subject of Salvation. I used to be very keen on this and it figures in most of my early short stories, and a little in my novels up to *A Passage to India*, from which it has almost disappeared. It has now disappeared from my thoughts, like other absolutes. I no longer wish to save or be saved, and here is another barrier that has interposed between myself and revealed religion whether Christian or Pagan. Nor do I wish to escape; how can one escape from a universe that is said to expand? What I would like to do is to improve myself and to improve others in the delicate sense that has to be attached to the word improvement, and to be aware of the delicacy of others while they are improving me. Improve! – such a dull word but it includes more sensitiveness, more realization of variety, and more capacity for adventure. He who is enamoured of improvement will never want to rest in the Lord.

Thus ends a Presidential address. Maybe I have softened my loss of faith retrospectively, and underwent crises and tumults which my subconscious has suppressed. Or maybe a Humanism which has been gained so softly may not stand by me in the hour of death. I should be glad if it did. I do not want to recant and muddle people. But I do not take the hour of death too seriously. It may scare, it may hurt, it probably ends the individual, but in comparison to the hours when a man is alive, the hour of death is almost negligible.

[1963]

Age

Recollectionism

The past is always with us. Though whereabouts? As each of us chonks along, carrying mixed goods in his interior like a grocery van, whereabouts are the labelled parcels of the years? Difficult to locate among the joltings and the obscurity. But perhaps the labelling is on different lines. Is the past packed up not by years but by subjects, that is to say, by the preferences of the heart? For instance, had I better look for a parcel labelled 'Love of Wiltshire', rather than for the year 1904, when I first realized my love? Wiltshire today – scarred, militarized, droning, screaming – how best can I sink through its ruins thirty years downwards into Figsbury Rings above the Winterbourne, where Wiltshire seemed indestructible and eternal? Or Cambridge – Cambridge today? When I see that Babylonian incinerator, the tower of our new University Library, how best can I blow it back into its native smithereens? Where is my spiritual dynamite? Or Oxford – the Oxford of tomorrow? When I hear that the generator of our incinerator is to build the Bodleian extension, how best shall I finish this sentence? It only leads me to write another sentence, on the subject of Dorking. The town councillors of Dorking are just now proposing to cut an enormous cock on the chalk escarpment of Box Hill. This they would do in honour of the Coronation. It is to stand out for centuries as a memorial of Surrey's loyalty and good taste.

Thoughts like these – they are confused and querulous, but the past is confusing, and frequently involved in recalling the future – thoughts like these run in and out of one's poor head as one peers into the grocery van, and rummages after the stuff. How best can one get at it? Through chronology or through subject matter? I can't myself manage chronology. The River of Time must be left to historians and Matthew

Arnold. Most of us see the past as a swamp. Events do not flow past us; they neither go down into the mighty ocean nor are they lost in the sand; no, their behaviour is otherwise; the moment they move out of our physical reach they begin to sway and interlock, and they remain quite near. It is no wonder that amateurs all through the ages have indulged in incantations, and have hunted for the Word, the Gesture, the Sensation which should evoke their unburied dead, and bring back the richness and sweetness which had scarcely ceased to breathe. The taste of a cake, the unevenness of a tile, were sufficient to regain all childhood, all Venice, for Proust. Homer poured out blood, drinking of which the ghosts put off their ghostliness and conversed with men. In mythology, as in experience, only a low barrier divides the present from all the pasts. One step, and we're over.

Why is the step so rarely successful? It is not that incantations are difficult to arrange: a crinkly, paper passport, a really honest piece of sealing-wax, a Victorian shilling, the Victorian constellation of Orion, a kitchen table leg clawed by pre-war cats, a few words of French as it used to be talked before servants (*pouvez – non – cuisinière – bon*, etc.) – these are some of the trifles which may hook up a tangle of memories. They do in my own case. But, as in all magic, there is a catch. The devil nearly always tricks those that trust him, and here he contrives that the process of memory shall alter the nature of the thing remembered. For an instant the past is seen as it was, the sleeping beauty breathes in her tomb; then she crumbles or hardens, and the practitioner is left with a pinch of dust or a lump of clay. Events seem to die two deaths. The first occurs when they pass from us physically, the second when we remember them and so destroy their nature. And that is why it is so depressing and so futile to think of someone whom one has cared for and who is no longer accessible; if the voice re-echoes, the face fades; if the face remains, the body melts. And that, again, is why dreams, in spite of their silliness and horror, sometimes preserve an emotional truth which no waking moment can command. Dreams remember the essential past, however wildly they distort its forms. And Consciousness, as if aware of their reality, does all that it can to forget them. 'My tablets – meet it is I set it down.' But the tablets are never to hand and the dream floats away, carrying all Wiltshire in its folds.

Still, there are two solid reasons for remembering, or trying to remember. The first reason seems to me really important and the second evidently appeals to my contemporaries. Memory gives mental balance. That's partly why I practise it. The present is so heavy and so crude and so vulgar that something has to be thrown into the opposite scale, or one will live all lopsided. I throw in my own past. It may not be much, yet it is a counterweight to Mussolini, the Dorking cock, the Coronation, the incinerator. The past is not a series of vanished presents, of superimposed Mussolinis, as the historians have to assume: it would exercise no effect if it were. It is a distillation, and a few drops of it work wonders, even though they change colour on exposure to the air. This is not a private fancy of mine; all races who have practised ancestor-worship know about it, and Ulysses went down into the underworld to acquire better balance for his course in this. 'One foot in the grave?' Yes , I should hope so. Impossible to walk steadily if it wasn't.

The second reason for remembering is a simpler one: there may be material and money in the past for a book or even two books. This is an age of autobiographies and recollections, indeed, I don't suppose that the human memory can ever before have been so remorselessly called into print and so gallantly responded. That bishops, burglars and butlers should publish their pasts seem proper enough; for professional reasons they have had much to conceal, and so they should have much to say. That creative artists should be equally chatty surprises me. They might be expected to have said what they wanted to say in their works, and, in the deepest sense, to have drained themselves dry. Still, recollect they do, and frequently to our delight. I could point to some eminent recollectionists who have added to literature, and to others who seem just to be knocking up extra royalties; though to none who resemble my own great-grandfather. He, a banker and an M.P., seated in the King's Arms on January 7th, 1795, thus sets the pace:

> On this morning after some previous and occasional Deliberation I determined to begin to keep a Diary. – My motives for it are the following.
>
> I think I have discovered that my religion consists too much in active duties and in efforts to edify and convert others and too little in serious self-examination and attentive reading of the Scriptures, prayer and secret self-denial.

The diary continues in this strain for about a hundred octavo pages. It is never bright. Then it concludes:

> I may consider myself highly favoured by Providence, for how few can I discover round me who have half my Prosperity or who can look with so little reason for apprehension on a numerous family of children?

What could he make of us and our methods of thought? We can look back on him with gentle amusement and even with respect and with a sort of gratitude, but how can he look forward? Our quick jazzy minds, our trickiness with time – they would be quite outside my great-grandfather's comprehension, he would scarcely know that we and our memories existed, even if Ulysses called us all to drink blood together.

[1937]

De Senectute

During recent years I have put down a few remarks about old age, and now seek publicity for them. I will start by distinguishing old age from two kindred subjects, namely death and growing old.

Death, though it interests me personally, for I am bound to experience it, is at present an unfashionable subject. It is regarded as insufficiently communal. Thanks to two world wars and to the possibility of a third, the present century has become very offhand and gruff on the topic of death. Get on with your job! If you fall out of it, someone else will carry on. I realized what was coming a few years ago, when I referred in a broadcast to a poem of Matthew Arnold's ('A Southern Night') in which he laments emotionally, and I thought appropriately, on the deaths of his brother and his brother's wife. I received as a result a rather dry letter from a member of the Arnold family, who took my sentimentality to task. Softness and weakness, he implied, might have been pardonable in Victorian times, but were unacceptable today when thanks to our heavy casualties we have achieved another and a juster view of the value of individual life. I disagreed; that is to say I reserve the right to be frightened at the thought of my own death and to mourn the deaths of those whom I have loved or haven't even known. I deplore this smug rejection of mourning, this glib return to one's job from the graveside, if indeed one has ever been there. I consider that the present century has become too curt over bereavement just as the nineteenth century was too expansive over it. Both of them are endangering the human norm. Who then mourned correctly? The Greeks. They wept, they recovered, they recalled. Anyhow my correspondent was in closer touch than I can be with contemporary taste. He had duly relegated death to the statistical. He at all events was unlikely to confuse it with old age.

The identification of old age with growing old must also be avoided. Growing old is an emotion which comes over us at almost any age. I had it myself violently between the ages of twenty-five and thirty, and still possess a diary recording my despair. At twenty-five I thought a human being was in its prime, and there are moments when this is still my opinion. After twenty-five decay starts, one is not what one was, hair thins or might thin, one is unattractive, is a bore, finds examination papers more difficult to finish, gets rattled by the lapse of time, etc, etc. This unpleasant sensation (rendered bearable only by self-pity) is only intermittent except in a few special cases. It comes and it goes, and it is probably only another form of the sensation of being too young, which irritates adolescents. It is one of the ways in which we indicate that we don't feel altogether at home in the world of time, and are partly bound for another place. That place is not, however, old age.

Old age is a state to which too little intelligence has been devoted. Both by its practitioners and by its observers it is approached too rhetorically and on too sustained a note – the whine of the gnat, the thrumming threnody, the organ pedal diapasoning, the boom of the bittern, are among its musical accompaniments. The old person is assumed, and often affects to be all of a piece – disgusting, pitiful, pretentious, peevish, noble, ingratiating, moody, and so on. The eulogy or the satire is set like a mechanical carillon; the Ulysses of Dante or the Strulbrugs of Swift intone their appropriate chants and old age gets summarized by a steady noise. It is really more varied. It is really a seductive combination of increased wisdom and decaying powers. On that combination I offer a note.

Through experiences, and through the pattern into which memory composes experiences, it is natural that A, at fourscore, should have an attitude which is impossible for B, who at twenty-five has had fewer experiences, and whose memory, though more reliable, has had less material to handle. A has also secreted a larger body of subconscious stuff, which may have further modified what was pumped into him as a baby. The outcome of his acquisitions may be wisdom, and the belief that wisdom is always the outcome, and that it is communicable, and that it is helpful when communicated form the triple foundation of the Senatorial Heresy. 'I would have this audience of young people in whom lies the future know. . . . Let me once more as a very, now a very, old man urge upon them to. . . .' The audience slips out. Many old people are foolish, but even when they are wise they find it impossible to convey their wisdom. Their old mouths address young ears. And their memories, though extensive, are usually inaccurate; wisdom is inevitably connected with the decay of powers. As a prophet or guide the Senator is quite useless. He can, however, be esteemed as an exhibit, and on that narrow pedestal a case for him can be made. Like one of the wire baskets which I hung up in a solution of alum when I was a child, he can demonstrate what accretes round a skeleton when conditions have been favourable. A few Senators are works of art; or, to attempt more precision, they display ethical deposits which can be regarded aesthetically.

I find myself being invited to define wisdom, and becoming mystical about it. I do regard it as an immensely important human achievement. I connect it with length of years, and I distinguish it from intuition which may occur at any age. It has nothing to do with making decisions or with the conveyance of information, it is only indirectly connected with the possession of knowledge. It does not specialize in sympathy. But it has the power, without proffering sympathy, of causing it to be perceived, and it is certainly not cynicism. The possession of it arises from human relationships, rightly entertained over a long period. When it is intermittent – and it may become so through weakness or disease – it is most alarming to watch, and has the effect of witchcraft.

For mixed up with this noble achievement of wisdom is the failure of the physical powers. The theory that failure here indicates the thinning of the corporeal frame, through which the soul may now more clearly shine, must be reluctantly dismissed. It is possible though that decay, when it is not of the cancerous type, may assist concentration elsewhere. The arrival of sexual impotence for instance – a mild case can be put up for it. Provided it is not a worry it may be a help in removing distractions, or it may even stimulate creativeness, as it did for Yeats. Sometimes physical decay seems to have no mental effect at all. To refer to myself, I know that I am getting deaf because when the telephone rings I often don't hear it when others do. The lesson learnt is immediately forgotten, and until the telephone rings again and is again missed by me, I have the illusion that my hearing is as good as anyone's. When I went to Provence last time and never once heard cicadas, I assumed they must have hopped elsewhere. I was told that they had not. Some day I shall be convinced that I am somewhat deaf, and when this happens I shall admit that in one particular direction I am older.

These notes are concerned with the borderline between Shakespeare's fifth and sixth ages. The grey-beard still saws impressively and keeps passably up-to-date, but already he stretches out his feet for his slippers. The seventh age, sans everything except pain, lies outside my observation as death did. I will here state that old people (except when they are actually suffering or are wanting to be impressive or detestable) usually report old age as the same as youth . . . with incidental if severe limitations.

More research remains to be done. Quite enough has been said in literature and in conversation on the relation of age to youth, too little on the relation of one old person to another. This subdivides into (a) old people who have been in touch all their lives (b) who meet again after a long interval (c) who meet for the first time.

The first – the 'golden wedding' class – is of great social importance, and any civilization that hinders it from coming into being has failed. It includes as its highest achievement the married couple who have not quarrelled too much, who have produced children and have not alienated them, and who have received, as their final reward, the collusion of their grandchildren. Such couples cannot be numerous, and no statistics are obtainable. With them must be classed, though less excitingly, old people who have seen each other constantly over a long period, and want to go on seeing each other. The true history of the human race is the history of human affection. In comparison with it all other histories – including economic history – are false. It has never been written down and owing to its reticent nature it cannot be written, but it has continued from generation to generation ever since the human race became recognizable, and this 'golden wedding' class is its highest manifestation.

Class (b) – the 'reunion' class – tells another and a more poignant story. Old people who meet again after a long interval are inevitably distressed by the experience. Each sees the other as he would not himself wish to be seen, thinks '*I* cannot have turned into that', yet knows that he has, and is appalled at the discovery. The first glance is the worst. After it there is an attempt at transfiguration, each seeks for the vanished lineaments of youth, and in American reunions the attempt is sometimes assisted by a sash round the paunch, bearing the date when the wearer was young. It is possible to meet an old friend after a long interval and to start again with him. But one must taste, and must administer, some bitter waters first.

Class (c) – the 'Introduction' class – is wholly comic. Old people meeting for the first time present a most entertaining spectacle. The other day, at a public reception, I had the advantage of observing one distinguished old man introduce a second to a third. The newly-mets shook hands in a spirit of determined amity, which was shared by their genial go-between. 'Situated as we both are, I am sure you will not let me down', they seemed to say, and they glanced at each other's medals, ribbons, necklaces, and decorated buttocks without envy, yet without contempt.

[1957]

Books Reviewed

Baker, Ernest A., *The History of the English Novel*
Bannerjee, Gauranga Nath, *Hellenism in Ancient India*
Baring, Maurice, *Diminutive Dramas*
Belloc, Hilaire, *Europe and the Faith*
Bentwich, Norman, *Hellenism*
Brentford, Viscount, *Do We Need a Censor?*
Brooke, Stopford A., *Naturalism in English Poetry*
Burton, M.E., *Women Workers of the Orient*
Byrne, M. St. Clair (ed.), *The Elizabethan Home*
Caudwell, Christopher, *Studies in a Dying Culture*
Cecil, David, *The Stricken Deer*
Clemenceau, Georges, *The Strongest*
Cockerell, S.C., *Friends of a Lifetime*
Coleridge, Samuel Taylor, *Unpublished Letters*
Dostoevsky, F., *An Honest Thief, and Other Stories*
Doughty, C.M., *Mansoul*
Ford, Ford Madox, *The English Novel*
Gairdner, W.H.T., *The Rebuke of Islam*
Gauguin, Paul, *Lettres à G.-D. de Monfreid*
Gide, André, *Prometheus Ill-bound*
Gow, A.S.F., *A.E. Housman*
Greene, Graham (ed.), *The Old School*
Hall, H. Fielding, *Love's Legend*
Hamilton, Clayton, *Materials and Methods of Fiction*
Housman, A.E., *More Poems*
Lampedusa, Giuseppe di, *The Leopard*
Lawrence, D.H., *Pornography and Obscenity*
Lawrence, T.E., *The Mint*
Lee, Sidney, *King Edward VII*
Manning, Frederic, *Scenes and Portraits*
Marcosson, Isaac F., *Adventures in Interviewing*

Martin, E.O., *The Gods of India*
Murry, J. Middleton, *Son of Woman*
Nevinson, Henry W., *More Changes, More Chances*
Pollard, S., *In Unknown China*
Renier, G.J., *The English: Are They Human?*
Rodocanachi, E., *Etudes et fantaisies historiques*
Rowland, Benjamin, *The Art and Architecture of India*
Tchehov, Anton, *The Bishop and Other Stories*
Tolstoy, Leo, *What Then Must We Do?*
Tyndale-Biscoe, C.E., *Character Building in Kashmir*
Wadia, A.S., *Reflections on the Problems of India*
Wells, H.G., *The Outline of History*
Wharton, Edith, *French Ways and their Meanings*
Wilcox, Ella Wheeler, *Poems of Problems*
Woolf, Virginia, *The Voyage Out*
The Mark on the Wall
Kew Gardens

Sources

BOOKS

TO SIMPLY FEEL
New Weekly 8 August 1914

A NEW NOVELIST
Daily News & Leader 8 April 1915

BREAKABLE BUTTERFLIES
Athenaeum 6 June 1919 (Signed E.M.F.)

KILL YOUR EAGLE!
Daily News 17 June 1919

VISIONS
Daily News 31 July 1919

ALMOST TOO SAD?
Daily News 23 August 1919

THE END OF THE SAMOVAR
Daily News 11 November 1919

LITERATURE AND HISTORY
Athenaeum 2 January 1920 (Signed E.M.F.)

FRENCHMEN AND FRANCE
Daily News 3 January 1920

COUSIN X—
Daily News 3 February 1920

WHERE THERE IS NOTHING
Athenaeum 27 February 1920 (Signed E.M.F.)

THE SCHOOL FEAST
Daily News 28 May 1920

A GREAT HISTORY and A GREAT HISTORY II
Athenaeum 2 & 9 July 1920 (Signed E.M.F.)

MR WELLS' *OUTLINE*
Athenaeum 19 November 1920 (Signed E.M.F.)

A CAUTIONARY TALE
Nation 9 October 1920 (Unsigned)

EDWARD VII
Calendar of Modern Letters April 1925

PEEPING AT ELIZABETH
Nation & Athenaeum 8 August 1925

POVERTY'S CHALLENGE
New Leader 4 September 1925

LITERATURE OR LIFE?
New Leader 2 October 1925

MR D.H. LAWRENCE AND LORD BRENTFORD
Nation & Athenaeum 11 January 1930 (Signed E.M.F.)

THE CULT OF D.H. LAWRENCE
Spectator 18 April 1931

THE HAT-CASE
Spectator 28 June 1930

SCENES AND PORTRAITS
[?] [About December 1930]

WILLIAM COWPER, AN ENGLISHMAN
Spectator 16 January 1932

COLERIDGE IN HIS LETTERS
Spectator 10 September 1932

ANCIENT AND MODERN
Listener 11 November 1936

A BEDSIDE BOOK
Listener 7 November 1940

GEORGE CRABBE
Listener 29 May 1941

THE MINT by T.E. LAWRENCE
Listener 17 February 1955

THE CHARM AND STRENGTH OF MRS GASKELL
Sunday Times 7 April 1957

FOG OVER FERNEY
Listener 18 December 1958

THE PRINCE'S TALE
Spectator 13 May 1960

THE ARTS IN GENERAL

TATE VERSUS CHANTREY
Daily News 26 May 1915

THE EXTREME CASE
Athenaeum 4 July 1919 (Signed E.M.F.)

REVOLUTION AT BAYREUTH
Listener 4 November 1954

DIVERSIONS

DIANA'S DILEMMA
Egyptian Mail 26 August 1917 (Signed 'Pharos')

SUNDAY MUSIC
Egyptian Mail 2 September 1917 (Signed 'Pharos')

HIGHER ASPECTS
Egyptian Mail 5 May 1918 (Signed 'Pharos')

THE FICTION FACTORY
Daily News 23 April 1919 (Unsigned)

GREEN PASTURES AND PICCADILLY
Athenaeum 22 August 1919

THE SITTERS
Nation 24 July 1920 (Unsigned)

PLACES

ROSTOCK AND WISMAR
Independent Review June 1906

A BIRTH IN THE DESERT
Nation & Athenaeum 8 November 1924

THE EYES OF SIBIU
Spectator 25 June 1932

INDIA

IRON HORSES IN INDIA
Golden Hynde December 1913

THE GODS OF INDIA
New Weekly 30 May 1914

THE TEMPLE
Athenaeum 26 September 1919 (Signed E.M.F.)

JEHOVAH, BUDDHA AND THE GREEKS
Athenaeum 4 June 1920 (Signed E.M.F.)

MISSIONARIES
Athenaeum 22 October 1920 (Signed E.M.F.)

REFLECTIONS IN INDIA I and II
Nation & Athenaeum 21 & 28 January 1922 (Unsigned)

WOODLANDERS ON DEVI
New Statesman & Nation 6 May 1939

THE ART AND ARCHITECTURE OF INDIA
Listener 10 September 1953

THE ENGLISH SCENE

THE CEREMONY OF BEING A GENTLEMAN
Spectator 27 June 1931

BREAKING UP
Spectator 28 July 1933

THE OLD SCHOOL
Spectator 27 July 1934

THE POLITICAL THIRTIES

NOTES ON THE WAY
Time & Tide 10 June 1934 & 2 November 1935

THE LONG RUN
New Statesman & Nation 10 December 1938

TREES – AND PEACE
Manchester Evening News 15 July 1938

MEMOIRS

RECOLLECTIONS OF NASSENHEIDE
Listener 1 January 1959

HOW I LOST MY FAITH
Bulletin of the University Humanist Federation Spring 1963

AGE

RECOLLECTIONISM
New Statesman & Nation 13 March 1937

DE SENECTUTE
London Magazine November 1957

Annotated Index